To Andy
with love
from Mom and Dad

other books by John White

THE COST OF COMMITMENT
DARING TO DRAW NEAR
EROS DEFILED
THE FIGHT
THE GOLDEN COW
HEALING THE WOUNDED
(with Ken Blue)
THE MASKS OF MELANCHOLY
PARENTS IN PAIN
THE RACE

other fantasy by John White

THE TOWER OF GEBURAH

booklets by John White

BIBLE STUDY
PRAYER

The IRON SCEPTRE

John White

Illustrated by
Elmar Bell

INTER-VARSITY PRESS
DOWNERS GROVE
ILLINOIS 60515

InterVarsity Press is the book-publishing division of Inter-Varsity Christian Fellowship, a student movement active on campus at hundreds of universities, colleges and schools of nursing. For information about local and regional activities, write IVCF, 233 Langdon St., Madison, WI 53703.

Distributed in Canada through InterVarsity Press, 1875 Leslie St., Unit 10, Don Mills, Ontario M3B 2M5, Canada.

ISBN 0-87784-589-1

Printed in the United States of America

Library of Congress Cataloging in Publication Data

White, John, 1924 (Mar. 5)-
  The iron sceptre.

  SUMMARY: Wesley, Kurt, Lisa, and Mary aid the forces
of good in the mythical kingdom of Anthropos and fight
the evil witch, Mirmah.
  [1. Fantasy] I. Title.
PZ7.W5837Ir   [Fic]   80-36727
ISBN 0-87784-589-1

17 16 15 14 13 12 11 10 9 8 7 6 5 4
95 94 93 92 91 90 89 88 87 86

To Aaron, Emmet and Mason

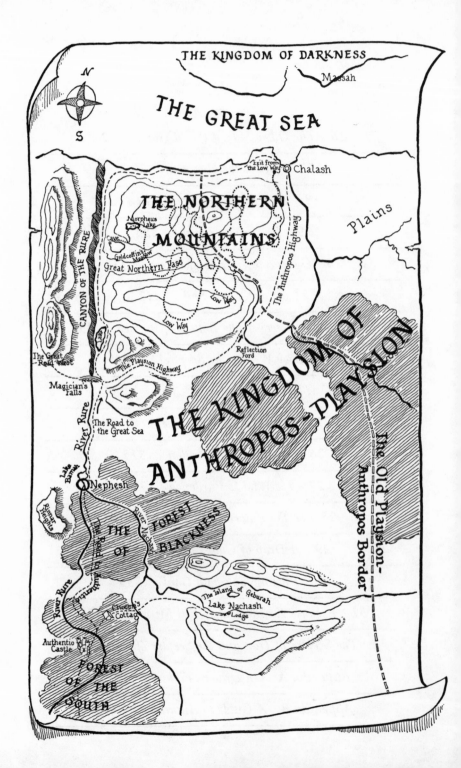

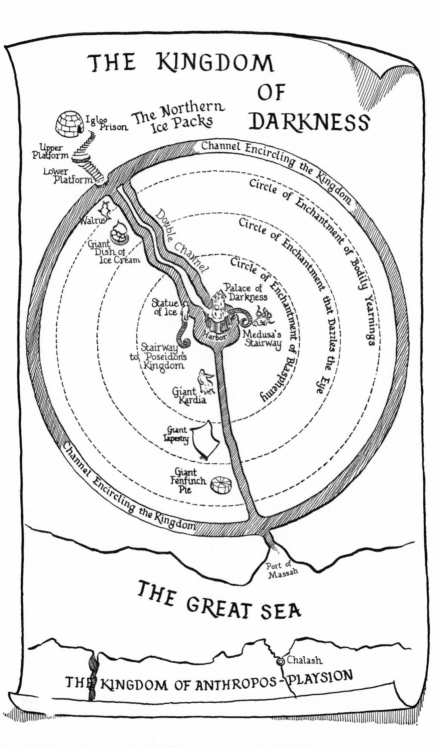

I

Miserable Mary McNab

Mary stared from her pillow through the window at the lamplit trees on Grosvenor. In spite of the attic's oppressive heat she felt chilled and hugged her sleeping bag around her shoulders.

She had tried all five of the television sets on either side of her bed, but none of them worked. Then she had cried for an hour or more wondering why everyone hated her, even her cousins here in Winnipeg.

Mary had what grownups call a weight problem. She had no real friends. The boys and girls at her small private school in Toronto had called her elephant, fatso, hippo and many other names that were worse still. She was so fat that her pimples (which worried her more than her weight) escaped ridicule. Mary was sure that if only she were thin and pimple-free, people would be nice to her.

Supper that night had been unpleasant. It had begun happily enough with her kindly Uncle John and her three cousins Wesley, Kurt and Lisa. Wesley, the oldest, had been polite. Lisa had smiled at her from time to time though Mary saw her surprised looks at the mountains of potatoes and gravy she had heaped on her plate. Only Kurt, the youngest of her cousins and a year older than Mary, had stared at her, puzzled, throughout the meal.

"Toronto's much bigger than Winnipeg," she had said for the third time.

Uncle John once more agreed politely. He had spoken little at supper because he was thinking of the extra mortgage he had to take out and was wondering how he would pay for the repairs to the roof.

"New York's bigger still," Kurt had mumbled peevishly. "So's Tokyo. So's London. Toronto isn't really that big."

"It's bigger than Winnipeg."

Kurt must have forgotten the warning Uncle John had given them all before her arrival. "Mary's a strange kid," he had said, "very bright, but she takes a bit of getting used to. It's not her fault. She's had a rough time for the last few years. I want you all to be kind to her and let her know we're happy she's here. Her stepmother (who was your Uncle Peter's second wife) wants to get rid of her. Poor kid didn't even know she was her stepmother until this morning. Thought she was her real mother. And now your Great Aunt Felicia is after her too. Wants to adopt her."

"You mean our crazy aunt? The one who used to be a dentist?" Kurt asked.

"You mustn't call her crazy. She's—well, a little different."

"But surely they won't let her," Wesley protested.

"No, I don't imagine so. For one thing Felicia's nearly eighty. But she's arriving from Chicago tomorrow evening. I tried to dissuade her over the phone, but nothing doing. I'll do all I can to prevent her from seeing Mary...."

"Does Mary know her?" Lisa asked.

"Yes. She used to have her dentist's office in Toronto. That's how Mary knows her."

"How d'you mean?"

"Your Aunt Felicia used to insist on being Mary's dentist. As a matter of fact, the only view Mary ever had of her was from a dentist's chair. And it was at a time when Felicia was a little 'crazy,' as Kurt put it. Poor kid was frightened to death."

"You're not kidding! Fancy being hunted by a crazy dentist when your stepmother throws you out!" Kurt mused sympathetically. "I hope you'll be here when she arrives."

"Aunt Felicia? Yes, I'll be here. As I said, her plane doesn't get in until tomorrow evening. But I want no more 'crazy aunt' talk. Felicia is good enough at heart. She just seems to have a problem keeping friends. It's not going to be easy, but at least we can be nice to her."

"Sounds like we're gonna have to practice being nice to a bunch of nuts," Kurt murmured after Uncle John had left the room.

But long before suppertime Kurt had forgotten his uncle's warning to be kind not only to Great Aunt Felicia, but to Mary McNab. Lisa bit her lip as she saw him glare at their cousin from Toronto. She tried to say something soothing.

"Well, I think you'll like it here even if Winnipeg is small. You'll have lots of friends."

For a moment Mary forgot how mean her school

friends had been to her.

"I went to private school in Toronto."

"Did you like it there?" Wesley asked.

"One girl in our class has a father who makes a million dollars a year. But he's divorced."

No one made any comment. Thinking she had impressed her cousins Mary went on, "Mummy thinks you can't trust the doctors in Winnipeg. All the good doctors go to the States or to Toronto. She says it's the same with the schools. There aren't any really decent schools here."

Mary never saw Kurt look at Uncle John nor at the frown he gave Kurt. Wesley also put his finger over his lips, saying without words, "Take no notice. Just let her talk."

Once or twice, it seemed to Mary that they wanted to change the topic, but Mary was used to controlling conversations. "Mummy says the cultural activities here are overrated. The Royal Winnipeg Ballet's never in Winnipeg and the Art Museum should be called a mausoleum."

The Friesen children (Uncle John was their uncle too) stared at Mary in astonishment. Wesley felt she sounded silly. Lisa knew she was just showing off. But Kurt, ignoring his uncle's warning signals, said, "And who's Aunt Polly to set herself up as an authority? She can't sing. She can't play a note. She can't even run a business. Her lousy boutique's gone bankrupt."

Above the babble Mary's own voice rang out. "She's a lot better than your mother. She didn't leave me in Canada to go in the stinking diplomatic corps!" (Their parents were in a "troubled spot" and so the children had to be sent back to Winnipeg for the time being.)

Before Uncle John could finish clearing his throat Kurt said, "If Toronto's such a neat place and your mother's so marvelous, why did she send you here? Why don't you just go back?"

Kurt had not meant to be as cruel as he sounded and was instantly sorry for what he had said. Mary stood up enraged, her face at first red, then very white. Staring at Kurt she choked over the words "I hate you. I wish you were dead." As she turned to run from the room, she accidentally knocked her milk glass off the table and onto the dining room carpet.

Matters only worsened when, three hours after she was in bed and thirsty for the milk she had not been able to drink at supper, she went down to search the kitchen refrigerator. She had not meant to eat all the cake that Lisa had baked for the next day's dessert, but it had tasted better than she expected. Lisa seemed unfriendly when she stumbled half asleep into the kitchen to find Mary, surrounded by crumbs and spilt milk, finishing the last mouthful.

Hugging the sleeping bag round her, Mary sat and rocked herself backward and forward as she had done so often at home in their Toronto apartment. "Everybody hates me; everybody hates me; everybody hates me."

Her mind went back to the mother Kurt had been so rude about. Did her stepmother love her? Certainly she had called Mary "precious" and "my beautiful." Certainly, too, she gave her money, clothes and toys. Sometimes she would even take Mary to a movie. But there were many bitter quarrels between them. And there were long, long times when Mary would sit alone in the apartment twisting the television controls or staring vacantly at the flickering colored tube.

She had never known her father. Until six months ago she had lived with her mother and a man Mary called Uncle Alan. Uncle Alan used to call her "sweetie" and hold her on his lap. He smelled of cigars and whiskey and shaved infrequently, so that he scratched her face when he kissed her. Sometimes he would pinch her and tease her. Yet she liked to sit on his knee and let him call her his "cutie pie."

But there were many times when she lay in bed trembling as Uncle Alan shouted and her mother screamed. Then on a never-to-be-forgotten night, she heard the sounds of blows, of dishes being smashed, of her stepmother's sobbing voice saying hoarsely, "Get out of here, you drunken bum, and don't ever come back! This time I mean it! This time it's for good!"

It was the last Mary ever saw of Uncle Alan. She had cried herself to sleep for several nights.

But there were compensations. For the first week after Uncle Alan left, her mother had taken her to five different movies. There were parties (not very successful ones) for her schoolmates. But little by little she again began to see less of her mother, until most of her free time was once more spent staring vacantly at the television.

Three nights before her arrival in Winnipeg, "Uncle Pete" (tall, handsome, wearing silk suits and an earring) had moved into their apartment to live. Mary disliked him from the moment she saw him. Their meetings were few and stormy, and the night before she was flown to Winnipeg she had sat up tensely in her own bed trying to shut out words which sickened her.

"Get rid of that brat, Polly. I can't stand her! Either *she* goes tomorrow or *I* go. Can't you persuade your precious in-laws in Winnipeg to take her under their wing?"

Did her stepmother love her?

Mary rocked herself back and forth.

Does it mean a grownup loves you when she calls you

"my precious one," "my little baby," "my precious little baby"? That's what her stepmother had called her later in the night when she explained about the "little holiday" Mary would be having in Winnipeg. Mary had screamed and stamped her foot, but it had been useless.

Events took control of themselves. The alarm had gone off at five, and the cab came along at six. In the early morning cold, Mary had had feelings only of tiredness as her mother rushed her through the airport.

Hurrying along wide carpeted corridors, bumping against passengers walking to their gates, she had listened with growing fear to her mother's nervous voice.

"Mary darling, there's something I've never told you. You know I love you, don't you, dear? Well, I don't really know how to say this but while I love you like a mother . . . I'm not your real mother. I'm your stepmother. You see. . . . " She went on talking but Mary could only hear the shocking words "I'm not your real mother." They turned themselves over and over in her mind. She had not looked up. She wanted to withdraw her hand from the cold hand that grasped it, but she was being pulled forward too rapidly to do so.

Suddenly they were at the gate. Her mother was still talking and hugging her in nervous spasms. She glanced at her face, seeking out the mole above the left eyebrow. Then in a daze she found herself being handed over to a stewardess. She turned to see her mother waving, but quickly turned her back on her. For a few seconds she felt she wanted to scream, scream not with sorrow but with rage. Instead she slammed a door in her mind, and as she passed inside the aircraft she locked Toronto, mother, private school and Uncle Pete firmly out of her mind.

She could remember little of the flight. The one nice thing that happened was that the stewardess had given her an extra breakfast when she complained she was hungry.

And now, she thought as she rocked on, they probably hated her here at Uncle John's in Winnipeg. Well, she would hate them back. Yet what if, what if they sent her away from here too? Was this only a holiday? Or had she been sent away from home for good? The thought of her stepmother's nervous face, the mole above the left eyebrow and the sound of the words "I'm not your mother" chilled and sickened her.

Her heart stopped with a sudden bump, and she would have stopped rocking, but something strange happened. The bed began to rock gently with her, and the mattress slowly rose behind her back, as if to comfort her. She was too scared by the thought of having no home to be frightened of a bed that cradled itself round her and rocked her back and forth. In a way the bed reminded her of Uncle Alan, except that she could smell no whiskey.

But it comforted her, oh, how it comforted her! Was she dreaming? She didn't care. She didn't care when she found, staring up, that there was no roof over her head and the walls around her had disappeared. She didn't care when she felt herself floating, floating as well as rocking, floating she knew not where. She only knew that the closeness and firmness with which the mattress and pillows held her, the warmth they began to make her feel, comforted more than Uncle Alan and more even than her stepmother crying and calling her "my precious baby."

Where was she going? What happened to the street lights outside her window? Why did the stars whirl so quickly round her? Why did she feel so safe? Was she in the air, or wasn't she?

Suddenly a blast of cold wind brushed her face and fine powdery snow filled her nostrils. But the bed only hugged her more closely.

Stars shining down from the night sky above her lent a soft radiance to the snow that stretched like an endless carpet for miles around. Sometimes it would swirl gently, and sometimes drift in low white lines across her field of vision. Eventually it settled into stillness and quietness. The stars stared down, large and unwinking. The snow had fallen asleep and the bed continued to hug her tightly.

"I hope I don't wake up," she whispered to herself.

She had no idea how long she remained there. Presently it seemed that away in the distance something like a faint blue light was moving toward her. She struggled to sit up higher and the bed, like a huge nurse, lifted her gently to let her see better, then tucked her carefully into its cradling, warm arms again.

Ever so slowly the light grew larger as in sleepy contentment she watched. Before long she saw it was a man, a man shining pale blue. Curiously he seemed to be walking. He should have been skiing or snowshoeing. But he was walking, walking with a swinging stride, and as he got closer she could see he was kicking the snow carelessly with every step. She wondered why he did not sink.

He wore a long robe, and it was this that glowed with pale blue light, softly lighting the snow around him. Yet he looked solid enough. His skin was brown, his long hair and beard were white and a sword hung from his side. He wore sandals. Otherwise his feet were bare.

As he looked down at her she knew, without being told, that he had brought her here, and that he had arranged for the mattress to hold her tight and comfort her. She did not know how she knew. She just knew.

"I am Gaal, the Lord of ice and snow, Mary," he said.

Mary stared at him wonderingly. The blue light from his robe had transformed the surrounding snow crystals into tiny gems that glittered with pale lavenders, greens, pinks, coral reds and yellows. "Snow flowers," Mary thought, but she was looking at the man who called himself Gaal.

He unbuckled the sword with its scabbard from his belt and held it out, handle first, to Mary.

"Take it," he said. "Give it to your cousin Wesley. Tell him that when the time comes he must plunge it to the hilt in the center of the yellow circle."

"Tell him what?"

Gaal repeated his instructions patiently. "Tell him that when the time comes he must plunge it to the hilt in the center of the yellow circle."

Mary still did not understand, but her memory was excellent. She would never forget the words, and she supposed Wesley would understand what they meant. She reached forward and was surprised at the weight and the warmth of the sword. It felt too solid, too real for a dream sword. Gaal's deep voice was rolling toward her from the circle of light. There were other words, he said, which Mary must also teach her cousins:

Gaal is the Lord of far and near.
Gaal is the Lord of light.
Gaal is the Lord of sea and fire.
And Gaal is the Lord of ice.

Gaal is the Lord who rescued you.
Gaal is the Lord to obey.
When Gaal the Lord says, "Go," you must go.
When Gaal says, "Stay," you must stay.

In Anthropos King Kardia reigns,
While birds in the forest sing;
Upon its fields the sun pours gold,
That fruit from the ground may spring.

Like a child delighting to please a new teacher Mary repeated the words flawlessly. As I already told you, she was very clever in that way. Gaal watched her intently as she recited, and nodded.

"You learn well," he said. "That is why I called you here. I want Wesley, Lisa and Kurt to come back to Anthropos to aid Queen Suneidesis and King Kardia, and to deliver Anthropos from peril.

"Tell them they must pass through the three Circles of Enchantment in a Kingdom of Darkness. The first circle is the Enchantment of Bodily Yearnings, the second circle, the Enchantment that Dazzles the Eye, and the third, the Enchantment of Blasphemy. They will pass through all three unharmed, for I will protect them. Yet they must beware of my enemies who will seize them if they leave their vessel before they are bidden. Therefore they must on no account leave the boat in which they travel until they reach the gateway to Poseidon's Kingdom."

In the silence that followed, Mary stared at the glowing figure who transformed snow crystals into jewels and flowers. Gaal, Lord of ice. Strange that he should seem so warm and so full of life. She liked him. She liked him even more than she had liked Uncle Alan—the man who used to call her "cutie pie." She wondered whether he liked her and with all her heart she wanted him to. *Gaal.* Why did she feel so drawn to him?

"There's one more thing I want you to tell Kurt. Tell him that the rooster that crows the loudest is the rooster

22

that flees the fastest. Can you remember all that I have told you?"

"Yes, Gaal." Every word was engraved in her memory. It never occurred to her to question what she was to do, but there were two questions that did float like bubbles to the surface of her sleepy mind. "But please, Gaal. . . . "

"Yes, little one?"

"What is Anthropos? And will I see you again?"

Gaal's eyes looked deep into Mary's until she knew he was reading the secrets of her heart. Yet she did not care. It was as though his eyes grew bigger and brighter. They were like a sunlit ocean in which she longed to swim. Sleepily she heard him say, "You, too, will come to Anthropos and find me there. But you will suffer before you do."

The ocean grew bigger and warmer until the bed that was holding her slid gently from the snow bank to be cradled in its swell. The snow disappeared. The last thing she could remember was floating in a bed that held her tightly and the gentle rolling of an ocean.

2

What Mary Tells the Others

"Pass the milk, please," Kurt asked Mary a little hesitantly the next morning.

It irritated him to notice how two cereal boxes, the peanut butter jar, marmalade, sugar and milk had all congregated around Mary's plate. The four children were sitting together at the kitchen table. Uncle John had already left for the office.

"I had a dream last night," Mary said as she passed the milk.

"Thank goodness there's no school today," Lisa sighed. "More toast, anyone?"

"No, but I'd like some coffee." (Both Wesley and Lisa drank coffee.)

"I had a dream last night," Mary repeated.

"So did I," Kurt said. "I dreamed I had to stay on till the end of June and take the exam."

"Here's your coffee, Wesley," Lisa murmured. "Cream and sugar?"

"My dream, . . ." Mary began.

"Are you sure no one else wants toast? There's a piece sitting here in the toaster," Lisa asked again.

"In my dream there was a message for you, Wesley," Mary said a little peevishly.

"Was there now?" asked Wes. "I'll have the toast after all, Lisa. Mebbe you could butter it for me. The butter's over at your end."

"Don't you want to know about the message?" Mary asked.

"Oh, of course. Sorry, Mary. Breakfast is always a mixed up kind of meal. Not too much butter, Lisa, please."

"Well, it was from a man called Gaal."

"*Gaal?*" Three voices had spoken at once. Lisa sat with the butter knife poised over Wesley's toast. Wesley rattled his coffee cup and slopped coffee into the saucer. Kurt paused open mouthed, his spoon slowly sinking back to the cereal bowl. All three Friesen children stared at Mary in silence.

A struggle went on inside Mary. She was pleased to have startled them all even if she couldn't understand exactly why. She felt important and wanted to hold their interest as long as she could.

"What was the message?" Wesley asked quietly.

"I . . . I don't remember." She eyed each of them in an attempt to read the expressions on their faces.

"Surely you must remember something."

"Well, there was snow."

"Snow?"

Their interest was not lessening. They continued to stare at her.

"You guys were mean to me last night." Mary looked as though she were going to cry. "You said my mother was no good and you didn't want me."

"Oh, shucks," Kurt said. "I guess that's my fault. I'm sorry, Mary."

Mary sniffed. "I still don't remember," she said.

A strained look came over Wesley's face.

"Try," he urged. "Please try, Mary."

"I want some more toast," Mary said sulkily.

Lisa and Wesley exchanged glances. Lisa kicked Kurt's foot under the table to warn him to be quiet. She handed Kurt his toast and said, "Don't bother her now, Wesley. It's probably not too urgent. Let me make you some more toast, Mary. Your stomach's more important than your dreams."

This, of course, was very clever of Lisa who knew that nothing would be more likely to make Mary speak than to pretend they had lost interest in her dream. Wesley saw what Lisa was doing and smiled to himself.

"The name Gaal is probably just a coincidence," he said. "I guess it could mean anything."

"He said that when the time comes, you must plunge the sword into the heart of the yellow circle."

If Wesley was interested he showed no sign of it. Fortunately Mary did not notice Kurt's startled face.

"I see," said Wesley, as casually as he could. "Did you put some toast in for her, Lisa?"

"Well, aren't you interested?" Mary sounded anxious.

"Interested in what, Mary? The toast?"

"No. The sword, stupid."

"What sword is that, Mary? Oh, you mean the sword you were dreaming about."

Mary's stool crashed backward as she pushed herself from the kitchen table. She stamped out of the room, and they heard her running up to the attic.

"Oh, shucks, now you've done it!" Kurt said in dismay. "That was her stormy exit routine. I bet we won't see her for the rest of the morning." But a moment later Mary ran through the kitchen door holding above her head with both hands a magnificent sword in a jewel-studded scabbard.

Two more kitchen stools crashed back onto the floor while a third was pushed back more gently. There was a look of awe on Wesley's face.

"It's the Sword of Geburah!" he said softly.

Mary saw the awe in their faces. Never in her life had she been able to create so great a sensation, or to be so thoroughly the center of everyone's attention. For a moment she struggled with the thought of getting back at her cousins by refusing to tell them anything more, but the temptation to be at center stage was too much. She would tell them everything. Crossing the kitchen floor she handed the sword to Wesley saying again, "And *when the time comes,* you must plunge it to the hilt in the center of the yellow circle."

The children crowded round with gasps of wonder.

"You remember the room underneath where the Sleeper was?" Lisa breathed.

"D'you remember Inkleth crawling across the grass to us all bloody and groaning?" Wesley chimed in excitedly.

Kurt looked gloomy. The incidents on the Island of Geburah were etched deeply and painfully into his memory. It was the one part of their adventures that he never wanted to remember.

"Don't let's talk now."

Mary's ears were wide open. What were they talking about? Geburah. Sleeper. Inkleth. She could see they were not making anything up. Evidently they shared secrets she longed to share with them. She determined at once to be a part of whatever it was that bound her cousins together.

Wesley looked hard at her. "Did he say what yellow circle he was talking about, or when the time would be?"

"No. I thought you'd know. He seemed to think you would."

Kurt was still suspicious. "What did he look like?"

"He looked *real neat.*"

"Yes, but how?"

"He came walking across the snow...."

"The *snow?*" three voices chimed.

"Yeah. He came walking across the snow in sandals...."

"But there *is* no snow...."

"It's summer...."

"In Anthropos...."

"Do you want me to tell you or don't you? You asked me what he looked like and I'm telling you!" Mary shouted.

There was a moment's silence.

"Sorry, Mary. It's kind of exciting for us to hear anything about Gaal, and I guess there are things about him we don't know," Wesley said.

"Well, whether you believe it or not, he was walking across the snow in his sandals, and he kind of made it light up with real pretty colors. It was dark when I saw him. He wore a long white ... thing, with no sleeves. It had a gold belt. An' he had a beard."

"What color was his hair?"

"It was white, I guess. But mebbe it wasn't. I mean, he was *young.*"

"You sure?"

Mary looked puzzled.

"No, I'm not sure. He could have been old too."

"She really did see him. That's what he looks like— old and young at the same time," Lisa said.

"Of course, I saw him. And he called himself Lord of the ice."

"Lord of the what?"

"Of the ice."

The Friesens stared at one another in silence.

"Let's go and sit in the living room so you can tell us all about it," Lisa suggested sensibly. "At least, that is, if you really want to."

Mary didn't wait for any further invitation but instantly turned toward the living room. Kitchen, breakfast, dirty dishes were all forgotten. It took only a moment for them all to snuggle on the settee or on their favorite chairs. The Sword of Geburah was placed carefully on the coffee table. It lit the whole room like a fierce tropical bird. Outside through the lace curtains morning sunlight threw a dappled green pattern through the elm trees onto the lawn.

Mary drew a deep breath.

"Gaal said I must teach you these words:

Gaal is the Lord of far and near.
Gaal is the Lord of light.
Gaal is the Lord of sea and fire.
And Gaal is the Lord of ice.

Gaal is the Lord who rescued you.
Gaal is the Lord to obey.
When Gaal the Lord says, "Go," you must go.
When Gaal says, "Stay," you must stay.

In Anthropos King Kardia reigns,

While birds in the forest sing;
Upon its fields the sun pours gold,
That fruit from the ground may spring.

"Sounds just like Gaal," Kurt said slowly.

"He never called himself the Lord of ice before," murmured Wesley.

"I suppose there's a whole lot we don't know about him," Lisa said.

"Why does he want us to learn the rhyme?" Kurt asked.

"Don't ask me," said Mary. "He just did."

"Will you teach us?" Lisa asked.

"*I* learned it the first time he said it."

Kurt's face went red.

"Well, mebbe you could repeat it slowly so I can write it down," Lisa said quickly getting up for paper and a ball-point pen. "We're not all as good at remembering as you are."

"Half an hour ago you said you couldn't remember anything," Kurt muttered surlily.

"I don't have to tell you any more if I don't want to. I won't even tell the poem again if you're not nice to me."

Lisa returned with the paper.

Wesley said, "Mary, if Gaal wanted you to tell us, you should tell us because *he* said so."

The memory of the strange beauty and of the comfort she had experienced in the snow flowed back into Mary's mind. She disliked what Wesley said, but the thought of the tall white-haired man made her friendlier. Almost without thinking she began to dictate the words she had heard to Lisa.

"I don't see why Gaal should use someone like *her* to send his messages," Kurt continued. Mary never heard him, and a moment later looking at Wesley he added, "But I guess I'm not the one to talk."

"What does it all mean?" Wesley asked when the dictation was over.

"I don't know," Lisa said. "Was there anything else, Mary?"

"Well, you're all to go back to Anthropos."

"We *are?*" Kurt sounded more excited than when he first heard the name *Gaal.*

"You might have guessed as much from the sword," Wesley said.

"Yes, you're to help a king and queen called Kardia and Suneidesis."

"To help them? How?"

"He didn't say. He just said something about Anthropos being in peril."

"It sounds the same as it did last winter," Lisa said. "I wonder what it's all about. Didn't he tell you, Mary?"

"He said you were to pass in a boat through three enchanted circles in a dark kingdom. He said you weren't to get out of the boat at any cost but that you had to go right through until you reached the entrance to Poseiden's Kingdom.

"The first circle was called the Enchantment of Bodily Yearnings; the second, the Enchantment that Dazzles the Eye; and the third, the Enchantment of Blasphemy." Mary felt very proud as the long words came effortlessly from her lips. She had no idea what they meant.

The Friesens were silent for several minutes.

"Can you make any sense of it, Lisa?" Wes asked.

"Not much. Except that we ought to go."

"The sets have never worked once since last winter."

"No, but they might now."

Again there was a pause. If any of them had been looking at Mary's face, they would have seen a look of wicked glee.

"There was a special message for Kurt," she said slowly. "Gaal said, 'Tell him that the rooster that crows the loudest, flees the fastest.' "

"You're just making it up." Kurt's face was suddenly pale.

"I don't think she is, Kurt. But it could mean anything."

Lisa and Wesley both knew about Kurt and roosters. It had begun when he was four years old during a visit the children had made to a farm. The crowing of a large rooster had filled him with delight, and often he had tried to mimic its song. But one day in the farmyard it had attacked him fiercely, flapping its wings in his face, and he had slipped and fallen, screaming in terror. He received no injury, but the feel of wings beating against his face and of his panic-stricken flight when he could finally get up had haunted his dreams for years. No longer was he delighted by a rooster crowing. In fact, the sound always awakened the memory of his terror. He was ashamed about his fears and never again walked across a farmyard if he could help it.

Lisa saw his pallor and looked anxiously at Mary. "Let's clean up the kitchen, then go up to Mary's room and see what we can do with the old TV sets," she said.

3

Great Aunt Felicia

Neither Kurt nor Wesley were keen on cleaning the kitchen. For that matter, neither was Lisa. The sight of the Sword of Geburah, the pounding of their hearts, the thought of a second visit to Anthropos, the mysterious instructions, and above everything else the possibility of seeing Gaal combined to make kitchens and dishes seem very uninviting. But Lisa had insisted.

"We're not going to leave another mess for Uncle John to clear up," she said firmly. Uncle John McNab was a favorite with them all. But he could be strict.

"D'you think he'll mind if we go off again?"

"We were only gone a couple of hours last time."

"I know. Yet it was days and days in Anthropos."

"He won't mind," Lisa said, reaching up to stack unused dishes in the cupboard above the sink. "He's been there himself, you know."

"I wish I was more clear about what we had to do," Wesley frowned, clattering knives, forks and spoons into their respective slots in the drawer.

"We didn't understand a thing last time when Lisa disappeared into the television."

Wesley grinned, "No, we were scared out of our wits, eh!"

"You were. I was . . ."

". . . all cool and collected. All ready to stay behind and take charge of things!" Wesley teased. Kurt smiled ruefully. He, too, had been scared on their previous journey.

Mary had no relish for cleaning kitchens. Indeed kitchens and dishes were light years from her mind. "The sets," they had said. So the TV sets were the clue to it all. They were the secret for getting to Anthropos, whatever Anthropos was. And if Mary knew the Friesen children (which she didn't), they would certainly try to stop her.

Well, she would outsmart them. She would get there first. And once she got to Anthropos, Gaal would stop them from sending her back. With a beating heart she slipped from the room and crept up to the attic where her bed was, and where the strange old television sets were lined against the walls on either side of it.

"Where's Mary?" It was Lisa who asked as she stacked the plates in the dishwasher.

"Avoiding work."

"What are we going to do with her?"

Lisa, who had been kneeling before the open door of the dishwasher, stood up and faced her brothers. "We can't leave her here."

"Oh, Lisa. Do we *have* to drag her along?" Kurt sounded irritated.

"Well, after all, she's been there already."

"You mean she dreamed she had."

"The sword wasn't a dream."

"But whoever heard of snow in Anthropos?"

"We were there during the Anthropos summer, remember?"

"But Lisa, she'll spoil the whole fun of it."

"Fun? Last time wasn't fun. Some of it was sheer terror."

Wesley interrupted. "She's a nuisance and none of us like her. But that's beside the point. We can't leave her alone in the house. She'll just have to come with us and that's all there is to it."

Kurt said, "We'll be taking her into danger, you know."

"If Gaal knows about her, you can be sure he'll take care of her," Lisa replied quietly. "Now, the kitchen looks pretty decent. Just give me a minute or two to restack the dishes, and we can all go to find her and try to explain."

At that moment there was a ring at the doorbell.

"You answer it, Wes," Lisa pleaded.

Wesley hurried along the worn carpet that lined the hallway between the dining room and living room and opened the front door. He found himself looking up at the tallest old lady he had ever seen. Her arms were folded, her shoulders back, and her head held high. She looked down at him fiercely.

"You needn't pick up my luggage. I shall be staying in a hotel if we can't get a reservation back to Chicago this afternoon," she said loudly.

Wesley's jaw dropped. He had never seen the lady before and had no idea what she was talking about. An ancient leather portmanteau lay in the porch beside her, and as he glanced at it he noticed she wore old-fashioned, black-laced boots. The way she dressed reminded him of Mary Poppins. Her midlength gray coat was plain and severe, but the bonnet she wore was a frivolous cloud of flowers, totally at odds with her beaked nose and her fierce gray eyes.

"Here, have a cigarette!" she said suddenly flashing a gold cigarette case before him and flipping it open expertly. Wesley wanted to snigger but with a huge effort he controlled himself.

"No, thank you. I don't smoke. I . . . er . . . what is it you want?"

She snapped the cigarette case closed and stuffed it into her coat pocket. She then pushed past him unceremoniously and began to stalk down the hallway. "I want Mary McNab. I'm taking her to Chicago with me."

So *this* was the mad dentist! This was Great Aunt Felicia! Wesley left the front door ajar and hurried after her, his head spinning. Hadn't Uncle John said she would be arriving that evening? What on earth would they do with her until he got back? Was she really mad? Maybe he ought to hide Mary away somehow. Where was Mary?

Felicia peered into the living room. "Not bad," she said. "You ought to get a new cover for the chesterfield, and the plaster needs to be touched up. How much does this place cost to heat?" Then, catching sight of the Sword of Geburah on the coffee table she strode toward it, picked it up and whistled expertly. "My stars! Does that fool John know what this is worth? Where on earth did he pick it up?"

Before he could answer, she had dropped the sword, turned round, crossed the hall and was into the dining room. Wesley trailed behind her.

"So John got cousin Bertha's dining room suite after all!" she said, planting her hands on her hips. "Bertha always did have a soft spot for him. It could do with some

wax polish. Does John have a housekeeper?"

He would have had no time to answer, even had he known what sort of answer to give, for she was already pushing the kitchen door open. Kurt and Lisa were staring at her in surprise. Lisa had a wet plate in each hand and one of the plates crashed to the ground as Felicia seized her by the shoulders and held her at arms length.

"My, oh, my! What a pretty thing you've turned out to be now you've lost all that puppy fat! Give Aunt Felicia a kiss!" She relaxed her grip on Lisa's shoulders, bent down toward her and thrust a down-covered chin into the girl's face. Lisa dropped to her knees.

"Oh, excuse me. Let me pick the broken bits up first. Are you Great Aunt Felicia?"

But Felicia was not to be denied. She pulled Lisa to her feet, pecked her cheek in a thoroughly no-nonsense fashion and said, "Go and get your things packed. I'm taking you to Chicago."

"But this isn't Mary. This is my sister, Lisa—*Lisa Friesen,*" Wesley interjected quickly.

Great Aunt Felicia glared at them angrily. "It was very wrong of you to deceive me," she said to Lisa. "I may be an old woman, but I will not be made a fool of. Where is Mary?"

"She's upstairs in the attic. That's where she sleeps."

The words were out of Kurt's mouth before he could stop them. Aunt Felicia swept through the kitchen door with Wesley running after her, like a piece of paper sucked in the wake of a speeding truck.

"Where's the attic?" She had already found the staircase and was mounting the steps purposefully.

Back in the kitchen Kurt and Lisa looked at each other in dismay. "She really *is* crazy!" Kurt whispered in a horrified voice. "I wish I hadn't told her where Mary was."

"She'd have found her anyway, Kurt."

"What can we do?"

"We could phone Uncle John." Lisa was mechanically holding shattered fragments of the plate in her hands.

"But he says we should never call him at the office. Besides, what if she catches us?"

"I don't care if she does." She tossed the broken pieces into the garbage pail, reached for the kitchen phone and began to dial.

"Could we call the police? What if she drags Mary off with her before Uncle John gets back? What if. . . ." Kurt was panicking.

Lisa was speaking into the phone. "Hello? Is that . . . oh, yes. Is Mr. John McNab there, please?" There was a pause. "Oh, I see. When will he be back, please? . . . Could you ask him to call home as soon as he comes in? Tell him its very urgent. . . . Message? Could you tell him Great Aunt Felicia arrived? . . . Felicia. F-E-L-I-C-I-A. Great Aunt Felicia. Yes, that's right. . . . Thank you. Bye." She slammed the phone down nervously, and drew in a deep breath. "He had to drive to Steinbach this morning to see a lawyer there. I guess I'd forgotten. He's on his way back to Winnipeg now."

"Then how are we going to stop her?"

Lisa had forgotten the remaining fragments of china on the floor. All thought of clearing up the kitchen had gone from her mind. They could hear footsteps descending the main stairway and strained their ears to listen.

"Has she found her?" Kurt whispered.

Again they listened. Aunt Felicia's powerful voice echoed from the foot of the staircase. She was evidently talking to Wesley. "I'm not going to leave this house until I see her. Bring my bag in from the porch. You can tell your sister I'll have a cup of tea in the living room. Two sugars and just the tiniest drop of milk."

Kurt and Lisa held their breath. Floorboards creaked as their great aunt made her way into the living room. Then came a slam of the front door.

"Guess that must be Wes bringing her luggage in."

Lisa took the electric kettle and filled it with water.

"Get me the china teapot from the dining room cabinet and a tray—not the silver one—just any old tray. There's a matching creamer and sugar bowl by the teapot." She sighed, and Kurt left obediently, returning a moment later.

"I brought one of those special china cups. I hope it'll keep the old buzzard happy."

"Good. I'll fix her the tea she asked Wes for."

At that moment Wes joined them, visibly shaken, the Sword of Geburah in his hand. He saw them stare at it. "I didn't like the way she looked at it. I sneaked out with it when she turned round. Hope she doesn't notice." He handed it to Lisa. "She wants some tea in the living room. Says she won't leave here till she sees Mary. Is that tea you're fixing?"

"Yes. We heard her ask. She didn't find Mary, eh?"

"No. She wasn't in her room."

"You sure?"

"Yes. The bed wasn't made, but there was no sign of her—just her unmade bed, a pile of clothes and her suitcase."

"She couldn't have been hiding?"

"She might have been under the bed. Mebbe we should sneak up and look again."

"O.K. But let's give Great Aunt Felicia her tea first. It might keep her quiet."

"Quiet?" Wesley snorted. "She asked for a hammer

and nails. She never stops talking."

"Hammer and nails! Whatever for?"

"She says the pictures in the living room need rearranging. They're all too high or too low and in the wrong positions. She has most of them on the floor already. Where does Uncle John keep the toolbox?"

He left the kitchen to hunt in the basement without waiting for an answer. The electric kettle began to simmer.

4

Pass through the Glass

Mary had been in the attic all the time. She had, as the children suspected, hidden under the bed. But before matters had gone that far, she had surveyed the TV sets. "They probably didn't work last night because they weren't plugged in." So peering behind the first of the sets, a look of bewilderment clouded her puffy eyes. "No cord. There's no cord," she said. "No plug either. No wonder it didn't go on. I wonder...."

Eagerly she checked behind each of the other sets, inserting her fat little body between the wall and the old sets to push each away from the wall for a better look. But from none of them hung the familiar electric cords, and nowhere could she see a plug.

She sat pondering for several minutes on her unmade bed. Were these the sets? Could there be a magic set in some other room in the house? Had she heard right down in the kitchen?

She frowned at the oldest set in the far corner of the attic. It was by far the shabbiest, its white paint chipped and scratched and most of the knobs broken or missing. Only the volume knob seemed intact. Yet there was something mysterious about the crude white box.

Slowly Mary rose to her feet and approached it. She sat on her haunches and let her finger rest on the volume control. Would it work if she turned it? She had the strangest feeling that it would. Perhaps. . . .

"Mary!"

The shout came from somewhere below. It was at that moment that Wesley had begun to search for her. Mary heard voices and the sound of approaching footsteps. She could distinguish at least two—Wesley's and a woman's. The woman's voice was vaguely familiar. Who could she be? It sounded as though they were coming up the attic staircase.

"I think she may be in her room, but I really wish you'd wait till Uncle John comes home. We weren't expecting you till tonight and he wanted to talk to you before you spoke with Mary," she heard Wesley say.

"John isn't going to keep me from my own flesh and blood. I'm going to take Mary back to Chicago *this morning.*" At the sound of the woman's confident take-charge voice Mary clapped both hands over her mouth to stop herself from screaming. It was the voice of Great Aunt Felicia, the mad dentist. She was coming to take her away!

"You can't take her with you! That's kidnaping!" Wesley's own voice had risen to a high-pitched squeak. There was a sound of a scuffle on the attic stairs.

"Here, let me get by. Don't you dare stop me!"

Mary began to shake. Where could she hide? There

was no closet. Desperately she scrambled under the bed and hoped she would not be seen.

They were coming through the door. She lay still but felt sure the booming of her heart must be heard all over the room, even over the heavy panting of Great Aunt Felicia.

"She's not here. Where is she?" Mary stopped breathing.

"Aunt Felicia, *please.*" Wesley's voice from above the bed was desperate. Mary could see his sneakers and a pair of old-fashioned black boots that must belong to Great Aunt Felicia.

"Young man, you have deceived me. I am an old woman and climbing stairs is not good for my heart. You knew all along that she would not be here. Where is she?" The door slammed and the sounds of their departure were muffled.

Mary's limbs were still shaking. She lay under the bed listening for an unbearable length of time. Would she be able to get away? Would they come back? Suddenly she remembered the TV sets.

She scrambled from under the bed, grasped the volume control of the old set and switched it on. Instantly she felt a faint vibration and heard a low hum. First there was a purple dot in the center of the screen, and then familiar horizontal lines leaped to fill it entirely.

For a moment nothing more happened. Then from the top left-hand corner, computer letters began to jiggle themselves into place.

Look all thou wilt at the pictures and see.
List' to whatever they say to thee.
The pictures you see are but one, not four,
And each to the others may serve as a door.
Once mayest thou enter by climbing the frame.

Once mayest thou enter but never again.
Once, yet I pray thee to shatter the bond
And pass
Through the glass
To what lies beyond.

Mary had no idea what the words meant. She bit her lip in frustration. The computer letters continued to appear. The rhyme would print itself repeatedly, rather like a weather report, wipe itself off and begin all over again. The only phrase that made sense to her was the one about passing through the glass. Clearly it was an invitation to get into the television set. But how could she?

Mary sat on the edge of her unmade bed and frowned anxiously at the screen. Suddenly she heard a creaking as stealthy footsteps mounted the attic stairway. She turned off the set to see if she could get back under the bed. But as she looked she was shocked to discover that *there was no longer any attic*. It was gone. Her bed was gone. So were the television sets. There were no walls. But it was darker now than in the attic. Snowfields stretched around her as far as she could see.

"Varmint!"

An enormous bear was speaking into her face and its voice was gruff and unfriendly.

"Varmint!" it said again. "Who told you to come into this territory? You're trespassing! That's what you're doing—*trespassing*." It rolled the word round its tongue as if it were a new word it was showing off. "I'll have to do with you what I do with all trespassers."

For a moment he stared at her, then slowly rising to his full height, he growled with a volume and a fierceness that chilled Mary far more than the snow could ever have done.

The three children crept as quietly as they could toward the attic. Kurt led the way and Lisa followed, hugging the Sword of Geburah. As Kurt reached the door he stopped suddenly, "I'm sure she's there," he whispered. "I can hear her move." Slowly he opened the door. "No! Oh, *no!* She's gone. The TV's are working again!"

Wesley and Lisa pushed by him to stare for themselves. Mary's unmade bed occupied the middle of the floor. To the left, in the alcove opening from the sloping ceiling a window looked down on to Grosvenor. Mary's open suitcase lay on her bed, clothes spilling onto the floor. But it was at the five old television sets that the three children were staring. Two of the screens were blank. Three of them shone with still, silent, colored pictures.

One showed a tall, tall woman standing on the steps of a throne surrounded only by intense darkness. On her head was a crown so big that it looked rather like a Christmas tree hung with hundreds of egg-shaped jewels. Beside her stood an enormous rooster.

A second picture showed a ring of men and women in ancient dress around the table of a stone-walled council chamber. The Friesen children stared at the costumes of the counselors and a king and queen whose faces seemed familiar yet whom they did not immediately recognize.

The third TV set showed a hill of dark green ice, crowned with a palace of ice whose windows glowed with ruby-red light.

"She's gone," Kurt repeated. "There's no other way. She must have."

"They're both blank," said Lisa, staring not at the illuminated screens, but at the dead ones.

"And we'll never know where she's gone," Wesley said softly.

"We could run them through again," Kurt suggested.

"It wouldn't work. In the first place we don't know how many times she let the jingle run through. In the second place the screen would come up blank again. Don't you remember how it happened with Lisa? Once she went inside the picture we never saw her again—at least not until we'd been in Anthropos for ages." He shuddered as he said it.

"She must be *in* Anthropos," Lisa said.

"I wish we could be sure," Wesley said in a worried voice. The council scene looks like Anthropos, but the other two. . . . "

"How in the world did she figure out how to do it?" Kurt asked.

"The same as we did, I suppose," his brother replied. "And in any case the magic only seems to work when Gaal wants it to. You know how many times we've fooled with the sets since last winter. Magic doesn't seem to keep to rules."

Lisa sat down slowly on the side of the unmade bed.

"We must go ourselves," she said. "We can't stop now even if we want to. Who knows what sort of mess she'll be in!" They little knew how frightened Mary was.

They continued to stare at the remaining pictures.

"One of them's got to come alive if we wait long enough. And if it does we'll go inside it and hunt for her, just like you two hunted for me."

Wesley's face was grave. "I don't know. Don't forget the jingle said, 'Once mayest thou enter but never again.' "

"Yeah, but maybe that means we can only enter each television once," Kurt offered. "There's still a couple sets we haven't gone through."

"I don't know," Lisa replied slowly. "Not that it matters. Gaal*said* we were going back, anyway." She clutched the sword tightly. "Not that I feel enthusiastic right now."

"You went through some real danger before we got to you last time."

Her face was expressionless. She thought of the evil jinn, of the sorcerer Hocoino, of being chained in darkness to a high altar and of her desperate flight into the House of Wisdom.

"In the end it was *I* who found *you*," she said referring back to Wesley's remark. "Though before that happened, it was Gaal who found me."

"I don't like the look of the tall queen person," Kurt said. "Doesn't the rooster. . . ."

"Oh, yes, the *rooster!*" Lisa exclaimed. "That must be the rooster Gaal's message was about!"

"I still don't like it," Kurt said. "The woman looks like a witch."

"I'm not sure the one of the city on the hill is any more inviting," Wesley murmured. "Let's stare at the one that looks like Nephesh Palace. Mebbe if we concentrate on it." They looked at the picture of the council chamber.

"I don't think we'll need to concentrate," Lisa said with growing excitement in her voice. "Can't you see what's happening?" Before their eyes the television screen melted and the three children found themselves looking at a tiny puppet theater on which miniature figures seemed to talk eagerly around a semicircular table. They heard the sound of footsteps ascending the attic stairs.

"I need more nails," came Great Aunt Felicia's voice. "Are you children up there in the attic?"

"Quick! Hold hands tightly, everyone! I'm going in!" Wesley whispered hoarsely.

And then as he pushed one foot in the television, in the strangely familiar way it had happened to them six months before, the whole scene seemed to swell and to sweep over them until they found themselves standing on a stone-flagged floor in an ancient council chamber, surrounded by the semicircular table. All movement stopped and twenty faces turned to stare at them.

5

Anthropos Betrayed

They knew they were in Anthropos. More than this they knew they were in Nephesh Palace. Wesley could now recognize the council chamber by the tapestries on the wall, and Lisa by the familiar black surface of the long semicircular table that curved round them. But who were the men and women facing them at the table? Where were King Kardia and Queen Suneidesis?

Wesley stared at two dwarfs at one end of the semicircle. Inkleth! Gunruth! And the woman—young and lithe, her gold hair falling over the shoulders of her blue gown—surely that was Chocma! But who were the other people?

"So you have come! After thirty-one years you have come back!" It was the king's voice. They all recognized it immediately. But when they turned toward the source of the voice, instead of the young, virile man they expected, they saw a face that was as gray as the man's hair and beard. Wesley jumped as he saw what looked like a dark green glass dagger protruding from the old man's chest. The voice was feeble. "My lord Wesley, my lord Kurt, dear lady Lisa! Welcome back to the Kingdom of Anthropos. You come as you came once before in an hour of peril." He seemed to have difficulty breathing and spoke in gasps.

"Your majesty!" Lisa's voice was shocked. "You are old ... I mean, you look ill! We didn't recognize you! And that dagger. . . ." She sounded almost as though she was about to cry.

Kardia (for it was indeed King Kardia) smiled wanly and turned to the council members seated on both sides of him. "My lady Chocma, gentlemen, bid our guests welcome! Bring them chairs that they may be seated."

It was only then that Wesley realized that the blank stares that had greeted their arrival had in reality been from people too stunned to grasp that the children were really there. Broad smiles and growing excitement began to register on the staring faces. One after another the council members rose to their feet to crowd round the ends of the table in their eagerness to greet the children.

"Inkleth. . . ."

"Gunruth, how good to see you!"

Kurt and Wesley found their breath being squeezed out of their rib cages by the mighty embraces of the two Matmon. Gunruth's beard was a little more gray now while Inkleth's beard, once bright red, was now showing signs of becoming salt and pepper. Of course the dwarfs had aged more slowly than the humans. For a few moments there was a hubbub of eager conversation.

Lady Chocma was holding Lisa's face between her hands. "Gaal sent you!" she cried. "Now need we fear no

51

longer!" Lisa stared back into her face, smooth yet age-less. She had known Chocma both as an old, old lady and as the young and lithe woman she now appeared to be.

"Your cottage," Lisa said, "is it still small on the outside and enormous on the inside?" And without waiting for an answer she hurried on. "What *is* the matter with the king?" But Chocma gave her no reply.

Wesley had caught sight of Nocham. "Sir Nocham!" he cried. "Your hair's almost white!"

Gunruth corrected him. "It is *Lord* Nocham of Authentio, now," he smiled. "And as for our hair, we have passed through more than thirty summers since you were with us last!"

The sound of excited talking slowly swelled, then died again as the council members resumed their places behind the table on either side of the king. Silence fell and Lisa, dismayed to see the king's drawn face said, "The dagger, your majesty! Can't it be taken out? Isn't there a doctor somewhere? You'll die...." She turned to the members of the council, "He'll die if you don't do something about it! How long has he been like that?"

Kardia replied, a smile hovering round his pale lips. "It is an enchanted dagger, little lady," he said quietly. "It is of enchanted darkness, and unless the bewitchment can be undone it will remain inside my heart." He paused, his breathing still labored. His face, covered with sweat, glistened in the light of the oil lamps on the walls. "We were meeting together to consider her majesty's danger...."

"The queen?"

"Suneidesis?"

"Yes, Suneidesis. She left us but nine days ago with my son, Tiqvah. We fear they may be in the hands of one who calls herself the Lady of Night."

"The Lady of Night?"

"Who is she?" Kurt could not restrain the question.

"The same who plunged this dagger in my bosom!"

"But how?"

Lord Nocham was about to interrupt but by a gesture the king prevented him. He paused again to regain his breath. "It is said that she is a witch from ancient times. Some say she came from the frozen north, others that she has lodged for centuries in Goldcoffin's Palace, deep in the heart of the northern mountains. It is her vaunted goal to rule the world with darkness. For some reason we do not understand the Sceptre of Anthropos is the key to her conquest of the world." He glanced at the ornately wrought, black iron rod, symbol of his rule in Anthropos, lying beneath his pale fingers on the table before him.

After a moment he continued. "Gaal gave me this when I was restored to power in Anthropos, some weeks after the Battle of Rinnar Heights. It was no ordinary gift. By it I am made a real king. Without it I am less than a beast. Should any man try to steal it from me while I slumber, he can no more do so than he could tear out my heart, so great is the power that binds it to me. Let a man try to wrest it from my grasp while I am awake, and though he have a thousand times my strength he will never succeed. In jest we have played the game a hundred times to see who could tear the sceptre from the hands of Kardia, king of Anthropos, and none has ever done so. Yet, and this is passing strange, if I choose I may yield it to whom I will."

"You must be very strong," Lisa said, looking puzzled.

"Nay, 'tis not a question of strength. All Anthropos knows my love of fenfinch pie. Yet many a man has torn a plate of it from my grasp!" He laughed, almost lightheartedly. "But the sceptre is another matter. It is bound to me by the laws of Gaal. Only when I break those laws that make me king can it be seized against my will."

Old Dipsuchos, a fussy courtier in a blue velvet robe interrupted the king. "No one can take the sceptre from his majesty," he squeaked. "Even this witch has no power to take it. None can snatch either sceptre or power to rule from Kardia of Anthropos!"

Kardia resumed his story. "Ten years past our days and our summers began to grow shorter, while our nights and our winters grew longer. The sun shone paler. Crops took longer to ripen and the fruit in our orchards remained acid. Some said our winters were colder, while in midwinter, even at midday the sky in the northern horizon was veiled in a curtain of night.

"The ancient ones among us assured us that such things had happened before, and that after a few lean years light and warmth would return. But their words have proved false.

"Now rumors reach us that this creeping darkness is part of an enchantment that threatens to engulf the world of which we are a part.

"Some days ago villagers from Playsion's northern coast came to beg lands in the south of Anthropos, for their crops had been ruined and starvation faced them. Nothing would dissuade her majesty (is she not rightful queen of Playsion?) from traveling to visit their lands and fields. With her she took his royal highness Prince Tiqvah. Strongbeak the eagle was sent with her as were their Lordships Ramah and Oqbah and a cohort of men-at-arms. We had expected word by now, but of Strongbeak there has been no sign. Then two nights ago there came a vision of pale beauty that stood beside my bed. Tall, she was, with a face the color of the moon, and wearing a crown the like of which I have never seen. . . ."

"Sort of like a Christmas tree?" Kurt could still not suppress his excitement.

"A Christmas tree?" Kardia sounded puzzled.

"He means a very big crown," Wesley interposed, "with diamonds hanging from it the size of pigeon's eggs!"

The king's eyes widened. "Then you have seen her?"

"Only on TV."

Again Kardia's frown deepened. "You speak of matters too high for me."

Lisa hastened to explain. "TV's a sort of vision. Like the *tele*vision that I told you about when I came here last time."

"Ah, yes. The proseo stone! So you have again come to us by means of a proseo stone. And you have seen the Lady of Night in it as well."

He paused, and there came a faraway look in his dark eyes. "Her voice was sweet and low. 'Give me your sceptre, Kardia of Anthropos, and I will restore the Tobath Mareh Tapestry to the wall of your banqueting chamber.'

" 'The sceptre is not mine to give,' I replied, 'and as for the Tobath Mareh Tapestry, it cannot be restored. It has been destroyed by fire.'

" 'Yet it was a thing of great beauty I am told,' said she.

" 'Of a beauty for which men sold their souls,' I replied, 'and for generations have my ancestors cherished it. But it is no more. It was burned in a palace fire ten years past.'

" 'What would you give me, Kardia of Anthropos, if I were to restore to you the Tobath Mareh Tapestry?'

" 'Who are you?' I asked. 'No mortal could restore the tapestry's beauty! The skill and cunning of the ancients is no more. Their secrets have died with them. No one living could weave it again.'

" 'Did you not weep, Kardia of Anthropos, when it was destroyed?'

" 'Aye,' I replied, 'and half the kingdom with me, for it was the delight of our eyes.'

" 'I am Mirmah, Lady of Night and Empress-to-Be of the Darkness that Swallows the World. I know the secrets of a thousand ages. I will restore your tapestry in exchange for your sceptre.'

"Dearly would I love to have the Tobath Mareh Tapestry again, and sorely was I tempted. But I received the sceptre from the hand of Gaal, who brought it to me from the skies above Lake Nachash, bidding me keep it all my life and give to none but him. And thus did I tell the Lady Mirmah.

" 'The sceptre is not mine to yield,' I told her. 'I hold it in fealty to Gaal, and to none but him will I yield it.'

"At this and before I could move, she pulled from the sleeve of her robe a dagger of dark green stone, plunging it into my chest. 'Let me see if this will change your mind,' she said—and was gone! I can feel its darkness there now. I am dead, yet I am not dead. I will not speak of pain, but the only strength left to me seems barely enough for me to hold on to the sceptre. And *that* I will not let go whether in life or in death, save that Gaal himself should come to take it." His head fell forward on the hands that gripped the sceptre, cold sweat soaking his gray locks.

Chocma's voice cut the silence that followed. "We have no clear knowledge, but ancient prophecies speak of Mirshaath, a witch who will try to conquer the world by hiding the sun. Whether it is Mirmah of the north and of Goldcoffin's mountain haunts, we cannot tell. Yet it is said that her power will not be enough unless she gains the Sceptre of Anthropos. We suspect she may have the queen and the prince in her power, and that she will hold them to ransom for the sceptre. But his majesty refuses—even should it mean their lives—to yield it.

"Some citizens of Anthropos speak of fleeing south to escape the coming dark age, but we know that if Anthropos falls, the enchantment will grip the rest of the world and no one will escape its power. Yet I see from your faces that you know something."

Wesley cleared his throat. "We have a cousin whose name is Mary McNab. For all we know Mary may be in the power of the witch you talk about. Last night she saw Gaal, though where or how we don't know. Yet she brought me the Sword of Geburah in token." He raised it to show them all.

"She gave us some pretty weird instructions from Gaal. We have to memorize a poem, though we don't know what the poem is for. We have to go by boat along a channel that passes through enchanted ice, and we may only leave the boat when we reach the heart of what Gaal called the Kingdom of Darkness. Somewhere—perhaps there—I must plunge this sword to the hilt in the center of a yellow circle. It doesn't make a lot of sense, but those are our instructions."

They were interrupted by a knock at the door of the council chamber. A soldier entered and bowed to King Kardia. Behind him was a troubled looking youth in a purple gold-laced jerkin and soft leather breeches. His blond hair fell over his shoulders and he held a sealed letter in his hand.

"Enter, Kaas," the king said. "Do not be afraid. What do you bring us?"

Wordlessly the boy crossed the stone floor, knelt before the king and handed him a sealed scroll. Slowly

Kardia broke the seal. As he read the letter aloud his face darkened.

To his Gracious Majesty Kardia of Anthropos, Lord Protector of the Realm of Playsion.

Greetings.

I am bidden by her Ladyship, Mirmah of the Night, Empress of the Darkness that Devours, to advise you that though her majesty Suneidesis of Playsion, and his Royal Highness Prince Tiqvah are safe for the present; nevertheless the darkness which surrounds the queen will choke her in a matter of days unless measures are taken to restore her.

Her ladyship has no wish to bring tragedy upon the reigning families of Anthropos and Playsion but deeply regrets that in the best interests of your citizens she will be obliged to sacrifice both your family's life and your own, unless the Iron Sceptre of Anthropos is delivered within a fortnight into her hands. It may be delivered at the entrance to her majesty's kingdom, which lies in a harbor of ice twelve leagues across the sea from the Playsion seaport of Chalash. I find it singularly distasteful to be the bearer of such tidings and only pray that your majesty's mercy will prove as great as your wisdom.

Your humble servant,

Ramah.

Kardia stared at the boy. "The letter is from your father, who went east to protect the queen." The boy nodded, still kneeling, his head bent low. "This letter bears no date. When came it into your hands?"

"It did not come by courier, your majesty. My . . . my father gave it to me before he left. He forbade me to deliver it to you until he had been gone ten days. He said that were I to do so sooner, your majesty might lose his life."

A roar of excited voices filled the room.

"Then Ramah was already in the pay of this so-called

Empress-to-Be before he left here! The queen was delivered into a trap!" squealed old Sir Dipsuchos.

"He knew before he set out that the queen would be betrayed and captured!" Lord Nocham growled.

"Ramah himself was one of her betrayers!"

All the time the youth crouched low before them.

"Seize him!" Inkleth cried, "To the dungeons with him! Let us see what else he knows."

The boy's face looked up into the king's, his eyes filled with fear. Chokingly he said, "Let you majesty deal with me as you see fit. But if I may give my life to undo what I have done, give me, I beseech your majesty, an opportunity."

"Don't listen to the rascal! He knew what was in the letter!"

Kardia raised his head. Weak and in pain as he was, he dominated the council by his mere presence. "He knew nothing of the contents of the letter. Could he not have lied and told us he had received it but today? And who among us has not seen that the boy who kneels before us was beaten, spat upon, abused and mocked throughout his life by the man who calls himself his father? The question that must be settled is, Does the letter speak truth? How do we know the plot succeeded? Is my wife in the hands of this upstart witch or is she free? Would her own subjects in the north of Playsion betray her or would they fight for her?"

Chocma quickly got up, excused herself and hurried from behind the table, past the children to a small round pool of water six feet across that lay in the floor of the council chamber behind the children's chairs.

"The mirror!" she cried, as she ran. "The waters are stirring!"

There wasn't room for everyone, and it is a miracle

that no one fell into the water. Kardia was helped and supported until he could sit on its edge, the dagger of dark green stone still protruding from his chest. Chocma, Wesley, Kurt and Lisa sitting near him had a clear view.

At first there was little to see. The waters were broken as though an invisible hand stirred the surface. Fractured images of their own faces and broken reflections of red torchlight mingled in confusion.

Then all was black and still. Slowly, as when mist fades, a scene grew clearer. It was as though they were staring at events taking place in the distance.

The foreground was filled with people, villagers and soldiers, soldiers who were chaining the villagers in long lines. Some lay on blood-stained grass. It was impossible to say whether they were dead or wounded. The center of the scene was dominated by a large sailing vessel.

"Some of those soldiers are of Anthropos," Lord Nocham murmured.

"And I could swear that others are of Playsion," Chocma added.

Beside the ship was the woman with the tall crown the children had seen on the TV screen, and beside her was an enormous rooster. "That is the one," they heard King Kardia murmur, referring doubtless to the witch.

A small knot of people was being herded toward the vessel and again they heard Kardia catch his breath. Looking sideways at him, Lisa saw his pale cheeks glow and his eyes flash. And as she looked back she saw the upright figure that she knew was Suneidesis and beside her, a tall, young man who she guessed was Prince Tiqvah, moving, their heads held high, to climb the steps of a rope ladder until they disappeared from view over the side of the ship. Kardia groaned softly. The villagers too

were marching in chains toward the ship.

Beside her, Lisa heard a low sob. She glanced at the boy Kaas, who had brought the letter. He didn't seem to be talking to anyone in particular but the words came despairingly from his mouth. "They've chained him too. I wish he hadn't gone." Lisa's heart softened toward him, and she quickly looked back in the pool to see what had caught his attention. Two men dressed in purple velvet the color of the boy's jerkin were climbing the rope ladder to the deck of the ship. Then the pool grew dark again, and they were able to see no more.

6

The Igloo and the Animals

"It's human all right, but it's the wrong color—too light,"
said Mrs. Ermine.

Mary McNab peered at the beautiful, long creature,
almost invisible against the snow wall of her prison.
Above her head a smoky oil lamp burned. Why the
speaker should think of Mary as too light was not clear.
Mrs. Ermine, apart from the black tip of her bushy tail
was, like all the other animals in the jail, pure white.

"It'll die if it doesn't put some more skins on," Mr.
Ermine replied.

Normally Mary hated people talking about her as
though she wasn't there. Some of the children in her
school in Toronto did the same sort of thing. Only when
they did it they would cast sideways glances at her to see
what effect their words had and whether Mary was getting mad or not. The children did it to tease her. But Mr.

& Mrs. Ermine talked about her in a very grown-up way as though it didn't matter whether she heard or not, or as though she was too young to understand what they were talking about.

But Mary was cold and too miserable to care what Mr. & Mrs. Ermine thought. Her head ached from the cuff the grizzly had given her before he had tossed her unceremoniously into a snowy domed room lit by two oil lamps (not unlike pictures of igloos Mary had seen in our own world, only rather bigger). She had skinned her knees as she fell on the ice floor, so that what with smarting knees, a headache, uncontrollable shivering, and a terrible anxiety about what would happen to her, she had little thought left for talking ermines.

The six animals who were her fellow prisoners had tried politely to ignore Mary as she was bundled unceremoniously into the jail. Mr. & Mrs. Arctic Fox abruptly dropped a bitter argument they were having about whose fault their imprisonment was and watched her out of the corners of their eyes. Mr. & Mrs. Arctic Hare had not been talking. They had simply snuggled closely together, but both of them had felt sorry for the strange creature that had come among them, who seemed so helpless and out of place.

"If it had any sense it would put some of *those* on," Mrs. Ermine continued, nodding her quick pointed nose at a pile of caribou parkas and trousers lying in a heap on one side of the prison.

"Well, obviously it doesn't have any sense," Mr. Ermine rejoined. "I wonder how long it will take to die? They generally don't last too long when they stray into these parts."

Just at that moment Mary almost felt she didn't care if she did die. Anything would be better than what had happened. She had been terrified when the grizzly raised itself to its full height and growled something about trespassing. Then, whisked upward, cracked violently on the side of the head and flung through a tunnel into the igloolike jail, she felt very frightened indeed. The bear thought he was being gentle, for Gaal had strict laws about brutality, but the grizzly was a raw recruit in Gaal's service.

"Gaal asked me to come here," she had sobbed, crawling to the tunnel entrance. "You've no right to treat me this way."

"I've heard that sort of tale before," the grizzly had called back. "You stay where you are and do what you're told." He was not hardhearted as grizzlies go but he was not very bright either. It never seemed to occur to him how cold Mary might be.

The Ermines, of course, were exaggerating. Inside the snowy prison the temperature was above freezing. Mary would be uncomfortable, but she was not likely to die though the Ermines continued to discuss the possibility quite heartlessly.

"Oh, I don't know. Sometimes they last for hours."

"Usually they die pretty quickly."

"Outside, maybe. But not in here."

"You may be right, but it's pretty cold. Not like our own lovely, warm home. Whatever made you suggest we set out today on our expedition? I wish to goodness they'd let us go. This place is miserable."

"I wonder where the human came from."

Mary stopped listening. She was crying softly, shivering and crouching, since she couldn't sit. She was wearing, not jeans, but a dress. It is very cold when you sit on ice without proper clothing. But after a moment, turning to look at the pile of skins the Ermines had mentioned, it began to occur to her, in spite of her misery, that there might be some sense in looking for warmth in the pile of fur. She picked up the piece lying on top and discovered that it was some sort of garment and that it was heavy. There were sleeves and there was a hood. It was in fact a parka, the kind you have to pull over your head because it doesn't open at the front. The fur was thick and soft. The hood was trimmed with a darker fur, and the bottom edge of the parka and of the sleeves were trimmed with a thick, woolly white fur.

She was just about to pull it over her head when a gentle voice said, "You put the other one on first." She turned and saw that it was one of the hares (Mrs. Arctic Hare, in fact, though Mary couldn't have told the difference) that had spoken.

"Which one? I mean, which one goes on first?"

"I'm sorry, dearie. It's really not my place to be telling you what to do, but that's the way the *other* humans put them on."

Mary stood staring at her, the caribou-skin parka hanging from her hand. She had no idea what other humans the animal was talking about, but she sensed the kindness in Mrs. Arctic Hare's voice, and did not doubt for a moment that Mrs. Arctic Hare knew all about the parkas.

"If you'll look at the pile there, I think you'll find one with the fur on the *inside*," Mrs. Arctic Hare said. "At least there *should* be one. Excuse me, I know I've no right to interfere, but if we're to get you warm let's get you really warm. We wouldn't want you to get sick now, would we?"

As she spoke she hopped over to the pile of skins. Her husband hopped after her. "Yes, Mrs. Hare," he was saying, "let's get the kitten properly covered up. We mustn't have it getting sick on us."

"Of course, Mr. Hare, my dear."

Mary was a little taken aback by being referred to as a kitten (which is what artic hares in Anthropos call their own young) but once again the obvious concern Mr. Arctic Hare showed comforted her.

The hare tugged busily and energetically, dragging a fur-lined skin parka from the pile, while Mr. Arctic Hare, his mouth filled with another skin was saying, "Zees sings for ze legsh go on, . . ." he dropped the skin, " . . . go on first, I believe, dear." Mary picked up the fur-lined trousers Mr. Arctic Hare had dragged out for her inspection. "Put them on," he said. Mary did, finding them warm, very cozy and only slightly tickly. Surprisingly they fit her perfectly. But how could she keep them from slipping down?

Mr. Arctic Hare had dragged another pair of skin trousers from the pile, only unlike the first pair the fur was on the outside, and there were shoulder straps to hold them up.

"There, my dear. You put these on over the top of the others," Mrs. Arctic Hare was saying.

"You mean I wear two pairs?"

"Yes, dear, one with the fur inside, and the other with the fur outside."

Mary had quite a struggle getting the second pair on, but eventually she succeeded, hitching the straps over her shoulders. Her legs felt wonderfully warm, but awkward inside the thick skins. ("Something like wearing a space suit," she thought to herself.) By the time she had the second pair hitched up Mr. Arctic Hare was waiting with a fur-lined parka.

"This one first, then the one with the fur on the outside," he said.

Mary found it even more of a struggle to get into the

parkas. Mr. & Mrs. Arctic Hare gave what help they could, tugging here and there with their teeth. Eventually it was all in place and she found herself kicking her shoes off and tugging on beautiful mukluks, both lined and covered with fur. A pair of furry mitts completed the outfit.

All the time Mary had, with the aid of the Arctic Hares, been dressing, the Arctic Foxes had resumed their quarreling, snarling and snapping at each other.

"Idiot! It was all your fault."

"Idiot yourself! Why didn't you run when I told you to? He couldn't have gone after both of us."

"Don't take any notice of them, dearie," Mrs. Arctic Hare said. "They've been at it ever since they came in. You know, you look beautiful in that outfit. It really suits you. Might have been made for you. Doesn't she look nice, Mr. Hare?"

Mary was beginning to perspire inside the heavy fur skins. They had a strange smell, but she didn't mind. The warmth and the friendliness of the hares comforted her. She longed to pick them up and cuddle them, but somehow it didn't seem right. They behaved too much like protective adults. Yet she couldn't help but pull off one of her mitts and reach out to touch Mrs. Arctic Hare's soft white fur and say, "Thank you." (Mary McNab didn't often say, "Thank you.") "You've been very kind."

"The creature does look a lot better," said Mr. Ermine.

"But she obviously hadn't the remotest idea how to use the skins," sniffed Mrs. Ermine. "Not very intelligent, I would say. Probably won't survive anyway once she gets out of here."

"Take no notice of *them* either," Mrs. Arctic Hare whispered. "They're very conceited animals and look down their noses at everybody, don't they, Mr. Hare?"

"That's right, Mrs. Hare. Think they're above everyone else. But they never seem happy. I think they just talk like that because they're envious of the rest of us."

"That may well be, Mr. Hare. But it's very rude and unkind of them to talk like that about a frightened kitten."

The "frightened kitten" was beginning to like Mr. & Mrs. Arctic Hare very much. She felt just a little uncomfortable at their remarks about the Ermines. Was she herself so critical and proud (she had certainly been pretty boastful with her cousins) because she envied other people's happiness? Certainly she wasn't happy very often. She shut the thought out of her mind, and let her fingers caress Mrs. Arctic Hare's thick white fur.

Suddenly all talk inside the snow jail was silenced by a growl that made the very walls shake. "It's the polar bear," said Mr. Arctic Hare softly. "He's the head of the patrols."

"You mean you threw them all in here as prisoners?" came the terrible growl from outside.

"Well, sir, yes, sir," they heard the grizzly say. "I mean they had no right to be in this area in the first place. It's been closed off, hasn't it? I thought, sir, meaning no disrespect, sir, that it was my job, sir, to guard the area."

The growl that came from the polar bear grew to a roar. "You were meant to protect Gaal's creatures from the dangers of this area. The prison was meant for any prowlers from the Kingdom of Darkness."

"But the human. . . ."

"I know all about the human. We'll talk about her later. Now, have you warned the animals you took as prisoners that this is a dangerous area?"

"Yes, sir."

"And what did they say?"

"We told him to mind his own business and that we could look after ourselves!" yapped Mr. Arctic Fox.

There was a moment's silence from outside. "Come out here, whoever said that!" The polar bear's growl was low and menacing. Mr. Arctic Fox licked his lips nervously and began to shake. "I said come out here!" The growl was softer, but somehow more terrible than ever.

Mr. Arctic Fox rose to his feet. His head was held low, and his beautiful white brush dragged on the floor between his legs. He was shaking from head to foot. Slowly he approached the exit passage, Mrs. Arctic Fox following him, equally cowed.

"So you told him to mind his own business, and that you could look after yourselves?" the growl went on. There was a pitiful, low yelping sound from Mr. Arctic Fox, then a terrified squeal. All of them inside could imagine the little creature being picked up by the great polar bear. And when there came a half scream, half yelp—they all could picture the massive paw of the polar bear cuffing Mr. Arctic Fox's head.

"Now let that be a lesson. This area is dangerous. Next time you come something worse might happen to you." Mr. Arctic Fox's yelps died rapidly away as he ran off into the distance.

"And what of the rest?"

"Well, the human...."

"We'll come to the human in a minute. What of the other prisoners you took. Did they show any tendency to ignore your warnings?"

"Well, no sir, not exactly."

"What d'you mean by 'not exactly'?"

"Well, sir, in fact not at all. I just thought, sir...."

"Thought! You *thought*? That's the last thing you did.

We don't imprison Gaal's subjects for no reason. Come outside, all of you!"

The Ermines were already sinuously streaking into the passage. Mr. & Mrs. Arctic Hare looked up at Mary.

"Good-bye, dear. Don't be scared. No harm will come to you. Good-bye!"

Mary watched them hop into the entrance tunnel and suddenly felt alone and frightened again. She could hear the polar bear apologizing to the Ermines and to Mr. & Mrs. Arctic Hare, and warning them at the same time of the danger in the area.

"What danger?" Mary wondered.

"Now, human little girl!" It was the voice of the polar bear rumbling softly. "I'm too big to come through the tunnel, but I've brought you some food. Come to the entrance and get it."

Mary was terrified but she was also hungry. Crawling through the passage she felt the hairs on the back of her neck prickle as she saw the silhouette of the polar bear's head in the dim light. A massive white paw pushed two bundles toward her across the icy floor. Mary's heart beat suffocatingly, but she seized the bundles and crawled back into the jail.

"Eat well, little girl. Gaal will decide what is to be done with you. I'm sure he won't leave you here for long."

Mary quickly discovered that one of the bundles was a skin bottle of milk. The other package, also of leather, contained crisp, freshly baked bread whose smell made her mouth water, and cold roast meat. Greedily she began to eat and drink.

"Where in the world did you find her?" she heard the polar bear asking.

"I don't really know, sir," the young grizzly replied. "It was like seeing a picture in a piece of ice and the piece

71

of ice grew and grew. Then there wasn't any ice. It was like crates washed up on the shore," his voice sounded very puzzled, " . . . and, sir, she was hiding under a sort of crate, at least I thought it was a crate . . . and, sir, she was obviously hiding, . . ." his voice trailed away.

"Well, she's here anyway. And we must await further instructions from Gaal. Meanwhile you'd better get off watch and get some sleep. I'll get one of the Koach to watch the entrance. Here's one of the wolves now. White-fur, come and take over guard of the cell."

Mary never heard the soft padding of the wolf's feet. From outside came the slowly mounting sounds of a howling wind, as though a blizzard was beginning. She found the milk strange but very satisfying while the bread was delicious. She ate the whole loaf. The meat tasted strong. So she decided to leave it. In fact she felt uncomfortably full, almost as though the milk and bread gave her indigestion.

But Mary had other things on her mind than indigestion. One of Mary's problems at school had always been that she didn't believe what people in authority told her. Danger? What danger was there in *snow*?

She wiped her mouth with the back of her hand, slipped on her new mitts and pulled the furry hood of her parka over her head. By now the wind was screaming and she should have known that there was a full blizzard.

Her curiosity was rising. She crawled on her hands and knees to the entrance of the passage. There was no wolf to be seen. In fact, there was nothing at all but an impenetrable gray-white that dimly reflected the lamplight from inside the igloo as the howling wind whipped powdery snow in a white sheet across the entrance.

Mary had heard people say you should never leave shelter during a blizzard, but a few yards wouldn't mat-

72

ter. As she emerged from the tunnel a fierce and frozen gale snatched her breath away. Fine snow particles pelted her face and forced themselves into her nostrils.

She stood up precariously. Leaning against the tremendous wind, she tottered a few steps forward until her feet sank into a shallow drift. The next moment a powerful gust bowled her over, and she found herself rolling helplessly, blown by the awful gale.

Somehow she struggled to her hands and knees and turned toward her former prison. But there was nothing to be seen but a dense blackness while snow whipped her face. It was only after she had crawled for several minutes, exhausted now by the struggle, that she began to realize that even in so short a time she was lost in a blizzard.

7

A Giant Dish of Ice Cream

Mary was so exhausted that for a moment or two she gave way to the luxury of lying down in the soft snow. It felt good to relax and to let weariness drain from her limbs. The blizzard screamed across her. She was warm from her efforts, even perspiring, but the wind's piercing cold brought intense pain to her forehead and cheekbones. Panic was rising in her.

"I can't be more than a few yards away," she said to herself anxiously, thinking of the snow jail house. "I must have been going in a circle."

If I had been Mary I would have been frightened too, and Mary assured me (when we talked later) that she was very scared indeed. She paused to rest a little longer and forced herself to think about the problem more carefully. "Yet if I've been going in a circle, I should be back at the snow house by now. I should wind up where I started. Mebbe I've not gone far enough."

Mary, as you can see, was a pretty intelligent girl, however disagreeable she may have been. She struggled to her hands and knees, whimpering and forcing herself in spite of her weariness to go on.

"I'm *bound* to get back sooner or later," she half sobbed. Yet doubts rose in her mind. Was it true that you went in circles in a blizzard? Were they exact circles or did you sort of spiral? Perhaps she had passed the snow house already. Was she crawling in a circle of which the snow house was the center? If so, oughtn't she to go at right angles?

She had a brief impression of a deeper darkness looming above her, felt her mitts slipping, and then her whole body slithering headfirst down a slope. A moment later she slid onto a platform of ice. Instantly the blizzard stopped. She seemed to be somewhere underground. Something, or someone, then seized her from behind. It had happened too suddenly for her to feel anything except a tinge of shock. She had slipped down a tunnel of ice across the entrance of which the howling blizzard, its scream now muted, continued to hurl fine snow crystals. Below her, green steps of ice led to hidden depths.

The something that seized her was holding on to her parka and growling. She lay still as a frozen river making no attempt to escape. The growling something let go of her and began to sniff. As he moved round to where she could see him, she discovered that he was a large and stiff-legged husky. Not entirely satisfied with how she smelled, he stood by her feet, growling.

Mary never made a move. The husky's lips were pulled back, showing his teeth. He snarled. "Who is Gaal?"

"Who is Gaal?" Mary repeated, bewildered.

"You heard me. I'll only ask you once more. Who is Gaal?"

Her mind was spinning. Then between gasps for breath the words came tumbling out:
Gaal is the Lord of far and near.
Gaal is the Lord of light,
Gaal is the Lord of sea and fire.
And Gaal is the Lord of ice.
The husky's lips lowered and his teeth disappeared. He began to look more friendly.

"No one told me you were coming," he said. "Did the patrol bring you?"

Mary was still recovering her breath. "Well, not exactly," she panted. "The chief polar bear gave me some food."

The husky looked puzzled. "I suppose it must be all right. You knew the password. Go ahead to the bottom of the steps. Be careful you don't slip. The seal will tell you what to do next."

Mary did the only thing she could have done under the circumstances. She had evidently stumbled on something, and tired or not there seemed no way but to go on with her adventure. For a moment she thought of asking the husky to show her the way back to the jail house, but the thought of the buffeting, screaming blizzard changed her mind. On the other hand, what might she find at the bottom of the steps? The husky had talked about the steps as though they were very ordinary. He had even mentioned a seal at the bottom. "The seal is sure to be friendly," she told herself. The only seals she had ever seen had been at the zoo where they had performed interesting tricks and had played "God Save the Queen" on old automobile horns. She decided to go on.

Her legs felt weak. Awkwardly, bloated by the fur parkas, she waddled to where the narrow staircase began, relieved to see that though the steps stretched down a long way (too far down for her to see the bottom) they were lit with pale blue lamps. Taking care not to slip, she began her descent. Down she went and down, down, down. Soon her legs were like columns of jelly, and she sat down shakily to rest.

Weren't icebergs mostly under water? Was she under the water level now? Mary tried to think of her geography lessons. Was this Hudson Bay? Or Greenland? She did not know she was in another universe, another *kind* of universe in another age. She gave up the problem and leaned against the pretty, blue ice wall, waiting for her legs to recover.

Then down and down she went for another half-hour, stopping for several more rests. When at last she saw that the steps were opening onto a second platform, she began to hurry and in doing so, slipped. If you've ever slipped on ordinary stairs you'll realize Mary's problem. Steps of ice, lined by walls of ice, with no banister or handrail make it difficult to regain your balance. Mary rolled, slithered and bumped her way to the level area in as undignified a fashion as she had slithered onto the upper platform. Fortunately she was too well padded by fur clothing to hurt much.

She stopped abruptly when she bumped into a solid, dark mass of flesh and fat. As she scrambled to her hands and knees, she found herself facing the curves of a friendly, old seal, his flippers stretched out on the ice and his gleaming, little eyes staring at her above long whiskers.

"Who is Gaal?" barked the seal.

This time Mary was ready with the answer. The seal looked pleased.

"Good. You got it right the first time. Good job for you that you did." His eyes twinkled. "I'm pretty strict with people who get it wrong. And I wasn't expecting you so soon. There were to be four of you. Where are the other three?"

Mary stared at the seal. It began to dawn on her that he was talking about Wesley, Kurt and Lisa. So *they* were expected here. And she had arrived before them. Well, she wasn't going to wait for them to find her. They might send her back. The seal was expecting an answer.

"I'm afraid I don't know," she replied, reasonably honest. After all, where *were* the Friesen children at that moment?

"What would you like to do? Wait for them or go ahead?" He was obviously trying to be helpful.

"I . . . I think I'll go on ahead."

"You sure? It's pretty dangerous. The Kingdom of Darkness lies ahead, you know."

"Yes, I know." She didn't know, but she knew enough from the message she had given to the Friesen children that it was not exactly safe. After all, you don't find swords or help kings and queens on Sunday-school picnics. "Only I don't know the way to the . . . to the enchanted circles."

She felt rather clever about bringing in the enchanted circles. It would be sure to convince the seal if he still needed to be convinced that she was supposed to be there.

"Well, that's my job, to set you on your way. You'll have to go by boat from here. And remember, *don't* get out of the boat. But I expect you've had that drilled into you already."

Staring around her Mary was awed to see that they were in a dim cave of ice, a cave so vast that she could not see the roof. All around them was the same blue light she had seen on the stairway, but deeper in the cave beyond where they stood red light glimmered menacingly among black shadows. From where the red light came she could not tell.

Just beyond the platform a broad canal crossed the front of the cave. So far as Mary could see the canal seemed to go in a great circle all around the sides of the cave. Immediately beyond the canal, and opposite to where Mary was sitting, two narrow channels stretched back toward the center of the cave. From the left-hand channel green water glinting with blue light tumbled and frothed into the canal, while the right-hand channel sucked water avidly into itself. The left-hand channel spewed water out; the right one gulped it in.

"It's the channel on your right that you take," the seal said. "You won't have to worry about paddling or sailing. Just let the current carry you all the way to the Kingdom of Darkness—and *don't* get out of the boat too soon. You won't do that now, will you?"

"Oh, no. Really, I won't." Mary was anxious to be on her way before the Friesen children arrived. The seal humped and flopped his way to where a group of boats was drawn up at the water's edge. There were birch-bark canoes, canoes called umiaks made with walrus hide stretched over a wooden framework, and kayaks. The seal selected a small kayak.

"You'll find it a bit wobbly," he said, pushing it toward her with his nose. Mary grasped the prow with her mitts and pulled. The kayak was extraordinarily light.

"Ever been in one of these?"

"Er, . . . no, I haven't."

"Well, the channel's narrow and you can hold your paddle," Mary had already picked up the two-bladed paddle, "above the ice on each side. Once you're in the channel you'll be O.K. Soon get used to it." He pushed

79

the kayak into the canal and slid gracefully into the water beside it. Mary saw his head on its far side holding the boat steady for her.

"Get in," he barked, "I won't let it tip."

Cautiously she sat on the edge of the ice, dropped her feet through the opening in the kayak and then pushed her legs forward and sat down. Several times the little boat almost turned over, but the seal expertly kept it upright.

"Now, hold your paddle up so the blades are above the ice on either side of the channel. Then you won't tip over. I'll push you across the canal and into the entrance."

Mary was not hungry, but food was never far from her mind. "How will I eat?" she asked.

"Leather pouches of food stowed all round the inside," barked the seal.

The nose of the kayak was now entering the channel and before she had time to think she found herself moving rapidly forward. "Keep your paddle up! And don't forget the other passwords!"

She turned her head to see the seal receding into the distance. "Passwords?"

"Yes, you know. He says, 'The sun is dead,' and you say, 'Darkness reigns and ice has come to worship it.' And then there's. . . ." But he was now too far away for her to hear what he was saying. The rushing water drowned out other sounds.

Mary concentrated on keeping the kayak upright as she began to travel forward at an increasing speed. "The sun is dead. . . . Darkness reigns and ice has come to worship it," she muttered to herself over and over again.

Hours passed.

The sides of the cave had disappeared long since. The only sounds were those of rushing water in the two parallel channels. Mary was gliding swiftly into an endless dark red void. She had eaten . . . precariously. The first time she tried she almost lost her paddle. Then she succeeded in wedging it into the narrow opening in the kayak.

There was milk and bread—the kind the polar bear had given her—and Mary was growing to like them more and more. She still found the meat strong, but she ate a little of it.

She could neither tell how far she had traveled nor how long, since her watch was in the attic of Uncle John's house. She had eaten three times. However, Mary's mealtimes tended to get closer together when she was alone. She was about to consider a fourth meal when she sensed she was getting toward the end of the cave. Something about the sound of the water was changing. What lay ahead? She could not be sure. She strained her eyes for several minutes.

Gradually a black arch began to take shape. Getting closer she could see she was facing a wall of ice above and around the arch. It turned out to be the entrance into a wide tunnel.

The current slowed and she drifted, hardly moving at all. She was startled to see a huge walrus lying on her right. She was sure he was waiting for her. His tusks pointed down but his head was raised, and his right flipper hung over the edge of the channel.

As she drifted past him, his flipper stopped her and rested heavily on the kayak, tipping it slightly forward. Staring into the one eye she could see, she wondered whether he was looking at her. Or was he staring straight ahead of himself?

"Perhaps it's like Disneyland," she said rather unconvincingly to herself. "He's probably not a real walrus."

The walrus began to speak in a silly sing-song way. "Welcome to the approaches to the City of Ice. May you shiver in the dark forever! May your bed freeze over for at the end times there will be darkness, darkness, everlasting darkness."

"It's all recorded," Mary thought. "I wonder if I ought to reply?"

Then, quite suddenly, with no change in his tone of voice he said, "The sun is dead," and Mary, remembering the last words of the seal, said, "Darkness reigns and ice has come to worship it." She hoped there was nothing more to it and that the words would be enough to make the walrus raise his flipper. They were. The released kayak began to drift past him. Mary asked, "Is it far to the enchanted circles? How long will it take to get to the Kingdom of Darkness?"

The walrus stared straight ahead as though she were not there and said, "Dark was. Dark is. Dark ever will be."

Mary shrugged her shoulders. "I guess it can only say three or four things."

The walrus continued to stare straight ahead. The kayak moved more quickly, and she left him behind. His last sing-song words floated through the red light to her. "In water you may travel fast, but once the water freezes you never move again. You will stay in the dark forever and ever."

The current was faster now, and a moment later the little kayak shot into the black tunnel. Would the water freeze here in the dark? Was there any way of stopping the kayak? Of turning back? She had no experience paddling kayaks.

Red light began to alleviate the darkness again. Red letters glowed on an archway ahead. As the kayak sped toward it Mary caught a glimpse of the words "CIRCLE OF THE ENCHANTMENT OF BODILY YEARN-INGS" and then passed it, entering what seemed like another cave so huge that it was like going into the open air. The Circle of the Enchantment of Bodily Yearnings. Strange as it may seem, the words comforted Mary a little. She little knew how great her peril was.

The kayak slowed to a halt. On her right Mary could see something huge. The darkness made it hard to see clearly. It looked like a very large dish, heaped high with food. "It could be a dish of ice cream with a whipped-cream topping," Mary said to herself. "I know the walrus said I mustn't get out, but the kayak *has* stopped. What else is there to do? I can't stay here forever."

To tell you the truth, she was scared of tipping and was sitting like a statue. But anything shaped like food interested her very much. Slowly she thought matters over. It *did* look like a giant dish of ice cream. If this place was like Disneyland then the giant dish could not be intended for a real giant. It might not even be edible. It might only be made of plastic. Still the kayak did not move. Gingerly Mary tried to stand up, and a moment later had the awful sensation of a boat swinging sideways under her feet. She grabbed the sides, froze into stillness, and it settled down.

"I'd better just jump," she muttered desperately.

But when you jump you need something steady to jump from, and the kayak was anything but steady. As Mary leapt the kayak shot away from the bank, tipping sideways as it did so, and flinging Mary ungracefully on the ice at the water's edge. She got up just in time to see her boat drifting away into the red darkness. For a moment she watched it. Then, shrugging her shoulders she walked across the ice to the thing that looked like a giant dish of ice cream.

And it *was* a dish of ice cream—chocolate fudge ice cream full of walnuts (the size human beings are used to) and topped with twenty gallons of whipped cream and a giant cherry the size of a soccer ball. I forgot to tell you the chocolate fudge ice cream with walnuts was Mary's favorite. There was a wooden spoon beside the dish—the kind you stir Christmas cakes with. Mary picked it up, scooped herself a bite, tasted it, and drew in a quick breath of delight. She then took a large mouthful of the ice cream and sighed with sudden relief.

She kept eating, eyeing the cherry from time to time and slowly deciding she would have to leave it, at least for the present. Somehow the idea of climbing up a slope of chocolate ice cream did not appeal to her. She liked whipped cream. But she would hate to fall face forward into it and smother. Besides, what could she do with a cherry the size of a soccer ball?

Before long Mary began to feel very full. Her fur clothing grew tight and constricting. She struggled to ease the pants down a bit but found she could not for they were gripping her too tightly. Unfortunately Mary never knew when to stop eating ice cream. Again and again she dug the spoon into the lovely mixture and stuffed it into her mouth. She began to swell like a balloon. Even her face was swollen.

At last she could eat no more. She felt very, very uncomfortable. Never in her life had she eaten so much. She pulled off her mitts and when she saw her hands she gasped with dismay. Have you ever blown up a rubber glove? If you have, you might have an idea of what Mary's hands looked like. They were enormous, the fin-

gers sticking out at curious angles.

The tightness of her clothing had grown painful. Every moment she seemed to be swelling more. "I'm going to blow up!" she gasped in panic. "I'm going to burst like a balloon. Oh, Gaal! Gaal! Where are you? It must be the ice cream that's doing it. Oh, Gaal, how was I to know? Gaal! Gaal! Can you hear me?"

I'm sure Gaal must have heard her, though if Mary had known what he would do I think she would never have cried out for him. For she began to feel sick. Before long she knew that she was about to lose all the ice cream she had so eagerly swallowed.

She turned in disgust and loathing from the dish. "Oh, dear," she said. "I'll never eat chocolate fudge ice cream again. Never! Not *ever!*"

Then she knelt on her hands and knees and vomited. Now I know it's not nice to talk about people vomiting, but I'm afraid I'm going to have to. I don't know how to explain it, but what went into Mary was *not* what came out of her. What went in was chocolate fudge ice cream and walnuts. What came out was pale blue, shining and froze into a mirror, a mirror in which she could see her own reflection.

Her face was even more swollen than her hands had been. When she saw herself she began to cry. "Oh Gaal, what can I do? I didn't know it would make me this fat!" Then she vomited some more.

The next time she looked into the mirror she could tell that her face was a little less swollen. Her clothes, too, though still tight were less painful. Even her hands were more normal. But the sight of her swollen and pimpled face made her cry and vomit once again.

The process must have gone on for half an hour, and by the end of it Mary felt she had nothing left inside her.

Around her the blue and shining mirror reflected back at her the face she had always known against the background of a giant dish of ice cream. She put her mitts back on.

"That's better," she said as she surveyed herself. Anything was better than the way the ice cream had made her. Then a shock pierced her. The mirror she stared into slowly grew black as night. Beside her own reflection the mirror showed the reflection of a tall and beautiful woman, bearing on her head the largest crown Mary had even seen. Above her left eyebrow there was a mole —just like the one Mary's stepmother had. Mary froze with fear, not daring to look up. She never forgot the contrast of the two faces, her own face round and full of pimples and the lady's face, oval, white, with beautiful amethyst eyes.

"Darling, what a lovely mirror! But it's dangerous, you know. Did you find it here?"

Still Mary did not look up.

"I . . . I vomited it," she breathed softly.

Suddenly she was snatched up into the powerful arms of the Lady of Night. "My darling," Mary heard her say, "you mustn't look into a mirror that came from inside you. You will never be beautiful that way. Come to my palace and let me give you a *magic* mirror, a magic mirror far better than your blue one. I think you're already beautiful, very beautiful, but if you wish, I will give you my kind of beauty, and your very own mirror to see yourself."

Mary was surprised to find how warm she could be in the arms of the lady. She was not in the least afraid. Suddenly everything grew totally dark. The last thing she remembered was the sensation of flying.

8

The King Sends a Letter

For several minutes Kardia sat motionless, staring into the pool. Its surface was settled and calm, reflecting the people who surrounded it, and the torch flames wavering against the walls of the council chamber. After several minutes, he rose to his feet and was helped by Lord Nocham to his chair. Once the king was seated there was a general movement as everybody else resumed their seats. Only Kaas beside Wesley's chair remained standing.

Wesley who had attended student council meetings, felt how very different a royal council was. The red lamps flickering on people's faces made him conscious that they were in another world and another age. The dim light emphasized the solemnity on everyone's face—on Lord Nocham's, Chocma's, Gunruth's, Inkleth's and above all on Kardia's. It flickered also on the hilt of the glass dagger still protruding from Kardia's chest. Wesley could see by glancing sideways at Kurt and Lisa that they too were solemn and a little frightened.

The king was the first to speak, slowly and painfully. Turning to Chocma he asked, "The pool does not lie?"

"No, your majesty. It speaks only truth."

"Then my wife and son are now in the hands of this evil woman."

"Yes, your majesty. Let me, I pray your majesty, serve you a cup of wine from my home in the forest. It will ease your majesty's pain and give you strength." The king nodded wearily, and at Chocma's word a servant left to return a moment later with a silver cup which Chocma herself held to the king's lips. "Drink deeply, your majesty. You have need of strength and courage at such a time as this."

The wine was evidently no ordinary wine. As he returned the cup to her his shoulders straightened, his face regained some of its color and a sparkle returned to his eyes. Had it not been for the hilt of a dagger protruding from his chest or for the gray in his hair and beard, he might have been the young king the children knew on their previous visit to Anthropos.

"There were signs of fighting in the vision."

"Yes, your majesty," Lord Nocham said. "Her majesty the queen and Prince Tiqvah were not taken easily. Someone fought to protect them."

"Aye," the king retorted, "but who fought to defend them, and who fought to capture them?"

"Some of the soldiers wore strange uniforms," Chocma said, "yet I could swear they were men of Anthropos and Playsion."

"Traitors," Inkleth said. "Traitors serving the witch and that absurd roosterlike creature. Those who died defending her majesty were villagers of Playsion. For it was villagers who were herded toward the ship, and it was the soldiers who herded them. Why would they wear the witch's uniform unless they had accepted her service?"

"It was even so," replied Kardia, "and it would seem that treachery exists not only in my court and in this very council (for were not their Lordships Ramah and Oqbah members of it?) but in the ranks of our armies. How widespread is this treachery? How much of a threat does it now pose to us? Who are our friends and who are our foes?"

There was an uncomfortable silence, broken after a moment by a hesitant cough from Sir Dipsuchos, the old man in the blue velvet robe and the black skullcap. "Your majesty will pardon me," he said, "if I again express concern for her majesty and his royal highness. . . ."

"I too am concerned for my wife and son," Kardia replied a little testily. "Do you suggest I lack concern?"

"By no means, your majesty, though should his royal highness be harmed, there will be no one to succeed your majesty as king. I realize how delicate is the matter I raise. But your majesty must consider your own peril. From your body a dagger protrudes. Your son and heir is threatened with death. What will happen to Anthropos should both of you die?"

"In that case Anthropos will be governed by whomever Gaal appoints. The ancient and noble family of Ratson has a claim to the throne. What matters, my good Dipsuchos, is not that I or mine continue to occupy the throne, but that the throne continue, and above all that the sceptre remain in the kingdom."

"Yet consider, your majesty, how disturbing to the citizens your death would be at such a time of crisis. The sceptre is a valueless thing of iron. If it were part of the kingdom's treasures, it might be different. Might it not be better for us to accede, in some measure at least, and perhaps only temporarily to the demands of this woman?"

"For *us* to accede?" There was an edge to the king's voice. "Did I not hear you tell us firmly and clearly half an hour ago that I and only I am able to yield the sceptre and that no one can oblige me to yield it up?"

"Of course, your majesty. . . ."

"And did I not hear you say that he who holds the sceptre, of mere iron though it be, will rule Anthropos and that no army can snatch the kingdom from him?"

"You heard aright, your majesty. '

"Then let us have done with this word *us*," Kardia said quietly. "If the sceptre is to be yielded up, it is *I* not *we* who will yield it. Let it be known by all here that I choose not to yield it to any save the Lord Gaal."

"But if your majesty should die . . .?"

"I do not intend to die."

But your majesty must face the possibility."

"Dipsuchos, I am not dead yet, nor are my wife and son. And since it is the will of Gaal that I yield the sceptre to none but to him from whom I received it, I have confidence that *should* I die he will be there to receive it from me. Until then let us have done with talk of yielding it—temporarily or otherwise. Are you for Anthropos or for her enemy?"

Dipsuchos rose suddenly from his chair. "Your majesty!" He sounded close to tears.

"Nay, I do not doubt your loyalty, Dipsuchos," Kardia said more gently, "but your counsel would spell ruin not only for Anthropos but for the rest of the world."

Dipsuchos sat down. He reminded Wesley of an old

dog who has been whipped. His shoulders were rounded, and humiliation clouded his face. Kardia continued, and Wesley shivered with ecstasy at the magnificent boldness of his words when death protruded from his chest.

"The facts are clear. Our peril is dire. And not only our peril and that of Playsion but of the whole world to the south of us. It is evident that this witch has both power and cunning. As yet we know not the extent of what she has done, but no longer can we doubt that she has power to blot out the light of the sun. This Kingdom of Darkness of which Gaal spoke to our helpers from another world," here he nodded at the three children, "evidently is established. She has enchanted or seduced members of our inner council and controls soldiers from our army. Worse, she holds to ransom our sovereign cohort, her majesty Queen Suneidesis and his royal highness. The dagger protruding from my chest testifies both to her powers as an enchantress and to her ruthlessness.

"If it is true that I have but a few days left before I, my wife and my son die, then I intend to use those days to do whatever damage I may to the so-called empress and her plans. The question is, How? First, I refuse to relinquish the sceptre. So long as I hold *that* the witch has no power to advance. But that is not enough. It is not my wish to sit idly holding a sceptre till death comes. In what way may we take action against this witch?"

"Your majesty," said Lord Dilogos, a smooth, urbane man in red silk robes, "how can we take action against her? We can proceed to this port of which she speaks, but she is not likely to expose her person to any risk. And if we attempt any course other than the one she plans, she is likely to harm her majesty and his royal highness. Indeed it would seem that we shall endanger them by any action we take."

"The witch is not a fool," King Kardia replied. "It mayhap that she plays a game of bluff. Her real desire is not to murder my family but to win the sceptre. She knows as well as we that only of my free choice may I yield it up. There is no means that she can devise to force me to do so. She also knows that Gaal, not Kardia, is her real enemy.

"She will soon become wise to the fact that, . . ." and here his voice shook, " . . . that I am prepared to lose both my wife and my son . . . as well as to give up my own life sooner than yield her a sceptre which is not mine to yield. Whether she will proceed to murder us remains to be seen. But if so, it will be from spite, not from any advantage she will gain. For she will still have neither the sceptre nor the power to lay her hands on it. It may occur to her to devise some other plan once she knows my readiness to sacrifice our lives. Let it hap as it may.

"But my first wish is to let her know clearly the firmness of my intent. How quickly can a letter be taken to the entrance to her kingdom?"

"In four days, your majesty."

"Good. Scribe, write as I dictate."

The scribe, whom none of the children had noticed before sat on the king's left. A large piece of parchment and a bottle of ink lay before him while beside him stood what looked like a large saltshaker. "It's got sand in it . . . to blot the ink," whispered Kurt to Lisa, proud of his knowledge of history.

From behind his ear the scribe plucked a feather, the end of which had been cut to serve as a pen. He turned to the king and looked expectantly at him. Like all of them in the council room he wondered what the king would say. Kardia's voice was firm, not only from the benefits of Chocma's wine, but because of his determination.

93

"From Kardia, under Gaal, King of Anthropos, co-sovereign of Playsion, Lord of the Further Isles: To her that styleth herself Mirmah, Lady of Night and Empress-to-Be of the Darkness that Swallows the World."

"... Darkness that Swallows ... the World," repeated the scribe, scratching away busily.

"Be it known unto you that neither the death of her gracious sovereign and royal majesty Queen Suneidesis of Playsion nor of our son his royal highness Prince Tiqvah of Anthropos, heir to both kingdoms, nor yet of our own threatened death by the enchanted dagger placed in our sovereign person. ..."

"A moment, if it please your majesty ... 'the enchanted dagger' ... what came next?"

"... placed in our sovereign person, ..." the king repeated.

"'... placed in our ... sovereign person.' Yes, your majesty?"

"... shall in any wise induce us to yield the sceptre of Anthropos to any but to Gaal the Shepherd, Son of the High and One True Emperor, under whose protection, as you well know, the sceptre rests." There were several more pauses while the scribe, whose tongue protruded from one side of his mouth, licked and scribbled frantically to keep up with Kardia. "Be it known to you furthermore that harm done to our royal persons will not only prove fruitless to your purposes but will be avenged by the High Emperor, and that your plans are doomed to failure and your personage to destruction and perdition."

"Boy, I like his style," whispered Kurt to Lisa. "I don't understand all the words, but he sure is giving her heck."

"Yes, he's not budging an inch," Lisa's voice was shaking a little. "You know he cares terribly about Suneidesis

94

and Tiqvah. I can't bear to think of Kardia himself dying. I feel scared. But, you're right. It's glorious to listen to him."

"Beware what you do," the king continued. "Desist from your evil designs. Return to those dark regions in the north whither you truly belong.

"We fear you in no wise. Whatever your power, you oppose greater powers. Whatever your determination, you face our royal confidence in Gaal the Shepherd.

"Whatever you do—beware!"

" 'Whatever . . . you . . . do . . . beware . . . exclamation mark!" breathed the scribe, who then took a huge breath, sprinkled sand liberally from the silver sandshaker, jiggled the parchment so that the sand would spread, then after waiting a minute brushed the sand from it.

"Your majesty may wish to read the missive before signing it," the scribe said, carefully placing the parchment before Kardia.

While Kardia bent over the letter Wesley had been watching the faces of the counselors. Inkleth's, Gunruth's, Lord Nocham's and Chocma's faces registered sadness, admiration and approval. Sir Dipsuchos' eyes were shining. He seemed to have recovered from Kardia's put-down. But Lord Dilogos, while he said aloud, "Your majesty's great courage and wisdom are highly to be commended," was at the time frowning a worried frown and biting his lower lip. Wesley wondered what was going on behind his face. Lord Dilogos' expression had been smooth before. Why had he begun to frown?

"And who will have the courage to deliver this letter for us?" the king asked softly.

"Your majesty, it will give me great pleasure to go with it. Give me two men-at-arms and horses and I will leave at dawn," Lord Nocham said.

"Your mission will be perilous. Have you thought of what may happen to you?"

"Your majesty cares not what happens to your royal person. You have taught us that it is what happens to Anthropos and its sceptre that matters. I would share your majesty's peril."

The king looked gratefully at him. "Then go, my lord, and may the protection of Gaal cover you."

"Be careful, your majesty. You are dripping water onto the parchment," said the scribe hastily shaking more sand onto it. Only the children saw where the water was coming from.

"The hilt of the dagger is melting," Wesley's voice was hoarse with excitement. "It's as if it were made of . . . ice or something!"

"It's losing its shape," Lisa breathed.

Rivulets of water were running down it and wetting the king's robes. A spreading wet patch darkened the royal purple. Soon, other council members began to realize what was happening. Protocol was forgotten. They jostled round excitedly.

"By thunder, your wine hath powerful properties, lady Chocma. I feel an easing and a warmth in my heart that I have not known for many an hour."

"Nay, your majesty. My wine has done nothing to the dagger. The witch's sorceries are being undone by courage, the courage your majesty has shown this night. Enchanted stone cannot stand the heat of fearlessness. It is your majesty's letter that is melting the dagger. You have shown us what direction to take in dealing with the Lady of Night."

The king's robe grew very wet. The hilt of the dagger slowly disappeared until there was nothing—nothing but a wet robe and a smiling Kardia. He pulled the robe aside to reveal a wet and hairy chest. There was no sign of a wound from where the dagger had protruded. There was laughter and merriment around the king. "Fenfinch pie, your majesty! Now you will eat fenfinch pie again!"

"Fenfinch pie! Fenfinch pie!" other voices echoed with more laughter. Kardia's appetite for fenfinch pie was legendary. In his youth he had once disguised himself and won a silver cup at a pie-eating contest where he had consumed eleven and a half pies at one sitting. Fenfinch pies were served constantly at the palace tables and Kardia's moods and health were measured by his appetite for them.

The king was smiling. "Bid the cooks scour the pantry for fenfinch," he cried. "We shall sup on fenfinch pie and mead before we sleep!"

"Greetings, your majesty," the voice was powerful but almost unbearably high-pitched. "I rejoice to behold you in good health." All eyes swung to the open window at the side of the room from which the sound came.

"Strongbeak!"

A very different Kardia, a Kardia alive with strength and purpose, sprang to his feet and walked toward the window where a magnificent eagle with black piercing eyes surveyed the room. "What news do you bring?"

"That I was put in a cage, your majesty, by some of your majesty's former soldiers, some of whom I killed in the struggle and others who will be long recovering from the wounds inflicted by my claws and my beak, to say nothing of the limbs my wings broke." The eagle preened himself delicately.

"Bravo, Strongbeak!" Kardia laughed heartily. "Come to the council table. Perch where you will. The cage did not hold you permanently then?"

"As your majesty can see."

Kardia returned to the throne and the great eagle spread his wings, floating to Lisa's dismay to perch on the back of her chair. She sat stiffly even though she knew she was probably safe. She was not used to eagles, especially at such close quarters.

"And what is your news, Strongbeak? We already have seen the capture of her majesty and Prince Tiqvah in the mirror pool. We also know of the witch's threats and of an ice port across a narrow straight, east of the village of Chalash."

"Your majesty knows much. But does your majesty know that there are many who have sold themselves to the witch?"

"Sadly, yes. But how widespread the treachery is, that I know not."

"Happily, your majesty, there are those who have formed a movement of loyalty to the crown, who meet in secret to support your majesty. It is their object to oppose the witch's supporters, discover all those who are disloyal and to foil their plans." The eagle paused and slowly looked at everyone in the room. He stared particularly long at Lord Dilogos. Then rather pointedly he said, "Loyal groups may be found in every city and village of Playsion and of Anthropos. But it would be better for me not to speak of such matters in the present company."

An uncomfortable silence followed his words, a silence which no one broke. Strongbeak continued.

"Theophilus VI, flying horse and son of the flying horse Theophilus V, he who refers to himself as an equine angel," Lisa's heart missed a beat as she remembered Theophilus, "bids me inform your majesty that some children from worlds afar are to go to the aid of her majesty, the queen, and Prince Tiqvah and of their own kinswoman, the lady Mary. He tells me they have already been given some of their instructions.

"They must now proceed north along the east bank of the River Rure, beyond Magician's Falls to join the old road north until they are well to the north of the Great Northern Pass. Strange adventures will befall them, and they will discover the roots of the mountains and the depths of the seas. But they need have no fear. All will be well if they remember their orders and carry them out."

Again, no one spoke. The Friesen children had been startled by the reference to Mary. Nobody else seemed to have noticed. The king had a puzzled expression on his face.

"But north of the Great Northern Pass lies nought but wilderness," he said slowly. "There is no way to cross the mountains there."

"I understand there *is* an ancient road leading north."

"Yes, so it was in time of war long ages past, but it leads to the north coast far to the west of the port that of which Mirmah speaks."

"I do not understand the instructions, your majesty. I only repeat them."

"Strongbeak, I cannot suffer the children to go alone. I must go with them."

"Your majesty, the Lord Gaal bids you to remain with the sceptre and that you not approach the enchanted kingdom for the sceptre's sake."

"Nay, but why would Gaal bid children go on a mission while I remain here? I must go, Strongbeak, I must!" For several minutes the talk went back and forth from the king to the eagle to others at the table, but the children were finding the sequence of events hard to follow. Adventure was still opening up before them. Yet a strange tiredness was dragging at their eyelids.

"I will myself accompany them, your majesty," Strongbeak said at length, "but Gaal also bids that horses be prepared with food and supplies. Such men as your majesty can trust may accompany them on their journey." Reluctantly, the king nodded in agreement to this compromise plan.

Throughout all the meeting Kaas, the son of the traitor Ramah had never moved but had stood stiffly and silently beside Wesley's chair. Now he stepped forward and knelt before the king. "Grant me, your majesty, the chance to undo my father's ill. Give me leave, your majesty, to go with the three from other worlds." He knelt unmoving, his head bowed, and for a moment Kardia stared at him without speaking.

"The young man seems a little overeager," Lord Dilogos murmured quietly. "At a time when treachery abounds, and when the young man's father has shown himself so treacherous. . . ." Lord Dilogos did not bother to finish his sentence.

Lisa never knew why she did it, but she too stood and approached Kardia. "Please, let him come, your majesty!"

From behind her came the high-pitched voice of Strongbeak. "By all means let it be so, your majesty. I shall kill him should he show any sign that leads me to suspect him. My wings," and he spread them wide, "could smash his skull. And as for my beak and my claws. . . ."

The king laughed grimly. "Be not overeager to kill, my good Strongbeak." He paused for a moment, then said, "The boy shall go."

Lisa sighed with relief. She could not understand why she had felt so strongly.

Weariness continued to drag on the children's eyes. They had been only two hours in Anthropos, and a great deal had happened. It felt as though they had been there much longer.

"There is much to do," they heard Kardia saying. "Let our guests be shown to the royal guest chambers. I would speak with Chocma, Gunruth, Inkleth and Lord Nocham. The rest of you are dismissed. Take courage all. From this point we are not defending but attacking."

Afterward the children could not remember being led to their rooms. They only remembered the deep softness and warmth of goosedown mattresses and eiderdown pillows.

9

A Sleepless Night for Everyone

Several hours later when everyone else in the palace was asleep, Kardia, who had been dreaming of the Tobath Mareh Tapestry, woke with a start. Silhouetted against the moonlit window a man was creeping across the royal bedchamber toward him. The lamp in the room shone too dimly to show the man's face, but it glinted briefly on a naked sword in his hand.

"Hold! Who dares approach his sovereign with a naked sword? Pages! Ho, there! Pages! Treason!"

Swiftly Kardia rolled out of the far side of his bed, snatching his sword from the scabbard he kept by his bedside. Clearly someone was after the sceptre which he now kept constantly with him. The man hesitated.

There was a sound of scuffling from the antechamber behind the curtains where the pages kept watch. Kardia and his assailant, swords in hand, were facing each other as two sixteen-year-old pages, one carrying a lamp and both likewise armed with swords, sprang into the room. In the lamplight the face of Lord Dilogos showed clearly. "Dilogos! Drop your sword!" Dilogos did not move. Kardia, wearing only a linen tunic and having neither shield nor armor, leapt across the bed with an agility amazing for his age, his sword raised high. The pages leapt forward at the same time. In a flash Dilogos dropped his own weapon and jumped through the open window. From below they heard the clattering and scrambling of horses' hoofs on the cobblestones of the courtyard. By the time they reached the window they were able by the moonlight to see three riders galloping toward the open gates of the palace.

Kardia's voice rang across the courtyard. "Ho, there! Guards! Seize the horsemen!! Guards! Guards!" But only the echo of his voice sounded over the clatter of the galloping horses. The riders rode unhindered through the open gates and the sound of their horses died into the night.

Kardia whirled to the pages. "Summon the captain of the watch. Let him be brought to me in whatever condition he may be found. Call the second watch and bid them replace the first immediately. Rouse the emergency guard and bid them pursue the riders."

Both pages ran from the room. Already lights had begun to appear and voices to be heard. Soon the palace was alive with shouts, more lights, the sounds of feet running along corridors and across the courtyard, and the clatter of horses emerging from the stables.

Lord Nocham strode unceremoniously into the royal bedchamber where Kardia sat thoughtfully on the edge of the bed. "Your majesty is unharmed?"

"Happily, yes. But there may be treachery among the

palace guard. The gates were ajar and no one responded to my call."

"Drugged?"

"That I know not. But that I shall know."

"Your majesty would prefer that I stay here and send someone else with the missive to the witch?"

The two men looked at each other, the king smiling. His tension had relaxed and something of his old light-heartedness was emerging. "These adventures begin to please me, my dear Nocham. I have not felt such a surging of my blood since I met you on the walls of Authentio. Fear not! I shall root out the treacheries here. And then, mayhap, I shall leave here—whatever Strongbeak says. My only concern is that harm may come to you at the hands of the witch. As for me, the pulse of victory is in my veins."

"Then if your majesty will excuse me, I must prepare the horses and supplies for my journey."

"Go, my good lord, and may Gaal protect you!"

Kardia continued to sit on the side of his bed, wondering in what state the captain of the watch would be brought before him—drunk, drugged, trembling, bound or dead.

An hour later, as the hubbub had begun to die, Wesley was still wrapped in slumber. In his dream he was standing at the bottom of a deep pit. From the rim far above him Kurt was shouting, "Hey, stupid! Get up! Come on, get out of that pit." Wesley struggled to climb the steep sides but constantly fell back with a groan to the bottom again. "Come on, sleepyhead! Wake up! We have work to do!" In his final desperate struggle the walls of the pit dissolved and Wes felt himself shaking his head. His eyes refused to open.

"Wes. Wes!" It was Lisa's voice this time. "Wake up, Wes!" When Wesley finally struggled into a sitting position and opened his eyes, he felt quite sure for some minutes that he must still be dreaming. The room he shared with Kurt (Lisa had her own room) was brightly lit and crowded with animals. There were more wolves, sitting and panting, tongues hanging out, than he could immediately count. Strongbeak the eagle was perched on the open windowsill and beside him a tiny skylark. Kurt and Lisa had resumed their seats on Kurt's bed, and draped between them were two large raccoons, their ears perked up and their bright eyes surveying Wesley curiously. Wesley rubbed his eyes hard, opened them and blinked. But the scene remained unchanged.

The high-pitched voice of Strongbeak broke the silence. "We regret to disturb you, my lord Wesley, but matters move quickly. I address you as the leader of the delegation from worlds afar."

Wesley stared stupidly at Strongbeak, who ruffled and then preened his feathers. He had no idea what the eagle was talking about.

"They want to come with us, Wes, but they won't unless you say so," said Kurt.

"To come with us?"

"Yes, you know, on the journey we have to make!"

"*Who* wants to come with us?"

"The wolves, Mr. & Mrs. Raccoon and the skylark. Strongbeak's coming anyway."

Wesley was always fussy about things like permission and had the vague feeling as he grew more wide awake that he really had no authority to give permission for a bunch of animals to accompany them. Surely he ought to ask someone else. But whom? Kardia? Kardia himself seemed not to have any say about their trip. He scratched his head as the animals, the birds and his brother and sister all looked expectantly at him. "Just what is the idea of all this?" he asked, stalling for time and trying to gather his wits.

Strongbeak spoke again. "You will need a patrol, an invisible patrol (or at least one that is as invisible as possible), to cover your movements. You cannot expect to set out on a journey like this and not be attacked. An attempt was made to murder the king himself an hour ago."

Then Wesley became wide awake. "Wh-at?"

"He's O.K., Wes," Kurt cut in, "but they haven't caught the guy. It was Lord Dilogos. A regular plot as far as we can make out."

"The point is, my lord Wesley," said Strongbeak, who seemed to be heading the animal delegation, "that if the king's enemies are so desperate, they are likely to try to stop any attempt to rescue the queen and Prince Tiqvah. Your reputations here are greatly feared. History has recorded your actions of thirty-one years ago. Your return to Anthropos and your mission have caused consternation in the ranks of the king's foes. I have no doubt that your party will be attacked and attacked fiercely as you travel, and great as are my personal watchfulness and strength, . . ." Strongbeak paused at this point and looked at the ceiling modestly for a moment. "As I say, great as are my watchfulness and strength, I cannot protect your party alone. I need help." You can see that Strongbeak was a little vain. But he had a good heart, and his mind as well as his beak was strong.

"But there will be soldiers to protect us."

"Your enemies know that. They will take it into account in their plans. What they will not take into account is an animal patrol."

An old white wolf walked stiff-leggedly over to Wesley's bed, sat down slowly and looked at him.

"My lord, I am Garfong, son of Garfong, son of the Koach leader you knew so well during your last visit. I have with me eight of my younger sons. They are young but well trained. They work as a team. They can track silently through woods or over plains. They can attack either man or beast in superb coordination. My father learned much from the Battle of Rinnar Heights. They can divide and attack more than one enemy at once. Their leader is my older son, Garfong III."

Wesley stared at the wolves. Nearly all were gray but a slightly larger one was white like his father and his grand-father. The muscles rippled beneath their shining coats. Their eyes were clear. Wesley's heart stirred as he re-membered their last adventure together, and his affec-tion for the brothers Garfong and Whitefur. He caught his breath and marveled that he was now looking at Gar-fong's grandsons. Deep down he knew that what the older Garfong said made sense.

"My lord," Strongbeak said, "it is important that no one but yourselves should know of our mission. There is a difference between ourselves and humans. Our loyal-ties do not change. We can be trusted. But no one knows at this point who among yourselves can be trusted. If word were to leak out of our enterprise, . . ."

Wesley nodded. "O.K.," he said, still a little anxious about the decision, "I accept your very generous offer."

"Attaboy, Wes!" Kurt bounced excitedly up and down on his bed, rocking the two raccoons. Lisa said nothing but smiled her approval.

"Now tell me more about your plans. I see we have a skylark with us."

"Ah, yes, let me present Twitterpitter," the eagle said gravely.

"Welcome, Twitterpitter. Could you tell us. . . ."

"Oh, I just *love* to sing," piped Twitterpitter. "I just love it. I sing and sing and *sing*. It's my whole life. I. . . ."

"But as she sings she rises higher and higher, and the higher she rises, the more she sees."

"Ah, yes," the twittering went on, "and the more I see, the more I sing but, . . ." Have you ever heard a skylark sigh? Twitterpitter *sighed*. "I keep on singing but I have to start watching. I watch for movements anywhere near my nest."

"Well, it's most kind of you to offer to come, Twitterpitter, but what about your nest now?" Wesley was trying to be kind, but once more he felt confused. What earthly use could a skylark be—especially such a silly one as Twitterpitter?

Twitterpitter puffed her chest out. "My young are all grown and gone. And I want to do something *interesting* between now and my next mating. Mr. Strongbeak says I can spell him off. . . ."

"Giving more all-round daytime observation," Strongbeak said.

"And giving *me* a chance to sing," Twitterpitter said.

Wesley couldn't help smiling. "And if either of you," said Wesley turning to the birds, "see something, how will you let the wolves know?"

"Oh," twittered the skylark excitedly, "I can drop like a stone, and no one would guess why I was dropping. Whoever heard of a skylark dropping on a wolf?"

"And there are signals and calls," Strongbeak said. "We have worked out a code. . . ."

Wesley's eyes widened. "It seems you've been thinking all this out very carefully."

He looked at the two raccoons, relaxed yet so keen eyed. He did not want to sound skeptical lest he offend the party. And he was a little afraid of Strongbeak. But he would have to make sure what was being planned.

"And you two, where do you fit in?"

"Distraction," said Mr. Raccoon laconically.

"Timmy really can manage on his own now," Mrs. Raccoon answered by way of explanation.

"Timmy?"

"Timmy's our youngest. Well, not our *youngest,* but he was the runt of the last litter. Stayed with us after all the others had taken off to start their own lives. But it really is time for him to go, and we thought the expedition would be an ideal opportunity to give him . . . well, to give him a gentle push—didn't we, my love?"

"Yes, Mrs. Raccoon."

"You mean you plan to bring Timmy with you?"

"Oh, no. My gracious, no! That's the whole point. If we join the expedition he'll have to look after himself. And goodness me, he *ought* to be able to. He can fish, he can. . . ."

Wesley was confused. He still couldn't quite see what Timmy had to do with the expedition. "You said something about distraction."

"That's right," said Mr. Raccoon.

"What exactly d'you have in mind?"

"Oh, keep 'em on edge, like. Especially if they have dogs."

"And how will you do that?"

"Well, see, Mrs. Raccoon and me works together. We sneaks around the camp and gets all the dogs barking. Then if the men lets 'em go, we leads 'em a merry chase in the woods. We tricks 'em. Sometimes we can keep 'em going all night. Dogs get all worked up and sometimes men don't know what they're worked up about. Think there's maybe other men around. We gets 'em as far as possible from their camp, and we tries to lose 'em in the woods." Wesley's eyes lit up. "Sometimes we drowns the dogs. We leads 'em on to thin ice, like, or we gets 'em in deep water and goes for 'em. Dogs don't fight well in water." Lisa shuddered. It sounded horrible to her.

The more Wesley heard, the more impressed he became. "You're sure they will come after us?"

Strongbeak ruffled his feathers. "We can't be sure of anything," he said, "but it does no harm to be on the watch. A trip in the woods will do us no harm, even if no one decides to attack you. But my bet is that they will. They can't afford to let you go on a rescue expedition. They'll trail you at a distance and go for you when you're far from help. And I am in a mood to go for more eyes."

Wesley felt a chill of fear. "How will we know where you all are?"

"Leave that to us. It's our job to be watching out for you, not yours to be looking out for us. All we want is your approval and consent."

Wesley firmly put his inner uncertainties aside. Very carefully he made a little speech. "Mr. Strongbeak, I think your plan is well thought out. On behalf of my brother and sister I want to accept the noble offer you have all made and to tell you how very grateful we are for your proffered help."

"Well it's not just that we're thinking about you, but Anthropos, the witch, and our queen and prince."

"Of course."

Dawn was breaking. Animals do not stand on ceremony. The raccoons were the first to glide to the door. Mr. Raccoon peered cautiously into the corridor and listened. Mrs. Raccoon waited beside them. Then without a sound they were both gone. Next Garfong, son of Garfong, was at the door. In ones and twos the wolves glided into the corridor. Wesley wondered whether they could get out of the palace unseen. Strongbeak stretched his great wings and floated out into the open air with a lazy flap or two.

Twitterpitter was the last to go. "Isn't it exciting?" she said. "I feel like a good sing." Then she too fluttered from the window, and from outside in the early morning air came the sound of a skylark's song, growing fainter as Twitterpitter circled higher and higher into the sky. The three children were alone in the room.

Lisa was too excited to go back to sleep once she got back into her room. From her window she stared at the empty courtyard as the early morning light turned the blackness into a cold gray. So much had happened since their arrival. Her mind was spinning with the events of the council the night before, the dramatic announcement of the attempt on the king's life, the exciting and dangerous journey that lay ahead of them, and now the animals—the Koach, the raccoons, Strongbeak and Twitterpitter.

Her meditations were broken by the sound of horses' hoofs on the cobblestones. A group of men entered the courtyard, three of them leading horses saddled and with side packs. Among the men Lisa saw Lord Nocham. She dived into the closet behind velvet curtains for a robe. "He's setting out for Chalash," she murmured to herself. "I *must* say good-bye to him."

She ran with bare feet along the corridors and out into the courtyard. The men were making a final check on the tightness of the saddle straps and fussing generally around the horses.

"My Lord Nocham!" Lisa cried, running awkwardly to him, for the cobblestones hurt her bare feet. The big man swung round and caught her in his arms.

"My dear little lady! What can I do for you?"

"Oh, nothing. I just wanted to say good-bye and, well, I *do* hope everything goes well."

Lord Nocham held her to him closely, then released her. "I never had a daughter," he said slowly. "But if I had, I would want one like your ladyship."

Out of the corner of her eye Lisa saw, or thought she saw the round-shouldered, skull-capped figure of old Sir Dipsuchos.

"My lord, I too would bid you farewell," she heard his voice say as he joined both of them. "I wish you well on your journey. I fear for you, but I know my counsel was wrong."

"It takes a man of character to admit a mistake."

"My lord, you well know I am not a man of character. My life seems to have been a series of wrong choices. I would to Gaal I had your lordship's firmness of resolve— or even that of her ladyship here."

For a moment nothing was said. Lord Nocham was looking at Lisa. "It is because of the lady Lisa that Anthropos still exists today. It was at her ladyship's discovery of the Mashal Stone, lost for many a century, that our fortunes in our darkest hour began to turn."

A look of delight came across Lisa's face. "The Mashal Stone! Where is it? D'you think his majesty would let me use it again? It could be terribly useful." The Mashal Stone had many properties. It could both make its wearer invisible and give the power to see things that human eyes do not normally see. But its effects were powerful only if the wearer were acting in the service of Gaal.

"I'm quite sure his majesty would have no hesitation in letting you use the stone. Ask him yourself, my lady. It lies in the royal treasure house and has not been used since your ladyship was last in Anthropos. Dipsuchos, you have the keys. You would know where it is?"

Dipsuchos seemed strangely agitated and lowered his head. He was rubbing his hands together.

Lord Nocham looked at him keenly. "You do know where the Mashal Stone is, do you not, Sir Dipsuchos?" he asked quietly.

There was a long pause. Then Dipsuchos said, "No, my lord. To my shame I do not know where it is." There was another long pause. Sir Dipsuchos remained with bowed head and rubbing hands. Finally he said, "My lord, the Mashal Stone has not been among the royal treasures for fifteen years. I do not know where it is. I was persuaded to give it secretly to someone who told me his majesty's life was in danger and that there was one who could use it to save him."

"And to whom did you deliver the stone?"

Sir Dipsuchos took a deep breath. "To Lord Ramah, my lord."

There was another long pause. "So it is now in the hands of our enemies."

"I know not, my lord."

"And though this took place fifteen years ago you never reported it?"

"No, my lord. I thought, I thought. . . ."

Lord Nocham gave a snort of contempt. He turned and climbed into his saddle. Though the light was not enough to show it, his face was red, his actions angry. None of the men around them had been listening to the conversation. The two men-at-arms mounted their horses mechanically. "Unhappily I have no time now to look into this matter. There are more important things to attend to. Farewell!"

He swung his horse round to the gate and set out at

a gallop, the men-at-arms following him. The little crowd dispersed. Lisa and Sir Dipsuchos were alone in the courtyard. The old man fell on his knees before Lisa.

"My lady, I beseech you, do not reveal this to his majesty. I am not a traitor—only an old fool." Lisa had no idea what to say. The light was growing and had a rosy tint. To her surprise she saw tears running down his wrinkled cheeks. Part of her was sorry for him and part of her terribly embarrassed. It felt very strange to have a dignified old man kneeling to her and pleading with her. "Please, your ladyship, I beseech you."

He seized her hand and was about to kiss it when Lisa pulled it away sharply. "Oh, *don't.* You mustn't kneel down to me like this. It isn't right. I don't know what I'll do. You'll just have to let me think. Now please get up and go. I'm confused. Just go!"

It sounded terribly rude, but Lisa found herself growing angry inside, without understanding why. She could not make herself look at Sir Dipsuchos and half turned from him. Out of the corner of her eye she saw him trying to get off his knees. He seemed to be very stiff and had difficulty in straightening out his old knees and back. Lisa neither moved nor spoke.

She saw him turn, his miserable shoulders slouched once again. He began to hobble uncertainly across the courtyard away from her. Once he stopped, turned and seemed about to speak. Then he changed his mind and hobbled on until he had rounded a corner.

Lisa noticed her feet were icy and that she was shivering. The anger with which she dismissed the old man had drained away. And the adventure that an hour before had seemed, however dangerous, to promise excitement had lost its appeal. Slowly she walked to her room feeling more miserable than she had felt for a long time.

10

Fire on the Mountain

The children began their journey north on the east side of the River Rure not many hours after Lord Nocham had galloped off to deliver Kardia's letter. They shivered in clammy mist that lay over a forest of giant cedars, hiding all but the trees nearest to them. So heavy was the mist that they could never be sure whether to call it mist or fine rain. It thoroughly soaked the warm cloaks the children had been given in Nephesh. Whenever they stopped they could hear nothing but their own muffled breathing and the heavy drip, drip of water from the lower branches of the cedars. Awed and excited by the size of the trees, the Friesens wished the weather had been clear, for the mist revealed only the lower part of enormous trunks, which loomed darkly as they passed them.

"As wide as a little cottage," Lisa had marveled as they stared at one of them.

"Just like the redwoods in California," Kurt said unromantically.

Lisa's mind went back to the wakening elms and oaks that they had encountered on their previous visit to Anthropos. She wondered whether the cedars had ever awakened, and if so whether they had ever marched against an enemy, and whether they would be friendly or treacherous. Looking at their great girths, she was sure they would be friendly—frightening perhaps, but definitely on Gaal's side. After all, did he not *smell* of cedar?

All day they journeyed north along an ancient road paved with flat stones. Wesley, the least experienced rider among the three children, passed his belt and the Sword of Geburah to Kurt, to the latter's great delight. The children had been overjoyed to find that in addition to six men-at-arms, the two Matmon lords, Inkleth and Gunruth, had been assigned to protect them. They wiled away the time listening to news of all that had happened since their first visit, and hearing tales of the ancient days of Anthropos. Kardia himself, chafing still under Gaal's instructions, had remained in Nephesh.

Toward evening the sky cleared to reveal the most spectacular scenery the children had ever seen. For almost half an hour they had grown conscious of a steady thunder in the distance, that grew louder as they advanced. "Magician's Falls," Inkleth had told them, without elaborating. Then without warning they found themselves at the head of the most awesome canyon they had ever seen, whose tree-carpeted floor three thousand feet below them was flanked by walls of sheer rock. The Rure poured itself over the cliffs at the head of the canyon to fall as a stupendous cataract into mist-covered whirlpools far below them. From there it continued its

course north to the sea.

Crossing the river at the point where it made its spectacular downward plunge was a massive seven-arched bridge that spanned the river. " 'Tis of the same masonry as was the Tower of Geburah," Gunruth told them. "Legend has it that the cohorts of Shagah, the great sorcerer, built it in the days before he took refuge in the tower. He was angry, they say, with the mountain tribes in the north. For a time past the Northern Mountains were mountains indeed, rising far above the level they now reach. Snow and ice crowned them eternally."

"They still look pretty big," Wesley said, glancing at the mountains that overlooked the canyon.

"Shagah cursed them, bidding them sink. But his power, great as it was, was not enough. They settled and the whole earth shook, but the rage of Shagah was not appeased. So standing on the bridge before us he flung his wand in the water, bidding the earth beneath to split and to open a gap in the mountains, that the Rure might flow into the northern sea."

"You mean it didn't used to flow north?"

"They say it was once fed by the snows of the Northern Mountains, and that it flowed into the swamps that surrounded Lake Nachash."

"And its flow was reversed?"

"Its flow was reversed."

"And that's why they call the falls Magician's Falls?"

Gunruth nodded. "If we crossed the bridge, the road would take us to the lands of the west."

Just as they passed the bridge the party paused, stunned by the panorama below them. But at last they moved on away from the river over more rugged ground. There was no sign of pursuing enemies, nor did they see or hear anything from Strongbeak, Twitterpitter, the raccoons or the Koach. Now that they were safely on their way, Wesley confided to Gunruth the strange story of their arrangement with the patrol.

When darkness fell Gunruth allowed them to halt. That night they slept stiff, sore, damp and cold. Two of the men-at-arms and Inkleth took turns keeping watch. The children did not fall asleep until dawn was breaking. Their sleep was troubled and dream haunted. When they woke, they found themselves staring up into a deep blue sky. The smell of a wood fire and of frying bacon tempted them out of the snug shelter of their blankets. But my! How stiff their muscles were from the previous day's riding!

They were delighted to discover that they had camped on the shore of a small lake, having left the forest of giant cedars, and entered one of pines, firs, spruces, larches and birches. Wesley sat up sharply, catching his breath at the sight of rocky peaks, reflected through streaks of mist on its mirrorlike surface. Dark green cloaks of evergreen warmed the shoulders of the mountains and flowed down luxuriously to the edge of the lake. Great boulders of granite, blanketed with vivid green moss, lay scattered between the trees around their campsite. Wesley sucked at clean, cool air, shivered a little and crawled out to admire what he saw.

Breakfast was a hurried affair. Gunruth seemed nervous about the column of smoke rising slowly from the fire on which their breakfast was cooked, and insisted they stamp it out as soon as the meal was prepared.

That day the road wound north, parallel with the Rure, climbing along the sides of mountain slopes, but dipping occasionally into valleys. The weather was dry. Their horses moved more slowly than on the previous day. The children, still stiff and sore, were not sorry.

About midmorning Gunruth called the party to a halt. "Hist!" He craned his neck backward, staring into the sky. "Didst speak of a skylark, my lord Wesley?" he asked.

"Yes. Twitterpitter." Faintly, from far above them came the lark's impudent twittering. "There she is! Singing fit to burst!" Kurt cried excitedly.

"Where? I can't see her."

"Right there!" Kurt said, pointing almost directly overhead. "Can't you see? She's just a tiny dot, going round in little circles!"

Their spirits had been lifted when they resumed their way. It was reassuring to know that a watch was being kept. No one had realized how tense they had been feeling until they felt the warm relief of knowing the "invisible" patrol was active. As the day wore on they also saw Strongbeak wheeling and soaring above them.

And so it continued till darkness fell and they camped by a stream on the southern slopes of the Great Northern Pass. That night children and soldiers slept soundly. Only Gunruth, keeping watch, a black silhouette against the starlight, heard the distant baying of hounds and knew that their enemies were behind them. His eyes twinkled and a smile creased his bearded face. "Methinks the little furry ones are leading them a merry chase," he murmured.

They crossed the pass in the early morning, gazing long from its northern slopes to see if they could discern any movement in their rear. But they saw nothing. It was not until midday, while they were finishing a hurried meal, that they heard word of who it was that pursued them.

Strongbeak glided down on them as they ate. He seemed ill at ease and made no mention of his powerful beak or wings. The soldiers, the Matmon and the children stared expectantly at him. "A score of soldiers, all mounted, under one Lord Bogedoth advance toward you," he cried in his high-pitched voice.

"From whence?" Gunruth asked quickly.

"They are two leagues behind you on the road you are on."

"Then we may hide among the trees and let them pass."

"They have dogs, hounds trained in the hunt, who have the scent of your horses."

"The furry ones cannot distract them?"

"I have told the furry ones they may return to their own lands." There was a stunned silence.

"But Strongbeak, why?" It was Lisa who spoke.

Strongbeak preened his neck feathers with his fearsome beak, all the while fixing her with one wicked, little eye. His piercing voice sounded unconcerned. "The forest is on fire less than a league to the north of you as well as on the slopes below you. A strong north wind fans the flames to such a fury that by nightfall the whole of this mountain will be burning."

Again for a moment there was silence, but this time it was broken by a clamor of questioning voices. Several of the soldiers jumped to their feet to see whether they could see smoke, but the high trees surrounding them shut off the view.

"So our foes are behind us while fire advances from below and above."

"Your enemies are heavily armed. They are spurring their horses, determined to catch you. As yet they know nothing of the fire. Your only escape will lie in scaling the mountain. Some distance above you lies a wide meadow through which runs a stream. It may prove a haven from the flames. If you had wings I would urge you to fly. As it is, I shall stay with you until I know your fate."

In seconds the campground became the scene of feverish activity. Horses were unsaddled, their noses turned south. They were sent on their way with a slap. Taking only water bottles, bows, arrows, swords, a blanket apiece and a little food, the small company abandoned their luggage and equipment. No one smiled. Fear lay heavily on all of them.

Before long they were scrambling grimly upward. Twice Kurt tripped as the Sword of Geburah got caught between his legs. He hoped Wesley would not notice. Gunruth insisted that the party keep together and would allow no one to go ahead or to lag behind. Sweat began to run down their faces. Strongbeak wheeled and turned in the sky above them. Then when a thinning in the trees enabled them to see better, they could perceive black smoke rising in a long line of cloud below them and to the north. Even as they watched, a column of flame exploded upward from the crest of a ridge a mile or so to their left.

" 'Tis nearer than we thought," Inkleth said uneasily. "How far do the meadows lie of which the eagle spoke?"

"He didn't say," replied Kurt. "Oh, *look!*" A stag moved swiftly through the trees, taking no notice of the Koach or the human beings, springing and bounding with desperate speed toward higher ground.

"Would that we all had such legs," Gunruth said grimly. "But with what legs we have we must make do. Let us be on our way!"

A smell of smoke added to their fear as they peered upward steadily. There was no underbrush, yet before long their chests were heaving, their thighs had turned to rubber, while salt sweat burned their eyes. A strong wind blew cold on their faces. Lisa longed to stop, but she bit her lip and doggedly put one foot after another. Wesley sensed her distress.

"Here. Give me your blanket and your water bottle. I'm not feeling tired yet. Hang on to my left hand, and I'll give you a pull. It's getting steep here."

There seemed no end to their climb. More animals appeared, some crossing their path toward the south, but most of them moving upward as they did themselves. There were several squirrels, a brown bear and two does, none of which took any notice of them. Upward, ever upward the party scrambled. Treetops tossed wildly in the wind. The children's chests were now torn with pain as they struggled to fill them with air. Then came an abrupt halt as they found themselves without warning facing a wall of rock that rose from the forest into the sunlight.

"Now what?" panted Kurt, leaning his back against the rock.

Flapping and fluttering through the trees, Strongbeak settled among them. "The meadow lies right above," he screeched. "Follow me." He half hopped, half glided southward along the foot of the precipice to where a clear stream bounced down a narrow cleft in a series of little waterfalls.

They paused briefly to plunge hands and heads into the water and to rest. The climb would not be difficult. Yet the smell of smoke was now stronger and the urge to get to safety grew powerful within them. Men and dwarfs struggled to their feet, testing their watery limbs gingerly.

"Not far now!" Wesley said encouragingly to Lisa.

But Lisa was staring with a worried frown at Kaas whose face was gray and who looked ill. "Are you all right?" she asked. Kaas nodded his head without saying anything. He struggled to his feet then lifted up a small, but obviously heavy, wooden barrel.

"Did you carry that all the way up?" Wesley asked, awe in his voice.

"What is it?"

"Oil." Kaas turned and began to climb. Wesley, Lisa and Kurt followed.

"Did he bring that thing all the way up here?"

"He must have."

"I wonder what he wants with it."

"It's nearly killing him. You can see he's all in."

"No wonder!"

In five minutes the whole group stood on the upper edge of a rocky outcrop that rose high above the forest. Before them lay the meadow of which Strongbeak had spoken, and beyond it more forest and the mountain peaks. But it was what lay below them that arrested their attention. They saw a long line of fierce red light topped with a curtain of billowing black smoke less than a mile to the west. More frightening, they perceived as they looked north that the raging line of fire had clambered up the mountainside and was rolling toward them from a ridge about a quarter of a mile away. A fierce wind carried the smoke across the mountain to where they stood. It was frightening. Wesley drew in a deep breath. The panic he felt arose less from the danger itself than from a feeling of responsibility to Lisa and Kurt. "I shouldn't have brought them," he thought. "I could have come alone. It's my own stupid fault."

"Will we be safe here?" Lisa asked.

"I don't know. Look at the grass."

"It's dry."

"And knee high."

"Will it catch fire?"

"You bet it will."

"Oh, Wes! Where can we go?"

Where could they go? Wesley's palms were sweating. "Oh, *why* didn't I leave them in the house?" he muttered. His misery was intense.

Gunruth, Inkleth and Kaas were talking together. Kaas was pointing to the northern end of the meadow, and it seemed as though they were arguing heatedly. Strongbeak spread his wings, ready to leave them. "I shall see how the Lord Bogedoth and his party fare," he screeched. "Then I will watch you from above." Wesley was too concerned with the danger to which he had exposed his brother and sister to spare any thought for their enemies. The fire was a living, powerful thing devouring the mountain and threatening to devour them too. He turned from everyone and strode toward the forest to hide the misery in his face.

"Inkleth is beckoning us all over to the edge of the forest," Lisa said. Kurt and Lisa followed Wesley to join the Matmon and the men-at-arms among the trees. Kaas had chipped a hole in the barrel with his axe and was pouring oil on the grass in a long line along the northern edge of the meadow where it met the trees. From their shelter Lisa and Kurt watched him.

"What's he doing?" Lisa asked.

"I have an idea, but I'm not sure. I think he's going to set the grass on fire."

"Oh, Kurt! Is he crazy? Why?"

"If he burns it off before the forest fire reaches this point, we'll have a burnt-out area to stand in. And it'll be safe. See, he's using his tinder on it now. Pretty bright of him if you ask me."

Inkleth and Kaas stared intently at what they were doing. Before long, dull red flames were licking the grass and spreading over the meadow in a smoking line. They could hear the grass spitting and crackling from where they stood.

"Good old Kaas! He's proved his usefulness as well as his loyalty," Kurt cried, slapping Lisa on the back. "Isn't it exciting?" Neither Lisa nor Wesley answered. They watched the fire springing to life, now leaping, now crawling, now standing still and dying away only to leap up anew. The wind blew fiercely on the flames, chasing them like chickens among the grass and tossing burning pieces of grass in the air to drop them where they could start new fires. In the wake of the flames the grass lay blackened and smoldering.

It did not take long for the fire to cross the meadow. Nor did it stop at the far side. For a moment it seemed to have burned itself out. Then with a crackling roar two trees on the far side of the meadow burst into dull reddish flames. Within half an hour the forest line on the south of the meadow was ablaze.

It may have been a good idea to burn off the grass, but the burnt-off meadow was far from pleasant to stand in. For one thing smoke still rose from it. The ground was hot underfoot. There were places where a little spurt of flame would start over again. And when they stamped on the flames, thin black dust would rise up, making their eyes run and causing them to sneeze. The wind picked up the dust and the fragments of burnt grass and whirled them in dust devils over the meadow.

Smoke from the forest was now denser and they could hear the approaching roar of a forest fire and the occasional crash of falling trees. Sparks and sooty particles blew over their heads. Through the smoke that dirtied the sky above them they could see that Strongbeak still wheeled and soared. Sometimes it seemed as though he were dropping toward them, but if so, the smoke and the hot air would drive him away from the meadow repeatedly.

The little company gathered by the stream in the center of the meadow, where fresh green grass was still to be found. The wind that blew in their faces had grown uncomfortably warm. Above the trees on the northern edge of the meadow dense smoke poured fiercely.

"I wish it would hurry up and get it over with," Kurt said. "It's worse than waiting in the dentist's office." Even as he spoke fire began to consume a tree on the northern edge of the meadow. Within minutes the meadow would be ringed on three sides with fire. The men-at-arms seemed not to share Kurt's nervousness. They had begun to sing together, oblivious of danger. Clearly they felt they must be safe for the moment. Kurt found himself sitting next to Kaas.

"That was a pretty good idea of yours. Thanks for lugging the oil up. You probably saved our lives."

"My lord, it was a small thing."

"Small, my foot."

"Your lordship?"

"I mean it wasn't a small thing at all. We're very grateful for what you did."

Kaas seemed not to be listening. He was staring in the direction of the cliff edge below them. When Kurt looked in the same direction he was startled to see two lithe wolves loping along the banks of the stream toward them. Two more followed and then another two while on the far bank two raccoons loped determinedly toward the sitting men and dwarfs. Fluttering behind them in hops and spurts was Twitterpitter.

"The patrol!" Kurt cried, tripping once again over the sword he carried. Lisa ran past to throw her arms round the leading Koach. Koach and raccoons were at first too winded to speak.

What Twitterpitter said made little sense. "Oh, dear, . . . we thought they'd never follow us into the fire, . . . " she said.

Inkleth had recovered from his surprise to ask, "Of whom do you speak?"

"Strongbeak said to go home," Mrs. Raccoon said, coughing and panting pitifully.

"They're on their way now," squeaked Twitterpitter.

"Who's on their way?"

The leading Koach addressed himself to Inkleth. "My lord, we harried them from behind, and they pursued us. We could not shake the hounds of which there were fifty or more, and this was the only direction we could follow. Soldiers and dogs will be upon us in a minute for they are close behind."

Gunruth stood beside Inkleth. "How many men and how many dogs?" he asked.

"My lord, nearly three-score dogs and as many men."

Above the howling of the wind and the roaring and crackling of the burning trees they could now hear the baying of hounds. Gunruth swung round to face the children and the men-at-arms. "To your feet!" he cried. "Unsheath your swords and follow me!"

Yet even as he cried, the baying of the hounds broke over the meadow. Tumbling and yelping they bounded over the edge of the waterfall. Wesley stared at them in dismay. He hated violence and his heart was beating suffocatingly. He tried to remember how well he had fought on the Heights of Rinnar. But the pigeon was on his shoulder then, and there was no pigeon now. It seemed that everything was happening in slow motion. Each detail stood out in Wesley's mind— the bristling hair on the necks of the hounds, the snarls and bared teeth of the Koach, the men-at-arms stumbling to their feet and looking uncertainly at Gunruth, the shouts of unseen men climbing up beside the waterfalls, the wind tearing at his clothes, the crackling and roaring of the forest fire and the beating of his own heart.

But Strongbeak saw something that neither Wesley nor anyone else in the royal party saw. Wheeling far above them and watching them with his beady red eyes, Strongbeak alone witnessed the strange column of dense black smoke that writhed like a living thing from out of the forest behind them to wrap itself round men-at-arms, children, Koach, Matmon, raccoons and skylark. In a moment it swallowed them up. And in another moment it had dispersed in the wind and with it the whole company.

Over the edge of the cliff came more hounds and panting, sweating men with drawn swords. Some of the hounds were moving in ragged circles, sniffing and snuffling the unburnt grass where the little company had been but a moment before. Strongbeak soared higher and higher, wondering what it all could mean. But of the royal party there was no sign.

II

Grateful Even for a Witch's Hug

"She should wake soon. The spell lasts but a week." Mary McNab heard the words through a haze of sleep. Who was speaking? Where had she heard the voice before?

"I don't understand why you brought her. What use is she?" a man's voice asked.

"She was calling for Gaal."

"So? There are many who call for Gaal."

"But such was her call that an enchanted mirror surrounded her." There was a pause. The woman's voice, rich and deep, hovered pleasantly on the border of her memory. Such a lovely voice! Whose ... ?

"Don't you consider it dangerous?" the man asked again.

"I do."

"What is she doing in the Kingdom of Cold Darkness if the powers of Gaal are about her?"

"That is a question to which I must find an answer."

Sleepily Mary opened her eyes. Flickering light penetrated the almost black green of the ice above her. Ice. Ice? At once she remembered the terror of the enchanted circle, and the lady with the mole over her left eye and a dazzling crown on her head. She rolled over gently to see a hideous old woman wrapped in a torn gray shawl, her eyes glittering in the light of a ruby red fire whose flames flickered on her wrinkled and filthy face. Between where Mary lay and the ruby fire was the black silhouette of a tall man in a pointed hat and a long cape. His was the second voice Mary had heard and as she stared at his pointed hat he spoke again.

"You are not afraid then to seize a servant of Gaal?"

"She came willingly. She was glad to see me."

"One does not play games with Gaal. You should not have meddled with her."

"And leave someone with the power of the Name loose in my kingdom?"

"Mirmah, you are a fool. You could have watched her." Whom were they talking about? Surely they could not be talking about her. She scarcely breathed for fear caught at her throat. The black silhouette went on talking. "Let us send her by a speedy ship to Playsion to avert danger. So long as she remains we are in peril."

"I intend to make use of her." The beauty of the hag's voice contrasted with her bony fingers and her long blackened fingernails.

"To use a servant of Gaal against him?"

"Gaal is a formidable opponent, but I intend to be bold in the game we are playing."

The black shadow shifted uneasily. "The risk, Mirmah, the risk! No one has ever dared!"

"When danger is great, it is the bold who win. Those

who before me have challenged Gaal lost their courage and lost the game. So I shall be bold. The child will prove useful."

The *child!* Then they were talking about her. At any rate they thought she was important, and the old woman seemed to value her. Mary stared at the unnatural ruby flames. How had they made a fire like that? Did they use special chemicals? And why did she think she recognized the voice? Surely she knew it!

"What world does she come from?"

The words startled Mary. In spite of the talk of the Friesen children, she had not believed that she had really left our own world behind. Strange though her adventures had been she was sure she was only somewhere in the far north of Canada. The terror that now began to grip her went beyond any of the experiences she had already undergone.

"You asked what world?" A dreamy look came into the old hag's eyes. "What world indeed! She comes from no world we could ever know. From another universe comes this one and from a time that is not now nor will be for ages yet to be. Across timeless voids where new stars are born she was drawn by the power of Gaal."

The witch, for surely she must be a witch, was making it up. She was making up a story out of her own head! They were *not* in another world or another age. The thought of timeless voids where new stars were born made her pulse race.

The black silhouette continued. "And you suppose, Mirmah, that you can match the power of a Gaal who can reach beyond space and time to touch other universes and other ages and bring here a child like this?"

"I may not be able to match his power but I can outwit his cunning. And by subtlety I will learn the secrets of his power."

Mary began to shake. She *was* in another world! The peril of her situation began to grow more clear to her. There might be no way of getting back. She was trapped beneath ice in a world belonging to a different time and universe. Her quarrel with the Friesen children seemed unimportant now. But the pain of being given up by her stepmother woke again inside her chest, and she wanted to return to familiar houses and to see familiar faces. She tried to stifle the sob that rose from deep inside her, but it pushed powerfully and broke out of her explosively.

At once the old woman was at her side, and the smell of her was like last week's garbage. "My darling! My precious darling!" (Who used to say things like that to her? Why did she not like the words?) "My poor little bird! We frightened you, didn't we?" She snatched a handful of ashes from below the red fire and flung them into Mary's eyes. Instantly the man in the cape was gone, and instead of an ugly, old woman stood the tall Lady of Night with a crown of dazzling jewels on her head. It was the witch with the mole above her left eyebrow.

The lady swept her into her arms and carried her across the room. Sobs came freely and tears were blinding her. She no longer cared how embarrassing her tears might be.

"I want to go home! I want to go home! Take me home! Please take me home!"

The Lady of Night sat down on a throne of ice beyond the fire and Mary felt herself being rocked, tightly grasped in her powerful arms. But the rocking did not soothe her. In a low voice the lady sang,

Blood from a viper's heart, tongue of a lizard,
Dust from the never-seen face of a moon,

Scale of a dragon and ear of a mangy dog,
Sweat from a murderer hung at high noon:
Purge from her memory all that disturbs her,
Burn with the flames of the fire on my floor,
Seal up inside of her all that molests her,
Fasten the chamber and lock tight the door.
  Blood from a viper's heart, tongue of a lizard,
  Dust from the never-seen face of a moon,
  Scale of a dragon and ear of a mangy dog,
  Sweat from a murderer hung at high noon.

If the spell worked on Mary it probably only half worked. Gaal must have been protecting her. The music was wild and sweet, but the words added to her terror. Was this black magic? The witch's voice seemed to sound from inside her own head, sometimes softly, sometimes loudly, but always terrifying. As she continued to be rocked, it seemed even to fill her body. Yet, in spite of her fear, her sobs subsided. Why had she been crying? She struggled hard to think. She wasn't sure. How long had she been here? She did not know. Yet she was more afraid than she had ever been in her life.

The Friesens? Yes, yes, she knew the Friesens. They were her cousins. Yes, her stepmother had sent her away. Yes, she *was* in another world. Again at the thought terror rose within her. Her own world seemed like something on television—bright, but flat and inaccessible. Who were the people she had met?

She struggled to sit up and opened her eyes. "Where's the man with the cape and the pointed hat?" she asked fearfully.

"He left," the lady replied.

"Who was he?" Mary was fearful and suspicious.

"My chief magician."

"Is he a *good* magician?"

The Lady of Night paused for a moment. "He has powers gathered from the dawn of the world," she said slowly, half to herself. "Sometimes I fear his powers are too many. But he is useful."

"Can I go now?"

The lady laughed. "My sweet child, *you* are going to be useful too. And I love you more than anyone I have ever met. Who made you so beautiful?"

She hugged Mary tightly again. And when she did so something happened to Mary. The hug achieved something the spell had failed to. For Mary needed a hug right then and was grateful even for a witch's hug. You might think she would have been too afraid to enjoy it. Yet in spite of all her fears and suspicions she felt comforted, marveling again at the softness and warmth that came from this beautiful woman. She was thankful that somebody loved her—even if the somebody were a witch in a far-off world. The lady lifted her with powerful arms and set her gently on a fur rug at her feet.

"Here," she said, leaning over her and handing her a clear ball of crystal that she had plucked from the massive jeweled crown on her head. "Have you ever seen one of these?"

"Yes," Mary replied cautiously, "my mom took me to see a fortuneteller at the Exhibition, and the fortuneteller had one. But I couldn't see anything in it." She stared at the sphere, watching two reflections of the ruby fire, one of them upside down, tiny and flickering. There were other reflections too, some of them too small to see clearly. "Is it magic?"

"Place it on the fire and see. It's yours. You may keep it."

"Oh, thank you. But on the fire? Will anything bad happen? I don't like magic."

135

"There, there, dear. Would Mirmah try to hurt you? I love you like my own daughter, sweet child. Don't be afraid. The ball will grow and you will see pretty pictures."

Mary looked at the ruby fire and back at the crystal ball. She was afraid to do it yet even more afraid of angering the witch, so she leaned forward, extending her hands until the heat of the fire hurt her fingers, then tossed the ball into the flames. She knelt on the rug and watched it with a beating heart.

For a moment it floated like a bubble on the tips of the flames. Then it began to swell, growing steadily before her eyes without changing its shape. In seconds it was as large as a soccer ball and still growing. Moments later it was the size of a pumpkin. The lady knelt beside her and they watched together. Still it grew until it towered above them. When it almost filled the ice-walled cave, it extinguished the ruby fire with a hiss, and they seemed to find themselves at the bottom of the sea.

There was no water at the bottom of the sea. At least it didn't feel as though there were any. Mary wasn't wet and she could breathe. Yet everything looked as it does when you open your eyes under water. There was sand underfoot and rocks all around. Seaweed rose from among the rocks, waving slowly in currents that Mary could not feel. Her heart beat fast as she saw an octopus staring at her with unwinking eyes from a rock a dozen yards away. It beat even faster when she kicked her foot against a stone, only to find that the stone was a skull.

"Where are we?" she asked fearfully, knowing all the while that they were under the sea.

"We are in Poseidon's Kingdom," the witch replied. "Come quickly and I will show you my prisoners."

"Is it safe?" Mary asked. "Will we be all right? Perhaps

we'd better go back before anything happens."

The lady seized her arm urging her forward. "Darling, you're not scared. You're too beautiful to be scared. What a lovely girl you are!"

She went on talking rapidly as she dragged Mary across the sea bed, but Mary was not listening. It was curiously unpleasant to be told how lovely she was and even worse to be dragged. It reminded her of something. But of what? She had the strange feeling that everything that was happening had happened to her before. Glancing up she saw the mole above the left eye on the witch's beautiful, pale face and recalled the airport in Toronto and the rush to catch the plane for Winnipeg. She remembered the words, "I'm not really your mother," and as she did so her feelings about the witch grew more confused than ever. The witch had told her she was beautiful. But her stepmother had called her "my precious" and had sent her away in the end. Perhaps all grownups were like that. They were good at saying nice things but they sent you away when they no longer had any use for you. Well, in that case she would make herself useful to the witch. At least she would have someone to belong to.

The Lady of Night stopped abruptly and Mary lost her balance and almost fell. Several yards away a cave mouth opened, before which rose the biggest sea anemone you could ever imagine. It must have measured five yards across its base while from its circumference rose serpentine tentacles reaching far and wide above and around it, as though it were searching for something.

"What *is* it?" Mary asked in breathless alarm.

"That is Medusa."

"It's a *what*?"

The witch drew Mary close to her and ran her icy fingers tenderly through her hair. "It's not a *what;* it's a *who,* dear. Her name is Medusa. She's a daughter of the old gods. You'll have to be careful of her for she's dangerous when she's angry, and she's angry most of the time. I use her to guard my prisoners."

The more Mary stared, the more the waving tentacles looked like long snakes. She could not be sure, but she thought she could see flickering tongues at the tips of many of them.

"Are they . . . are those things . . ."

"Yes, dear, they are. They're snakes. Medusa has snakes for her hair. She's not very pretty, is she? Not like you, dearest."

Looking beyond Medusa, Mary saw that in the cave mouth the creature guarded, there stood a tall and graceful white-robed woman with long black hair. Beside her was a boy of twenty or so, dressed like a page in stories about King Arthur, and wearing a sword in the leather belt around his blue tunic. Neither looked at Mary, their whole attention being fixed on the waving, serpent hair of Medusa.

"That is Suneidesis, Queen of Anthropos, and her son, Prince Tiqvah. They are the two whom I am holding prisoner," said Mirmah softly.

"What are they doing?"

"They are trying to escape."

"Are you going to let them?"

"Not just yet. Would *you* like to set them free?"

"I don't know. Why do you keep them there?"

"I want to see if the queen's husband has the courage to come and rescue her. If he does, he will make me a worthy husband."

Queen Suneidesis and Prince Tiqvah, their eyes still fixed on Medusa, were cautiously leaving the cave mouth. They did not seem to see the witch and Mary. The prince had drawn his sword. Just when it looked as though they might escape, Medusa's long hair streamed toward them both. The queen drew back while the prince stood his ground, his face set sternly and his sword slashing fiercely at the serpents. Yet the more serpent heads he sliced the more appeared until it seemed that they would wrap themselves around him and drag him to his death. But his mother seized him by the belt and pulled him back into the cave. The serpents drew back and Medusa's long hair grew shorter again.

"They will be too afraid to venture out for a while," the witch said.

"It doesn't look like . . . I mean, she doesn't look like a person," Mary said, referring once again to Medusa.

The Lady of Night gripped Mary's waist in her powerful hands and swung her effortlessly high above her head, advancing toward Medusa as she did so. The waving snakes parted to reveal an enormous face, filling the center of the giant anemone. Evil red eyes the size of volleyballs and overgrown with blood vessels stared with unblinking hatred into Mary's own. Enormous purple lips parted slowly as though they were trying to suck Mary into the opening between them. Suddenly she felt herself being pulled in the direction of the face.

She screamed.

As the lady swung her back onto her feet and hugged her protectively again, Mary had the impression that she was shaking with laughter. Yet her words were comforting and kind.

"There, there, dearest. Don't be frightened. She has a horrid face, doesn't she? But I won't let her hurt you. You're quite safe with Mirmah."

Folded in her sheltering embrace Mary waited with

her eyes closed until the beating of her heart subsided. "Take me home," she pleaded, her head still buried in the deep softness of Mirmah's dress. "I don't like it here. I'm scared. Please take me home."

"First I must teach you to control Medusa," the lady said firmly.

Mary's arms were shaking and her legs felt weak. "I don't want to control her. I just want to go back. Please take me back. *Please.*"

Mirmah's arms still held her tightly. They felt comforting and safe and Mary found her fingers were clutching through her mittens at the dark substance of Mirmah's dress. For a moment the witch said nothing. Mary tried to shut out the memory of Medusa's appalling face.

"Listen, darling. You know I love you, don't you? I think you are the loveliest little lady I've ever seen. And I know you're brave too. Don't be scared of Medusa. The tiniest jewel from the crown of my head will shrivel her to almost nothing. All you need do is to toss one into her mouth and her power will be destroyed for many hours."

Gently but firmly she pushed Mary from her. "Look at me, darling," she said, raising Mary's chin with a bony finger. Reaching up with her other hand to the jeweled crown on her head, she plucked two green stones from it. Mary could not see where they had come from for the crown was encrusted with more jewels than you could ever count. "Here," she extended her hand to Mary and dropped them into the palm of her mittened hand. They were the size of large marbles. "Now, dear, I want you to throw one into Medusa's mouth and see what happens."

Mary's throat was dry. As she looked into the face of the Lady of Night she knew with absolute certainty that she was left with no choice. She did not know how she could obey. The thought of approaching the revolting

140

creature (she still could not think of Medusa as a person, daughter of the gods or not) filled her with terror. But the look in Mirmah's eyes was more terrifying still. Her red lips were smiling, but her eyes were merciless.

"Will you come with me if I do it?"

"Sweetheart, the spell will not work if I come with you."

"Why not?"

"It just won't, dear."

Mary described it afterward as a nightmare. The only difference was, she said, that in some nightmares you want to run and your feet won't move, but here she wanted to stand still yet her feet kept walking toward Medusa. Try as she might to slow down or stop she had no power to. Her rebellious feet carried her relentlessly on. The anemone tilted toward her and with dismay she saw again Medusa's red eyes and her bloated purple lips licked by a thick black tongue. Still Mary walked nearer. The snakes weaved in a stream toward her, forming an arch above and beside her through which she advanced to Medusa's cavernous mouth.

Only as she was about to step into the mouth itself did she remember the green stones. Quickly she tossed one ahead of her and the purple lips slapped together, closing inches in front of her. The face shrank like a deflated balloon and Mary found herself staring at nothing more than a sea anemone not much bigger than her thumb.

Her head grew light and giddy. She turned and felt the lady's arms about her. Her knees folded beneath her and the last thing she heard was the sound of Mirmah's laughter and the smell of an old, old woman who had never cleaned her teeth and who drank something that smelled like Scotch.

12

The Darkening of Six Kingdoms

An evening meal was being served in the dining chamber of Nephesh Palace just seven days after the children had set out. Candles lit the faces of eight diners and eight serving men behind their chairs, and threw flickering shadows against the tapestried walls. The light was too dim and the shadows too dark to see the pictures the tapestries bore.

Kardia glanced gloomily at the tapestries. They reminded him of the Tobath Mareh that ten years before had been destroyed by fire, and that the witch Mirmah had offered to restore in exchange for the Iron Sceptre. There had never been any tapestry like the Tobath Mareh, a history of early Anthropos woven in gold and scarlet, silver and blue, russet brown, copper and Anthropos green. When people wanted to express how lovely the sky was, or a girl or a flower or any work of art, they would say it was "beautiful as the Tobath Mareh." The tapestry had shown the building of the ancient Tower of Geburah and of the battles that raged because of it. It had depicted the murder of Gaal by the cave in ancient times and the arrival of the boy John Wilson from distant worlds. Kardia shook his head sadly as he remembered the Tobath Mareh Tapestry, now lost to Anthropos forever.

The diners were sitting on either side of a heavy oak table. Lord Nocham sat on the king's left, a frown creasing his normally cheerful face. He had returned the previous day bearing the strange news that a giant cockerel in Chalash had plucked the king's missive from his hands, and flew north with it, low over the sea. The queen's chair, like many others, was vacant. Lord and Lady Qatsaph, Sir Chush and Lady Marah, old Sir Dipsuchos the widower, and the lady Chocma filled the remaining places opposite and beside the king. Between them the table was filled with silver platters bearing food, and flagons of wine and mead. The king's Iron Sceptre lay on the table among the dishes. Not only had he never been parted from it since the night Lord Dilogos had tried to seize it, but there seemed to be a strange attraction between the sceptre and the man, a magnetism that held the two together. Several of the courtiers had noticed it.

Eel soup had been served and the bowls taken away. Faces were grave and the silences between remarks long. The diners seemed absorbed with their plates, now filled with fenfinch pie, venison and cold duck.

You will remember that Kardia once won a prize for eating fenfinch pie, and that there was no other kind of food that pleased him more. Where you or I might sneak down to the refrigerator at night to make up a sandwich and pour a glass of milk, Kardia would descend to the royal pantries to cut a generous slice of pie and pour a beaker of mead. If he was sick, the first sign of his recovery would be that he requested fenfinch pie. It was ordered every day for the evening meal and no banquet was complete without fenfinch pies and pastries. But tonight Kardia merely picked at his food and left his slice of pie partly uneaten.

"Matters are grave indeed," Sir Dipsuchos said, laying his dagger beside his plate and looking at the king.

"Grave enough," replied Kardia briefly.

"Three kingdoms, then, are under her power?" Nocham asked.

"Certainly the Kingdom of Klemma has fallen. An unearthly darkness covers her, for the sun's warmth is felt no more. Her rivers and lakes are frozen and snow covers the land," Kardia said slowly.

"Snow in June?" Lord Nocham murmured wonderingly.

"Did their emissary tell you when they expect their king to return?" asked Lord Qatsaph, a man so fat and heavy that his chair groaned constantly.

"They doubt he will ever return," Kardia responded quietly. "It is rumored that this self-styled Empress-to-Be of the Darkness that Swallows the World gains her power over any kingdom by breaking its royal sceptre and pronouncing a spell over it."

"Why did their royal majesties yield their sceptres?" Sir Dipsuchos asked. "Your majesty refused to yield yours."

"No one knows, my good Dipsuchos. Certainly she has been more courteous and more gentle in her invitation to other rulers than she ever was to me. She invites them to a feast and offers them her magical powers to aid them in prospering their realms. Then she befools them, or so I suppose, and breaks their power by breaking their sceptres."

"How were matters in the Kingdoms of Chamash and Mispach?" The words came from Sir Chush, a tall, thin man who constantly drummed his fingers and bit his lip.

"Likewise wrapped in blackness but without snow," Kardia said. "The messenger from Mispach told of crops that do not ripen and of blighted orchards."

"Surely they will starve!" Lord Nocham said anxiously.

"Nay—it seems she has enchanted the hearts of the people. They sleep a deathlike sleep, falling to the ground wherever the darkness caught them. They are dead, yet not dead, rigid and unmoving. Only few escaped the spell and came to warn us."

"Your majesty will forgive what I say—but all three kingdoms deserve to suffer," said Lady Marah, her dark eyes flashing.

"Aye, they have not been the best of friends to Anthropos, and many are the times we fought them and would fain have done them ill. Yet what has befallen is a dastardly fate to wish on them."

"Her magic is powerful," Chocma said softly.

"Powerful enough to darken three kingdoms, but not powerful enough to keep them dark for more than half a year unless. . . ."

"Unless what, your majesty?"

"Unless she shall break the Sceptre of Anthropos, and that, please Gaal, shall never be. Rumor has it that if she can but conquer all seven kingdoms, then will her power last forever, spreading to kingdoms across the sea, chilling and darkening the whole world."

Kardia paused and drank a draught of golden mead.

"She now has three of the seven, then," Lord Qatsaph

said, his round red face looking full at the king.

"As like as not she has six," Kardia replied. "The sovereigns of Chaiyah, Perachim and Elim have answered her summons. Like silly sheep three more rulers have gone to the slaughter, carrying their sceptres with them."

"Do we have news of them?" Sir Chush asked, still drumming his fingers on the table and moving restlessly in his chair.

"None," replied Kardia shortly.

Sir Chush continued, "Then if it please you, my liege, I would urge you to reconsider an attack upon this vile witch. Only you, your majesty, have shown resistance to her, and your opposition has harmed us not one whit. Why, the very dagger in your majesty's bosom melted and disappeared when you wrote your letter of defiance."

The serving men bore away the platters on which the diners had eaten their meat and brought others to replace them. The king cut himself a slice of mulberry pie and transferred it to his plate. For a moment he said nothing. Then once he had swallowed his first mouthful he spoke slowly. "Most dearly would I love to fill a fighting ship with men-at-arms, sail to the heart of her kingdom and destroy it! Gaal has bid me stay here, yet my spirit chafes within me."

"And what of her majesty the queen? And his highness Prince Tiqvah?" Lord Qatsaph asked, bending his enormous body forward.

Kardia's face darkened. He was about to speak but Chocma spoke first. "If Gaal has given instructions for his majesty to stay here, then we may be sure that Gaal can protect our queen and prince."

"*If* Gaal has given instructions!" Lord Qatsaph's fat

jowls were shaking indignantly. "How do we know that Gaal has spoken? The only word we have is the word of a bird—a bird that came and went who knows where. Shall we trust the destiny of a kingdom—nay, of half the world to the ravings of a mad eagle?"

Sir Chush bit his lips till a trickle of blood ran down his chin. His wife had placed a hand over his restlessly drumming fingers.

"Bid me provision a ship, your liege, and commandeer troops! What hinders us? Gaal has not bid *me* stay, and I would sail within three days! Let us not remain idle lest we lose the kingdom."

For a moment Kardia's face twisted, as pain and frustion chased themselves across it. Then his expression became stern. "Dearly would I love to storm the Kingdom of Darkness," he said. "The waiting is most difficult. Can Gaal truly know the straits we are in?"

Silence fell and slowly the group resumed their meal. For a few moments mulberry pies, blackberry pies, pastries, preserves and fresh Anthropos fruit occupied the attention of the diners.

Suddenly with a roar of grief there burst through the chamber door the strangest figure you might ever expect to see. The lower part of his body was that of a large bear but his head, arms and chest were those of a giant. He towered above the diners and their servants crying, "Woe to the Kingdom of Chaiyah! Woe, woe is befallen us!"

Kardia had risen to his feet. "Who are you, and what tidings do you bring?"

The giant's fists beat upon his head as he roared, "I am the marshall of Dob from the Kingdom of Chaiyah. Scarce three weeks have passed since our sovereign left by ship at the bidding of the Lady of Night, and now a horror of shadow has fallen over us. Drowsiness has drugged us all so that we sleep in deathlike slumber. Only a dozen of us remain. We beseech your majesty's aid!"

Kardia shook his head. "Right sorry am I to hear your tidings. Your fate is the fate of Klemma and Chamash and Mispach. But I have no power to undo the spells of a witch. Doubtless your lord and sovereign has yielded his sceptre to her. Bid your survivors come and shelter in my kingdom for here, at least, you will be safe from her."

Excited conversation had broken out among the diners. At an order from Kardia a serving man led the messenger from Chaiyah to the servants' quarters to be fed. Lord Quatsaph had settled his fat body on his chair and was again about to speak when a high-pitched wail was heard from a solitary window high on the side wall. They turned to look and as they did so a slender dryad leaped with agile grace to the chamber floor and a moment later a nyriad followed her. The dryad stood shivering so that her leafy gown rustled ceaselessly. Her face was turned to the floor causing her silver hair to cover it. "Our kingdom is under a spell," she cried, wringing her hands, "and our subjects all are dying. Darkness is come upon us and with it a chill like we have never know. The sun is no more. Winters we can survive, but not cold and darkness such as this. The firs and pines might bear it, but the beeches, oaks, larches, birches, elms, willows and countless more will perish. Wind strips our summer leaves away and drives ice needles through our bark. A-ah, how dark it is and how very, very cold!" She was shaking convulsively.

"Your majesty was right," Chocma said. "First Chaiyah and now Elim and Perachim. It is clear that all six sceptres are broken."

The dryad moaned and fell crumpled on the stone floor. A gasp of horror broke from the group as they

watched. For a moment a sinister darkness hovered where she had stood. Then in the place where she fell there was nothing but a pile of withered leaves.

Beside the leaves the nyriad stood shivering. Her tinkling tunes broke over them. She stood no more than eighteen inches high, her little face framed with a bonnet of rose petals above a dress of leaves. "Most of us were in full bloom," she cried shrilly. "The bees that come to sing for nectar lie dead upon the grass. Others of us have not had time to open. The sun has gone, the endless night is come, white petals of the dead float down from the clouds and we are cold. . . ." She continued to speak but her voice was too faint to hear. Slowly her head bowed, then her shoulders. She shuddered like the dryad had done and fell. All that remained of her was a heap of rose petals.

Nobody spoke for almost a minute. Then Kardia ordered, "Take away the food and leave us." Again the serving men sprang forward and deftly removed food, utensils and linen cloths from the oak table. In little more than a minute they were alone in the room. Chocma got up from her place and gathered first the withered leaves, and then the petals, placing them on the table between them.

Lord Qatsaph's jowls were shaking with agitation again. "This changes matters, my liege," he said. "Anthropos-Playsion alone survives on this whole continent. Surely your majesty now sees that we must act!"

Kardia's face was troubled. "The witch does not conquer with armies but with sorcery, and no sorcery can touch us so long as this sceptre be not broken. Yet I fear to go against the bidding of Gaal. And yet . . . have you not all noticed that now I *cannot* be separated from the sceptre? It is as though it were a part of me. I cling to it and it to me. What witch could rob me of it now?"

"Then it would be perfectly safe, your majesty, to invade her kingdom with men-at-arms. So long as your majesty and the sceptre are bound in a bundle of life, our kingdom is secure! Let us attack, your majesty, let us attack!" Sir Chush's eyes gleamed and the fingers of both hands drummed restlessly on the table as he looked at Kardia. Again his wife placed her hand over one set of drumming fingers, but Sir Chush drew his hand sharply away.

Kardia said nothing. He was looking at the leaves and petals that lay around his sceptre. "Poor creatures," he said, "what harm have they ever done to mortal soul? These kingdoms were our friends, our allies." He picked leaves from the table and looked at them in his palm. "You talk of this woman's power. It is her cruelty that fills my heart with bitterness. Who would kill forests and flowers to sate a senseless greed?"

"Mirmah the witch kills forest, flowers, beasts and men," Lord Qatsaph said testily. "Why do we wait to kill her?"

"Enough!" Kardia spoke sharply. "Say no more. It may well be my will that we act. But for a little longer we shall wait. Remember that the servants of Gaal from other worlds may be even now in the witch's kingdom. Let us await word from them." Then he glanced at the window and gasped. There, perched above them was the eagle. "Strongbeak!" he called. "What news?"

Strongbeak spread his wings wide and floated over to perch on the back of the queen's empty chair, and to preen his feathers. "What news, my good Strongbeak, what news?" Kardia knew he could not hurry the eagle, but he was impatient as all of them were to know the fate of the children.

No one spoke while Strongbeak ruffled his feathers, cocked a small black eye, in the direction of all of them by turn and said in his high-pitched voice, "Strange tidings, your majesty, most strange!"

Kardia pressed his lips together and said nothing. Lord Qatsaph smashed his fist against his palm and Sir Chush continued to drum his fingers. Lady Qatsaph clenched her hands so tightly together that the knuckles showed white. Sir Dipsuchos shuffled his feet and said, "Ahem! Ahem!" Only Chocma remained calm.

"When last I saw them they were ringed by a forest fire," Strongbeak said at last, pausing to watch the effect of his words and pleased by the gasp of anxiety he heard. "A band of men-at-arms were rushing them with drawn swords, but. . . ." He paused and looked down at his claws.

Kardia's voice shook a little but he sounded patient. "But what, my dear Strongbeak, but what? Is it well with them?"

"I know not, your majesty. It was very strange." Still he hesitated. I hate to say it, but I know he was enjoying the tension he created. Finally he said, "As the slaughter was about to begin a cloud of smoke enveloped them, and they were gone!"

"Gone? How could they have gone? You mean, you couldn't see them for the smoke?"

"There was no trace of them when the smoke left, your majesty. Those who attacked them remained, for the meadow was safe from the fire. But of the children from other worlds, of sundry animals and of the Matmon there was nothing more to be seen. For four more days I sought them through every mountain and valley."

"Where did this strange event take place?" Kardia's voice was strained.

"In Goldcoffin's Meadow, your majesty."

"Goldcoffin's Meadow!" several voices echoed.

Sir Dipsuchos drew a deep breath and said what everyone was thinking. "Then the enchantment of the mountain has come upon them!"

Kardia stood, grasping the sceptre in his right hand, his face white. "Thank you, my good Strongbeak," he said at last, and turning to the rest, "I would meet with my Lord Nocham, my Lord Qatsaph and with Dipsuchos, Chush and the lady Chocma here, tomorrow at dawn. Until then—good night!" With that he turned on his heel and left the chamber.

13

Mary's Mission for Mirmah

Mary opened her eyes sleepily to stare at walls and ceiling of ice. In spite of her parkas and mukluks and the skins on which she lay, she did not feel completely warm. Yet she sensed it would be colder once she got up, so she snuggled down a little further among the furs and tried to sleep.

Through half-closed eyes she watched the ruby fire. She remembered the crystal ball and wondered what she had done with it. How had they got back from Poseidon's Kingdom? When had she come to bed? She went back in her mind to her strange adventure under the sea and to her frightening ordeal with Medusa. How *had* they returned? Struggle as she might she could not remember.

Come to think of it she could not even remember arriving in this strange room for the first time. She could remember meeting the beautiful Lady of Night in the

Circle of Bodily Yearnings and then. . . . And then what? A puzzled frown creased her forehead, and a knot of anxiety tightened somewhere under her rib cage as she recalled the conversation between the ugly, old woman and the magician whose face she had never seen. How would she get back to Winnipeg? Never again would she go into the attic in the house on Grosvenor if ever she got back there. She would insist they let her sleep someplace else. Those TV sets were dangerous. Yet in the meantime, however scared she might feel, she would have to make herself useful to the lady. Nothing would be gained by antagonizing her.

Where exactly was she? She was in a room, a room with a ruby fire and walls of dark green ice, but where was the room? However hard she tried she could not remember what happened between the Circle of Bodily Yearnings and this room, or even between the ocean and the room. What had made her sleep? She could not remember *falling* asleep. Her mother (it was hard not to call her mother) used to give her Nembutal to put her to sleep whenever she threw a party in the apartment. But with Nembutal you always got dizzy and could snuggle under the covers as the noisy conversation and dance music in the next room washed over you like a lullaby. And you could remember everything next morning, too, even if you did have a hangover that made you fall asleep in school. Did the lady make her sleep somehow? She didn't feel as though she had a hangover.

Slowly the suspicion grew that the witch must have done something to her since otherwise she would be able to remember *something*. What was the last thing she could remember? Had the lady given her a pill? She was sure she hadn't. The last thing she could think of was the lady's arms folding around her. Did she hypnotize her?

Or did she use magic?

Mary remembered how she had begun to cry when she first realized she was in another world and how the witch had lifted her to rock her and sing to her. She had felt very strange then. Maybe that was it. Maybe there was some magic that made you lose consciousness when the Lady of Night put her arms around you. It was her arms that did it. She must watch out before letting her get too close. Those arms could be dangerous. Yet it had been so comforting, so very comforting to feel them round her. How could she *not* want arms round her when she was lonely and scared?

The more Mary thought about the witch the more confused she grew. She was afraid of the strange lady and she was sure she could not trust her. Yet she hoped against hope that she could win the lady's love. It was like her stepmother all over again. Yet surely she meant *some* of the nice things she said.

She shivered a little and wondered whether it would be worthwhile to get up and warm herself by the fire. The ruby flame leapt with unearthly beauty. She threw off the heavy skins, swung her legs over the edge of her solid ice bunk and crouched by the fire. She pulled off her mitts and stretched out her hands, pleased by the flickering red that played over them. The fire was not very warm, in fact she felt no warmth at all, so she held her hands close. Suddenly burning pain made her pull her hands back. But they were still cold. Cautiously she tried again, spreading the fingers at a safe distance. No warmth. She moved them closer. Still no warmth. Further still—and again, burning pain. With an angry cry she jerked her hands back and nursed them under her armpits.

A musical laugh above her made her look up to see the

Lady of Night standing beside her, a glittering smile be-low her dazzling crown.

"I don't see what's so funny," Mary said peevishly. "It's a dumb kind of fire that doesn't warm you." Slowly she replaced her mitts.

"Only weak people need warmth and light," the witch answered gently. "Strength lies in darkness and cold. Think how feeble water is and how hard and strong is ice."

Mary scarcely heard her. "I'm nearly freezing! I don't like it when I'm cold."

"Ah, but then you've never been really cold. To be truly cold, to let the dark ice penetrate to your very heart is to be strong. If that ever happens to you you'll never be sad again, never be scared, never know any more pain."

Mary said nothing. The lady looked so very beautiful and her voice was like music. She had knelt down beside Mary, bringing her face on a level with the girl's. In spite of her growing fear Mary's eyes widened as she saw the loveliness of the complexion. The mole was still there, but it looked like a beauty spot. Only the eyes like dead but glittering amethysts made her uneasy for she couldn't see where the eyes were looking. There was a bad smell, too, a smell like teeth that had never been brushed.

"Her arms," thought Mary, "if she puts her arms out I'll roll away from her." But the lady made no move. "I love you, Mary McNab." How did she know her name? "I love you very much. Don't be frightened, dear. I know how it feels, not to know where you are."

"What is this place?" Mary asked her guardedly.

"It's your very own ice room, dear."

"But where is it?"

"Where, darling? Why, it's in the heart of my palace in the Kingdom of Darkness."

"How did I get here?"

"I brought you, dear. You have been sick. You were nearly dead when I found you in the Circle of Bodily Yearnings. If I hadn't found you and brought you here, I don't know where you'd be now. You became unconscious only seconds after I found you. Poor darling!"

"And am I better now?" Mary's heart was beating. It was all very confusing. One part of her wanted to believe all the comforting things the lady said, but another part of her knew that the lady was lying.

The lady extended her pale fingers and rested them gently on Mary's forehead. For a brief second they felt terribly cold, but in an instant warm and pleasant. She eyed the lady's other arm carefully, wondering whether she would attempt to take her into her arms again. The unblinking amethyst eyes stared blankly at her. The lady withdrew her fingers.

"Good," she said.

"You mean I'm better?" She tried to sound childlike and to look pleased.

"Really better this time. I thought you were better when I took you down to Poisedon's Kingdom. But I was wrong. I nearly lost you again."

So that was what happened. She had passed out under the sea. No wonder she had felt so strange.

"I heard you laughing. You were laughing at *me*."

The lady laughed again.

"Oh, yes, I was laughing, dear—but not at you. Poor Medusa! She hates it when someone feeds her the jewels from my crown. You were really very clever to do it so well."

As the memory of the face of the sea god came back to

her, Mary's skin crawled. She shivered. "I'm cold."

"I could cure you of feeling cold forever, Mary. I could make you strong as ice. Once you have dark ice in your heart, you never will feel cold, only strong and beautiful."

Beautiful? Would she be thin? Or was it a trick? "Could you take my fat away? And my pimples?"

"If you had darkness in your heart, dear, you could look almost exactly like me."

"Like you?"

"More beautiful, dear, more beautiful than I ever was."

There was a pause. The queen was still staring at her. Mary's heart beat fast. What did she mean?

"You saw how ugly I used to look."

Then Mary remembered the first time she had opened her eyes in that very room when the man in the pointed hat had been talking with the hideous old woman. If the lady could transform herself from a hag to the Lady of Night, then perhaps she really could make Mary beautiful.

"You mean you really were that . . ." Mary was about to say "horrid" but quickly changed her mind, " . . . that old lady?" she asked, scarcely daring to look at the witch, but hoping she sounded innocent and pleasing.

"Yes, sweetheart. That's what I used to look like. Sometimes I change myself back that way to remind me what it was once like. But when darkness entered my soul I became like you see me now. Do you know how old I am?"

Mary shook her head.

"I am six thousand, five hundred and ninety-nine years old. Do I look like it?"

Mary stared. Her stepmother used to spend hours applying her make-up and had made jokes about having a face lift. Somehow the Lady of Night looked as though she never needed make-up. To look like the lady would be, would be something else! But could she be trusted?

"How did the darkness enter your soul?"

"Ah, my dear—that's a secret!"

"Aren't you going to tell me?" Mary pretended to be sweet again.

"I might."

"Please?" she pouted prettily.

"Well, dear, you have to pass the test before it happens."

"The test? What test?"

The Lady of Night stared at her again, but the amethyst eyes were impossible to read. "You really would like to be beautiful?"

Mary nodded. She wondered why her heart was racing. Could the witch really do what she said?

"How about clothes?"

"Clothes, dear? You could have any you liked. Not my Crown of Anan of course, but a little one of your own."

"Really? You really mean it?" She tried to sound eager.

"Of course, dear. You'll have to pass the test."

Test? Mary's thoughts raced to her last report card. Surely she would be able to pass it. Her only low grade (a D) was in phys. ed. The rest of her subjects were A or A+. Her marks were one of the things that made her so unpopular at her private school. Thank goodness she had not done as she planned and worked at getting low grades. She was sure the witch would be impressed.

"I'm no good at phys. ed.," she said, "but if it's English or French or math, . . ."

The Lady of Night was not looking at her. "I'd like you to visit a king for me."

A king? What could she mean? Mary had never even

seen a king. She'd seen the Duke of Edinburgh and Prince Charles on TV—but a king!

"His name is Kardia," the lady continued. "You saw his wife and son in the cave Medusa was guarding, and he lives in a palace in a country called Anthropos." *Anthropos.* Now her heart was really beating, and she hoped the lady wouldn't notice. If she went to Anthropos then there might be some hope of getting back to Canada. The Friesen kids might even be there.

She waited eagerly to hear what the Lady of Night would say. The lady was smiling. "I'd like to marry him. But you mustn't tell him that for he's too much in love with his wife at the moment. Let me tell you what I want you to do. Remember your crystal ball? Pull it out of the pouch in the front of your fur garment."

"She must mean my parka," Mary thought.

"Ah, yes, *parka*," the lady said instantly.

The lady had said *parka* the instant she had thought it! Yet previously she'd called it a fur garment. Could the lady read her thoughts? Had she overheard her thinking about Anthropos? She tried to stop thinking, but found she couldn't. Mary pulled the crystal ball out of the pocket and was holding it in her mitted hands. How had it got into her parka?

"You can go anywhere you want with the crystal ball," the Lady of Night said. "All you need is a fire. You just place it on the fire and think of the place you want to go."

"Anywhere?" Mary said. "Anywhere at all?" But again her mind was racing furiously. Perhaps she could get back to . . . but no, no, *no.* She mustn't think it! She must keep it out of her mind. If the witch could read her thoughts. . . . But on the other hand did she really want to go back to Winnipeg right away? Maybe she could be made beautiful before she went back.

"Anywhere, dear? Well, anywhere in *this* world. Anywhere you like."

Did the lady know? Mary felt herself blush and did not dare look up into the amethyst eyes, staring instead at the crystal ball. "What's the test?" she asked.

"You must go to King Kardia's bedchamber, dear, and do exactly what I tell you."

"Do I go by the crystal ball?"

"Yes, dear—just like we went to the bottom of the sea."

"Will it work?"

"Of course."

"And how do I get back?"

"You will find the ball is still either in your pocket or else around your neck. It may be small, but it will be the same crystal ball. All you do is place it in a fire and wish your way back here."

The witch had said *pocket*. Somehow the word sounded wrong. Hadn't she said something else last time—bag? No. Something diplomatic. *Pouch,* that was it, pouch. Then the lady *could* read her thoughts. She was getting new words from her all the time. Should she ask her just to make sure? But *no*. Once again she became frightened and wanted to have thoughts that *nobody* could read, and again in her anxiety she tried to stop herself thinking. Because she was *just about to think something she must not let the witch know. She could feel the thought coming and there was no way to stop it.*
Hickory dickory dock.
The mouse ran up the clock.
The clock struck one, the mouse ran down.
Hickory dickory dock.

Quick! She must think of another nursery rhyme and stop any thoughts leaking out!
There was a pretty girl

With a very pretty curl
Right in the middle of her forehead.
When she was good
She was very, very good,
And when she was bad she was horrid.

"It would be horrid, wouldn't it, dear, if you couldn't get back? But don't worry; the crystal ball will never leave you. It is yours forever, now."

Mary felt her throat close up. For a moment she couldn't breathe. But the Lady of Night didn't seem to notice.

"You will find him fast asleep, and there will be nobody with him."

"But what shall I say?" Mary's mouth was dry.

"You won't say anything at first, dear. On the table beside his bed you will see a long iron rod. It's called a sceptre. I want you to take it and lay it very quietly on the floor as far from the bed as you can. If it stays where you put it, then all you have to do is pick it up again and bring it back to me."

"But why shouldn't it stay where I put it?"

"It might not, dear, but I don't want you to worry about it just now. Listen to what you must do. If the sceptre doesn't stay perfectly still, just forget about it and waken the king. Now, will you be able to remember what I say?"

"I'm very good at remembering."

"Very well. You must say to him, 'I am Mary McNab from a world far off, your majesty. The Lord Gaal has sent me to bid you arm a sailing vessel with your fiercest warriors and sail into the heart of the Kingdom of Darkness. The Lord Gaal will watch over you and will enable you to destroy it. Do not be afraid. Only hasten to do the bidding of Gaal!' "

"What are you going to do? Will he really destroy this place?" Once more she tried to make herself sound silly, like a little girl.

"I want him to come here and marry me."

"What about the queen and the prince?"

"They will be all right, Mary. I will let him rescue them, but I shall put a spell on him so that his wife will seem ugly. She really is not very suitable for him, dear. He will be much happier with me."

"But suppose he doesn't believe me?"

"He will, dear. You will make him believe. After all, you're going to be beautiful, aren't you?"

Mary took a deep breath and stood up. The Lady of Night also got up and stood beside her, and turning to look into her eyes Mary repeated word for word the message from Gaal. All the time she could smell the unbrushed teeth and stale Scotch.

"Did Gaal *really* say that?" she asked, though she knew the answer to her question.

"Of course not. I like to play jokes with Gaal. It's a little game we have. It's fun to fool him."

Mary's head was whirling. There were so many things to think about. She wanted to be beautiful, and it would do no harm to try to do what the witch said. Yet she couldn't let herself think about anything else but becoming beautiful for the moment. She longed to get away from this lovely but dangerous person—at least until she could sort her feelings out—and the crystal ball was her only means of doing so. She tossed it into the ruby flames and watched it begin to swell.

She could see the king's bedchamber as the ball grew bigger. Moonlight flooded through leaded windows to trace a delicate pattern on the white bed cover beneath which King Kardia lay sleeping. He was on his back, his left arm flung out to lie across an ornate iron rod on a low table by the bed. So that was the Iron Sceptre.

By now the scene was very clear. She could even see the patterned rug covering most of the floor and black beams supporting the ceiling above the bed. Hardly thinking what she was doing she stepped forward and at once the witch and the Palace of Darkness were gone.

She was standing in the king's bedroom inside the royal palace in Anthropos, and though she didn't know it, the crystal ball through which she had stepped, was already hanging from a chain round her neck.

14

Beneath the Northern Mountains

The contrast was unbelievable. One minute his ears had been filled with roaring, crackling, the baying of hounds and the shouts of men, and the next minute with silence. The wind that had been tugging at Wesley's clothes and blowing hair in his eyes was suddenly stilled. The sight of angry hounds and enemy soldiers, of spurting flames and smoke had been blotted out in an instant by total darkness.

Stillness, silence, blackness. Wesley shrank into himself scarcely breathing, straining his ears for any sound above the pounding of his heart. He stretched his arms cautiously in front of him for the darkness was too thick for him to see. Was he alone? Ought he to call out?

The blackness slowly lifted. A bright moon shone from a sky of blue velvet on the little company beside the stream. Men-at-arms, swords half-drawn, still looked expectantly at Gunruth. Koach teeth were bared and glinting in the moonlight, but the growls had died in their owners' throats. Kaas, Kurt and Lisa stood wonderingly together. Only the raccoons seemed unsurprised.

Twitterpitter fluttered to where Wesley stood. "Oh, dear. Oh, dear! I never thought *this* would happen. It's too bad. I really only came to sing. I feel lost without Strongbeak, and I don't feel well. May I get inside your pocket?" Wesley held his jacket pocket open to the soft, warm little bundle of feathers.

"What happened?" Kurt asked Lisa in a whisper.

"The hounds and soldiers have disappeared!" Lisa said softly.

"There's no forest fire."

"It looks as though there never was a fire!"

"Well, I'm sure we didn't dream it."

"Mebbe we're dreaming now."

"It doesn't feel like it."

The men-at-arms had begun to put their swords back in their scabbards, shaking their heads and muttering as they did so. Gunruth and Inkleth stepped across the stream to where Wesley was cautiously fingering the feathery ball in his pocket.

Gunruth's voice was grave. "My lord, this is deep magic. Time has changed."

"What happened, Gunruth?"

"I thought that you would know, my lord." Wesley shook his head.

Inkleth's face was creased with a frown. "The moon is full," he said slowly.

"And last night it was but new," Gunruth replied. "The magic is deep indeed."

Inkleth's look grew excited. His face became aglow

with delighted anticipation. "Wist ye not that we may be in Goldcoffin's Glade?"

Gunruth's eyes widened. "How so?" he asked, sharply.

The impish look on Inkleth's face reminded Wesley of the Inkleth he had once known before he had crawled, bloody and mangled, out of the ruins of Geburah. As they watched him Inkleth began to sing a mournfully jaunty song that matched the roguish look on his wrinkled face.

Hard by the glade that the brook runs through
To splash down the rocks night and morn,
'Neath a full moon he who finds will rue
Day that he e'er was born.

Moon stands still and a cave gapes wide
Once in a hundred years.
Let him take heed, he who goes inside,
Lest he weep pools of tears!

Fa la la, fa la la,
Fa la la, la lal la la,
Lest he weep pools of tears!

Gunruth sounded peevish. "There be many glades crossed by brooks in the mountains."

But Inkleth was not to be daunted. "And if the moon stands still?"

"Who could say if the moon did stand still? What eye could see it?"

"The Koach's eyes could, my lord Gunruth. Shall I call one?" His eyes still gleamed with merriment. Watching his expression, Wesley grew still more anxious. He remembered the night when Inkleth's willfulness had ended in his hanging by one leg from the mouth of an ogre. Premonition of danger crept icily beneath his ribs.

Inkleth called one of the wolves. "Ho, there, Garfong, son of Garfong, son of Garfong!" The white-furred Koach bounded toward them.

"The moon, have you seen the moon?" Garfong growled. "What does your growl mean, friend Garfong?"

Garfong growled again. "I fear, my lord Inkleth."

"Why so?"

"Since I was a cub all stars and planets have been alive. But now, . . ."

"Now what?"

"Most unnatural it is, my lord. The hair on my brothers' backs rises with fear."

"And what do they fear, good Garfong?"

"The moon, my lord. It hangs like a dead thing in the sky. It is as still as a frozen river and has ceased to prowl the heavenly grasslands."

Only Inkleth was smiling. "Well, my lord Gunruth?"

Then without waiting for Gunruth to reply he went on singing.

Now that a hundred winters have passed
Goldcoffin wakes again,
Spreading his treasures across the floor,
Madd'ning the eyes of men!

Goldcoffin under the mountain sits
With Murder, Envy and Greed
Serpent and lobster and naked bird
Waiting on humans to feed.

Fa la la, fa la la,
Fa la la, la lal la la,
Waiting on humans to feed!

"Who's Goldcoffin?" Wesley asked Gunruth.

"He was the grandson of Bjorn, father of the race of Matmon. At the birth of Anthropos before Gaal had created man, Goldcoffin in his greed for wealth stole from his brothers. He slew Rathson, Bjorn's favorite. It is said that Bjorn banished him and all his treasure to a prison on the great Low Way under the Northern Mountains, and that once every hundred years the gateways to the ancient Low Way are opened for any who want to see him."

"Is the story true?"

Gunruth would say no more, but got the party to sit down and eat while he sent wolves and raccoons down through the woods. "I know not what enchantment lies upon us," he told them, "and I cannot see the highway from this place. I fear it may have been spirited away. Go seek it, and bring us word again. Is this indeed the meadow where we sheltered from the fire?"

During the meal they discovered something strange about the stream. "It's just like Jello!" Kurt said to Lisa.

"You mean to taste?"

"No, to look at. It's stopped."

"Stopped? What d'you mean?"

Lisa turned to look at the water. It was true. It was not moving, but seemed to have been arrested in midmotion. Ripples and wavelets stood stiff like molded gelatin or like a model of a stream in a museum. Yet the water looked real enough, gleaming in the moonlight.

Kurt reached out and touched it. To his surprise his finger penetrated the surface. "Oh, it *is* water," he said. "It's still wet!" Two or three of the men-at-arms had also noticed the strange phenomenon and were successfully filling their water bottles from the brook.

"Can we drink it?" Lisa asked. She got down on her

hands and knees and put her face in the water. It felt shockingly cold. She sucked it in through her lips to find that it tasted and felt like water anywhere. Yet when she lifted her face the water was undisturbed. No new ripples appeared around the place where her face had been, and no droplets fell from her.

"Why has it stopped?"

"Goodness knows! Streams don't stop. They dry up. Wesley! Wesley, come and look!"

Wesley was as perplexed as his brother and sister. "Garfong said something about the moon standing still. Now it's the stream as well."

"And the trees and the grass."

"How d'you mean?"

"Well, haven't you noticed? Nothing is moving except us. There isn't a sign of movement anywhere. It's just like we were on a movie set."

"Except that everything's real."

"I know. But everything, everything has ... has stopped." Lisa caught her breath, shocked by what she had said.

"It's impossible!" Kurt said.

"But the stream. . . ."

"I know! Let's go down to the waterfalls. Let's see what a stopped waterfall is like."

The children half ran to where the stream entered the cleft. As they did so they stared at the water almost as if they expected it to start moving again. But it remained as still as a picture.

"Look! Just look!"

There could be no doubt. The Friesens stared in awe at a waterfall as tall as Kardia that was as still as if it were frozen.

"The spray! Look at the droplets of spray!"

171

"My sainted aunt! Did you ever see anything like it! They're just suspended in the air!"

"It's ... it's beautiful!"

Kurt leaned forward and picked a droplet of spray between his forefinger and thumb. "Oh, it squashed!"

"Silly, what d'you expect it to do? It's water."

"I know, but it looked solid. Gosh, this is weird!" They stared at a static waterfall, suspended in midmotion.

"Let's look at the others."

There were several small falls between the meadow and the forest below, all looking like photographs snapped at a fast shutter speed. Behind one of them a cave mouth opened. "I never noticed *that* before," Kurt said.

"We were in a hurry when we came up," Lisa answered slowly.

Wesley stared at the cave. "Inkleth was talking about a cave that opens only once in a hundred years," he said uneasily. "He sang a song about the moon standing still and about some character called Goldcoffin who's been imprisoned under the Northern Mountains since the beginning of time."

They wandered toward the cave mouth and peered into a dark interior, too black for them to see anything. Neither Wesley nor Lisa had any wish to go exploring. But Inkleth had. When Kurt (to Wesley's dismay) described their discovery to him the Matmon clapped Gunruth on the back. "The Low Way," he said eagerly, "The ancient Low Way! Thus shall we pass the mountains— not above them, but beneath them!"

Gunruth was far from happy. He objected, sensibly enough, that the cave probably led nowhere and that the ancient Low Way was a matter of legend that no one had proved. But Inkleth and Kurt were eager to explore the cave to see where it led. If there were a chance of going beneath the mountains to Playsion, Gaal's instructions would make sense. The debate went on for what seemed like an hour beneath the unmoving moon. Gunruth, like the moon, refused to be budged. Then the Koach and the two raccoons returned, and for the moment the discussion was interrupted. Garfong's tongue hung from his mouth.

"The road," Gunruth said gravely, looking at him with obvious relief, "is it still passable?"

"My lord, there is no road."

"There must be a road," Gunruth's voice had an edge of alarm.

"My lord, we searched well. The woods below are not the woods we passed through heretofore. Briars and thorns crowd densely among tree trunks. A Matmon, let alone a man, could never pass through them. We found ways where animals could pass—but, my lord, there is no road."

"Then that settles it, doesn't it, Gunruth?" Kurt asked eagerly.

"The road *was* there," Gunruth said slowly, "and may be there still. On the other hand what else have we but the dark mouth of a cave? You talk as though the Low Way were already opening before us."

"We can at least go and see," Kurt said. Which is what they did. In less than five minutes, when the whole company had gathered around the cave by the unmoving waterfall, the debate broke out again, Inkleth taunting Gunruth, Gunruth quietly but stubbornly holding his ground, and the rest listening in troubled silence. Wesley, unable to rid himself of his anxiety over Inkleth finally interrupted.

"Inkleth! Are you for Gaal or against him?"

"My lord!" The Matmon's face, mischievous only seconds before, suddenly darkened.

"I'm not accusing you of anything, Inkleth. I just want to know. It's thirty-one years in *your* time since we met, and, well, I mean . . . it bothers me the way you're arguing with Gunruth. The rest of us are pretty unhappy. . . ." Wesley faltered lamely to a halt as he saw the whole company staring at him.

Inkleth's voice came low and clear. "My lord, you saw on the Island of Geburah how the powers of darkness treated me. You observed my pitiful condition when Shagah gave me up for dead. You knew likewise that I had betrayed all of you and had mocked the name of Gaal.

"Yet it was Gaal who in spite of my treachery healed my wounds and pardoned me. I swore then that I would serve him, and I will never change. Do not question my love for Gaal for he has won my heart forever. I tease, I mock and, like the mosquito I am, I bite and irritate." His solemn look disappeared like a cloud and a smile broke over his face again. "Do not slap at me, my friends, for I am sated with your own blood. I will bite no more. Pardon me, good Gunruth. One petition only do I make, and it is that he who carries the Sword of Geburah advance ten paces into the cave. If the sword shall show us a way, then we may decide."

Kurt drew the sword and with a beating heart walked to the cave. The men-at-arms parted to let him pass while the raccoons padded after him as though they were his bodyguards. In a moment he had stepped past the silent waterfall and into the black opening. As he did so the sword became a shimmering blue light, humming and vibrating as it flung metallic rays to all parts of the cave.

A murmur of excitement ran through the little group

outside and all moved forward to see what was happening. The Koach pushed among the legs of the humans, eager not to be left behind. Only Gunruth and Wesley were left in the unnatural stillness.

"I guess we might as well go and see," Wesley said hesitantly. He was afraid Gunruth might be offended. He was also afraid Gunruth might be right. Who was to say what lay beyond the cave mouth? Suppose they were walking into a trap? Supposing there was no turning back?

"My lord, it is my business to stay with you wherever you choose to go." He smiled ruefully. "I can no more control our fate than Inkleth can. Let us hope that the Lord Gaal has eyes that can see us."

The floor of the cave was wet and sloped downward before them. It proved to be the first in a series of small caves twisting this way and that, all leading deeper into the earth. Stalactites drew the tips of stalagmites up from the floor to meet them. Voice echoes mingled with echoing footsteps and the constant dripping and splashing of water.

At the far end of the seventh cave, the smallest of all, was a perfectly formed archway. It led them to where they could stand beneath a small dome on a circular platform of smooth rock. No sooner were they standing on the platform than Wesley, who was staring at the domed ceiling said, "Oh, look! The ceiling's going up! It's moving!"

Heads tilted back as everyone looked. Lit by the glimmering light from the Sword of Geburah, the dome seemed to be stretching upward before their eyes into the rock. I say *seemed* to be because what was really happening was that the circular rock platform was sinking down, but sinking so smoothly that they felt nothing. Rocky walls glided past them as the dome receded further and further. Soon they could no longer see it. All the time their speed was increasing until they were hurtling silently and swiftly into the bowels of the earth. Then both Wesley and Gunruth knew the true reason for their reluctance. Whatever perils awaited them, there was now no turning back. All hope of regaining the cave mouth was gone.

They seemed to descend for about an hour, while smooth rock walls rushed into darkness. Koach and raccoons had long since lain down and gone to sleep. Twitterpitter had poked her head out of Wesley's pocket, but all she had said was, "Where are we? Oh, dear! Oh, dear, dear!" and disappeared again. Wesley slipped his hand several times into his pocket to feel the soft warmth of her body and its rapid breathing. Finally he left his hand there, gently cradling her feathers, strangely comforted by the feeling that she wanted him to protect her. The Matmon and the humans sat down and talked in a desultory fashion. No one seemed excited, except for Kaas who had spent all his life in Nephesh and whose eyes were wide with wonder.

Eventually their descent slowed almost to a halt. Through an archway there lay before them the biggest cave the children had ever seen. It was lit with dim green light. Kurt sheathed the sword. As the platform came to rest with a soft thump, animals, Koach and men rose sleepily to their feet to stare at the cavern ahead of them.

"Goldcoffin's Palace," breathed Inkleth. "I swear it be Goldcoffin's Palace!"

"Have you ever seen it before?" Gunruth asked.

"What need to see it before?" Inkleth snorted. "Don't you remember the words of the song?"

This time echoes from his powerful voice filtered back faintly from the far reaches of the cave.

Lit by green fires from an emerald's core,
Silent as Morpheus Lake
From which it rises, upward to soar,
Who dares its treasures to take?

Hundred years gone! Though the hinges rust,
In go the travelers to see.
Then their eyes feast, and their hearts burn with lust.
He never lets them go free!

Fa la la, fa la la,
Fa la la, la lal la la,
He never lets them go free!

While Inkleth sang the Koach howled mournfully and Lisa shivered, partly from cold and partly from fear. "What does it mean?" she asked Gunruth. "Is that really Goldcoffin's Palace?"

"So I fear, my lady. In all the lore of Anthropos there is only one palace lit by emerald light—the palace where Goldcoffin lures his victims into the Prison of Greed."

"His victims. What d'you mean?"

"'Tis said he offers a share in his treasures to all who pass this way. The treasures curl round men's hearts so that they go mad to possess them. But all who touch them are enchanted forever and locked in the Prison of Greed."

The Koach had ceased their howling. Every eye stared at the distant, mysterious castle jutting steeply from the water.

"But surely not *everyone* gets enchanted and imprisoned," Lisa said questioningly.

"That may be so. Doubtless some have escaped. But the legends do not speak of those who escape, my lady, only of those who stay."

Mrs. Raccoon had pushed her little black nose between Gunruth and Lisa. "Nonsense, my dear! Don't listen to him. How dare you frighten the lady! Gold! Who wants gold? If he had *fish* now it would be a different story. But gold and jewels! I ask you! Of course we don't want them, do we, my dear?"

Lisa was about to say no when she saw that the question was addressed to Mr. Raccoon, who sneezed three times and said, "Of course not, my dear. I entirely agree!"

"Do we *have* to go inside?" Kurt asked. He too felt fearful at the sinister appearance of the castle, which seemed to be waiting for them like a spider in the center of a web. "Couldn't we just go round it?"

Inkleth shook his head. "The Low Way goes *through* the castle, not around it," he said. "The waters of Morpheus Lake are deep and treacherous. Only on the Low Way is there safety, and the Low Way is blocked by the palace."

It was an unpleasant prospect. Wesley said nothing as he fondled Twitterpitter's warm feathers in his pocket, but like the others he stared at the menacing mass of stone in the distance, certain that it was watching them.

Lisa's voice sounded thin and high pitched. "Let's go back! Please let's go back!"

But when they turned to look behind them they saw that there was no way back. The arch through which they had entered the cave was no longer there. Only a wall of smooth rock greeted their bewildered eyes.

Wesley drew his breath in deeply and slowly. "Well," he said, more confidently and cheerfully than he actually felt, "I guess we don't have much choice. We might as well be on our way to Goldcoffin's Palace."

15

Goldcoffin's Treasures

When Wesley used all his weight to pull the heavy bell rope he was surprised to find it lifted him right off his feet. From overhead came the hollow boom of a bell. Startled, Wesley let go of the rope and fell. Across the waters of Morpheus Lake from distant walls of rock, echoes reverberated like rumbling thunder arousing the guilt he used to feel when years before he rang neighbors' doorbells in River Heights and ran away to hide. He would like to have run away now, but there was nowhere to run.

It had taken the royal party about half an hour to walk along the Low Way to the castle, whose walls rose rough and high above their heads, while a gateway under the tower yawned like a mouth waiting to devour them.

With a clang, a rattle and a roar, the portcullis rose to let them pass. For a moment no one moved. Finally Gunruth stepped forward crying, "Let us be on our way. Salvation lies beyond Goldcoffin's Palace and we cannot go beyond until we have gone through!" He marched ahead of the ill-assorted little party across the courtyard to a tower whose windows and wide-open doorway were ablaze with light. Trembling they passed inside.

"Ho, there, travelers from the upper world! Who be ye and from whence in the upper world come ye? What is your mission?"

Staring at the grotesque figure on an ivory throne Lisa wondered how so great a roar could come from so small a person. Goldcoffin's chest was deep and barrellike, but his legs and arms were tiny while his white beard flowed like a foaming waterfall over his chest, his stomach and down between his legs to tumble over the steps in front of the throne. She wondered what he did with it when he walked. Did he lift it up in front of him? Or throw it over his shoulder? Or tuck it into his belt? Perhaps he hadn't walked for years. Perhaps he had remained seated on his throne for centuries while the beard grew and grew.

Beneath his bushy white brows fierce black eyes glowed. His great nose curved imperiously downward like an eagle's beak to where his chin might have been if you could have seen it. A jeweled crown sat rakishly on his bald head, and long earrings hung from his ears while seventeen rings encrusted his tiny fingers. All of them— crown, earrings and rings—winked and blinked with emeralds, rubies and diamonds.

"Who be ye?" he roared again. "Whence come ye? Whither are ye bound and wherefore?"

Nobody spoke. They all stared at Goldcoffin, at the frightening creatures behind him and the treasures in front of him. Standing twice the height of the throne, the Goblin of Murder, a great red lobster with a human

head, stroked Goldcoffin's shoulders with his delicate antennae and held murderous claws like nutcrackers above his head. A green snake, the Sprite of Envy, sat at the foot of the steps of the throne. She had a human skull for a head, staring from empty eye sockets at them. A black tongue flickered between her bony jaws as she hissed softly at the strangers. On Goldcoffin's left was the Goblin of Hatred, a black and shining beetle the size of a horse, tapping one foot with a clack, clack, clack that made Lisa want to bite her fingernails; while on his right a yellow bird, from whose featherless and naked head stared red and watery eyes, sharpened her beak against the side of the throne with deft strokes. She was the Spirit of Greed.

Lisa remembered a verse of the rhyme that Inkleth had sung, shuddering as she did so.

Goldcoffin under the mountain sits
With Murder, Envy and Greed,
Serpent and lobster and naked bird
Waiting on humans to feed.

Treasure in untidy heaps littered the marble floor between the throne and where they stood. There were swords with ivory hilts, swords with gold hilts and swords whose hilts were studded with stones. There were goblets of gold and goblets of silver, peacock feathers and necklaces of apes' teeth, silks, satins, laces, bracelets, finger rings, thumb rings, nose rings and earrings. There was a mountain of pearls, another of diamonds, others of emeralds, amethysts, opals and rubies. There were piles of soft yellow gold pieces, elephant tusks, tiaras and crowns, orbs and sceptres, chains, lampstands, and gold and silver candlesticks. There were idols and images, censors, vials, votive bottles and jeweled knives for the slaughter of sacrifices. There were ebony tables with inlaid mother-of-pearl and golden caskets full of queens' and princesses' fancies. There were silk dresses as fine and light as spiderwebs and satin dresses stiff with silver wire and jewels. Silver-coated suits of armor with jewel-studded helmets hung from the walls. Shelves were loaded with gold and silver tableware and great wine cups beaten with intricate and magical designs. And high above it all from a beam on the ceiling, hung a gold chandelier scattering light from a thousand wax candles through dangling diamonds the size of hens' eggs.

"Have ye no tongues? Speak! Or the Goblin of Murder will crunch your bones!" Lisa jumped as the lobster snapped his claws together. This was far worse than she had anticipated. How would they ever get away from this awful place?

Gunruth fixed his eyes upon the little dwarf on the ivory throne. "I am Gunruth, son of Guntug, of the sword Bloglin, which sword I now carry," and he drew the sword from its sheath, staring still at Goldcoffin, "and by which Akrath, dragon of the northern slopes was slain. My grandfather was Throssa, slayer of the serpent who held the Matmon Prince Galantash to ransom. I am descended from Rathson, grandson of Bjorn, whom thou slewest in the dawn of Anthropos."

Gunruth's words were bold and his voice firm, but his lips were white with fear and his forehead bathed with sweat. Goldcoffin never moved. He stared unblinking at the members of the party, fixing them one by one with his black eyes as Gunruth continued.

"With me is Inkleth, High Chieftain of the Red Dwarfs, son of Inklesh, son of Klingall, son of Lenglesh, first-born of the great King Kolungall.

"Their lordships Wesley, Kurt and the lady Lisa have come from other worlds at the bidding of the Lord Gaal.

They may speak for themselves."

Wesley's heart seemed to leap from his chest into his throat as the black eyes turned on him. Licking dry lips he did his best to speak in the same manner as Gunruth.

"We come at the bidding of the Lord Gaal," he said, dismayed to hear how squeaky his voice sounded, "who has charged us to invade the realm of the witch Mirmah (she who styles herself Empress-to-Be of the Darkness that Swallows the World) to rescue her majesty Queen Suneidesis and the Crown Prince Tiqvah. It is the will of the Lord Gaal that the witch and her kingdom be destroyed and with her the treacheries she has sown in Anthropos and Playsion." He stopped to clear his throat and catch his breath. His head was pounding but he felt pleased with himself.

Goldcoffin drummed his tiny fingers on the arm of the throne. "The will of the Lord Gaal may be disobeyed," he growled gently.

"Yet obeyed or disobeyed, the will of the Lord Gaal will prevail," Gunruth said, still white-lipped and trembling and with Bloglin still in his hand.

"The will of the Lord Gaal may bring pain to those who serve him." The growl was almost a purr. "Terror and dangers await the children from worlds afar. I am old and have no need of my treasures. It would please me to think that some of them might travel across the ages to other worlds in other skies." He searched the children's faces, his eyelids half-closed and his fingers still drumming. The lobster's feelers continued to caress his shoulders.

"What does he mean?" Kurt whispered to Lisa.

"He's trying to bribe us with his treasures."

"You mean he's actually *offering* us some?"

"Yes, but I don't trust him."

Gunruth slowly put Bloglin back in its scabbard. "It is said that none who touch your treasures ever leaves your palace," he said evenly. He stared at an archway beside the ivory throne where steps led into the dark. "Old tales tell of your servants Greed, Hatred, Murder and Envy who seize the subjects of Anthropos and fling them into dungeons where they waste and die."

The low growling continued. "No one steals the treasures of Goldcoffin. But I may give to whom I will. Return by the way you came and you may take all you will of my treasure. I can open the way back for you. You need not face the perils that lie ahead."

"We serve the Lord Gaal," Gunruth said stolidly.

"And how much does he pay you?"

Inkleth, who had been squatting on the floor, rose to his feet and stood by Gunruth. "He too has treasures," he replied, "treasures that would make the famous treasures of Goldcoffin look like tinsel. Yet we serve him for love. The Lord Gaal pours joy into our hearts so that we care neither for terror nor peril." Colored lights from myriad jewels played over his face, yet he stared scornfully at the heaps of treasure.

For a moment no one spoke. Goldcoffin continued to look steadily at the children. "The will of the Lord Gaal, ye say, will prevail whether ye take my treasure or no? The will of the Lord Gaal will prevail whether ye rescue the queen or no? Then the Lord Gaal has no need of you. He flatters only to let his servants perish. Have not many of them been slain with the sword? Go back to the safety of your world and take my treasures with you as a token of goodwill from Anthropos. These, my jewels, can bring happiness in any world."

Wesley thought of Uncle John's mortgage and of the cost of a new roof on the old house on Grosvenor. He glanced at a heavy gold crown encrusted with large and glittering stones, lying only a yard from his feet. One jewel from it would solve all Uncle John's financial problems, he was sure. He began to stare at it.

"Take it! Take it from Goldcoffin!" The ancient dwarf had followed the direction of Wesley's eyes.

Without thinking, Wesley slipped his hand into his coat pocket and felt the soft, warm bundle that was Twitterpitter. He could not explain the reaction that took place as he did so. Suddenly the thought of the crown and its value seemed foolish. The tiny bird's terror, yet her willingness to be the partner of an eagle in a dangerous mission, made him ashamed of his thoughts. Once more he heard his own voice, this time fierce and loud, saying, "We serve the Lord Gaal. No treasure can bribe the servants of Gaal." Yet something about the crown held his eyes. Where had he seen it before? His forehead creased in a frown.

"Take it, lord Wesley! It is one of two, alike as peas in a pod, crowns of the royal twins of Keshaph, Kashshaph and Anan." His black eyes darted over the piles of treasure as though he were looking for something. "The crown you see is the Crown of Kashshaph. There is another, the Crown of Anan, looking the same as the one you are looking at but worth more than all my hoard. . . ."

Wesley continued to stare at the Crown of Kashshaph. It seemed that the memory was about to come back, yet whenever he thought it would do so, it slipped away again. Lisa, too, was staring at the crown.

"The woman on the TV!" she said suddenly.

"That's it!" Wesley remembered now. "Mirmah! The Lady of Night! She was wearing it when we saw her in the attic!"

At those words a roar of rage filled the tower. Goldcoffin had jumped up on his little legs, his black eyes burning with fear.

"Mirmah, you say? Mirmah? Mirmah has taken the Crown of Anan! She whom I sheltered for a thousand years has robbed me!" The lobster's antennae froze into stillness. The green serpent ceased from swaying and hissing through its skull head. The beetle no longer tapped his feet and the bird stopped sharpening her beak. Goldcoffin's face was white with rage and his hands were shaking. One of them, Lisa noticed, was gripping something from which a thin gold chain hung downward. The chain, too, seemed familiar.

Raising the tiny fists above his head, the fine gold chain swinging from one of them, he gave scream upon scream. "The Crown of Anan! The Crown of Anan! Mirmah has taken the Crown of Anan!" In spite of her terror, Lisa felt pity for the grotesque little figure. It was hard to think that he had existed at the creation of Anthropos.

Then he stopped abruptly, tossed his long beard over his left shoulder and trotted with frightening daintiness down the steps of the throne. Winding his way through the piles of treasure he stood in front of Lisa, holding out the hand from which the gold chain hung.

"Go then to the Kingdom of Darkness!" he shrieked, "Go! Do the bidding of Gaal, and kill her! Kill her! Kill her! Here, take the very stone she gave me in payment for my shelter and use it to get close to her."

Lisa had been too busy staring at the grotesque figure to notice what lay in his palm, but when she did so she gave a breathless, "O-oh!" Filling Goldcoffin's tiny palm lay a gleaming blue stone that she remembered well. It was the stone she had talked to Lord Nocham about at dawn in the courtyard in Nephesh; the stone Sir Dipsuchos had wrongly released from the palace treasury; the stone she had discovered in a moment of terror on the floor of a dungeon in Authentio Castle. "The Mashal Stone!" she breathed.

"Take it!" the evil creature spat. "Take it and kill her!"

Carefully he picked his way back to the throne, his rage suddenly spent as he glared sullenly at the royal party. The Koach stood stiff and silent, their lips curled back and the hair on their necks bristling. They made no sound. Only Mr. & Mrs. Raccoon seemed unconcerned, sprawling on the floor and watching the Matmon and the children sleepily.

"Could there be treasure for us as well, your majesty?" The sergeant-at-arms looked appealingly at the dwarf. "Just little things to take with us as souvenirs from the palace beneath the mountains if it so please you, sire."

Goldcoffin stared at him dully. "The Crown of Anan is gone," he said. "Take what you will, but each of you may take one thing only. He who takes more shall suffer."

One by one the men-at-arms began to move among the treasures. At first they only looked, afraid to touch. Then one or another would reach with trembling fingers to feel the weight of a precious stone or to try on a crown or unsheath a sword. There were exclamations of wonder and gasps of delight. Soon there was nervous laughter and an excited hubbub of conversation. Goldcoffin seemed bored and unconcerned.

Then so quickly that no one could see how it happened, the four creatures around the throne ran toward the men-at-arms, seizing them all in beak, jaws, claws and torturous green coils. In vain they fought and struggled. In seconds they were gone through the archway behind the throne as their terrified cries echoed hollowly up the stairway.

The rest were too shocked to move. Staring stunned and wide-eyed at the archway they listened to screams which gradually grew fainter until they died away. It seemed that for an eternity nobody moved. Then, moving slowly, the Goblin of Murder, the Sprite of Envy, the Goblin of Hatred and the Spirit of Greed returned to resume their positions around the throne. The lobster, moving as though it were drowsy with content, reached down with his antennae, carefully set straight the crown on Goldcoffin's bald head and resumed the caresses of his master's shoulders. Wesley looked at the snake, the bird and the beetle. All seemed filled with the same sleepy contentment.

Gunruth exploded with rage. "Villain! Deceiver! My men are servants of Gaal! Restore them at once!" He pulled Bloglin from its sheath but did not move from where he stood.

Goldcoffin seemed unconcerned. "Those who have been eaten can scarcely be restored," he said carelessly.

"Eaten?"

"Men who give way to the lust of the eye grow tender enough for my servants to eat."

Gunruth was white with anger. "Enough! Bring back the servants of Gaal from your dungeons!"

"I have no dungeons, Gunruth, son of Guntug, of the sword Bloglin, whose forefather I murdered in ages past. I have only banqueting chambers where my servants swallow those who lust after my treasures. The servants of Gaal have been consumed. They are now digested. They are no more."

With a howl of uncontrollable fury Gunruth leaped toward Goldcoffin, his sword held high. Lisa screamed as she saw Inkleth follow him, and then Kurt, white-faced

and solemn, struggling to pull the Sword of Geburah
from its scabbard. With a rush and a roar a sheet of flame
flashed from floor to ceiling, and then the floor was
suddenly bare. Treasure, ivory throne, Goldcoffin and
demons had vanished. Only the chandelier with its thousand candles remained shining above the marble floor in
the center of which there now stood a large gold coffin.
Trembling they stepped forward to look inside. It was
empty. But on the gold bottom of its interior were engraved the names of the missing men-at-arms.

Suddenly a section of wall in front of them fell open
leaving a ragged archway through which they could pass
into the courtyard on the far side of the tower. Thirty
yards beyond was an open gate leading across Morpheus
Lake to the further side of the cave.

Lisa had never before seen Gunruth weep, and she
looked on with awe and pity as sobs shook him. Inkleth
took Bloglin from the Matmon's unfeeling hand, replaced it in its scabbard and led him gently through the
broken wall into dim emerald light in the courtyard. Silently the others followed.

They never again saw the men-at-arms.

Gunruth mourned as they traveled three weeks along
the ancient Low Way, blaming himself for what had happened and grieving to think of bereaved families he
would meet on their return to Nephesh.

They passed through tunnels, through narrow caves
and through great caverns; they crossed bridges over
underground rivers and chasms of fire. They saw neither day or night, and needed the blue light from the
Sword of Geburah to see their way.

Food supplies were gone yet they knew no hunger.
During the first week they would be terrified whenever

they slept by nightmares of Goldcoffin and his demons, until once in the last stages of fear Kurt had drawn the Sword of Geburah from its scabbard, so certain was he that Goldcoffin was upon them. In its calm light his fear subsided.

Inkleth was awake and watched him. "Leave it out of its sheath while we sleep," he said to Kurt. "It was forged from seven thunderbolts buried in the Garden of Peace and is engraved with elf runes. It may shed the peace of the garden over us."

And so it proved. Although Inkleth's explanation was mistaken, the sword being of logos-tempered steel, it did what he said it would do. Their sleep from that time on was deep and untroubled. While they lay on the rocky floor, the pulsing blue light from the sword wrapped them in warmth and peace.

By and by they came upon a perfectly formed archway leading into seven caves, all like the caves by which they had entered the mountains behind them in the west. And as they entered the seventh cave the same column of black smoke that first had wrapped them about in the meadow among the burning trees came again and placed them on a mountain slope in Playsion looking down upon the village of Chalash and the Great Sea.

It was early afternoon and the sunlight dazzled their eyes. They did not know that it was only a few days after they had left the burning forest for time moves little beneath the Northern Mountains.

16

The Other Side
of the Mirror

Afterward whenever Mary thought about her time in Nephesh Palace she remembered how anxious and uncomfortable she felt. One part of her might have enjoyed playing the heroine in the witch's plot. She was not scared—at least not as much as she had expected to be—even though she was being a real-life spy. She might have enjoyed thinking how impressed her friends in Toronto would be by what she was doing.

But she was too sick with worry to enjoy anything. Her worries had nothing to do with the danger of being found out. It never occurred to her to doubt that she would succeed in doing what Mirmah had ordered. But she was more troubled than ever about the witch herself. It had shocked her terribly to discover Mirmah could overhear what she was thinking.

How could she ever have let herself be fooled by the

nice things the witch had said? Yet whatever happened she must let the Lady of Night think she believed her. She wanted to get back to her own world and her own people. The crystal ball offered her a means of getting away from the Palace of Darkness. But when ought she to try to get away? For in spite of her fear, she still wanted to cash in on the promise of magical beauty. But if the witch once found out what she was thinking, she might never keep her promise. So she would have to wait (once she was beautiful) for a time when the witch was not watching her or thinking about her. And in the meantime she would have to concentrate every moment on not thinking anything that would give her intentions away.

Such were the confused fears passing through her mind as she stood at the foot of Kardia's bed. It was a relief to feel that for the moment she was free to think whatever she wanted without being overheard. But it would be unwise to suppose the Lady of Night could not see her. No doubt she was watching her at that very moment. She was determined to show by her actions how obedient she was being. And if the king woke she would speak to him in the way the witch had told her to.

So as I say, she felt uncomfortable, which when you think about it is easy to understand. She was trying to fool two people, one of them a king whom she began to like, as I shall tell you in a while (and it's never very enjoyable to deceive someone you like), and the other a witch who could sometimes hear what she was thinking and toward whom her feelings were very confused indeed. She struggled for several minutes to put her uncomfortable feelings to the back of her mind, almost forgetting where she was.

The sound of footsteps approaching the royal bedchamber woke her from her reverie. Instinctively she crouched down and raised the bed covers between the bed and the floor so she could steal quickly underneath it if she had to. But to her relief the person, whoever it was, passed the door and continued down the passage. Slowly she straightened up again.

She tiptoed along the bed toward the sceptre. A floor-board creaked loudly, and she froze into stillness while her heart bumped noisily, somewhere high up in her chest. But Kardia never moved. The sound of his breathing continued without any change, and her heart seemed to settle back down to where it belonged.

She took another step. Then two more. One more step would bring her within reach of the sceptre. She had an insane desire to start giggling for Kardia's hand was still resting on the sceptre, and she caught herself wondering what would happen if she were to tickle it. She watched his sleeping face and the more she watched it the more shivers ran up and down her spine.

Suddenly she jumped as he took a deep breath, sighed noisily and began to turn toward the window, lifting his left hand in front of him and away from the sceptre as he did so. Would he wake up? No. Once again his breathing settled and she stepped forward, gripped the rough iron rod with both hands, almost dropping it as she did so. Something about it felt wrong. It was heavy, but it wasn't heavy *downward* so much as *horizontally*. She stared at it, feeling it pull its weight against her hands, not toward the floor but toward the bed. Whatever could be happening?

There was no time to think. Grasping the sceptre firmly she struggled to carry it to the wall opposite the window and placed it quietly on the floor in front of her, still facing the wall and with her back to the king. Hardly had she done this than it rose from the floor and hit her shins, pressing against them. Startled she pushed it down again on the floor, but this time, almost as though it were alive, it jumped briskly and knocked her feet from under her so that she fell face forward into the wall. She struggled to her feet biting her lip with pain and turned round. The sceptre was once more lying on the low table, just as it had been when she entered the room. *It had been pulling toward Kardia.*

"Stupid thing!" she muttered angrily.

Suddenly she smelled unbrushed teeth and turned her head quickly. She was still alone. The smell made her think of funerals and burial grounds.

"I guess I'll have to wake him now," she thought. "Unless. . . . No, mebbe I won't. I'll take the sceptre to somewhere where there's a fire, and . . . " she felt in the pocket in front of her parka to realize with relief that the crystal ball was there . . ."and then I'll take it back through the glass to the witch."

"No, dear, you musn't do that. It wouldn't come with you. You must wake him like we agreed. It's really a part of him, as I suspected all along, so it can't be taken away from him until he comes to me." *The musical voice was coming from inside her chest and the smell was stronger than ever.* Was the Lady of Night inside her? For a moment she thought she was going to throw up. "Just shake him by the shoulder, dear, and then say what I told you. You're really doing very well. You're cleverer than I realized." This time the voice came from inside her head. Could Kardia hear it? Somehow she knew he couldn't. But of two things she was now terrifyingly certain. She had *not* succeeded in getting away from the witch, and the witch could still hear her thoughts. But had she heard everything? For the moment there was nothing to be done. She would have to do as she had been told.

Dismayed by what had happened and not caring now whether she made a noise or not, she strode to the bedside and shook the sleeping king's shoulder. He sat up and looked at her.

"Who are you?" His voice was firm and low.

"I am Mary McNab from a world far off, your majesty," the words came mechanically from her flawless memory. "The Lord Gaal has sent me to bid you arm a sailing vessel with your fiercest warriors and sail into the heart of the Kingdom of Darkness. The Lord Gaal will watch over you and will enable you to destroy it. Do not be afraid. Only hasten to do the bidding of Gaal!"

He must have looked at her for nearly a minute before speaking. "Yes, you are like them, though the clothes you wear are different. Tell me, what does the Lord Gaal look like?"

Mary thought for a moment.

"He's tall and straight and he wears sandals in the snow. . . ."

"In the *snow?*"

"Yes, he's the Lord of ice. Didn't you know?" She felt more at home now, sure of her ground. She liked the man with the soft gray beard, whose eyes twinkled in the moonlight and whose lips looked as though they might smile any minute. For a moment she felt tempted to tell him everything, but she didn't. She went on talking. "When he walks across the snow he doesn't sink down in it, but it kind of lights up with pretty colors, like jewels or like flowers. He gave me a sword called the Sword of Geburah, and I took it to my uncle's house. You should have seen their surprise!"

"So you really are the maid they spoke of."

"They? My cousins? Were they here? Have you seen them?"

The king nodded. "They came to rescue my queen and my son."

"Oh, I didn't know. Are they still here?" Hope flared up inside her.

"No, little maid. They have gone north on a rescue mission. But I fear for them. We know not what has befallen them, ..." his face was grave, " . . . but tell me. How did you enter our world?"

She was deeply disappointed, and her voice was flat and low. "I must have come through the TV. I thought it was something like Disneyland, but now I know it was real magic. A big bear grabbed me and threw me in an igloo," she paused. "D'you think they're all right—the Friesens, I mean?"

The king was frowning. He did not seem to understand. "An igloo? What is an igloo?"

"That's a kind of snow house. It was very cold. And I got these clothes there."

"But where were you? There is no snow in Anthropos."

The queen's voice sounded from her chest again. "Tell him you were by the northernmost outposts of the realm of the Lady of Night." Mary did so, but she stepped back a little in case he should smell the awful smell which by now was strong.

"But how came you here?"

"Tell him Gaal rescued you and sent you here." Again Mary repeated the queen's words.

The king smiled. "The Lord Gaal uses the strangest messengers. The maid Lisa came in a dark hour and rescued me from the dungeon of Authentio Castle. And now you come and tell me to sail into battle. Doubtless you, too, came through a proseo stone. It could not be better timed." He swung his legs over the side of the bed, and she saw that he was wearing what looked like a long nightshirt.

"Ho there, pages! Bring my clothes! And take the lady Mary to the guest chamber!"

The big door opened slowly and two boys about Wesley's age stumbled sleepily into the bedchamber, stopping when they saw Mary. "Your majesty?"

The king laughed. "Gaal has sent us another maid, kin of the lady Lisa."

"How came she here, sire?" one of them asked. "Did she enter by the window?" he looked at her resentfully.

"Aha! You have never seen a proseo stone, I'll warrant. She came through the wall!"

"Through the wall!"

"What is he talking about?" Mary wondered to herself. "He must know another way of doing it."

"Through a stone in the wall! A stone Gaal has given us in time of need. And dearly did I long for guidance this night! Conduct her with courtesy to the lady Chocma. Bid her call maids to light a fire in her room and bring food, water and changes of raiment to her chamber that she may refresh herself e'er she slumbers."

Events were happening too quickly for Mary, and she was too confused to do more than let events follow their own course. She was pleased that the interview with Kardia had gone so well, but it had been a terrible shock to know Mirmah had been reading her thoughts. She began to fear that escape might not be so easy.

Before an hour had passed she was alone in the circular bedroom on the third story of a round tower. Warmed by a fire, not the silent ruby firelight of her room in Mirmah's palace, but a real, crackling fire with smoke that went up the chimney, with dancing yellow flames and ashes glowing red. She had been comforted by a bath in an old iron bathtub, filled with water from steaming kettles, and had eaten a meal of soft white bread with a crisp and crackling crust, of cold meats, pickles, cheese and fresh fruit. The palace servants **had** been astonished at the amount of food she had **devoured**. It had made her feel almost cheerful.

But she was worried. Her clothes had been taken from her "to be brushed and made fine again," and though it was more comfortable and felt ever so clean wearing a long linen nightgown, she wondered what had become of the crystal ball about which she had forgotten in the hurry of the moment. She knew that if she was to be made beautiful she would have to return it to Mirmah, and in any case the crystal was her only hope of eventual escape.

She slid over the side of the soft feather bed (it had been like lying inside a warm cloud) and crept to the old oak wardrobe. The door creaked as she unlatched it. Inside they had hung three gowns for her, gowns of velvet and silk. Other clothes and shoes were in a chest of drawers. She examined them in the firelight.

Normally she would have been very excited at the chance of dressing up, but now she tried the dresses on apathetically and watched herself in the mirror. But once in a velvet gown of deep blue trimmed with gold she drew a quick breath as she caught a glimpse in the mirror of how well it fit. And fingering her neck she discovered the metal chain, from which the now tiny crystal ball hung. She tugged it over her head to examine it in the firelight. Was it really the crystal ball? The queen had told her it would never leave her. Ought she to try to go back now? Ought she to go back at all? Wouldn't it be safe to stay in the palace? But no. She was going to be made beautiful.

With a sigh she tossed the ball, chain and all, into the fire. For a moment nothing happened. Then as before it began to swell and in a few moments she stepped out of the circular, firelit bedchamber back into the chill of green ice walls and the silent ruby fire. Before her stood the Lady of Night.

But now she was not alone. Beside her stood a tall man in a red cloak and a high pointed hat, beneath which was the longest face she had ever seen. Skin like thin paper was pasted over a human skull. His eyes were two round holes of yellow fire.

"I am Archimago," he said in a hollow, familiar voice, "chief sorcerer and prime minister to her majesty Mirmah, Empress-to-Be of the Darkness that Swallows the World, Lady of Night and greatest of witches. So you are the pawn of Gaal. . . ." The cloak and the hat should have told her. She had seen only his silhouette before, but the voice was the voice of the man who had argued about her with the queen when first Mary had woken in the Palace of Darkness. She had no time to think for the witch was speaking.

"And how prettily dressed!" she said. "We think you did well on your mission in Anthropos. You talked very cleverly to the king—didn't she?"

In spite of her fears, the lady's warm words reassured her a little. She began to feel as though she had indeed been clever to trick the king of Anthropos, though the pleasure did not last. The sorcerer looked frightening, and the more she saw of the Lady of Night, the less she trusted her. Instinctively she put her hand to her throat to see if the chain and crystal ball were round her neck. They were.

"You'll never lose it now, dear," the witch said. "It will be round your neck with a chain forever." Far from comforting her, the lady's words made her more afraid. She did not know whether she was imagining it but the little ball at that very moment seemed to grow heavier, making the chain pull unpleasantly on her neck.

"I'm cold," she said.

From the Crown of Anan the Lady of Night pulled a long green crystal. "Here," she said handing it to Mary, "swallow this. You have earned the right to be beautiful and to be free from cold. Swallow it now and your beauty will come upon you for an hour. Swallow another one tomorrow, and you will be beautiful all day. Swallow a third the next day and you will be covered by the beauty of darkness for a thousand years!"

Mary took the crystal. It looked too long to fit inside her mouth, and it burned her fingers. "How in the world," she wondered, "will I be able to swallow it? Do I chew it?"

"Just open your mouth, dear, and place it on your tongue. It isn't hard to do."

Mary did as she was told. Instantly the crystal tugged itself from her fingers and shot to the back of her throat. Pain pierced her chest and her very heart. She closed her eyes. Invisible hands began to press and pummel her, squeezing her head and face into new unnatural shapes, crushing her chest, binding her limbs so that she screamed partly from fear and partly because it hurt.

Then as quickly as they had begun the pain and cold were gone and the only feeling left was a feeling of being stiff and unnatural.

"How beautiful she looks!"

"Almost as lovely as your majesty!"

They were staring at her when she opened her eyes, the Lady of Night smiling vacantly through her amethyst eyes and Archimago grinning hideously through his bony jaws.

The lady embraced her.

"I thought you looked lovely before. But now you are a dream of beauty. My daughter! My very own daughter. How I've longed for a daughter!" The foul odor choked her. The witch released her and continued, pointing to the wall behind her.

"See, darling, I've given you a present—you're very own mirror. It has velvet curtains to cover it. Whenever you want to use it, pull the gold cord at the side, and you will see how beautiful you are. But don't—whatever you do *don't*—go on looking at yourself when your beauty begins to fade." They were still staring at her, the Lady of Night smiling, Archimago with a frightening macabre leer. Mary shivered now not from cold but from dread.

Mirmah turned to the sorcerer. "Time is short. We must work. Let us be on our way," and without pausing to say good-bye they walked through the ruby fire toward the back of the room. There was no throne there now, only a low doorway with a black curtain through which they passed. Mary was alone once again.

Trembling, she looked round the room. No sound came from behind the black curtain and she did not dare approach it. Her bed, a niche in the ice wall opposite the curtained door was still covered with furs. The ruby fire burned silently without fuel and without warmth. Not that she needed warmth now, for strangely, she no longer felt cold. The curtained mirror was the only other object the room contained, and she drew in a trembling breath, wondering whether the stiffness she felt was because she was now beautiful.

But what if she were no different? She touched her face. It felt different in shape—oval instead of round, smooth instead of greasy and pimply. She looked at her

hands and wrists and saw slender, long fingers and fingernails like pink pearls. "It really has happened," she breathed.

Remembering the change would only last an hour she hurried to the mirror, pulled the cord and gasped at what she saw. She was beautiful beyond words. Staring back at her, framed by long black hair was the oval face she had touched. Violet eyes gazed solemnly back at her.

She laughed. Made faces. Pretended to be a beauty queen. Frowned. Scowled. Even scowling she looked lovely. She could not tear herself away. It was too good to be true. One hour today; all day tomorrow; and then beauty for a thousand years!

The hour passed quickly and Mary was still staring at herself when something began to happen. "It's wearing off," she thought sadly. The witch's words came back to her, "Whatever you do don't go on looking at yourself when your beauty begins to fade."

"It can't do any harm, though," she thought. "I guess she just didn't want me to be disappointed."

The face in the mirror was changing, but it was not growing like the old Mary McNab, but becoming more beautiful, yet in some strange way proud and hungry. She reached up again to touch her face. To her surprise it now felt round and pimply. She backed away a little from the mirror, but the face beyond the mirror came nearer. With a shock she realized she was no longer staring at her own face but at someone else, someone or some*thing* that stared at her from the other side of the mirror. Its face was filled with hate, and it looked not unlike the Lady of Night's face. And like her stepmother's face. Worse still, it looked as though it was about to come through the mirror. Suddenly she knew, as surely as she knew that her name was Mary McNab that the thing wanted *her*.

With a scream she turned away, slipped on the ice and fell, but when she turned round, she saw that the curtains had covered the mirror again. Sobbing she climbed up into the niche where the fur coverings were, curled up into a ball, and continued to cry.

The chain around her neck was getting heavier. From time to time she stole a look at the curtained mirror. Was that *thing* still there behind it? She would never, *never* open the curtain again!

17

Ballet of the Heavens

Eventually Mary stopped sobbing from very weariness and closed her swollen eyes to sleep a restless sleep. Then she jumped. Gaal was standing by her bedside. She recognized the brown, bearded face, the long woolen robe, the gold belt and the sword that hung from his side. The same blue radiance was about him, the radiance she had seen reflected from the snow on her first night in Winnipeg. How had he got inside the Palace of Darkness?

"Come, Mary," he said.

She got up without a word and gripped the hand he offered her. It was warm and dry, holding her own hand firmly, neither crushing nor even squeezing it. The room around them disappeared, and Mary saw that they were standing under the open night sky on a path emerging from a wood to cross an open glade. Warm air caressed her skin.

It had happened so suddenly that she asked, "Am I dreaming?"

"In a way."

"What d'you mean—in a way? If this is a dream—and it doesn't feel like one—it's a dream."

"*I'm* not dreaming, Mary. The things you will see, too, are real things."

Her mind was at a loss. "Well, where am I then?" She fingered the chain round her neck. "Are you taking me away from *her*?"

"Do you want me to?"

She drew in a deep breath. "Yes, but—"

"But what?"

"Oh, nothing. I was just thinking."

Gaal drew Mary toward a tree stump at the edge of the glade. "Sit down and watch the sky," he said.

Mary sat. The ground was a cushion of moss and as she leaned back she found the stump comfortable to rest against. She let her head fall back. "It's like a planetarium," she said to no one in particular. And it was. Soft-colored lights trembled gently across the high arch of heaven. She could hear music. As she continued to watch, the lights took shapes not unlike the swirling skirts of giant dancers.

"Oh, it's the northern lights!"

Gaal did not speak. He was standing in front of her now, his silhouette outlined against the shifting light. But Mary was watching the transparent skirts of the dancers, listening to an audible swish as they swirled their delicate pinks, greens and pale blues high above her. It was far better than a planetarium for at times the dancers would leap majestically into the deeper skies and then arch down to brush the treetops. She caught her breath at the glory. The dance went on for an hour and the longer it continued the more exciting it became, never repeating itself but growing more magnificent all the time.

She listened intently to the music which was high and pure. There were icicle tinklings so chillingly delicate they made you shiver, and the clean singing of stellar winds. The thin sounds swept the refuse from her mind. She drew a breath of joy.

Then her skin tingled. "They really are dancers! It's not just the northern lights!" Her eyes widened as the slow swirling giants danced on. There were hundreds of them and none of them hurried. Sometimes they seemed not to move at all. Then would come the swirl and swish of a thousand scintillating lights. Did they have wings? Or limbs?

Again she caught her breath when a cloud of golden hair brushed the treetops around her. A dancer had performed a somersault. And now, flung by an invisible hand the dancer dived ecstatically upward into the deep heavens.

Gaal had not moved. He too was watching the dance. Something about his rapt absorption held Mary's attention. Could it be? She looked from Gaal to the swirling skirts, then back to Gaal again. Was there a connection? She was sure there was, though how she knew she could never have told you. They were dancing around him. He was the center of the dance. *They were dancing for him.* It was a command performance with only the two of them there to watch.

Then in an instant they were gone, and only stars remained, sparkling like jewels and singing notes that fell like rain showers over the forest to make a million leaves tremble with joy. The stars sang wondermusic, music that made you want to laugh and cry, or to leap and shout, both at the same time. Mary struggled to her feet, unable to sit any longer. She seized Gaal's robe and cried, "Gaal, why are they singing to you?"

He looked down at her for a moment, smiling his joy, then turned his attention back to the stars. They were moving, swaying as they sang, clapping their hands with claps that clackered high above the night. Mary clapped, happily weeping. She clapped for Gaal. She clapped because she wanted to tell him how wonderful he was and that the stars and the dancers were right. Suddenly she knew that there was no one in the universe like Gaal. Out of her throat came music she had never heard before, music that came from the stars yet also from the center of her heart as she sang of the glory of Gaal. The more she sang, the more she loved him, and the more she loved him, the more she sang till her voice was hoarse and her tears dried saltily on her cheeks.

She had no idea how long it all went on. The singing stars, the joy of clapping her hands and stamping her foot in time with them, the laughter gurgling up from the soles of her feet—a laughter she had never known in her life before—made her want to go on and on. Out of the corner of her eyes she could see that the trees were lifting their boughs to the skies and waving them. She felt one with them too.

The sky in the east grew paler and to the tinkling of the stars was added the thunder of drums. Soon there were only four stars, gleaming jewels in the paling sky and singing more beautifully than Mary could have dreamed possible. They sang in a language she had never heard, telling a story of something about to happen. The brighter the eastern sky became, the higher their song rose and the faster became the rhythm.

A rim of liquid gold streaked along the eastern horizon. Organ notes thundered making the ground shake. Then with a blast like a million trumpets the sun shot over the treetops. He stood still for a moment and bowed deeply to Gaal before continuing his wild race into the sky.

But Mary's attention was caught by a willow tree crouching before Gaal and shuddering, her leaves rustling on the ground around his feet, shaking the golden dew from her. "I didn't know," the willow rustled hoarsely, "I didn't know you had come again."

Gaal stooped to lift some of her leaf hair from the ground and stroked it tenderly. "Stand up, dear lady, and be joyful," he said. Trembling, the tree did so; and when they left her, Mary could hear her hoarse sobs of joy.

They followed the path across the glade as stones bounced along the pathway with them, rattling their merriment and flinging themselves recklessly around their feet. A chorus of chittering, chattering bird song began. Taking Gaal's hand again Mary marveled at how different it was to be with Gaal than to be with the witch. Around Gaal there was joy, but around the witch . . . ? She frowned, puzzled, watching the excitement of the stones on the pathway. The trees at the edge of the glade still waved their boughs.

"They seem to know you," she said.

"They belong to me," Gaal said. "They know that I care for them."

"You care for the trees? And stones? And stars?"

Across the glade a wave of color swept as sheets of flowers opened. "And flowers too," Gaal said quietly. "But I care most for people—people like Mary McNab."

"The witch is going to make me beautiful. She says she wishes she had a daughter like me."

Gaal stopped and turned Mary to face him, looking intently at her. "You want to be beautiful, don't you, Mary?"

"I wish I could stop being fat, and I wish I didn't have pimples. Can you make me thin, Gaal?"

"Would you like to see my beauty in you?"

"*Your* beauty?"

"Beauty comes from joy, Mary. I've already given you some of my beauty. Look at it!"

They had stopped by a pool of water, and in it Mary could see the night sky as it had appeared an hour or so before when the stars were swaying and singing. In the center of the pool she saw herself, her face turned toward the sky as it had been a little while before. She saw herself still fat but with glory on her face, a glory that made her gasp. Her face glowed as though a light were shining beneath her skin while her body and limbs were alive with grace.

"Oh, Gaal!" she breathed in wonder—and then because she could think of nothing else to say, "Oh, Gaal!"

"Well?" Gaal said after she had looked for a full minute.

Mary continued to stare at the pool—a look of wonder on her face. "I ... I was smiling," she said simply.

"Is that all?"

"Well, my face sort of shines, but that's because I was real excited!"

"Excited?"

"And glad."

"What made you glad, Mary?"

Mary did not want to turn her eyes away from the pool, so she seemed to be talking to herself. "Oh, I don't know. Everything, I guess. The dancers and the music...." She looked up at Gaal. "And the way they were all doing it for you—as though they *really liked you.*"

"They do!"

"Well, so do I!" The words had slipped out before she could stop them.

"And how did you look when you felt excited and glad?"

Mary's face reddened. "I guess I looked O.K.—not exactly beautiful—"

"Not beautiful?"

"Well, yes, I guess I did. But I thought I'd have to look *different* to be beautiful—like no pimples and no fat."

"You were beautiful with joy, Mary. You still are. Gladness shines from your eyes."

Mary stared at him. She did not know what to say, and though she felt embarrassed, she could not help looking into his face. The pool had disappeared. "You're not like the witch," she said slowly.

"No."

"You can make people beautiful—*and* glad."

"There's nothing like gladness to make people beautiful, Mary."

"Could we stay here forever, Gaal?"

"No, little one."

"Just for a little while?"

"Not even for a little while."

"Couldn't we build a cottage here and live in it?"

"I'm too big to live in a cottage, Mary. And don't forget, this is sort of a dream."

Mary sighed. "I don't ever want to wake up. Why are you making me dream it?"

"So you would know whom to trust."

"To trust?"

"Yes, I want you to trust me, Mary, to trust me to take care of you whatever happens."

Mary continued to look at him. She wondered what he meant. Was something going to happen to her? To trust him? She remembered the giant dancers, the singing stars and the weeping willow. *They* trusted him. Who wouldn't trust him?

"I do trust you," she said almost to herself.

They continued to walk and for a while neither of them spoke. It was Gaal who broke the silence.

"What do you have round your neck, Mary?"

Instantly she became aware of the weight of the crystal ball whose chain still dug uncomfortably into her skin. How could she have forgotten about it?"

"It's a crystal ball. The witch gave it to me. You can go anywhere with it."

"Why did she give it to you?"

Mary felt uncomfortable. "Well, she wants to marry King Kardia and. . . ."

" . . . she sent you by magic into his bedchamber . . . "

"Yes! How did you know?"

" . . . to deceive him."

"Well, kind of. It was a sort of joke."

"A joke?"

"To get him to marry her."

"Does he not already have a wife?"

Mary thought of the captive queen and Prince Tiqvah, her son. She looked at the ground, not wanting to meet Gaal's eye. People in Toronto seemed to get divorces every day. Nearly all her friends' parents were divorced. Yet there was something about Gaal which made her realize that he took marriage very seriously. She breathed deeply.

"Well, yes, he has," she said, still looking at the floor, "but maybe their marriage isn't working out." The phrase sounded good. She had often heard it from her stepmother's lips.

"It can hardly 'work out' when Mirmah has captured and imprisoned his wife and son, can it? Did you not know how much King Kardia is grieving over his wife and son?" Mary said nothing. "Mirmah will not marry Kardia, Mary. She plans to murder him. She captured his queen and his son in order to lure him into her kingdom. When she failed, she used you. She hopes to kill him as soon as he arrives and she plans to kill his wife and son too. A moment ago you said you trusted me, Mary."

"Yes, Gaal."

"Do you think you can trust the witch, Mary?"

The chain around Mary's neck seemed to grow heavier every minute. No, she did not trust the Lady of Night. She knew that more clearly than ever now. Yet perhaps she could somehow trick her. Two pictures danced before her eyes, both of them her own reflection, the one in the mirror that the curtain had covered and the other of the glory in the pool. Which beauty did she want? The beauty the Lady of Night gave her would make her more popular at school than Gaal's beauty. It was like the beauty of Helen of Troy, the kind of beauty that launched ships and that drove men mad. The lady was dangerous. Yet all Mary would have to do would be to wait until the witch slept and then use her crystal ball to come back to Gaal. And once Gaal saw how beautiful she was. . . .

"Mary!"

"Yes, Gaal?" This time she made herself look up at him.

"You must either trust me or trust the witch."

Mary said nothing. She knew Gaal could be trusted. She had no doubt whose side she would join eventually. When the crunch came she would certainly choose Gaal.

But so long as there was a chance. . . .

"You must accept either her beauty or mine."

Still Mary remained silent. The thought of possessing beauty like that of the Lady of Night tempted her strongly. For the moment she forgot the terror of the mirror. Suddenly she decided. She would wait until that dazzling beauty was hers and then join Gaal's side.

Gaal continued, "And when the time comes you must hurl the crystal ball from you forever! You must hurl it into the mouth of Medusa!"

She stared into his eyes and her thoughts were confused and troubled. His eyes grew bigger as they had when she first met him in the snow, and in them she could see a picture of her icy bed in Mirmah's palace. Still the eyes grew and the picture with them. Afterward she was not certain what happened, but she thinks she remembers Gaal covering her with furs and saying, "There is only one beauty, Mary, not two."

18

The Broken Sceptres

They must have gone somewhere and returned, for now on the other side of the curtain the murmur of their voices sounded endlessly. Mary grew tired of listening. Sometimes she let her fingers feel the outlines of her greasy, pimply face. She was once again the old Mary McNab and part of her was glad and part of her sorry. It had been good to be beautiful, but whose beauty had she possessed? Try as she might she could not shut out the vision of the creature on the far side of the mirror who seemed to be struggling to break through the glass to steal her body. Had she made the wrong decision? Would Gaal even want her if she once accepted the beauty the witch offered?

The voices beyond the curtain grew louder and, she crept around the ruby fire to listen more carefully.

"They must be stopped, Archimago," a grating voice

was saying. "They have been singing the deep words of Gaal, and before we can prevent them they will have gained Poseidon's Kingdom. You must stop them!"

Cautiously Mary peered around the curtain. Facing her was the ugliest woman she had ever seen—the old, old woman into whom the Lady of Night turned herself from time to time. Upon her head still rested the high Crown of Anan. Smells from her drifted like a cloud so that Mary almost choked. They were the same odors that had come from the crystal ball. Through rents in the filthy rags that covered her, the witch's wrinkled skin showed clearly. Her hair was greasy, tangled and matted from runny sores on her scalp. Her teeth were yellow and rotted. As she stirred the pot over the fire with an iron ladle, Mary could see that her bony fingers ended in long and dirty nails.

"They must be stopped," she was croaking now, having lost her beautiful voice for the first time since Mary met her. "Call down the toads!"

The man in the pointed hat whose back was to Mary, looked up at the ceiling and said words Mary could not understand. Then from above, their legs spread wide in terror, three old toads plopped croakingly into the iron pot the witch stirred.

"Spiders!" the witch cried. "And bats!"

Again the sorcerer pronounced a spell and materialized clouds of spiders and bats which floated down to sizzle and crackle in the pot she was stirring.

Against the wall, rigid terror on their faces, three statuelike rulers stared at Mary. She knew they were kings and queens because they wore crowns on their heads. Their unmoving hands were stretched out to her, as though they had been frozen into stillness while trying to reach her. "They can see me!" she thought, her

heart pounding up into her throat, "but they're frozen solid!" A strange creature, half bear and half man, held its head between two paws while its jaws gaped wide as though silently roaring. Beside it was the statue of a graceful giant woman draped in a robe of bark, whose twiglike finger had tossed a veil of leaves back from her face. Her eyes too pleaded in silence for Mary to set her free. And beside her a small icy statue of a flower fairy crowned with rose petals drooped in frozen despair. On the floor in front of the statues lay six broken sceptres.

"One more kingdom," the witch muttered darkly, "one more sceptre and a continent will be ours." She chuckled. "And even as we cook our spells, the Iron Sceptre of Anthropos comes floating to us. But first we must stop the children from far-off worlds. The brew is ready, my good Archimago. Summon the ghoul that will bring us the shades from Morpheus Lake!"

Archimago rose to hover over the iron pot, his tall hat wreathed in vapor. He held his hands out and swaying his body rhythmically began to chant. The walls of the room disappeared. Flames rose on all sides around them. Slowly a head rose over the rim of the iron pot, and after the head, the body of a creature whose ugliness turned Mary's bones to water. Black, scaly and red-eyed it spread its wings slowly over Archimago and Mirmah, hovering over them amid the swirling mists and flames.

"Go," said the woman. "Go to Morpheus Lake. Plunge to its depths and choose the darkest nightmares you can find. Send them to rest on the children from other worlds e'er they reach Poseidon's Kingdom. Go!"

There was a roar and a flash. The creature was gone. The flames died down. The iron pot ceased to bubble and the old hag and Archimago sat down again. The statues continued to stare at Mary, and the broken sceptres remained at their feet.

"One more sceptre," the witch croaked, "one more sceptre and the world will be mine."

"What will you do with the child?" the sorcerer asked. "You have kept her in sleep these past two days."

"The child?" The queen threw back her head and made the kind of noise people make when they are gargling. (Mary realized with dismay that she was trying to laugh.) She rocked to and fro, and as the gargling noise subsided, said, "Have I not offered her beauty?"

"It is not her own beauty you have offered her."

"She cannot know that."

"Mirmah, she was brought here by Gaal."

"She was brought into my palace by me. She is my lawful prisoner." Again the gargling noise.

"You cannot summon one of the dark ones to rob her of her body for she is a minion of Gaal."

"Cannot? Already I have summoned a shade to wait behind the mirror. It will clothe her with enchanted beauty and capture her mind. Let Mary McNab taste twenty-four hours of looking pretty, and she will never again be found. The mirror will break, Archimago! Think of that! The doorway will be destroyed, and this petty servant of Gaal will be lost in the Caves of Aphela forever. As for the evil one whose beauty she covets, it will be released to serve me. Do you think I am a fool?"

"Mirmah! *Gaal brought her here!*"

But the witch only gargled again and the sound curdled Mary's blood. Terrified she crept back to the alcove beyond the ruby fire in her room. The Lady of Night had never loved her. Mary now knew she had been a fool to have believed her. The beauty she offered was nothing more than a terrible trap. Her eyes were dry but her heart wept bitterly.

Again she fingered the crystal ball around her neck. Carefully she looked into it, and as she did she saw that it had begun to glow. It grew a little so that she could see a picture. The creature summoned out of the pot was flying above the canal of water cut through the ice along which Mary herself had come. Tirelessly it beat its scaly wings to cross a wild sea, and beyond the sea a green land where mountains rose above pine forests. By and by it entered a cave, and looking into the crystal Mary could follow it still, through tunnels, through more caves, across underground rivers till it entered a cave filled with green light where an emerald lake lay like glass around a silent palace. Into its waters it plunged and disappeared.

For several minutes she went on staring. Then from the waters rose a tiny thing like an inky green rag that jerked convulsively into the air. Another followed it, then another and yet more. They looked like bats, yet not like bats, darting and twitching purposefully, returning by the way the creature had come, along the tunnels, through the caves, across the chasms, out of the hillside and over the forests and the sea.

Then it seemed she saw a strange boat, and recognized again the red light and the channel where she had been herself before she met the Lady of Night. There was a dwarf in the boat, and a boy she could not recognize as well as a pair of raccoons. With a gasp of surprise she also saw Lisa and Kurt and Wesley. Far above their heads, unseen by them all, the inky rags twitched and twirled in the red darkness.

Mary closed her hands round the crystal ball to shut out the sight. What did it mean? What did the witch's words about herself mean? Who could be waiting for her behind the mirror? She knew now that she must get away. She closed her eyes to think.

"My beautiful child!"

She knew who was speaking, but now only anger and fear swelled up inside her—the same anger and fear she had felt when she had parted from her stepmother. She opened her eyes to see the witch, no longer old and ugly but tall and beautiful, standing beside her bed. She had taken the second ice crystal from her crown and was holding it out to Mary.

"Take it, my dear," she said. "Take it and be beautiful for a night and a day. Then let me tell you what I want you to do."

Suddenly all desire to be beautiful left her. She stared fearfully at the hand the witch held out to her. The crystal glittered on her cold white palm and she shrank back.

"Don't be afraid, my sweet. It will make you beautiful again. Here, take and swallow it!" There was a hard edge to her voice, and against her own will Mary took the crystal and put it on her tongue. Once more she felt piercing pain at the back of her throat, and once again there came the strange sense of being squeezed, pummeled and pushed as her face and body began to change.

"I want you to go down to Poseidon's Kingdom," the Lady of Night said. "You must go alone this time and make your way to the cave where I have imprisoned the wife and son of Kardia. Do not be afraid of Medusa. She will not hurt you. Once you are there you must wait. It may be that your cousins from worlds afar will arrive there. I have tried to save them the trouble and to welcome them here directly. But in case my messengers miss them, I want you to bring them to me. Bring also the queen and prince. I have prepared a feast for them all."

Mary said nothing. She had no choice but to obey, but knowing now that the witch had access to her thoughts, she began deliberately to count backward from a thousand, counting to her own heartbeats lest her longing to escape should give her away. Mirmah's beauty? She trembled now as she thought of it. She did not know why the lady was sending her beneath the sea again, but at all costs she must keep her thoughts to herself. It was her only and perhaps last chance to escape. She could tell by the tight bodily discomfort that the form of the thing behind the mirror was upon her again, and she felt only fear. With all her heart she wished she had chosen Gaal's beauty. "Nine hundred eighty-three, nine hundred eighty-two, nine hundred eighty-one. . . ."

"Throw the ball on the fire!"

Mary pulled the chain from round her neck and did so. The crystal swelled and before her eyes she saw the mouth of a cave where Queen Suneidesis and Prince Tiqvah stood staring through the glass at her. She stepped toward them and in an instant the witch and the Palace of Darkness were gone.

Suneidesis held her hands out to her, a look of wonder on her face. "Whence came you, beautiful maiden?"

Mary glanced round. She was indeed at the bottom of the sea. Behind her the baleful face of Medusa glared at her, and the serpent hair began slowly to weave toward her. A cry of terror broke from her throat.

Queen Suneidesis took her by the hands and drew her into the entrance of the cave. "Fear her not, lovely maiden," she said softly. "The goddess will not enter here. Where did you come from? I perceive your raiment is from Anthropos. If I mistake not, it comes from the palace in Nephesh."

Mary was trembling. She noticed the prince staring at her with a puzzled frown. "I mustn't think," she said. "I mustn't talk." Instinctively she pulled her hands from the queen's to feel around her neck only to find the crystal ball there still. The smell of the evil queen was still about her, and the crystal ball was heavier than she had ever known it to be. Her lips were moving.

"Nine hundred fifty-nine, nine hundred fifty-eight, nine hundred fifty-seven—please don't make me talk—nine hundred fifty-six. . . ."

The queen was staring hard at her. "She is fighting an enchantment," she said slowly, turning to Prince Tiqvah. "What it means I know not, but the amulet around her neck must possess an evil power." She looked again at Mary. "Take it from you, my child, and throw it away!"

Mary screamed. "No," she cried, "No! No! No!" The thought filled her with terror. From inside the crystal the witch's laughter echoed in her ears. The foul smell of unbrushed teeth still sickened her. Yet in spite of her terror she still wanted the crystal ball. *How* she wanted it! If only she could stop the witch getting to her thoughts perhaps the ball could become hers. Then she could escape forever!

"Nine hundred forty-five, nine hundred forty-four, nine hundred forty-three. . . ." Then as her head jerked back, gargling noises came from her lips, gargling that was not Mary McNab gargling, but the witch's laughter. She struggled to control it. "Nine hundred forty-two, nine hundred forty-one. . . ." Suneidesis swept her arms round Mary and dragged her deep inside the cave, to pass through an opening into a second, inner cave, lying beyond the first.

"The goodness of Gaal is in here," she said. "Her torment may be lessened once we are away from the ocean."

She laid Mary on a bed of straw, and slowly the girl stopped counting. A look of peace stole across her face, and a sigh of relief broke from her lips. She opened her eyes. "Thank goodness! The smell has gone!"

19

Journey by Kayak

"It can't be far now," Wesley said.

The three Friesen children along with Kaas and Inkleth (not to mention Mr. & Mrs. Raccoon) were crowded together in a long umiak that bore them toward the Palace of Darkness across the Circles of Enchantment. Much had happened since they had emerged from the Low Way under the Northern Mountains.

It had been good to see the sunlight again and to feel sea breezes blowing against their faces. Gunruth and the Koach had said good-bye to them. While Twitterpitter sang ecstatically high in the air above their heads, Gunruth embraced them one by one, his eyes moist and his voice hoarse with emotion.

The nightmares of Goldcoffin had ceased to haunt him just as they had ceased to haunt the rest of the party. But dreams of Kardia had never ceased to trouble him, and he had talked much of "the danger that seems to stalk his majesty." After much thought he had relinquished the leadership to Inkleth.

"My lords and my lady, I bid you farewell," he told them. "Gaal will guide and protect you. Those who would harm you are now too far behind to pursue you. The timeless magic of the mountains has taken care of that. I go to King Kardia's aid, for I know now that something is amiss. I shall tell the bereaved of the deaths in Goldcoffin's Palace."

The Koach too had licked the children's faces and wagged their tails, but a few moments later they had followed Gunruth as he stumbled down the steep hillside.

Remembering the arrival of Theophilus, Wesley smiled, his thoughts far removed from the ice world through which they were floating. Hardly was Gunruth out of sight than they had watched the flying horse glide down, not to alight before them, for Theophilus had no intention of doing anything unobtrusively. Once he had secured their attention he had wheeled, looped and soared (a little clumsily) finally dropping like a stone, spreading his wings at the last minute to avoid what seemed like certain catastrophe. Indeed it could well have been a tragedy for he was stiff with age and his performance lacked the finesse of years gone by. His two foals did a much better job. The children and Inkleth had seen it all before, but Kaas had stared open-mouthed. When eventually the three alighted, the children had run forward to greet them.

"Are you taking us somewhere?" Kurt had asked.

"My dear young man," Theophilus retorted, "how else could you cross the Northern Sea? Who but Theophilus Gorgonzola Rocquefort de Limburger V would have the daring, the audacity, the cunning and the determination to brave the perils that await us? Who but Theophilus Gorgonzola Rocquefort de Limburger V would have the stamina, the fortitude. . . ."

"Stupid old fool!" Kurt muttered. For Theophilus was really serious. He meant every word he said.

"I beg your pardon?"

But Lisa had run forward to throw her arms round Theophilus' neck.

"You dear thing!" she laughed, "You haven't changed a bit. I never thought we'd get to see you again."

"Changed? My dear young woman, equine angels do not *age*. Whatever made you think we could? Take yourself, now. Thirty-one years have passed, and you look. . . ." But as Theophilus stared at her a look of wonder passed over his horsy face. "Well," he said eventually, "some of us do *mature* with time." Lisa stifled her laughter by burying her face in the horse's neck. Wesley and Kurt knew what was happening but Theophilus continued. "Do not weep, dear lady. I know how my presence affects the fair sex, but you must compose yourself. We shall need stout hearts if we are to rescue the queen." The only effect his words had was to cause Lisa to make strangling noises until her shoulders shook, and Theophilus turned to nuzzle her gently.

"How have things gone in Anthropos since we left?" Wesley asked.

Theophilus looked up into the sky. "Things. Ah, yes —*things*. We have governed the universe pretty effectively. No wars. No riots. I told Gaal to leave Kardia to look after affairs here. I felt he'd learned his lesson and could manage pretty well on his own. And Gaal, happily for him, took my advice."

"Matters have sure gone wrong now," Kurt could not resist saying, but Theophilus pretended not to hear him.

The journey north passed quickly enough. Wesley and Kaas being the heaviest had mounted Gasus, the stronger of the two foals, Kaas clutching Mrs. Raccoon while Wesley (into whose picket Twitterpitter had found her way again) held the reins. Lisa held the reins of Theophilus. "Yes, I know how you feel about it, Theophilus, but I insist. We haven't forgotten what happened on the flight to Chocma's Cottage last time we were here. Sometimes you're too intelligent for your own good," Lisa told the indignant creature.

Inkleth and Kurt clambered on Peg, Theophilus' filly, Kurt clutching Mr. Raccoon and Inkleth handling the reins. With a giddy swirl they leaped into the sky and in a matter of moments they had left the mountains of Playsion behind and were high over the glittering Great Sea.

It would have been bitterly cold had Theophilus failed to bring them the same kind of skin trousers, parkas, mukluks and mitts that Mary McNab had found so comforting. Even so the icy winds froze their cheeks as they left the sea behind to pass for hours over the sunless Kingdom of Darkness.

Lisa had been careful to place the Mashal Stone deep into a pocket on her inside parka. She felt no temptation to wear it, but wondered at the strange way it had come into her possession again, and was lost in reveries about the time she had been invisible and had been able to see the jinn as he really was.

They had taken their leave of the flying horses at the entrance to the long stairway Mary had descended days before, and like Mary they had slithered and stumbled between the blue lights to the icy platform where the friendly seal awaited them.

"So you came at last!" he had said, staring at them quizzically. "I let the other one go on."

"The other one?" For a moment Wesley had been puzzled. Then, "Oh, *no*. You must mean Mary McNab!"

Kurt and Lisa gasped behind him, "Where did she go?"

The seal shook his head. "I set her up in a little kayak. She wanted to go on, so I pushed her into the channel." He nodded across the water to where Mary's boat had been caught in the stream bound for the Palace of Darkness. "She seemed to know all about the three circles. She didn't even wait for me to give her all the passwords."

Wesley's stomach had begun to sink toward his boots. Their adventures on the journey to Goldcoffin's Meadow and on the Low Way under the Northern Mountains had driven the thought of their troublesome cousin from Toronto out of his head. Now it all came back. He stared at the channel, suddenly menacing, that had swallowed her up days before. How had she got there so quickly? What would Uncle John say if anything happened to her? And what did Mary McNab know about kayaks? Where was she now? The rushing water boiled dangerously. She might have drowned. His heart sank.

He turned to see that the others were staring at him silently. The raccoons also looked back at him with their big black eyes.

"You know the passwords?" the seal was speaking.

"I don't think so."

"Well the first sentry will say, 'The sun is dead' and you say"—and the seal repeated the instructions he had given to Mary.

The children repeated the words carefully.

"We had to learn a poem, too," Lisa said.

Gaal is the Lord of far and near.
Gaal is the Lord of light.
Gaal is the Lord of sea and fire.
And Gaal is the Lord of ice.

"Aha! Then you know the deep words!" the seal barked, flopping excitedly toward them across the icy platform. "With those words you need no passwords. With those words the magic of the circles becomes powerless! Do you know all three verses?"

The children repeated them.

"Wonderful!" The seal was filled with strange delight. "The first verse will take you through the first circle, the second verse will take you through the second, and the third through the third. But before you leave the third circle you will come to a statue of ice that guards a stairway leading down to Poseidon's Kingdom beneath the sea. Cut off the arm of the statue with your sword and go down to the sea bed. There you will find Queen Suneidesis and Prince Tiqvah. Poseidon himself cannot stop you. Bid him do anything you wish, and in the name of Gaal he must do your bidding!"

Since that time they had been pulled swiftly forward through caves of red light, feeding on bread, meat and goat's milk, and keeping whatever evil there was at bay with the verses of the song Mary had taught them. They talked about her endlessly, Wesley always with a worried frown. But whenever the talk got too gloomy the raccoons frisked mischieviously about the umiak, rocking it dangerously until Wesley cried half laughing, half angry, "Stop it, you idiots, or you'll capsize us!"

"Stop it, my dear, or you'll capsize us," Mrs. Raccoon would repeat with mock indignation to her husband. "Didn't you hear what his lordship said?"

"Just let me get that tail of yours between my jaws," her husband would reply ferociously as he scampered madly after her over the sitting passengers while the boat rocked yet more dangerously. The pair were not beyond leaping into the water, sometimes disappearing for minutes at a time. It was impossible to rebuke them, for they would gaze so solemnly at whoever bawled them out. "You are all absolutely right," Mr. Raccoon would say. "They are quite right, my dear. We have behaved badly. It was thoughtless of you to upset their lordships like that, and most thoughtless of me to do the same." Such was the expression of contrition on both faces as they spoke that even though you knew they never meant a word of what they said, you had to forgive them.

Only Inkleth could retain a stern expression and even he could not always do so.

"I know not why we brought you," he would say staring at them balefully. "Your mission was accomplished long e'er we entered Goldcoffin's Cave. You little understand either the danger that faces us or the solemnity of our quest."

They would stare back at him unblinkingly, their black-ringed eyes registering innocent concern. Then Mrs. Raccoon would move toward him remorsefully, lay one paw on his knee and look earnestly into his eyes as she did so. For a moment Inkleth would struggle to keep the stern expression fixed upon his face, but the muscles around his eyes and lips would begin to twitch and a moment later an explosion of merry laughter would burst from him. Then in a flash the raccoons would be chasing each other around the umiak again.

Kurt alone failed to enter into the merriment. Since the beginning of their journey the memory of his terrible encounter as a child with the rooster had never left him. Nightmares of wings that beat against his face continued to haunt him. Often he would sing the song of Gaal to himself, hoping to keep away the giant rooster that Gaal had warned him about. Would it really happen? Did he have to face the monster? Each time he thought about it he grew sick with fear.

To Kaas the journey was a marvel beyond marvels. Lisa was sure that his eyes had never returned to their normal size since they had left Goldcoffin's Meadow. Kurt had labeled him Bug-eyes, but Lisa had refused to let him use the term. "It's rude. It would hurt his feelings," she said. But for hour after hour Kaas stared into the ominous red light surrounding them, murmuring in awe at their strange surroundings. During the hours when conversation died Lisa would take out the Mashal Stone and gain courage from its blue light while Wesley would look troubled as thoughts of Mary McNab haunted his mind.

Twitterpitter remained subdued. After her one brief flight following their release from the Low Way, when her liquid notes had spilled over them high above the slopes of Playsion, she had settled again in the pouch of Wesley's fur parka.

It was Inkleth who eventually spotted the statue. They had slept for the second time, crouching uncomfortably in the boat. It was their third morning in the enchanted circles ("You can't really call it a morning," Kurt had grumbled), and Inkleth was kneeling, staring ahead in the bow. During the previous twenty-four hours the boat had slowed steadily, and now it was scarcely moving.

"My lords, my lady—look!" Inkleth was pointing, and ahead of them on the right bank a statue of ice was pointing back at him. It looked almost as though the two were accusing each other, Inkleth in the bow of the boat and the statue of a tall man on the bank. Slowly they drew level with it and the boat stopped. The arm was no longer pointing at them, but back in the direction from which they had come. One by one they scrambled onto the ice, and stood in a semicircle round it.

"It looks, it looks as though it's alive!" Lisa expressed what was in all of their minds.

Kurt drew the Sword of Geburah from its scabbard, feeling a strange reluctance to use it. "The seal said to cut its arm off," he said doubtfully.

"Mercy, kind sirs, have mercy upon me!" came a faint voice from deep inside the statue, so faint that none of them could be sure the words had been spoken.

"Did you hear that?"

"I think so."

"Hush—listen carefully."

"Have mercy, good people, on one who is bound by the witch's spell. My arm points true. Follow it to Poseidon's Kingdom. Do not harm me, for pity's sake."

"Who are you, and what are you doing here?"

"In a sad day I displeased the Lady of Night, and I am doomed to spend my days pointing strangers to Poseidon's stairs. Do not harm me, good people. My fate is sad enough."

Kurt pressed his lips together. "The seal *did* say to cut the arm off," he repeated uncertainly.

A thin scream came faintly from inside the ice. Inkleth laid his hand on Kurt's shoulder. "Do it, my lord! The longer we delay the more the spell of this place will come upon us."

The sword pulsed blue light. It had grown heavy. Grasping it now with both hands Kurt raised it high above his head and swung it hard against the statue's shoulder, hacking again and again while screams continued until the frozen arm crashed on to the ice. A trickle of blood flowed from the stump, and the cries ceased.

A sigh of relief came from all of them, and to their surprise the frozen arm that had hung by the statue's side rose and pointed over the ice to an archway a short distance beyond them.

"Oh, come *on!*" Lisa cried suddenly. "Let's get away from this horrid place. I don't know what Poseidon's Kingdom is all about, but it can't be worse than a statue that cries and bleeds," and she stumbled and slithered in the direction the arm pointed. The rest followed her after Kurt, exhausted, passed the Sword of Geburah and its scabbard on to Wesley to carry.

Below them a broad stairway descended, lined by statues of mermaids, mermen, dolphins and sea lions. They never saw that the boat had begun to drift on its way to the Palace of Darkness. Some instinct made them sit on the top of the stairway, staring down and wondering what lay below them. But flitting convulsively down through the red light toward them came the obscenely twitching green kerchiefs from Morpheus Lake.

20

Ogres and Dreams of Ogres

They never felt the jerking green kerchiefs rest on their heads. They were asleep and dreaming before the obscene things lifted to jerk their way back to Morpheus. In their dream the children climbed down the stairway between statues of mermaids, mermen, dolphins and sea lions, down toward Poseidon's Kingdom. By and by they arrived at a broad platform beyond which the stairway descended once again.

Around the platform were more ice statues, this time of the seven-headed ogres the children remembered so well from their previous visit to Anthropos. In their dream it seemed to them that from every side the fourteen eyes of each seven-headed ogre stared glassily at them, transfixing them to the ice. With rising horror they watched the ogres' hands stretching toward them. The statues were coming to life!

Screaming with terror they tried to run farther down the stairway, but their feet were frozen to the icy platform. Struggle as they might, they were powerless to move. The hands came nearer and nearer while the heads threw themselves back seven at a time to bellow in a wild chorus of laughter. Sweat poured from the dreamers' faces as their muscles struggled vainly to lift frozen feet. Finally, they cringed as a forest of giant fingers began to fold around them.

But a moment later, so suddenly that they had no time to realize what had happened, a trap door beneath them opened and they were flung into a void, falling, falling between cliffs of red-lit rock toward a river of flame where far below them tiny, jumping demons waited to catch them in their outstretched arms and throw them into the fiery river.

They woke with cries of fear to find their clothing soaked with sweat. The inky green kerchiefs had lifted themselves from their heads and disappeared. But they still shook with fear. As they peered down the stairway to Poseidon's Kingdom, they knew they could never force their feet to follow it.

"I dreamed . . ."

". . . we were going down this stairway . . ."

"You too?"

" . . . and these seven-headed ogres . . ."

" . . . falling down and down . . ."

" . . . horrible . . ."

"Then we must all have dreamed the same dream."

For a moment there was silence. Then Lisa said what all of them were thinking. "I'm not going to go down those steps."

"It is an omen," Inkleth said. "It is a warning from Gaal! Danger and death await us down there. We have been warned not to go."

Mrs. Raccoon looked at him solemnly. "Seals don't lie," she said gently. "And the seal told us to go. We animals know. Nobody bewitches *us*. I don't know what you dreamed, but whatever it was, it makes no difference. The seal gave good advice. I could tell by his eyes. He's to be trusted more than dreams are, isn't he, dear?"

"That he is, Mrs. Raccoon," her husband replied.

For a moment nobody spoke. Kurt tried not to look at the two raccoons. Twitterpitter had found her way out of Wesley's pocket and had perched on his shoulder. She seemed to have lost her featherheaded silliness.

"Usually I fly skyward to sing," she twittered softly. "But it looks as though I must try to fly down to sing here. Why don't we three go ahead and spy? After all, we did swear when we banded ourselves together that we would help the party from worlds afar."

The raccoons nodded their heads sagely and without another word Mr. Raccoon turned, sniffed the air in a professional manner, and slowly and gracefully began to lope down the ice stairway. Mrs. Raccoon followed him. Trilling musically, Twitterpitter fluttered into the air above them filling the hollow ice spaces with the sound of an English April and moved in spirals above the raccoons as they ran down the steps. The children drew in deep breaths and the panic that gripped them abated a little. Slowly the two animals and the tiny bird dwindled in size, descending further into the ice. Soon they were lost to view, and the merry sounds of the skylark's song, so strangely out of keeping with their surroundings, faded into silence.

"I hope they'll be all right," Kurt said.

"We shouldn't have let them go," Wes muttered uneasily.

"Think of those ogres," breathed Lisa.

"We haven't come across the rooster, yet," Kurt said. "He's got to appear soon. Mebbe he's down there too. D'you think he'll run before we get right up to him? I wouldn't mind running at him if I could be sure he'd turn and run before I reached him. But the thought of running at a giant rooster *and then him starting to come at me....*" He shuddered. "I oughtn't to be afraid. It's wrong. But I can't help it."

The more they thought about it, the more ashamed of their fears they became. Yet it was one thing to be ashamed and quite another to find the courage to go down the steps to all that awaited them. Do what they might, they could not stop the nervous movements their nightmare had started. Minutes passed, but from below them there came no sound. They strained their eyes into the dim light but saw nothing. Surely no harm had befallen the raccoons and Twitterpitter.

"Listen!" Lisa cried suddenly.

They strained their ears.

"I can't hear anything," Kurt muttered.

"Shhh!"

A smile broke over Inkleth's face, and he rose slowly to his feet.

" 'Tis the bird," he breathed softly. "Hark!"

Soon all of them could hear the thin twitter which slowly grew louder and still louder until in the dimness they could make out a tiny speck that rose toward them. A moment later the skylark had reached them.

"Where are the raccoons?"

"What did you find, Twitterpitter?"

"Did you see the ogres?"

The bird settled on Wesley's outstretched finger. "Oh, dear me. Oh, my, my! What a journey! I'd much rather circle in a blue sky above a meadow! Oh, dear, dear!"

"But what did you *see?*"

"Are the raccoons O.K.?"

"Oh, my, my! I'm out of practice. I haven't sung in ages. The raccoons? They went on farther. They said they'd wait for you at the bottom of the steps."

"Did you see the platform?"

"Yes, yes. But my voice! I'm almost hoarse. I can't sing like I used to. I think I must be getting old."

"Twitterpitter, you must think," Wesley sounded stern. *"Were there any ogres on the platform?"*

"Oh, my, my, I'm out of breath."

"Twitterpitter, *think.* Did you see any ogres?"

"No, there was nothing there. Not even a clump of grass. Nowhere at all to build a nest."

"Never mind nests, Twitterpitter. What about ogres?"

"Ogres? What are ogres? But I don't think so—no, no ogres," the bird replied. "And not a single twig either, not a grasshopper, not a beetle and not a blade of grass. When shall we be back in Anthropos? Oh, dear me, I must put my head under my wing." And before anyone could protest she had hopped into the pocket of Wesley's parka and was asleep.

"D'you think she can be trusted?" Wesley sounded doubtful. "She didn't sound as though she had a clue!"

"My lord, surely the raccoons would have returned if there were danger ahead. Yet—and I am ashamed to admit it—my flesh crawls at the thought of going down." No one seemed inclined to move. Inkleth sat down again. "We could go on until we see the platform," he said slowly. "We do not have to descend farther. Should there be ogres we shall see them before we arrive."

"Supposing when we get there, they turn out to be frozen statues like these that we can see?" Kurt asked, looking at the mermaids and mermen.

"If they are statues, then they are statues," Lisa said. But even as she said it she saw in her mind a vision of the statues that began to move toward her, and she shivered.

When she thought about it later she realized she could have put the Mashal Stone (which lay forgotten in her pocket) round her neck, and made herself invisible. Moreover, with the Mashal Stone she would have been able to see whether the statues were just statues or whether they were something else. Nor would she have felt so scared, for the blue light from the Mashal Stone filled her with courage whenever she had worn it on her last visit. Irritated, she recalled how she had passed through an army of seven-headed ogres at the Battle of Rinnar Heights. Why had she not remembered in time? But it was too late when the memories came back to her.

"Did not your lordships say that Gaal is the Lord of ice?" Kaas asked suddenly.

The children looked at him. "That's right," Wesley replied.

"Then, may it please your lordships, statues of ice must obey his laws. They cannot move unless he bids them."

What Kaas said made sense, yet it took all their courage to get to their feet and face the journey downward. Kaas addressed them once more. "May it likewise please your lordships, I would like to lead the way." His face was white and his lips pressed together. "My father betrayed my sovereign lord, King Kardia, and I came with your lordships that I might atone for my father's wrongdoing. If there are perils below I go to face them. Let your lordships and the Matmon Inkleth follow several paces behind so that you may flee should evil overtake me. Do not try to rescue me but save yourselves." And without another word he began to hurry down the steps, slipping and falling in his haste but recovering his balance and pursuing his way determinedly down.

After that, as Wesley said later, the rest of them could hardly do anything else but follow. And though they had no intention of letting Kaas face unknown perils alone, they found that in spite of their best efforts they could not catch up to him. Whenever they increased their speed (not that they increased it much for they were still afraid) he seemed to increase his so that in the end they were content to follow him into the bowels of the ice.

And by the time they came to the platform Kaas was standing in the middle of it. There was not an ogre nor even the statue of an ogre to be seen. Kaas faced them.

"My lords, the platform is solid. The nightmare deceived us." Wesley's hand was resting on the hilt of Geburah which he was carrying once again.

"Perhaps if it had to bear all our weight it would give way to let us fall as it did in the dream."

"Then let us cross one at a time. You go ahead, Kaas, and we'll follow you one by one!"

But Kaas did not seem to be listening. His eyes grew round and staring and his mouth fell open. His finger was pointing to the stairway behind them. "Flee, my lords, flee!" he cried.

Wesley who had brought up the rear swung round. Twenty steps behind them was the huge bulk of a seven-headed ogre, its heads almost filling the width of the stairs while its thick and stubby legs felt for each step carefully before descending. The enormous hands reached forward, seven fingers on each curling in eager anticipation.

In a flash Wesley had snatched the Sword of Geburah from its scabbard. "Run!" he yelled. "All of you, run! Get down to the bottom as fast as you can."

For a moment they all froze. Then as a roar of rage filled the stairway, Kurt, Lisa and Kaas ran on across the platform while Wesley and Inkleth stood their ground facing the ogre. Inkleth, like Wesley, had his sword drawn as he watched the monster sway clumsily toward them.

"Hist!" Inkleth said. He stood a little closer to the ogre than Wesley. "We must fight from above. 'Tis an old one for its movements are slow. As soon as its hands reach down for me I shall leap forward and run between its legs. The heads will turn to look for me behind. When they turn, follow me through the legs, my lord Wesley."

By the time he had finished speaking, the ogre's arms were reaching out for him. Yet an instant before its fingers closed round his waist, Inkleth darted up the steps, sword in hand, under the archway formed by the monster's legs. Fourteen fingers clutched at nothing. Catching his breath Wesley dodged round the clenched fists and scrambled to follow the Matmon lord. Between the ogre's legs he slipped and fell heavily. A strong hand seized his left arm and he was pulled to his feet to find himself, to his huge relief, standing beside Inkleth behind the ogre on a level with the monster's waist.

Wordlessly Inkleth plunged his sword into the monster's hips and Wesley followed his example. The scream of rage so startled him that he plucked out the sword from sheer fright but instantly struck the ogre again. It was trying to turn. Above him he caught a glimpse of seven ugly heads turning this way and that and the shoulders swinging round. A seven-fingered hand reached down for his head. Wesley struggled to raise the Sword of Geburah, but his arm was tired and he lifted it too slowly. The hand wrapped itself round his head

and shoulders and he felt himself suffocating in its powerful squeeze. Around came blackness, then roaring redness. His lungs were ready to burst and his chest heaved vainly for air. Suddenly he felt himself dropping onto the ice, and for several seconds he saw nothing but whirling red suns as he gulped huge gasps of air. By some miracle he had hung on to the sword. Slowly his breath returned and the sound of the fight began to penetrate his hearing.

The ogre was facing up the stairway toward them. Wesley watched as to his right Inkleth struck blow after blow at the knees and thighs of the ogre who was roaring with pain and rage. Curiously, its hands made no attempt to seize either of them. Instead they were groping around the seven heads, trying vainly to seize a tiny fluttering creature which flung itself courageously again and again at one face after another.

"Twitterpitter!" Wesley gasped.

Furiously the bird plunged its beak into an eye in the fifth head, then another eye in the third head. Five eyes were already streaming with dark green blood. Big seven-fingered hands slapped viciously at the bird which seemed to elude them only by a hairsbreadth and to attack again without a pause.

Sobbing with delight Wesley grasped the hilt of Geburah and swung it once more to slash the monster's legs, from which green blood rolled and splashed down the icy stairway. Two streaks of gray and white fur shot up toward the monster's necks. The raccoons too had returned to help.

Wesley was so glad to see them that he paused for a few seconds and watched them as, leaping on the ogre's shoulders they proceeded to play a game of tag, dodging in merriment around the seven necks like a couple of children running among tree trunks.

He could not remember the order of events clearly after that. But at last their enemy began to stagger backward down the steps, and he and Inkleth followed swinging their swords as they advanced. With a heavy thud it fell back to sprawl across the platform. For a moment they both stood breathing heavily, not moving. The ogre lay on its back, one arm still groping for Twitterpitter while the other moved toward Mr. & Mrs. Raccoon who still seemed to think it was all a joke and were still chasing each other in and out among the seven blinded heads.

A loud crack startled them all. A wide split appeared across the platform which slowly began to dip down from the middle. Wesley and Inkleth leaped back up the stairs.

"Twitterpitter! Mr. Raccoon! Mrs. Raccoon! Get back here! Quickly!"

The crack was wider now. The platform was opening like the leaves in the trap door of their dream. The Raccoons scampered madly along the ogre's body and leaped for the stairway. Twitterpitter rose in circles above it. Then the jaws gaped wide to reveal a chasm of fire descending to an infinite depth and the black body of the seven-headed ogre fell downward, downward, downward into its depths. A second later the doors swung back into place with a boom and the chasm disappeared. On the far side of the platform Kurt, Lisa and Kaas stared with white faces at them. No one spoke until Twitterpitter broke the tension as she circled toward Wesley.

"Dear, dear me. Such a to-do. I won't sing for a month. Oh, my, my! What carryings on! My next mate won't believe a word of it." And so saying she disappeared, as her habit was, into Wesley's parka.

For some reason Wesley and Inkleth felt no fear of

245

crossing the platform. The whole thing, as Wesley later pointed out, made no sense. How could you have solid ice over fire? ("There's snow on the top of volcanos," Kurt argued.)

The fear of their enchanted sleep had left them, and with the victory over the ogre they felt exhilarated and filled with new confidence. Moreover they had so much to talk about, describing to one another just what had happened when and who had seen and done what, that they descended for three hours or more scarcely realizing how tired they were, until at last they found their feet resting on the sandy floor of the bottom of the sea.

21

Kardia Sets Sail

Kardia leaned back against a wind that buffeted him along the stony beach. Seagulls circled screaming above him. To his right green breakers thundered, rushing repeatedly toward his feet before retreating with the rattle and clack of loose rocks. He filled his lungs with damp air, pungent with burning tar and rotting seaweed, glad to be able to stretch his legs and careless of cold mist mingling with sea spray.

Yet his mood was as gray as the sky. Three mornings before, he had met with Nocham, Chush, Qatsaph, Dipsuchos and Chocma in the lesser dining hall of Nephesh Palace and had surprised them by announcing his intention of doing the very thing he had said he would not do the evening before.

His eyes had been red with sleeplessness.

"Last night I dispatched Strongbeak with instructions

to arm and provision Thunderhead," he stated quietly. Thunderhead was the largest man-of-war in the Playsion fleet. "Chush and Qatsaph will accompany me on horseback with half a dozen men-at-arms. I have arranged changes of horses by sending carrier pigeons ahead. We leave two hours before noon and will ride hard till we join ship at Chalash, from whence we sail for the witch's kingdom three days from now."

"Your majesty does not wish to avail yourself of the whole fleet?" Chush asked.

"With a fleet our intentions would be obvious. With one ship well armed and filled with men-at-arms, we shall be in the heart of the kingdom before Mirmah knows of our intent. It is not superior force we need, my lord, but superior cunning. The witch awaits us not with an army but with sorcery and black arts."

Little more was said and the meeting was soon dismissed. Chocma, Nocham and Dipsuchos were to take Kardia's place in his absence. Chocma remained behind to speak with him.

"Your majesty is certain of what you are doing?"

Kardia stared at her wearily. "I am sure of nothing," he said. "Yet it is easier to act than to remain here idle. And did not the maid speak in the name of Gaal?"

"Yet your majesty is sure of nothing."

"You know the maid has disappeared?"

Chocma looked startled. "I knew it not."

"The clothes she wore are still here. She is gone with garments from the wardrobe in her room. Neither man nor woman saw her leave. We have searched the palace thoroughly. Her door was locked from within and her window barred."

"So you fear her treachery." Chocma was making a statement not asking a question.

"I will swear she is the maid their lordships spoke of. She came to my bedchamber as the lady Lisa entered my prison cell years ago. How could she have come here but through a proseo stone?"

Chocma was frowning. "Why would she need to come through a proseo stone? Did not the children tell us *she was already* here?"

For a moment they stared at each other without speaking. Kardia broke the silence. "How else would she enter the palace or how could she have entered my chamber except through a proseo comai stone?"

"How did the witch Mirmah enter your majesty's chamber?"

"Yet she spoke of Gaal. Would the sorceress speak of Gaal?" He frowned in thought, then continued. "Strongbeak, likewise in the name of Gaal, bade me stay here when the children first arrived. Yet who knows where the children are now? Enchanted? Perished in Morpheus Lake? Who knows what has happened? Would Gaal allow his servants to perish?"

"He has promised none of us immunity."

But Kardia was not listening. "And now the maid is gone too. 'Tis strange. 'Tis passing strange."

"Your majesty, the pool in the council chamber may give us some sign."

The sign the pool gave them was confusing. As the waters settled they found themselves staring at Mary McNab. On one side of her stood the witch and on the other Gaal, and Mary stared first at one, then at the other. In seconds the waters stirred again and the picture was gone.

Kardia shook his head. "The pool reflects but the confusion of our own minds," he said slowly. "We did not need the pool to tell us what we know already. I am compelled to go on this mad journey yet deep within me I think 'tis folly."

The ride to Chalash had been difficult. Rainfall had been heavy for the unpaved roads were muddy and the fords of the river deep. Yet Kardia pressed on, never giving way to his own or his companions' weariness. They had slept as little as possible on both nights at royal lodges where their meals had been ill prepared, so that by the third evening on their arrival at Chalash they had been exhausted.

The next day the ship Kardia had chosen was all but ready. In an hour they would set sail. Kardia had walked a little beyond a headland and was pursuing his way along the beach, his back to the barely discernable shore of brooding darkness where Mirmah's new kingdom began. The wind that buffeted him was cold. The winds when they sailed would be contrary, and though the distance was short, their journey would take long. The so-called empress might welcome them, but the elements seemed to oppose their journey.

Kardia turned to face the wind, leaning into it now instead of back against it, stumbling forward, using the Iron Sceptre to support him, and fighting his way along the stony beach. The wind roared by his ears and the waves, now crashing and rushing and now retreating, deafened him with the rollicking, clackering sound of the loose rocks they dragged back over the beach.

The winds were not so contrary as to prevent their setting sail, and within two hours Kardia stood, still gripping the sceptre, in the bow of Thunderhead as heavy seas battered her and her sails cracked in the wind. He stared at the low coastline they were making for, wondering why the journey was so difficult and why his heart was so heavy. Gloomily he made his way below where scores of archers were to be found, some on watch by the arrow slits in the vessel's sides while others lay by their blankets playing dice, talking and jesting. Around them the timbers creaked and groaned. The waves boomed hollowly against the vessel's sides and the masts strained under the force of the gale. Kardia had not found his sea legs and stepped unsteadily among the men, making his way toward the after companionway. As he approached it he tripped over someone lying awkwardly near the foot of it, and fell heavily.

The sleeper over whom he had stumbled sat up sharply. He was short and stocky wearing a long gray beard and having bushy eyebrows that arched over sleep-bewildered eyes. Kardia rolled over and stared at him.

"Gunruth!"

"Your majesty!"

"What in the name of the High Emperor do you do here? How came you here? We thought you were dead or else enchanted beneath the Northern Mountains!"

"Beneath the Northern Mountains I did indeed travel, your majesty—even by Goldcoffin's Palace."

"Yet you live! And the children from worlds afar? Do they live too?"

"They are alive and well, your majesty, or were when I last saw them. By now, please Gaal, they may be with her majesty the queen and his royal highness, Prince Tiqvah."

The two struggled to their feet, swaying as the ship continued to roll, and embraced each other heartily. Then they sat on the lowest step of the companionway. Kardia stared hard at the Matmon, shaking his head as he did so.

"I can hardly credit my eyes! And all are well?"

"Their lordships Wesley and Kurt are well and likewise the lady Lisa. So also is the young man Kaas and the Matmon Inkleth. But the men-at-arms are no more."

The king's hand was on his shoulder, his eyes still staring in amazement at Gunruth. "Tell me of the strange thing that befell you all in Goldcoffin's Meadow," he said. Slowly, between the king's interruptions, his expressions of relief, and cries of amazement, Gunruth told of their strange adventures along the Low Way. His face paled and his lips trembled when he described the fate of the men-at-arms and their sergeant and for some moments the two sat in silence. Then between his sighs Gunruth continued his story.

"I left them on the mountainside above Chalash," he concluded quietly. "The Koach came with me, while the little beasts and the skylark remained with the humans. I set out to return to Nephesh to bear news of the bereaved, but after two days as I lay in the Inn at Reflection Ford I dreamed that Gaal came to speak with me. 'Return to Chalash!' he told me. 'Kardia has need of you. And see you look well to the sceptre.' Three times I dreamed the same dream. Therefore I returned, and came upon Thunderhead as she was being readied. I sought your majesty earlier, but it was clear you had many matters to attend to."

"Gaal said naught of our mission?"

"No, your majesty. Only he bade me look well to the sceptre. He seemed earnest when he said this."

The sceptre was propped between Kardia's knees. The king was frowning. "Then perchance he approves of what we do."

"Your majesty doubts it?"

"I am confused, Gunruth. There came to the palace the maid Mary from worlds afar, kin of the lady Lisa, bidding me sail here. But we fear treachery. She spoke in the

name of Gaal, yet she gave instructions which contra-
dicted those brought by the eagle Strongbeak. I know not
what to think."

"Might Gaal change his mind?" the Matmon asked.

"The legends say his word stands ever firm," the king
replied heavily. "Yet the die is cast. For better or worse I
go forward. Why did he bid you look to the sceptre?
None can take it from me."

"I know not, my lord. Yet he repeated it three times."

The king's face was troubled. "'Tis well he bade you return. I am right glad you came. At least I know three
things: that the children are well, that there is still hope
for my wife and son, and that Gaal has a concern for us
all. But these words about the sceptre trouble me." He
paused. "He spake not of my death?"

"Your majesty?"

"Do not hide anything from me, Gunruth. We have
known each other for many years."

"Gaal said nothing about your majesty's death. Your
majesty must not speak thus. Only he bade me return
here and look to the sceptre."

The king shook his head. For a few moments neither
of them spoke. Kardia rose to return to his cabin.

"Have you a berth, my lord Gunruth?" he asked.

"No, your majesty. The vessel is crowded and none
anticipated my coming."

"Then you shall sleep in my cabin."

The king's face was filled with sadness so that Gunruth
wondered how he could cheer him. Suddenly an idea
occurred to him.

"Your majesty, I am hungry."

"I have food in the cabin."

"Your majesty would not by any fortunate chance
have...." He hesitated.

253

"Have what, my lord Gunruth?"

"I was thinking of fenfinch pie, your majesty."

A broad smile chased the shadows from Kardia's face, and he slapped Gunruth heartily on the back.

"You have a good stomach in a storm at sea," he said, his eyes crinkling with new life. "So you too like fenfinch pie! Fenfinch pie it shall be then!" and he turned toward the cabin. Gunruth's idea had worked.

Slowly the hours passed.

Gales from the north hurled mountainous seas to vent their rage on Thunderhead's sides. Water and wind seemed determined to drive her back. At times all hands were needed on deck, but many archers and men-at-arms huddled in misery below, their dice and cards abandoned. Some lay and groaned. Some vomited. From time to time sea water washed across the decks and poured down one of the hatches that had not been battened down, dousing them all with cold misery.

Gunruth and the king had retired to Kardia's cabin in Thunderhead's stern. For a while they had continued to discuss the strange events that had befallen them and the six kingdoms that surrounded Anthropos and Playsion. From time to time Kardia would venture on deck, but the master of the ship begged him to remain in his cabin.

"Consider the danger, your majesty—five men already washed overboard. Your majesty's life can ill be spared."

"And when, sir master, shall we gain this so-called ice port of Massah?"

"Would to Gaal I knew, your majesty. The storm is driving us east of our course. Had your majesty's urgency to set sail been less, we might have gained time by waiting for better weather. As it is we shall not reach the ice cliffs before the night watches. And as for the port. . . ." He did not finish.

Kardia steadied himself on the sceptre as the Thunderhead rolled heavily and spray continued to drench both men. Assisted by the master he returned to his cabin, and, having instructed the master to call him once they neared Massah, tore off his wet clothing and rubbed himself with towels until his skin tingled. Then, wrapping himself in his blankets, he did as Gunruth had already done and fell asleep.

It was then that Kardia dreamed of Mary McNab, tiny little Mary dangling by strings from the hand of Mirmah the witch and beckoning to Kardia to join them. The finger that beckoned grew longer and longer, controlled by a string that the witch was pulling. Soon it was under his nose, tickling him roughly until he sneezed.

And when he sneezed he woke. Or thought he did. The storm had ended and the ship lay in such silence that Kardia could hear Gunruth's soft breathing. He sat up, pulled a cloak around him and opened the cabin door. Silent moonlight bathed the empty deck. The sails hung loose. No breath of air stirred above the sea that lay like glass.

Scarcely breathing, wondering where the crew had disappeared and how the sea could be so calm, Kardia walked slowly to the bulwark and stared at the unnaturally placid water. Suddenly he started and rubbed his eyes, peered at the sea and rubbed his eyes again.

And as he stared a second time he shivered and felt the hair rise on the back of his neck. He could see a white and ghostly figure that moved toward him across the surface of the water.

Gripping the bulwarks with both hands he drew in a sharp breath stiffening his body and hunching his shoulders. The figure approached without a pause. As it came nearer he felt sure the ghost, if ghost it was, was the ghost of someone he knew. There was something about the powerful stride and the swinging, bare arms. It was not until the apparition was a shiplength away that suddenly he realized who it was.

"Speak!" he shouted fearfully. "Speak! Nay, do not advance in such grim silence. Are you dead? Is this your ghost? Speak, for I fear you!"

A deep and musical laugh rolled across the water. "I am no ghost," the figure called out, "though you are not the first to think I was."

"Gaal!" Kardia's shoulders dropped with relief.

Soon Gaal was standing on the water, leaning with one hand against the hull of the ship and looking merrily up at the worried king who now leaned over the side to stare at him from above. Kardia's heart was racing.

"Did we do wrong to come?"

"Why do you ask?"

"Did we?"

"Do you not know already?"

Kardia sighed and dropped his head still further.

"I do know. I have known all along, Lord Gaal. Yet I did not know what to do. I am a fool." He paused a moment, then pleaded, "I beg you not to let those who are with me suffer any ill on my account."

"Did you not weigh the danger to them when you chose to come?"

"I put it out of my mind, Gaal!"

"You have brought them into danger."

"I know, Lord Gaal. I have done wrong, but why should my subjects suffer because of my folly?"

"When I gave you the Sceptre of Anthropos I gave you the power to do great good to your subjects. But I could not give you power to do them good without also giving you power to do them harm."

"I am concerned for them, Gaal. Mine, not theirs, is the blame!"

"I too am concerned about them. I know them all. And as for their faults—I know them better than you."

"Gaal, what have I done?" Kardia's face was twisted with pain.

A rope dangled over the side and rested in the water. Seizing it Gaal pulled himself vigorously up the side, leaping over the bulwark on the deck. He stood a full head taller than the king and he placed his hands on his shoulders.

"What you have done is done. Kneel before me, Kardia of Anthropos!" Kardia knelt, his troubled face looking up into Gaal's. "The past is behind you," Gaal continued. "Will you obey me in the future?" Kardia nodded. "Then go forward now and take the adventure that comes to you. It will be a strange and fearful one, but do not lose heart. You will pass, after all, through the Circles of Enchantment—the Enchantment of Bodily Yearnings, the Enchantment that Dazzles the Eye and the Enchantment of Blasphemy. Do not leave the ship until you reach the heart of the Dark Kingdom. You must neither eat nor drink in order that you may have power to pass through unscathed. The danger is greatest in the circles. Yet fear not. I do not abandon those who serve me. But remember that if you should fail to kill this witch who sets herself up against me, she will certainly kill you." He paused, resting his hand on Kardia's head. "Yet in life or in death I will still be with you."

The warmth from Gaal's hand seemed to pass through Kardia's body flowing from his head to his feet and filling him with joy. He closed his eyes, and then it seemed to him that the ship began to heave and shudder as if it was being pounded once more by an angry sea. He heard, too, the howling gale, the flapping of the sails and the creaking of timbers. But he could not feel the wind.

Wonderingly he opened his eyes. Gaal was no longer there. Kardia was lying on his bunk in the lamplit cabin where Gunruth still slept peacefully. "Was it a dream?" he murmured wonderingly. "Yet I can still feel the warmth of his hand on my head. Gaal was here!"

22

The Charioteer at the Bottom of the Sea

They did not know, of course, that they were walking on the sea bed, nor would they have believed you if you had told them. It was only later that they discovered where they had been. At the bottom of the sea one expects to be in total darkness, crushed beneath a billion tons of water. Instead they could walk, breathe and see tolerably well. It was true that the dim light did not allow them to look very far ahead, creating an effect like dull green mist before sunrise. There was no horizon, no sky and no ceiling so that they stared about them wondering how to proceed.

The most disturbing thing about the sea bed was that it didn't stay still. At first no one noticed what was happening for the movements were slow and gentle. Lisa had the best description of what was going on. "It was like we were standing on a great bed," she told me, "and there was a giant under the bed covers slowly moving around. Of course there *wasn't* a giant."

"No?" I said, trying to figure out what she meant.

"No, there was a sort of . . . a sort of bubbling fire."

"A *bubbling* fire?" I repeated.

"Yes—molten rock and hot gasses and stuff."

"You mean hot bubbles were forming underneath your feet?" I suggested.

"In a way, yes. But they were real big bubbles—and I mean BIG—eh? The one that Medusa's stairway led us onto was pushing the sea bed up against the ice. Mind you, we couldn't feel any heat—leastways not unless cracks and chasms opened up, like the one on the platform we had to cross on the way down."

"Sounds very scary," I said.

"Not scary—*weird*," she said, frowning. "See, we didn't realize it was the deep fires pushing up. All we knew was that everything kept slowly changing shape. Mebbe it was scary for the witch, if she knew."

"Like giant fingers of fire poking up through the crust of the world to get her."

"Wow, if you put it like that. . . ."

But I'm getting ahead of my story. The changing landscape was not the only "weird" experience they encountered, as they stared round them, wondering which way to go.

"There's a path. At least I *think* it's a path," Wesley said slowly noticing a shallow depression in the sea bed between two slowly rising "bubbles." But it only led them inside a circle of black rocks.

"No way through here," Lisa muttered turning to face the way they had come. "Oh . . . !" The fear in her voice made them swing round. Behind them, blocking the exit from the rocks was an octopus, two tentacles waving like antennae and two mournful eyes staring at them.

"Make haste!" Inkleth cried urgently. "Over the rocks lest it catch us in its lair!"

But it was too late. One octopus after another began to float like rising black suns over the rocks around them. In silent grace the creatures encircled them ("Just like a bunch of ballet dancers," Lisa said later), drawing closer and closer. Mr. & Mrs. Raccoon had scrambled in terror into Wesley's arms. The children, Inkleth and Kaas contracted into a tight bunch of bodies, pressing each other back to back because there was no way to escape. Tentacles reached out to feel them gently, caressing their faces and bodies. Kurt cried out in hoarse terror. All of them closed their eyes.

Kurt felt his body convulse as a soft and boneless tentacle gripped him, trapping his arms to his side, and smoothly pulling him up. He began to struggle but quickly desisted not only because his struggles were futile but because he saw on opening his eyes that they were gliding high above the rocks and sandy floor. Terror of the octopus was compounded by terror of falling.

They floated far from the rocks, and the silent ballet continued as the creatures whirled their captives in dizzy, spinning circles. Then Kurt was released and flung. Before he had time to yell he had been caught in the tentacle of another octopus. Their captors were indeed dancing and that part of the strange dance consisted of a complicated game of catch as they tossed their prisoners carelessly from one to another.

"Is everyone all right?" he heard Wesley call.

And apparently everyone was though the voices that replied sounded thin and scared. Kurt began to see a grotesque beauty in the dance. At one point Mrs. Raccoon fell with a squeal of terror. Yet without a pause or a change in the rhythm of the ballet one of the dancers caught the poor creature and flung her high above them to an octopus on the far side of the circle.

Afterward none of them were sure how long the dance lasted. Lisa said she thought it was about half an hour but Wesley was sure it was more like an hour. Kurt never got used to being thrown across empty space. Each time his stomach turned and for a second he couldn't breathe. But the worst of his terror had subsided.

By and by the dance whirled down to the sea bed, a long way from where they had been seized. They were bundled playfully onto soft sand while their captors glided upward and onward again, leaving them like so many abandoned toys they had grown tired of.

"Phew! I'm glad that's over!" Kurt said as he watched them go.

One by one they picked themselves up and looked about them, laughing nervously as they discussed their strange adventure.

"We're in the middle of nowhere." Wesley sounded puzzled.

"Hist! Something comes!" Inkleth cried.

They could see nothing, but a low rumbling grew steadily louder from the direction in which the dancers had disappeared. It reminded Kurt of heavy trucks going over a bridge, and Wesley of the beginning of an earthquake he once experienced in California. Indeed, after a moment or two the sea bed beneath them began to vibrate so that they grew anxious again. Yet what they heard was the thunder of galloping horses and the rumble of a chariot.

"I do not like this place," Kaas said.

"Nor do I," Inkleth muttered while Kurt said, "Me neither!"

Then neck to neck over the crest of a slowly rising hill fifty white horses came galloping, eyes wide and staring, nostrils aflare and manes streaming, pulling a chariot of iron behind them. The charioteer was awesome. His limbs were like ivory columns. His chest and shoulders swelled with power. His black and green hair streamed behind him, his beard being whipped this way and that by the fury with which he drove. From his left hand streamed fifty reins. From the trident in his right hand he flung lightning flashes to crackle above the heads of his chargers. His head was held high. His eyes shone. And from deep in his chest came mighty bellows of laughter to mingle with the thunder of two hundred pounding hoofs.

"He's doing it no hands!" Kurt gasped with admiration.

It was true. The charioteer had leaped from the floor of his chariot to balance with reckless confidence on the front wall of the chariot, gripping it with his toes and swaying his muscular body with easy grace as the chariot bounced and tossed over the sea bed. It was a magnificent sight. The children stared in wonder. But a moment later they were scrambling to their feet, their wonder turned to fear. It seemed for a few seconds as though the charging horses would run them down.

But they stopped in time. With a yell of exultation the charioteer raised his left hand high and tugged back on the reins, flinging a last awesome flash to scorch the sea bed in front of his charges. Some of them reared up neighing loudly. Others pawed the ground and shook their heads wildly from side to side. Yet not one fell and in seconds all were standing still while the charioteer, still balanced on the front wall of the chariot, surveyed the party contemptuously.

"'Tis the god Poseidon!" Inkleth breathed, awe in his voice.

Poseidon stooped down somewhere to pluck a gold goblet as large as a major-league trophy. It was full of something the god poured down his throat before flinging the goblet carelessly behind him. "Little ones!" he smiled, "You have missed your way. Know, you who are mortal, that mortals drown! This is territory of the gods. Yet it would grieve me to see little ones hurt. I will forgive you. Begone!" He waved his trident and Inkleth and the children jumped as lightning whipped and crackled inches above their heads.

Inkleth, white and shaking, took a step forward. "I am Inkleth, Chieftain of the Red Dwarfs, son of Inklesh, son of Klingall, son of Lenglesh, first born of the great King Kolungall." His tone was defiant but his voice was unsteady.

"The affairs of dwarfs and of other mortals do not concern me," Poseidon replied quietly. "They breed, they eat and in a few brief years they die. I am a god. Go back to where you came from, little dwarf." He paused, and then as though a new thought struck him, "Or is it that you crave a boon from me? You have come far and risked much. Poseidon is generous. Ask what you will before you go! Your boldness softens me!"

They could see from behind him that Inkleth's whole body was shaking. "I crave no boon!" he cried breathlessly. "In the name of Gaal we come. In the name of Gaal we demand passage across your kingdom!"

Rage transformed the god's face, twisting and distorting its features beyond recognition. He lifted his trident high over his head and for a second Kurt was sure that their last moment had come. Then lightning ripped apart the space between Poseidon and some horses far on

his right, striking ten of them mercilessly to the ground and cutting their traces, so that they shuddered and died.

"Oh, how awful!" Lisa gasped, but her words led to trouble. Poseidon seemed to notice her for the first time. The rage disappeared from his face as quickly as the shadow of a cloud sweeps across a field, and he burst into merry peals of laughter.

He leapt lightly down from his chariot, passed between the horses and approached them saying, "You please me well, mortal maiden. I shall take you back with me. As for this impudent chieftain of the dwarfs, I shall give him a thousand years of life to weep salt tears and quench the everlasting thirst of my daughter Medusa. Come, mortal maiden!"

His arms were stretched out, and he had almost reached them. Lisa flung her own arms round Wesley, who roughly pushed her behind him, and before he had had time to think what he was doing, pulled the Sword of Geburah out of its scabbard. As he did so, he found the hilt was alive with warm vibration and that from the blade came the same throbbing blue light that had so comforted them in Goldcoffin's territory below the Northern Mountains.

Poseidon stopped, motionless. "Who are you?" he cried fiercely. "Who are you? You come in the guise of mortals, yet you bear Imrah in your hands. The sword you have unsheathed is none other than Imrah, Imrah from other worlds brought here in the first years. Are you mortals or are you gods?" Wesley hardly knew how to reply, but as it happened he did not need to, for after a moment Poseidon went on talking. He was staring at them still through half-closed eyes. "I know who you are," he said softly, and for the first time there was a note of wonder in his voice, "You are servants of Mi-ka-ya."

He pursed his lips.

"We are servants of Gaal," Wesley replied, still confused by the turn of events.

"Gaal I know not. But I perceive you are servants of Mi-ka-ya. What is your bidding?"

"We come in the name of Gaal to rescue Queen Suneidesis and Prince Tiqvah."

"So they too are under the protection of Mi-ka-ya!" He paused, eyeing Lisa speculatively.

"And the maid? May I not take her?"

"No!" Wesley almost choked.

"I will feed her with food of the gods and quench her thirst with ambrosia!"

Wesley drew in a deep breath and gripped the Sword of Geburah more firmly.

But Poseidon was smiling again. "It is well," he said slowly. "I may not refuse ought to the servants of Mi-ka-ya. Five horses will I leave you that will take you where you want to go. But you must be gone from my kingdom ere the green light fades and the red of the deep fires begins to glow. But I perceive there is yet another mortal maid. Her I may take?"

Wesley had no idea what the god was talking about. "I guess so," he said, a note of vague worry in his voice. He was anxious for Poseidon to be on his way.

Poseidon began to laugh again and as he turned to go back to his chariot his shoulders were shaking with merriment. He leapt into it, seized the reins and raised his trident above his head again. "The servants of Mi-ka-ya may not lie!" he cried triumphantly. "The servants of Mi-ka-ya do not break their word. I will take the second maid! Farewell!"

Lightning snapped and crackled over his chargers, which started up snorting and pawing. In one magnifi-

267

cent sweep the line of horses wheeled, and behind them Poseidon swayed in the rocking chariot. The thunder of his laughter was drowned in that of the hoofs as he disappeared into the dim green mist. Silence fell. The dead horses too had disappeared, but five living horses, white like Poseidon's, were standing quietly beside them, saddled and ready to ride across the shifting sea bed beneath which deep fires bubbled slowly.

23

"Look Well to the Sceptre!"

No one but Kardia and Gunruth stood on the deck of the Thunderhead as she glided with furled sails along a broad canal that led to the heart of the Kingdom of Darkness. Red dimness obscured the ice ceiling far overhead. The two friends had been subdued by the eeriness of their surroundings since the Thunderhead passed inside the ice world. Their dismay was all the greater because of what had befallen the crew. The moment the ship had sailed beneath the entrance to the Kingdom of Cold Darkness, between motionless walruses watching them vacantly, the ship's crew, its officers, the soldiers and their officers had grown heavy with enchanted drowsiness. One after another they had crawled below decks, soon to be drowned in slumbers from which every effort to waken them failed. Now only Gunruth and Kardia, unaffected by the spell, stood together in the ship's bow peering intently ahead. Flickering torches round the gunwales and in the bow threw dancing shadows on the Thunderhead's empty deck.

"How mysteriously the vessel is drawn without wind or current, like iron toward a loadstone," Kardia mused, half to himself. "What powerful laws are pulling us?"

"Whose laws make the sun to rise or the rain to fall?" Gunruth responded. "Whose but the High Emperor's?"

"Nay, but here his laws are powerless." Kardia shook his head, and began to answer his own question. "In this place we drift through a world apart. Other laws, *her* laws govern all that takes place here."

For some moments Gunruth stroked his beard, a thoughtful frown creasing his forehead. Eventually he spoke again. "My liege, whose are the laws that make water freeze when the warm sun hides?" Who gave it power to harden? Do not the Emperor's laws rule even here?"

"But she has seized his laws and twists them to serve her purpose," Kardia replied. "He may have made the laws. . . ."

"And his power makes them work. . . ."

"Agreed! But it is she who uses them, and by using them she controls us. Even the men below deck sleep at her bidding."

"Yet she did not invent sleep, my liege. Nor could she make them sleep unless he let her. Is she stronger than he? He made even her, this Lady of Night. How can someone he made control his laws?"

"Do we not ourselves control them?" Kardia countered. "Do we not use his wind to grind our corn and channel his rivers to water our crops? If we can make use of his laws how much more can she?"

"Nay, but we work *with* his laws, using them for purposes he gave them for. But she, a creature made by him, uses his laws against him. How can it be?"

Kardia shrugged. "I know not. I only know that while we stand and argue she draws us toward her as a spider draws flies. We have placed ourselves beyond the reach of Gaal and the High Emperor. By my own folly I have set in motion unnatural laws that operate to our peril, pulling us into the heart of night."

Gunruth shook his head but said nothing. At length he murmured, "Your majesty must be hungry." The king had eaten heartily before the Thunderhead entered the Dark Kingdom but Kardia, remembering Gaal's warning, had fasted.

"Hungry?" Kardia chuckled grimly. "I could eat. . . ."

"Three fenfinch pies, your majesty?"

"Nay, five! But methinks a little fasting will do me no harm." He looked at Gunruth with mock sternness. "My lord Gunruth, let there be no talk of fenfinch pie nor of any other food in the presence of a starving king!"

Yet it was Kardia who began to talk of food. Before long the two were reminiscing, as friends do, about happy feasts of years gone by. They spoke of banquets under the shining Tobath Mareh Tapestry, and of the ballads the minstrels used to sing, telling of the first things, of the coming of John Wilson, and of how the proseo comai stones were blown throughout the world, of battles, of how Gaal conquered death, and of the terrible end of Shagah and Hocoino at the hands of Gaal.

They smiled as they talked and began to forget their isolation and the menace of the red mist around them. Suddenly Gunruth's eyes widened. "Your majesty will pardon the reference, yet as we talk I can almost smell fenfinch pie, fresh from the ovens of Nephesh Palace!"

"And I, my lord, not only *think* I smell it, but by the

tower I swear I *do* smell it!" As he spoke Kardia's face changed and he gripped the Iron Sceptre firmly.

They faced each other. On Gunruth's face too there was a look of wonder. "The cooks must be awake and baking," he said, "yet it seemed that all men slept." They listened intently. From the galley immediately beneath their feet there was no sound.

"Nay," Kardia said, "the enchantment is still upon them. You can still smell it?" Gunruth nodded, but Kardia was not satisfied. "And it is fenfinch pie you smell?"

"Fenfinch pie, your majesty!"

"'Tis enchantment then, and it makes rivers to run inside my mouth!"

"And in mine!"

For several minutes they sniffed, peered into the dimness ahead, looked at each other and peered ahead again. "The vessel is slowing," Gunruth said.

"She is well nigh heaved to!"

It was true. The Thunderhead was scarcely moving. Then by the port bow on the icy bank of the canal they saw something rise like a volcano from the ice. The Thunderhead slowly drew level with it and stopped. Their eyes grew so round that white showed all round them. Well might they stare. By the steam that wafted to them from the crater of the volcano they knew they were looking at the largest fenfinch pie that anyone had ever seen.

"'Tis a mountain of pastry baked for a giant!" Gunruth whispered, wonderingly.

"'Twas baked by no human baker, yet my stomach cries out to taste it!" Kardia replied. His legs were shaking, and his face was pale and sweating.

"Your majesty must not leave the ship!" There was a note of urgency in Gunruth's voice.

Kardia was not listening. "We are in the Circles of Enchantment, and this circle, I perceive, is the Enchantment of Bodily Yearnings." He sighed hungrily, gripping the Iron Sceptre.

"Gunruth!" he cried suddenly. Gunruth turned from the culinary mountain to look at him. The Iron Sceptre was writhing, twisting, jumping and tugging in the king's hands. Before long it was jerking his body this way and that while Kardia clung desperately to a rod that struggled to get away from him. Gunruth gasped as with one mighty wrench Kardia was pulled down on the deck and dragged toward the stern. Then, as it began to fly toward the giant pie, Kardia's body was dashed sickeningly against the gunwales, cracking three of his ribs. With a grunt of pain he dropped to the deck while the sceptre, tearing itself from his grasp, flew through the air to pierce the crust of the mountain and stuck itself like a fork in the pastry. Kardia struggled to his feet with a cry, and would have scrambled over the side of the ship, had the blow he sustained not robbed him for the moment of his strength.

" 'Look well to the sceptre!' " Gunruth breathed in wonder. Then crying out he said, "Gaal told me, 'Look well to the sceptre!' Stay here, your majesty!"

He seized a rope hanging over the Thunderhead's side, scrambled down to the ice, and up the slope of pastry to where the sceptre had impaled itself. It showed no inclination to resist. So with a vigorous tug the dwarf pulled the sceptre free. Then he began his descent, using it as a staff to steady him on the slope. But his task was not over.

Suddenly all round him the pastry crust began to break apart. First the yellow beaks and then the purple heads and crests of giant fenfinches thrust themselves through the pastry with piercing cheeps and twitterings. The heads alone were as big as Gunruth, and the noise was deafening. One after another the birds struggled to pull their gigantic wings and bodies from the pie while Gunruth frenziedly rolled and tumbled down the mountainside.

Out of the corner of his eye he could see them converging on him. In desperation he twisted round, pushed the sceptre into his belt behind him and leapt for the rope. Suddenly they were everywhere. The wind from their beating wings blew him this way and that and twisted the rope wildly as he continued to struggle up. Everywhere he could feel the whirring of giant wings and hear the raucous clamor the birds were making.

Then to his horror the sceptre was tugged from his belt, and he felt himself seized by the shoulders. Helplessly clinging to the rope he was pulled this way and that and, still clinging to the rope, dropped onto the deck of the ship.

For a moment he lay still gasping for breath. When he looked up he was alone with Kardia on the Thunderhead's deck. Of the birds there was no sign. Kardia leaned with his right hand on the sceptre and with his left was holding his painful chest. He looked at Gunruth with a twisted smile.

"So much for fenfinch pies, my lord!" Gunruth shuddered. "Where are the birds, your majesty?"

"Gone, my lord, gone! And the mountain with them!"

Gunruth caught sight of the sceptre. "Then all is well, your majesty!"

"Better than we might have hoped, friend!"

"I thought the birds had it."

"'Twas not for want of trying. It was not you they sought, but what you carried. At first I was sure they would succeed, and they well nigh did. So I hung over the gunwale, my poor cracked ribs making a bitter complaint, and seized it as soon as you came in reach. At once, by some miracle, the birds vanished. All that remained was to haul your lordship on board."

Gunruth sat up. "I am grateful for your majesty's help."

"Nay, my good Gunruth. I am the one who should be grateful, and not I alone, but all the Kingdom of Anthropos. Had you not placed your life in jeopardy, dark shadows might even now have been stealing like death over Anthropos." He paused. "This is a perilous place. In Anthropos none could snatch the sceptre from me. But here it takes unto itself a rebel's will and tears itself free." Then speaking in a low voice he said, "I should not have come."

"We cannot turn back, your majesty."

"No. And mayhap Gaal will still be with us. But I would that we had never come. I may not only have imperiled my kingdom, but placed my wife and son in greater jeopardy than before."

The ship was moving again. Neither of them felt sleepy. "I will never again eat fenfinch pie," Kardia said softly.

"His majesty may do as he pleases," Gunruth returned, a mischievous smile playing round his lips, "but as for me I will eat them with greater relish than ever."

"Nay, friend, it is not that I fear to, but that I am ashamed of my gluttony."

"Your majesty is no glutton. True, your weakness for the pies has become a legend. But your majesty never eats while others remain hungry, and at times you eat a little more pie only to live up to your legend. You know it pleases us and gives us something to jest about."

Kardia looked solemn. "Yet my delicacy nearly undid us."

"Your majesty, it matters little what form the enchantment took. We must not ask what the enchantress offered *but who offered it*. For the evil lies in taking anything—be it good or bad—that *she* offers. At the hand of Gaal we may receive anything, but at the hand of Mirmah even fenfinch pies were sin to take."

Kardia looked at the Matmon sharply. "You have wisdom, my lord," he said slowly, "and these adventures we pass through together are as great as any woven into the Tobath Mareh Tapestry or into the songs of minstrels. If Gaal should be pleased to rescue us, I swear I will set the women a-weaving once more. And on the tapestry we will see," and as he said it Kardia smiled broadly, "Gunruth the Matmon Lord winning the Battle of the Fenfinch Pie!"

But Gunruth was peering into the air above them. "Your majesty, do we pass beneath yet another arch?"

Kardia, too, looked up and then on either side of them. "It may be so," he murmured. "Methinks that walls of ice close in on us."

Little by little they found it easier to see the ice roof over their heads and the cliffs of ice beside them. Soon there could be no doubt that the canal was leading them into a wide tunnel. Lapping waters glowed and sparkled with red light and threw reflections on the black ice arching over them.

"Whither does it lead?" Gunruth asked.

"To the second Circle of Enchantment, I doubt not, the Enchantment that Dazzles the Eye."

"The pie enchanted *my* eye," Gunruth said grimly.

"Nay, it enchanted our noses and our bellies. Rightly was it called the Enchantment of Bodily Yearnings!"

Kardia laughed, adding more soberly, "And it tore the sceptre from my grasp. Had I not cracked my ribs so hard I would have pursued it."

"Your majesty, . . ." Gunruth hesitated.

"Say on, Gunruth."

"Your majesty will pardon my boldness?"

"What is it, Gunruth?"

"We know not what peril awaits us in the Circle of the Enchantment that Dazzles the Eye."

"No, friend. We do not know."

"Nor do we know whether your majesty's sceptre will break away from you."

Kardia gripped the sceptre till his knuckles showed white. "It will not break away from me while I have strength in my body."

"Your majesty, the enchantments have more power than mortals can resist."

"Your lordship, I *must* not let it go. I dare not. What would have happened beside the great pie if the birds had seized it?" Kardia groaned. "What a fool I have been, what a fool!"

"Yet if the sceptre does break from you, . . ."

Kardia groaned again.

" . . . your majesty must not attempt to follow it!"

The king's face hardened. "Must not? Thus did I say myself but an hour ago. Must not? Think, Gunruth. What value does my own life have if the kingdom is to be destroyed? Nay, my lord, . . ." he shook his head.

"Did not your majesty tell me the Lord Gaal forbade you to leave the ship in the Circles of Enchantment?" Gunruth asked softly. Kardia was silent. Gunruth continued. "Did he not also bid me look well to the sceptre?"

The king sighed. "May Gaal have mercy on us! What have I done?"

277

They were coming to the end of the tunnel and a moment later the Thunderhead entered a cavern so immense that its roof was lost in the darkness and its walls were too far off to be seen. Only the canal like a flaming pathway of ruby light led straight ahead of them while the torches on the deck bathed the ship in flickering yellow. They had become a glowing ship sailing through empty darkness along a ribbon of ruby fire.

Before long another light appeared in the darkness ahead of them. They stared at it, wondering. "What can it be, your majesty?"

"I cannot see what form it will take," said Kardia, his voice shaking a little. "But I fear it is the Enchantment that Dazzles the Eye."

"It will lie to our port side," Gunruth said as they drew closer. "It looks like a tall, straight tree made of torches."

It was a good description. The nearer they approached the more clearly they saw that the vertical line of light was indeed made up of many torches. As they drew level a surprise awaited them. They had been looking until then only at one edge of a vast sheet suspended from the ice roof far above. There were torches above and on both edges of it. As the Thunderhead slowly came to a standstill in front of it, the full glory of a tapestry broke over them.

"The Tobath Mareh!" Gunruth gasped. "How can it be?"

Kardia was speechless, his eyes feasting on familiar beauties. The blues, the Anthropos green, the reds, the russets had never glowed so vividly. Gold and silver threads glittered in the torchlight. Kardia was shaking his head in wonder, and a lump rose in his throat as he continued to drink in its loveliness.

"'Tis fifty times the size it was," the Matmon, too, was

stunned. Together they stared, overwhelmed by awe-some beauty.

"Would to Gaal we might have it back!" Kardia whis-pered.

Then, so swiftly that for a second he did not realize it the sceptre tore itself again from his grasp. As he felt the emptiness of his hands and saw it hurling itself at the center of the tapestry, he gave a cry of rage and despair. "Gunruth! The sceptre! The enchantment has won!"

But Gunruth was halfway down the rope. Dropping onto the icy bank of the canal, he leapt and seized the lower edge of the tapestry. What happened next took him by surprise. It was as if he had seized a curtain and dislodged the curtain rod. The tapestry fell heavily down about him, and he was crushed in the darkness by the weight of the cloth. The light of the torches was gone. Heavy material pinned him down, and he struggled des-perately to breathe, unable to move a finger.

But the tapestry came to life. The next moment he found himself being tossed and turned, thrown head over heels, twisted this way and that. Something hard hit the side of his head, and when his hands flew to his head, he found his fingers had closed round the Iron Sceptre.

Suddenly all movement ceased, and he could scramble to his feet. Standing upright and feeling with his feet and his free hand he discovered he was inside a cloth-lined tunnel. The tapestry had rolled itself up and by a miracle he was at the center of the roll. Quickly he groped his way along the tunnel to find his way out. But then the tapestry began to roll across the ice.

He was tossed and thrown, quickly losing all sense of where he was or in what direction he was going. "I must get out," he told himself, bumping painfully and bruising himself on the sceptre he clung to so tenaciously. It was all very well to tell himself he ought to get out, but soon dizziness overtook him.

Then without warning he was flung onto the ice, and the enchanted tapestry left him behind in the darkness. He lay for some moments clutching the sceptre. The universe seemed to turn over and over, and he was terrified lest he should fall off the ice. At times he seemed to be pressed against a ceiling of ice, and at other times against a vertical wall of ice. But before long he grew more sure that he was lying on a flat expanse.

Presently his dizziness subsided enough for him to stand unsteadily and look round. To his relief he saw a blob of light in the distance above a thick line of ruby fire. It was the Thunderhead. Stumblingly he made his way toward it, taking a half-hour to complete the trek. As he drew close he saw the ruby waters throwing their lurid light on the face of King Kardia who stared anxiously over the side.

"Gunruth!"

"Your majesty!"

"Thanks be to Gaal that you are safe! And the sceptre?"

"I have it here, your majesty!" Gunruth held it up. Then with no more ado he clambered on board. As he did so the vessel once again began to move forward.

The ship had entered another tunnel before either of them spoke.

"We have survived two of the circles, your majesty."

"One circle more," Kardia murmured. "And if in the goodness of Gaal we survive it, then shall we face the witch herself."

"Take heart, your majesty. Is not Gaal Lord of the ice?"

A bitter smile stole along the king's lips. "Heed not my

gloomy face, friend Gunruth," he said. "How feeble my grasp of the sceptre is! Battle I can face. Give me a horse and a sword in my hand, and I will fight. But sorcery has unmanned me."

"Yet your majesty has not drawn back from the adventure that comes to us."

"Drawn back? You yourself said we cannot!" The king laughed grimly. "We stand on the deck of an enchanted ship that moves against our bidding. Our crew and our men-at-arms are drunk with the slumber of sorcery. We have no choice in the matter. I could not flee even if I would. I am like a child being dragged to the puller of teeth."

Gunruth's eyes narrowed. "And who drags you?" he asked slowly.

"Can there be a question?" Kardia replied. "I have placed the ship in the power of the witch. I have entered her territory of my own folly. I have even forfeited my power over the sceptre. Who drags us? Why the Lady Mirmah drags us, pulling us like helpless flies into the heart of her web and playing with us awhile before she sucks our blood! Yet by Gaal's robe will I slay her, though I perish in doing so!"

"Nay, your majesty! Would Gaal hand us over to the power of the witch? Would he let his servants struggle like flies in the web of a spider?"

"'Tis of our own choosing, Gunruth—or rather of mine. Whose devilish magic baked the enchanted pie? Who dazzled our eyes with a tapestry that no longer exists? Who, even now, is preparing to humiliate us a third time?"

"Who snatched your majesty's sceptre up, delivering it from the beaks of giant birds? Who found your sceptre when it was lost in the folds of an enchanted tapestry?"

"You did!" the king said.

"Not so, by your majesty's leave! I followed the instructions of Gaal. He thrust the sceptre into my hands in the dark! He pulled me out onto the ice! Mirmah does not *play*, your majesty. She wants the sceptre, and even now is spitting out her rage because she failed to seize it twice. It is ours by the goodness of Gaal!"

"Perchance I do him an injustice," Kardia said.

"Is your majesty's folly greater than the faithfulness of Gaal? Will he let a witch destroy the lands he rules over? He may let us smart a little to teach us better ways, but his is the power that keeps these caverns from falling about our ears, and his is the rod that will smash the hand that pulls our ship, when the pulling has served his purpose!"

Once more they passed into a vast cavern. And once again the ship drew to a halt. But this time they saw nothing. Darkness and silence wrapped them round.

"Do you see anything?"

"No, your majesty."

"Do you feel anything?"

Gunruth hesitated. "I feel a presence—a very great presence, there on the port side. Your majesty can also sense it?"

"Not only do I feel it, but I begin to see it. Look! Do you not perceive? There—above us!"

It seemed almost as though an invisible giant was chalking the outlines of a three-dimensional colossus or as though stage lights were gradually revealing a scene.

"'Tis a statue the size of a mountain!"

"Nay, it is no statue. It lives!"

"It does not move—ah!"

It did move. And with a blinding rush of light everything became clear. Sitting upon a throne at the top of a flight of steps was a man dressed in the coronation robes of Anthropos. Yet his size was the size of a hundred men. And as he turned to face them, they saw that his face was the face of Kardia himself. They were staring at a young Kardia whose beard was black, not gray, at an enormous Kardia sitting on an even more enormous throne and smiling down on them, reducing them to pygmies.

They gaped with mouths wide open, Gunruth staring first at the Kardia beside him, then at the Kardia on the throne. "It is a perfect likeness—and it lives!" he exclaimed in bewilderment.

"It is no likeness," Kardia returned. "It is I myself! I am *there!*"

But more marvels were to follow. One after another the rulers of the neighboring realms climbed the steps, prostrating themselves before the throne, while Kardia on his throne smiled contemptuously. And up the steps ran Mirmah the witch to give him the Crown of Anan which he placed on his head while she like the other sovereigns flung herself prostrate at his feet. Last of all came Gaal, bowing low before the giant Kardia.

"'Tis blasphemy! 'Tis the Enchantment of Blasphemy!" Gunruth breathed in horror unaware for a moment of the scuffling and the gasps beside him on the Thunderhead's deck. For Kardia was again wrestling with the sceptre, his muscles bulging and his face suffused with blood. Back and forth went Kardia and the iron rod, now slamming with groans against the gunwales, now thudding against a mast, whirling, twirling, rolling, wrestling, leaping, bouncing, crashing, gasping. From Kardia's throat came a scream of despair as for the third time the sceptre eluded him and flew into the waiting hands of the Kardia that sat on the throne.

By this time Gunruth was aware of what was happen-

ing and had swung his body over the ship's side, burning the skin off his hands in his desperate haste to slide down the rope. But he felt no pain. In a flash he was tearing up the steps, pushing past the prostrate figures of the rulers, the witch and of Gaal himself, and scrambling madly up the skirts of the enthroned figure. Then, sweating and panting he flung himself at the sceptre the giant hands were holding.

The lights went out and he felt himself dropping. A moment later he crashed heavily on the ice below. He lay stunned. But as sense returned he became aware of the cold ice against his cheek, of the sceptre in his clutch, of the pains of his bruises and of the burning in his lungs that were fighting for breath.

When he got back to the deck of the Thunderhead he found Kardia lying face down, weeping bitterly.

24

The Crystal Ball and Chain

Slowly Mary rose to her feet. Here in the cave she felt a little safer, but fear still clawed at her heart. The crystal ball weighed heavily, the chain digging more painfully than ever into her skin. But there were no foul smells coming from it, and she realized that for the moment the witch did not have access to her thoughts. Yet she knew she was in danger. She had been a fool to think she could outwit the witch. How was she to escape? Queen Suneidesis and Prince Tiqvah could not help her. In any case they would never forgive her if they knew she had tried to steal the sceptre from Kardia and had lured him into the witch's clutches. As she thought of the Lady of Night's broken promises and lies, she trembled with anger that was mixed with dread. Queen Suneidesis had disappeared into the outer cave, and as Mary got to her feet, the young prince jumped up from the stone on which he had been sitting and bowed low before her.

"I am Tiqvah, son of Kardia, heir to the throne of Anthropos and Playsion," he said gravely. "Is there anything my mother, the queen, and I can do for you in your distress, for I perceive some ill has befallen you? Pray make your wishes known to us. I would that we were not prisoners of the evil witch Mirmah, for then we might truly offer help. Yet such aid as we can give, we will give gladly."

It was such a pretty speech, and he looked so handsome that for a moment Mary forgot her fear and would like to have made a pretty speech in return. Two things stopped her. For one thing she wasn't very good at talking the way Prince Tiqvah did, and for another there was something about the way he looked at her that made her uneasy.

"What is he staring at?" she wondered to herself. "Is it my dress? Have I torn it or spilled something on it? Maybe it needs pressing. I probably ought not to have curled up among the furs without taking it off."

Aloud she said, "Is there something wrong with my dress?"

Prince Tiqvah started and blushed deeply. "Pardon my discourtesy. I do not well to stare so hard. I thought, . . . but I am mistaken. No, fair lady, your dress becomes you well—if any dress in Anthropos could match the beauty of face and form like yours. What is your name, my lady? Never have I seen beauty so fair!" The flush on Tiqvah's face deepened and extended even to his neck and his ears. Once again he bowed, this time to cover his confusion.

"My name is Mary McNab," Mary replied, and remembering how her stepmother used to welcome visitors, "Won't you sit down?"

287

She sat down herself in the bed of straw and the prince squatted on a stone beside it. An unpleasant thought occurred to her. Perhaps he had recognized the dress she was wearing. After all it came from his father's palace. What would he think? Had it been stealing to take the dress? But Prince Tiqvah was smiling delightedly.

"Mary McNab!" he exclaimed. "I have never heard a name like that. Are you from Anthropos or from Playsion? Your speech is strange."

Mary shook her head, not knowing what to say. She liked the prince with his sparkling black eyes and his black curly hair, but the more she thought about the Lady of Night, and the fact that he and his mother were the lady's prisoners, the more uncomfortable she felt. She remembered their attempt to get away from the cave and the prince's narrow brush with death from the bites of Medusa's serpent hair. At the time it had all seemed unreal, as though Queen Suneidesis and her son were only actors on a stage. Now they were flesh-and-blood people who were showing her kindness, people she wanted to have as her friends. Outwardly Mary looked calm and beautiful, but inwardly she was sick with shame and fear.

Prince Tiqvah was telling the tale of their capture, and as she listened she realized how different he was from her friends in Toronto. "So we passed through the lands where the crops had failed, and we slept in the cottages of the poor." Then, his eyes flashing, he described their capture by treacherous Playsion troops in the pay of the witch, and of his mother's betrayal by two courtiers.

"One of them was called Lord Oqbah and the other Lord Ramah. Lord Ramah was the father of Kaas who is my friend." Tiqvah's face flushed with indignation and his hand rested on his sword hilt. "They paid for their treachery. This witch—this Lady of Night—this so-called Empress-to-Be of Darkness beheaded them both and along with them all the troops that served her. I was glad—till I remembered Kaas, my friend. Yet even then I was not sorry. For the Lord Ramah was an evil father who beat his son sorely every night. Often I wept with Kaas over his bruises and the wounds his father inflicted in drunken rages!" He sighed. "Where is my friend Kaas now?" Little did Tiqvah realize that at that very moment Kaas was riding on a white horse across the sea bed toward him.

But Mary knew what Tiqvah did not and was thinking of the witch's words to her. Were her cousins really coming? "Bring them to me," the Lady of Night had told her. "Bring also the queen and the prince. I have prepared a feast for them all." She knew now that the witch would prepare no feast. She had heard the lady's plans for her own destruction, and she could be sure that the same fate awaited them all. All they could expect was certain death. Yet what should she do? Could they escape by using the crystal ball? And what about the Friesens?

Tiqvah was still talking, describing his battle with Medusa. "Strongly did I wield my sword, cutting off many of the serpents' heads. But for every one I beheaded, two more appeared, and soon they were wrapping their evil bodies round me, dragging me into the mouth of the goddess. . . ."

"But your mother grabbed your belt and pulled you back!"

Tiqvah's jaw dropped. "How know you this?"

It was Mary's turn to blush. "Oh . . . I just guessed that was what happened," she lied.

Tiqvah was watching her keenly. "You were under an enchantment," he said. "What evil spell lies on you? And what, pray, is the amulet about your fair neck?"

Then Mary's flush was replaced by pallor. She looked down at her trembling fingers and fiddled with the folds of her dress. "The witch gave it me," she said in a low voice.

"The witch? The Lady Mirmah?"

Mary nodded miserably.

"Then you know her."

Mary nodded again.

"What is it? Why did she give it to you?"

"You can get to any place you want to go. It grows big when you put it on a fire and inside it you can see the place you're thinking of. You just step inside the ball, and you're *there*."

"Is that how you got here?" Tiqvah sounded puzzled.

"Yes." Mary was still looking at her fingers.

Queen Suneidesis was standing beside them. Neither of them had noticed her approach. "Why did you come here?" she asked gently.

"Mirmah made me come."

"*Made* you come?"

"Well, she said I had to." Mary took a deep breath. "She said I was to wait till my cousins came, and then take all of you back to a feast she was giving."

"*Are you her servant then?*"

For a second time a flush rose slowly from Mary's neck over her face and as far as the crown of her head, where it itched unpleasantly. Neither the prince nor his mother spoke for a full minute.

"The dress you are wearing," the queen said eventually, "is a dress I wore when I was a girl. It was in Nephesh Palace. Have you been there too with your crystal ball?"

290

"She made me go."

"Why?"

"She wanted me to steal the sceptre."

"Did you?"

"No." Mary hoped the queen would not guess that she would have stolen it if she could have.

"What did you do?"

"I told the king that Gaal said to come here and rescue you."

"Had Gaal said that?"

Mary's face burned the more fiercely and she bit her lip.

"And the gown? How did the gown come into your possession?"

"They were real kind to me. They took my own clothes and gave me a tub bath in a round bedroom with a big fire. The dress was in the closet. They thought I had come from Gaal. And I had—in a way."

"You came from Gaal? Did you not tell us you came from the witch?"

Mary sighed miserably, "I came from Gaal too. I guess he must have brought me here from Winnipeg in Canada—that's in another world, and I don't really understand how it works. Anyway the witch rescued me when I got into a mess in the Kingdom of Darkness. She took me to her palace, and she said I was beautiful and that she liked me. I thought she meant it. I knew I wasn't beautiful, so she gave me magic ice crystals to make me like this." She fingered her unnaturally beautiful face.

The queen sat on the straw bed beside her and gently took Mary's hands in her own. "The witch is not to be trusted."

"I know. I guess I've known it all along—but I didn't want to believe it. I wanted her to go on liking me. *I wanted it so much.* And I wanted to be beautiful." She paused and pulled her hands away from the queen's. "Gaal made me beautiful too," she said quietly, "but that was different." She looked up for the first time at Suneidesis and was strangely relieved to discover there was no mole above this queen's left eye. The dark eyes were thoughtful, looking directly into her own. Among the queen's black tresses she saw a thin circlet of gold in which large stones like rubies were set.

"Is that a crown?" she asked, forgetting her worries for a moment. "It isn't a bit like Mirmah's crown."

"It is a crown Gaal gave me. The stones are zabach stones. In fact it is because of the stones that we are safe in Gaal's cave."

"Safe? I thought this was the witch's prison!"

"The outer cave is. We knew naught of this cave until I stumbled against the wall of the witch's cave, and the coronet tumbled from my head, striking the rock wall. Then behold, an opening came and we passed into the stillness and holiness of this place! In here Mirmah cannot reach us. We are safe from her, concealed from her eyes in the depths of her own prison. That is why you were sent, to lure us from the Cave of Gaal."

"Why do you say it is the Cave of Gaal?"

Tiqvah interrupted eagerly. "Fair lady, do you not see the opening in the roof of the cave?"

Mary looked in the direction he was pointing. A shaft of pale blue light shone down to illuminate a flight of stone steps, and as she looked up she gasped in amazement to see a clear blue sky. "Oh," she cried, "let me see!" and would have darted up the steps had Tiqvah not held her back.

"What is it?" she asked.

"It is *the hole where time is no more*," he replied, and something in his voice made her stare at the opening in wonder.

"Can't we get out there?" she asked.

"No."

"Why?"

"Because our time has not come."

Mary felt a new kind of fear stealing over her—definitely fear, but a nice kind of fear. (And if you've never felt that kind of fear I can only explain it by saying it is the sort of fear that takes unpleasant fear away.) They turned to the queen again and sat down with her.

"What are you going to do, Mary McNab?"

The question brought the old kind of fear back, and Mary felt it so strongly that her hands began to shake again. "You said we were safe here."

"And so we are. There is fresh bread and fish for us every day in the Cave of Gaal, but we cannot stay here forever."

"Mirmah wants to. . . ." Mary was groping for words, " . . . wants to kill us all. Are you sure we can't get out of that hole?"

The queen shook her head. "Nor can we escape through the outer cave. Even if the old goddess were not guarding us, there is now an enchanted fire burning in the cave mouth, a fire we could never pass through."

Mary breathed sharply. "*All* red— a sort of *vivid* red, like?"

The queen nodded.

"Then it's *her* fire. It's the fire she wants me to throw my crystal ball in."

They went to look and it was true. Through a curtain of ruby flames filling the entrance of the cave, the baleful eyes of Medusa stared at them. Mary shuddered. Returning to the Cave of Gaal, they sat down.

Mary was watching the queen closely. "You don't seem scared," she said eventually.

"An idea has come to me," Suneidesis replied. "I may be very wrong, but Gaal has done stranger things. And I know he has not forgotten us." She paused and seemed lost in thought.

"Perhaps, m'am, you could tell us what it is you think," Tiqvah said courteously.

"I have read much in the book that came from the Tower of Geburah," Suneidesis said at length. "It tells of the doings of Gaal and of a holy bird and of the true and only Emperor. It tells the histories of the beginning of our time and of some who rebelled against Gaal. I also have read other writings about those who rebelled. Among them was a woman named Mirshaath, sister of the chieftain Atslah. Mirshaath gave herself to the study of evil and with her magic slew the priest of dark spirits. She was condemned to be hanged in a wicker basket from the bough of an oak tree until she starved to death."

"Why so?" Tiqvah asked. Mary merely stared with puzzled eyes at the queen.

"They said that her spirit must not be allowed to escape into the ground and that she must never be buried. So Mirshaath hung between earth and sky for a year, daily growing thinner but never dying. She neither moved nor spoke, scarcely seeming to breathe. In her left hand she clutched something, but none knew what it might be. Her body grew cool, but never cold. Some said she could not die. But a year to the day from the time she was hung in the basket she disappeared, and no one knew how or where.

"Then men began to say that Mirshaath had gone to the north lands to find the Spirit of the North who is the

Spirit of Darkness and to beg him to darken her heart that she might live forever.

"Some said the thing she clutched in her left hand was the first proseo comai stone torn from the primal rocks. Others said it was an elfin orb of frozen fire."

"Did she find the Spirit of Darkness, my mother? And did he darken her heart?"

"The books do not say," Suneidesis replied slowly. "Yet there are tales that tell of the wife of the Spirit of Darkness whose name was Migtar-of-the-Heart-of-Ice. Some say Migtar-of-the-Heart-of-Ice and Mirshaath are one. What is certain is that Migtar-of-the-Heart-of-Ice possessed the power to travel anywhere through a ball of ice and fire." She paused. "Mirshaath, Migtar, Mirmah—could all three be the same? Could Mirmah be the wife of the Spirit of Darkness? For the ancient books say Mirshaath will come again to conquer the earth with night." The queen frowned. "Mirmah," she said eventually, "must be none other than Mirshaath who is the same as Migtar. And as for the ball of ice and fire...." Mary's heart bumped suffocatingly. She knew what the queen was going to say. " ... as for the ball of ice and fire, I think it is the one that hangs round your neck, lady Mary."

Prince Tiqvah reached his hand forward eagerly to touch the crystal ball, but Mary pulled back and covered it with her own hands. "Please don't," she said anxiously wondering why the crystal was so precious to her. It was not just a possible means of escape to her. It seemed to have wound itself round her heart.

"I ... I don't want anyone to touch it!"

"Your pardon, fair lady," the prince said gravely.

"If I am right," the queen continued, "it can either bring our doom upon us or destroy our enemies, according to how the lady Mary uses it."

"I don't know what you mean," Mary said. The chain round her neck was by now making her whole head throb with pain.

"If the ball of ice and fire comes near the enchanted flames, we will be drawn into the witch's presence. But if you fling it beyond the flames into the mouth of Medusa, the goddess will be consumed from within and will turn into the ashes of a volcano."

"That's what Gaal said to do too," Mary said in a strangled voice. "He said that when the time came I had to fling it away from me forever—into Medusa's mouth. But I don't want to fling it away! I want to keep it! It's *mine!*"

"Your ladyship does not wish to destroy Medusa with it?" Tiqvah asked in surprise.

"Oh, but—yes, I *do.*" Mary's face was working and twisting. "Part of me wants to get rid of it. It hurts my neck and it scares me. But whenever I think of throwing it away I . . . I just can't. I . . . " and she shook her head in pain.

"My child, do you really suppose this witch would let you keep the ball of ice and fire?"

"Not if she could help it."

"Remember she defied death, clutching it inside a basket, hung between earth and sky at the dawn of time. Remember too that she took it across earth and sea and snow to reach the Spirit of Darkness and of the North, and has held it fast for thousands of years. It is tied to her by invisible chains, and so long as you wear it you are chained to her too. Either you must get rid of it, or it will destroy us all."

Then Mary moaned and trembled more than ever for she knew that what the queen said was true. In desperation she seized the crystal ball and tried to pull it over her head, but when her hands touched it, her arms grew weak and fell to her side. Again and again she tried but always in vain. Tiqvah and the queen tried too, but when they attempted to lift it, its weight was far beyond their strength, so that they marveled that Mary could still stand up with it round her neck.

"'Tis bound to you by enchantment," Suneidesis said. "For it is not that the ball of ice and fire belongs to you, lady Mary, but that you belong to *it*. It is your master and it rules you. Only Gaal can help us now."

25

The Easiest Thing Mary Ever Did

"Mary McNab!"

It was the voice of Gaal, calling her from the outer cave. She looked at the queen and at Prince Tiqvah to see a smile break over the face of Suneidesis.

"You must go to him," she said. "He can break the witch's spell!" Then to Tiqvah, who made as though he would also go into the outer cave, she said, "No, my son. We must wait here. For Mary McNab he called, and he has business only with her."

Gaal was standing with his back to the curtain of fire, and beyond it Mary could still see the baleful stare of Medusa. But she didn't care now. Her heart was beating fiercely and the palms of her hands were wet. Her eyes were on Gaal, tall and straight. One hand rested on the hilt of his sword, while he held the other up, palm facing her.

"Come no further!" he said.

When she heard him say that, Mary felt sure that there was no more hope for her. Gaal's face was stern and at the same time, sad. She wondered whether to say, "Don't be mad at me!" but the words never got as far as her lips. She wanted to cry, yet no tears came either. Her mouth was dry and her eyes were burning. At last she forced the words out hoarsely. "I couldn't help it. She almost shoved it in my mouth. And she made me come here. I know you said I had to choose between her and you. I know you said I couldn't trust her an' I didn't anymore. But it was too late. . . ." She shook her head miserably.

He lowered his hand. She longed to cross the floor to him and take hold of it. Still he did not speak.

"I wanted her to like me. I couldn't help that either. And at first I wanted to be beautiful—but after what happened I was too scared to want it anymore." Still she could not take her eyes off him, trying to read his expression. The memory of the northern lights came back to her. "It was, it was terrific being with you that night." How could she explain to him how wonderful it had been? But what was the use of telling him? He probably couldn't understand why she had let the witch place the crystal into her mouth. It had just happened.

"An' I can't take this thing off—this crystal ball. And," she lowered her voice in shame, "and I kind of don't want to either. But please—I *do* want to do it if you say so. Only I can't." Her eyes pleaded with him.

"Don't move yet, Mary," he said. "Just watch what I do. When I tell you to come, then cross over to me. But remember that when you do so, you will hear the witch and feel her power. Don't be afraid, for my power is greater, and I will not fail you."

Then sweeping his sword from its scabbard with a

ringing shish of cold steel he placed his left foot forward, raising his robe to his knees. A scar lay like a white star on his ankle and he stabbed it gently with the point of his sword, watching the red blood well up. Then replacing his sword in its scabbard he called her to him.

As she stepped across the floor of the outer cave she heard again the gargling laughter of the old woman and smelled her sickeningly foul smell. "So you are about to let the imposter who calls himself Gaal the Shepherd deceive you!" the voice said. "He will make you a slave, Mary McNab, and he will make you miserable and ugly. Ignore the red that flows over his foot. Come back to me, Mary McNab. Throw the ball in the flames and come back. I will make you beautiful for a thousand years!"

The volume and closeness of the voice shocked her, and she stopped in her tracks, looking piteously at Gaal. But he was bending over, wetting his fingers with the blood that came out of his scar. "Come, Mary. Don't be afraid."

As she reached him he said, "Kick off the shoe on your right foot!" She did so, letting her bare foot rest on the sand and trying not to think of the witch's voice, still talking in her ears. Then Gaal took the warm blood on his fingers and wiped it first on her big toe, then on the thumb of her right hand, and then, to her surprise, on the lobe of her right ear. A broad smile lit up his face. "Now you are mine," he said, "and the witch has no more power over you!"

At once the voice in her ears was gone, and there was no more smell. Faint sounds still came from the crystal ball, but she could not tell what they were about. More important she was in her own body again—overweight, pimply, but free. A rush of warmth rose from the soles of her feet. The joy she had experienced at the time she had heard the stars clap their hands exploded inside her again, and she flew like a cannonball at Gaal. His arms were wide apart and both of them fell to the sandy floor.

"Gaal!" she shouted in amazement. "Oh, I'm *sorry!*" They had fallen to the floor from Mary's impact. "You're really not mad at me? You still want me?"

He scrambled to his feet, pulled her up with him, and holding her by both hands burst into the merriest laughter. Then he twirled her in mad circles dancing and laughing with the laughter of deep heaven. "Why do you think I came all this way to find you?" he shouted back, "How long d'you think I've been chasing you, Mary McNab? *And now I have you!*" His voice rose in a wild song, and as they danced a new wonder came to Mary McNab. He had actually wanted her! Gaal was so glad about it that he seemed crazy with joy. Her legs were alive with energy, and she felt she wanted to go on dancing forever. She had one shoe off and the other shoe on, but what did she care about shoes? Yet as they whirled, the crystal ball was still banging heavily against her chest.

Suddenly a loathing filled her, and she snatched her hands from Gaal's. "This *thing*," she said, staring at it. Gaal stood stock-still. He was smiling but she did not know it for she was still staring down at her chest. She shuddered. "I hate it. Yet it still . . . it still—ugh!"

"You are free from it, Mary. It has no power over you."

She looked at him, saw his smile, then looked down at the ball again. Slowly her hands rose to touch it, and as she did so a look of wonder stole into her eyes. "I can lift it," she said.

"Take it off!"

She held it, hesitating. "Will it come off?"

"*It must!*"

Amazed, she lifted it over her head and turned to face the ruby flames, which still flickered menacingly in the cave mouth. She knew what she had to do. "Please come with me," she said. "That fire. . . ."

"The flame will not hurt you."

She felt his hand holding hers and as she stepped forward Gaal walked with her across the floor of the cave and through the ruby flames. To her surprise she felt no pain, only the warmth of his hand around hers. But now she was staring into the face of Medusa, and this time the snake hair did not approach her. Oniy the lips parted, and the great bloodshot eyes stared at her balefully.

Again she looked at the crystal ball now resting in her free hand. She was trembling and her mouth was dry. "You know I do hate it," she said, not daring to look at him, "but it would be kind of nice to keep it." There was silence. "Perhaps just as a souvenir?" she ventured, knowing all the time that she could not.

"Throw it into Medusa's mouth, Mary. You couldn't before, but you can now."

"You must think I'm awful," she said, depression settling over her. Already she had forgotten his great joy in finding her, but when she looked at him she saw to her amazement that he was smiling more broadly than ever.

"Throw it, Mary! Get rid of it!"

Then joy filled Mary, and stretching her arm back she flung the crystal ball with all her strength between Medusa's open lips. An explosion rocked the sea bed. Before their eyes a fire-filled cloud spiraled up to coil from the sea bed into the mists above them. For several moments Mary stared in awe, then turned to look at Gaal, her eyes shining. "I didn't really want it after all," she said. "I mean, I *did* want it, and then. . . . How does it work? I

wouldn't ever want to *touch* it again! And—and to see it do *that!*"

She let herself be folded in his arms again. But excitement began to rise anew within her. "I did it! I did what you said! I threw it into Medusa's mouth! I got rid of the horrid thing! Yuk! I just hate it!" and she pulled away and tried to grab his hands as if to dance again.

But he held her still and said, "It wasn't hard, was it?"

"Hard? It was easy—the easiest thing I've ever done."

"It won't always be that easy, you know."

"But I feel different inside."

"You *are* different inside. You're mine now—mine all the way through!"

She looked at him and took a huge breath. She had no words to express the tremendous thing she felt. "Wow!" she said. "Just . . . wow!"

He pulled a tiny, lead-crystal phial from his robe, unstopped it and bent to let the remaining drops of blood from his ankle flow into it. "Here," he said to Mary, "when next you see King Kardia, he will be in terrible need. Because you deceived him, the power of the witch surrounds him. When you find him, I want you to take my blood and do to him what I did to you. It is the only way he can be delivered."

He spoke gravely, and Mary's face grew solemn as she took the bottle. "Will I see the witch again?" she asked, slipping her right foot back into her shoe.

"Yes, you will."

"Oh, dear! Will she. . . . Will it be all right?"

"You belong to me, now. My blood is upon you."

"And can't she . . . ?"

"You won't let her!"

"Won't I?"

"No!"

"Whenever you see King Kardia, go straight to him. Tell him to take off his right shoe, and then smear the blood on his toe as I smeared it on yours."

"Yes, Gaal."

"You will not see me, but I will be there. So don't be afraid, Mary McNab."

"No, Gaal."

He stepped toward her, placed his warm hands gently on either side of her head and tilted her face to look up at him. His eyes seemed to be saying, "Good-bye."

"You're not going already, are you?"

He spoke slowly and clearly. "In one way I am. But in another way I'll always be with you. You can't get away from me now, Mary McNab."

"How can you go away and not go away at the same time?"

"You won't be able to see me as you do now."

"You mean you'll be invisible?"

"Invisible to you."

He released her, turned and strode into the green dimness, turning to wave before he was swallowed by the mist. Only then did she see that the spiraling cloud was now a wide stairway of hard volcanic ash climbing from the spot where Medusa had been moments before. Of Medusa herself there was no sign.

Slowly and reluctantly she turned to go back to the queen and Prince Tiqvah. As she was about to enter the outer cave her foot kicked a small parchment scroll that she did not remember having seen there before. Stooping she picked it up. It bore a blue wax seal, and there was writing on it that said, "To My Servant Wesley."

"He must have dropped it when we were dancing," she said to herself. "I guess the Friesens really must be coming."

She ran into the second cave and the faces of Suneidesis and Prince Tiqvah turned toward her as she did so. "It was Gaal," she said. "He broke the witch's spell, and he said I belong to him now!" They were staring at her strangely. "He actually danced me around. I thought he was mad at me at first, but he wasn't." Still they stared blankly at her, and she stopped talking, wondering what was the matter.

"Who are you?" Tiqvah asked slowly.

"I'm Mary McNab! I told you before when you asked. Don't you believe me? What's the matter?"

Light broke over the queen's face, and she rose and embraced Mary. "You're different," she said. "You wore an enchanted beauty before, but now there is the light of joy and peace on your countenance."

Mary giggled. "I guess I forgot about that. Did I scare you?" She giggled again, realizing now why they had looked at her so strangely. They had not recognized the old Mary McNab. Or was she the old Mary McNab? Her eyes shone when she thought about her reflection in the pool.

Tiqvah was laughing, too. "I recognized the gown your ladyship wore, and you had told us your beauty was enchanted—but your *face* . . ." and he blushed. "Your pardon, my lady. I mean no discourtesy. For there is a gentleness and a happiness about your own face that is warmer and clearer than any enchanted beauty." He bowed low.

Mary was eager to go on with her story, but they heard the stamping of horses in the cave mouth and the clamor of voices. They stood still.

"Poseidon?" Tiqvah whispered.

But Mary was sure she had heard Kurt's voice. "No, I think it's my cousins!" she half whispered, half squealed.

"Can you be sure?" The queen's low voice was concerned.

"Yes, yes, I'm absolutely certain."

The queen was smiling, yet her manner was stately. "We must greet them with every courtesy. They are visitors from distant worlds," she said. For Mary joy was being added to joy. Her nightmare seemed to be over at last. What did it matter that they were at the bottom of the sea in another world? Her cousins had found her.

From the mouth of the outer cave a conversation could clearly be overheard, and for a few seconds none of them in the inner cave moved.

"It's a cave! Let's see what it's like inside," they heard Kurt say.

"We might even find them here," Wesley replied.

"I think not, my lord," a dwarf's low voice continued. "If they were imprisoned there would be someone guarding them."

"Then be careful, Wes," they heard Lisa caution. "There might be guards inside."

By this time the rescue party had discovered the mouth of the Cave of Gaal. Suddenly Lisa, Wesley and Kurt were all standing in the entrance and Mary leaped to her feet shouting, "Wesley! Lisa! Kurt!" Wesley, who had been the first to enter, started in amazement. Lisa stood stock-still, her mouth gaping wide and her eyes shining. Only Kurt yelled at the top of his lungs. "They're here!"

Then there came a chorus of delighted shouts that echoed among the rocky walls. For a few moments everyone was talking at once. They embraced and bowed and curtsied. They laughed and chattered. Mr. & Mrs. Raccoon found themselves wandering among a forest of moving legs and looked up into flushed and excited faces, while Twitterpitter hopped and fluttered from one of Wesley's shoulders to the other cheeping, "Oh, my! Oh, my, my, *my!*"

Lisa curtsied hesitantly to the queen. "Your majesty!" she said, half laughing, half uncertain of herself. For when they had last met, Suneidesis had been little more than a girl and the two, who had shared many adventures together, had called each other by their first names. But on this visit Suneidesis was old enough to be Lisa's mother.

"You have not changed," the queen said, shaking her head. "You are no different than when you came here a quarter of a century ago while I am grown old and have a son. But you are still my friend, Lisa—and I must still be 'Sun' to you." And Lisa laughed and threw her arms around Queen Suneidesis.

But between Mary and the Friesens there were moments of hesitation and embarrassment. "Hello, Mary. I'm so glad you're O.K. We were worried about you," Wesley said rather stiffly. "We knew you'd got here but we were scared something might have happened to you."

Mary's face was red, and her eyes shining, but for a moment now that she had met them, she had nothing else to say.

"Much has happened to the lady Mary," Prince Tiqvah said. "Many and great have been the perils she has passed through."

"But Gaal made it all right," said Mary, finding she could speak after all, though her voice was hoarse and shaky.

"Oh, so *that's* how it is!" replied Kurt with a broad grin adding, "Yeah. I can tell. It's in your face." His tone was so warm and friendly that she knew she was now one of them, not an outsider from Toronto but someone who shared the secrets of Anthropos. She wanted to say something, but her lips were trembling, and she found she had to keep swallowing. So she just said, "Hi!" and hoped she wouldn't start crying. Yet she was happy not sad, happier than she could ever remember being.

Kurt put his arm around her shoulder. "I felt real bad about the way I talked to you when you first came to Uncle John's—you know, those things I said about your mom. I shouldn't have said them."

"It's O.K."

"It's *not* O.K. I was pretty stupid—eh?"

Mary looked up at him, smiling shakily through tear-filled eyes. "My nose is running," she said.

"Oh, shucks. And I don't have any Kleenex." Kurt looked so worried that Mary giggled and cried a little more and giggled again. "You'll have to sniff *real hard,*" Kurt said earnestly. Whereupon Mary spluttered into helpless laughter and told him to quit making her laugh.

They sat around on the floor in Gaal's Cave, and there were more cries of wonder from Inkleth and the Friesen children, who had sheltered in it from the deadly Qadar during their previous visit to Anthropos.

"How can it be here when it's on the top of a hill?" Kurt mused, wonderingly.

But the mystery of Gaal's Cave would have to wait for at that moment Mary remembered the scroll she had found on the floor of the outer cave, and she held it out to Wesley. "It's for you," she said. "I think it's from Gaal."

Wesley's eyes shone and his fingers shook as he took the scroll, broke the seal and unrolled it. While he stared at the writing no one breathed, waiting for him to start reading. At length, Wesley began.

Gaal, Lord of ice and fire and of that light which overcomes all darkness, with the High Emperor and the Holy One, Ruler of all that is: To my servant Wesley.

Greetings.

Your task has now begun. I commend to your care the Queen of Anthropos-Playsion and her son. You are to conduct them through whatever perils may lie ahead of you to the Playsion man-of-war Thunderhead. She who was once Medusa is now a stairway leading to a rising finger of fire through which you will be led to the Kingdom of Darkness and to the throne room of the wicked lady. Three perils await you. Poseidon will try to do you a great evil. Let your sister Lisa remember the value of the truth that lies in her hands. Then the sound that strikes terror and dismay will fill your brother Kurt with fear. For the real guardian of Poseidon's Kingdom is the giant rooster with deadly spurs. Him must Kurt slay, if you are to escape. Let Kurt remember that he whom Gaal pardons is pardoned indeed, and let him strike his foe with the Sword of Geburah!

Only Mary and yourself will enter the throne room. Your brother Kurt and my servant Inkleth will lead the rest of my servants down to the ship, where your brother will bid the ship's company awake.

The witch and my servant Kardia will be found in the throne room. You are to let one drop of my blood fall on the ice before the Lady of Night, and she will know her doom is come. Your cousin Mary knows her task already.

Fear not. I watch over you. Only flee to the ship when your tasks are accomplished. The time will be short.

He paused, still staring at the scroll.

"Is that all?" Kurt asked.

"What does it mean? Whatever is a finger of fire? And what's the Thunderhead?" Lisa wondered aloud.

"The Thunderhead is a Playsion man-of-war," Queen Suneidesis said slowly. "Kardia, my royal husband is coming then. Doubtless he journeys here on board the Thunderhead. But you are to find him in the throne room of the Palace of Darkness. As for the fingers of fire—there are prophecies that when Mirshaath brings the curse of darkness upon the earth, fingers of fire will reach up from the earth's core to consume her."

"And Medusa will lead us to a finger of fire!" Mary sounded scared.

"What about Poseidon?" Lisa asked. "Whatever is he going to do? A great evil! Sounds awful. And what d'you think Gaal means about . . . how did he put it?"

Wesley glanced at the letter again. "Here it is. 'Let your sister Lisa remember the value of the truth that lies in her hands.' "

"It doesn't make sense."

Queen Suneidesis pointed at Lisa's hands. "What *is* lying in your hands?"

"Oh, *this,*" Lisa replied, lifting the Mashal Stone by its chain so that its blue light danced on the walls of the cave. "I've been carrying it all the way from Goldcoffin's Palace. Sir Dipsuchos let someone borrow it from the palace treasury years ago, and I guess it got to Goldcoffin somehow via Mirmah. Goldcoffin gave it to me."

The queen looked grave, yet all she said was, "Even the evil of our enemies seems to be turning to our good."

"But it still doesn't solve my problem," Lisa said. "Gaal was talking about *truth* not about the Mashal Stone."

"Is it not a stone of truth?"

"Oh!" A look of surprised delight crossed Lisa's face. They crowded round to look at the beautiful stone, still gleaming as Lisa held it up. "Of course! It lets you see things *as they really are* when you put it on. And it also means that evil beings cannot see you. Mebbe that has something to do with truth too."

"I wonder what he means by one drop of his blood," Wesley mused.

It was Mary's turn to hold something up and, she showed them the crystal vial. "Gaal gave it to me," she said. "It's got some of his blood inside. I guess I could spare a drop. The rest of it's for Kardia." A hush fell over them all.

"His blood?"

"He stuck his sword into a scar in his ankle, and he smeared some on me. He said," and her face reddened with both shame and joy, "he said I belong to him now." Quietly she slipped the flask into the pocket of her velvet gown.

Kurt said nothing. When Wesley had read the words about the "sound that strikes terror and dismay," his heart seemed to settle slowly down to about the level of his knees. He knew now that he could not escape. He would get to hear the one sound he dreaded. And how would the rest of them escape if he failed to kill his terrible foe? He hoped none of the others would see how scared and how sick he felt, and he pretended to be interested in his boots. Why did Gaal have to choose something so impossibly hard? Was Gaal mad at him for some reason? Was this some kind of punishment? He pictured the enormous rooster in his mind, and it seemed to him that he could see the creature waiting for him, gloating over him. It seemed too as though it was the same rooster that had haunted him all his life. His terror grew and with it a sense of guilt. Had Gaal really forgiven him for what he had done so long ago in the Tower of Geburah? At the time he was sure he had. Yet he felt, illogically, that it was his own fault that he had to face the rooster. "I'm getting to be just like Wes," he thought.

No one had noticed Kaas and Tiqvah sitting in a dark corner at the back of the cave. Kaas had been weeping. His face was pale and his eyes red. Tiqvah's arm was round the boy's shoulders, and he was talking quietly to him. Wesley glanced at the queen enquiringly.

"He is my son's friend," Suneidesis said softly. "His grief is great for his father betrayed us."

"I know," Wesley said, "and on the trip he's been just tremendous. He said he wanted to atone for what his father did—and he really has. What happened to his father?"

"The witch beheaded him."

"Does he know?"

"He does now."

"Oh, I'm so sorry."

From time to time sympathetic glances were cast back at the two whose heads were bent together in the back of the cave. Everyone, for the moment, felt it better to leave them alone.

Queen Suneidesis was passing out pieces of a loaf of bread. Its crust was crisp and crackly, and its center warm and soft. They could smell the smell of baking. It seemed as she passed the pieces of it round that the loaf grew no smaller in size. There was fish, too, freshly cooked (though there was no means of cooking it in the cave) and steaming hot, which they took and laid on their hunks of bread. No one asked questions. "Gaal's bread and Gaal's meat," Suneidesis called it. Yet they all ate until they were filled, eagerly swapping tales of their adventures. They seemed to eat and to talk for hours.

Kaas and Tiqvah joined them, and Lisa squeezed Kaas's hand without saying anything. In spite of his grief, Kaas blushed with pleasure as they described the way he had made Goldcoffin's Meadow safe from fire and how he had run down the stairway ahead of them so that he would be the first to face danger.

They drank water from a cup they passed round. It

was cold and refreshing, and it sparkled on their tongues and their throats with a sense of life and strength. Their limbs grew strong, and their eyes grew clear. Slowly the storytelling grew ragged, interspersed with silences, and one by one they grew sleepy. "It would be well to rest," the queen said. "Once we set out we will need all our strength."

Her words made sense. Slowly they all found places in the cave where the ground was a little less bumpy, and one after another they were overcome by drowsiness. Within half an hour only Kurt lay awake, restlessly rolling from side to side as he tried to shut out of his mind the terrible sound of a crowing rooster.

26

The Peril of Poseidon

Wesley woke to hear a man's melodious voice. It was a deep voice that filled him with awe by its strangeness. He rubbed his eyes and sat up. Around him on the floor of Gaal's Cave everyone else was asleep. Kurt had huddled against the wall with Mr. & Mrs. Raccoon. The queen lay on the straw bed and on the floor beside her stretched Lisa and Mary. Kaas and Tiqvah lay together in the back of the cave where the prince had tried to comfort the bereaved boy some hours earlier. Inkleth, soldier as he was, had stretched himself across the mouth of the cave, to serve as a living door. Wesley groped for his sword belt.

The singing continued, and as Wesley listened he realized that the music was calling him, drawing him almost against his will into the outer cave. For several minutes he resisted the urge to move. It was like no other singing he had ever heard, for though he could not understand the words, the song conjured sea pictures in his mind, not pictures of the gentle blue sea, but pictures of crashing and angry seas, breaking in their fury over defiant black rocks. He could almost hear the cries of shipwrecked sailors and the fury of a gale.

Soon he could no longer resist the music. Cautiously he rose to his feet, strapped the sword belt round his waist and stepped across Inkleth's sleeping body into the outer cave. Then fear coiled coldly and tightly around his chest.

Poseidon sat on a rock, his back to Wesley, facing the mouth of the outer cave. Beyond him on the sand he could see the god's white horses and his chariot. His body was enormously powerful, the muscles rippling over his shoulders and back, yet the grace in his swaying movement and the strange sense of command and of majesty made Wesley realize that Poseidon could never be mistaken for a human athlete. His black hair, green-streaked, fell back over his mighty shoulders. When his song ended he burst into a roar of laughter, turned slowly round and drew himself to his full height on the rock.

As he did so his manner changed. The laughter left his face. His eyes narrowed, while his lips set in a straight line. "Servant of the great Mi-ka-ya," he said, "now I know you are indeed sent by Mi-ka-ya for I see Medusa is no longer one of us." He stood stock-still, staring at Wesley, whose head pounded uncomfortably. Poseidon continued. "Nevertheless I am come to hold you to your bargain. Soon the green light fades and the red begins to dawn. I am here to collect my prize."

Wesley drew the Sword of Geburah. "Your prize?" he asked.

"The maid you promised me, servant of Mi-ka-ya."

"The maid? What maid?"

Then Poseidon threw back his head and laughed until the cave rang with his laughter. The more he laughed, the more afraid Wesley became. "The servants of Mi-ka-ya may not lie, be they mortal or be they gods! Strange words you used when I spoke of the other maid who had penetrated my kingdom at the bidding of Mirmah. 'Her I may take?' I begged the servants of El. And you replied, ..." and then Wesley heard his own voice sounding across Poseidon's Kingdom, "I guess so!"

He could not tell why, and he still did not realize whom or what Poseidon wanted, but his heart began to sink. He had walked into some kind of trap. What other maid was there besides Lisa?

Then he remembered—*Mary!* So this was the peril of Poseidon that Gaal had warned them about! Poseidon had come to collect Mary and seemed to believe he had a right to claim her, and that he, Wesley, had given him that right.

"I never promised Mary to you. I didn't know what you were talking about."

A quietness settled over the god. Outside the white horses moved restlessly. Then he spoke calmly. "I shall wait, servant of Mi-ka-ya. Your promise will be kept. It is a word that cannot change. No servant of Mi-ka-ya can break a promise." He seemed to be looking above Wesley's head and Wesley began to feel, after a minute or so, that Poseidon had forgotten him. He seemed simply to be waiting to take Mary away in much the same way a customer who has bought a box of candy in a store waits for the clerk to wrap it.

Wesley grew desperate. "You don't understand," he said. "Mary can't stay here. In any case I didn't make any bargain. I told you already—I didn't know you were talking about Mary. It's a misunderstanding. Don't you see? It wasn't a promise at all."

It was as though Poseidon never heard him, as though he had turned himself into marble. Wesley had no idea what to do. He glanced down at the naked blade of his sword and felt foolish. Somehow the thought of attacking Poseidon with it seemed silly. You can't attack someone who ignores you. As he stared beyond the god he saw that the strange green half-light outside the cave was tinged with red. Twice Poseidon had talked about their having to leave the kingdom before the green light turned to red. It had sounded as though he were talking about traffic signals, but now the diffuse light in Poseidon's Kingdom *was* changing. Their time was evidently short. Something, Wesley had no idea what, seemed about to happen. His throat began to tighten.

A noise made him turn round. Suneidesis, Tiqvah and Inkleth were standing in the entrance of Gaal's Cave. The other members of the party also began to crowd through the door. The queen looked at Poseidon, and then at Wesley.

"Why is he here?" she asked in a low voice.

"He says I promised him that he could take Mary with him. But I didn't even know Mary was here. It's all a misunderstanding."

Suneidesis looked grave. "Keep her back inside Gaal's Cave," she whispered to Inkleth.

"When I tried to talk to him about it he just kind of froze—made himself like a statue," Wesley went on. He stared at Poseidon, half embarrassed, uncertain whether the god was listening to them or not. From the top of the rock he dominated the cave.

Inkleth returned and whispered something to the queen.

"Are you sure?" Suneidesis asked him.

"Quite sure, your majesty. It is only half the size it was."

Tiqvah turned to peer behind them at the inner cave mouth as Kurt emerged from it saying, "Wes, the cave is shrinking—Gaal's Cave, I mean. It's sort of squeezing us out like toothpaste."

Wesley turned to look. "Oh, *no!*" he said. "Whatever shall we do with Mary? Is she still inside? We've *got* to get away. The light is turning red too, and don't ask my why, but that seems to mean we can't stay here."

Something made him look up at Poseidon. The god was smiling down at him from the rock. "Can Mi-ka-ya not help you? No, I suspect he cannot. Not when you try to deny me my rightful prize. Aha!" He leaped down and strode toward them as he saw Mary and Lisa emerge from the inner cave. No one except Lisa had time to think. Poseidon brushed past Wesley and Kurt. His arms were held wide, and he was laughing hugely. In two bounds he was beside Mary.

"The Mashal Stone!" Wesley yelled.

But Lisa was already flinging the pendant over Mary's head. As the god reached for Mary he brushed Lisa aside. Then his arms wrapped themselves round empty space. Mary had disappeared.

The queen's voice rang through the cave. "Flee! All of you, flee at once! Flee to the stairway! Fly for your lives!" They scrambled in a mad rush for the mouth of the cave. Poseidon's roar made Wesley's ears ring. Lightning crackled and flashed around him blinding him so that he could scarcely see where he was going or where anybody was. He ran blindly, sensing rather than seeing that he was now out of the cave and near the foot of the stairway. He tripped and fell, and rough volcanic stone tore the skin on his bare hands. He felt no pain, but was up on his feet, stumbling, still blindly, up the stairway. Around him he could hear the others, and once he was sure he heard Mary laughing. But again Poseidon's roar, like a clap of thunder, made the stairway shake under his feet. Lightning exploded round him, dying to leave a thousand colored lights dancing in front of his eyes. Yet he dared not stop. Hoping desperately that the others were safe, he struggled clumsily upward.

He tripped and fell a second time and lay winded, unable to move for several precious seconds while he struggled to fight the awful feeling of suffocation. The dancing colored lights slowly died away, and as his breathing eased, he found he was lying alone on Medusa's Stairway a house's height above the ocean floor. Above him the rest of the party were looking at the sea bed. He looked himself and saw that Poseidon was again balanced recklessly on his chariot, the reins of fifty horses in his left hand and a trident flashing lightning from his right. He was making no attempt to pursue them. Fifty white horses were galloping madly away over the shifting sea bed. From time to time the god would turn and without pausing send yet another lightning flash to crackle around the base of the stairway, and continue his mad rush.

Hearing laughter behind him Wesley turned to see who was there. But he was alone. "It *is* just like Disneyland," Mary's voice sounded from thin air slightly above him. "He's not a god at all. He's made of some kind of plastic stuff, and there are funny little goblin things making him work. He's just an enormous puppet. I knew all along it must be something like that. I bet Medusa was a fake too."

"How d'you mean?" It came to Wesley then that Mary must still be wearing the Mashal Stone around her neck and that she was standing a little above him on the stairway.

"I was terrified when I came out of Gaal's Cave and saw him leaping at me. He looked so real, like he wanted to eat me. But when Lisa put this pendant thing round me, I could see through all the phony stuff. I wish you could have seen what he really looked like—just a great big doll to scare everyone. There were these funny little demons. One of them was making his face work, you know, making him smile and frown. Another one did the talking, and there were all sorts of them working his arms and legs. It was real neat how they did it."

Wesley listened fascinated, as below them the distant charioteer lashed his horses into the reddening mists.

"I thought some of these creatures couldn't be real when I first arrived," Mary continued. "I guess it's not really like Disneyland. It's more scary—evil, like. But it's *phony*. This pendant lets you see it."

What Mary said was true. Wesley's thoughts immediately went back to the Battle of Rinnar Heights on their previous visit to Anthropos. He himself had seen how Lady Sheriruth was no woman, and seeing her true shape he had been able to kill her with a good conscience. Yet it had never occurred to him that Poseidon might not be all he seemed.

Cautiously he got to his feet. "We'd better join the others," he said. "And you'd better take that thing off your neck, or I'll be bumping into you. Besides it's spooky to hold a conversation with an invisible cousin."

Mary giggled and promptly reappeared letting the beautiful Mashal Stone dangle from the gold chain in her hand. "I'd better give it to the queen," she said. "Lisa says it's part of the royal treasure. Looks like it's worth a mint."

No one was missing. Mr. & Mrs. Raccoon were in excellent spirits, and even Twitterpitter was gleeful. Mary returned the Mashal Stone to the queen.

They climbed for hours, quickly losing sight of the sea bed and stopping every so often to rest. They grew weary, hungry and thirsty. The stairway wound through misty space while the light grew dim and ever more red in color. Wesley said afterward that he felt like an ant crawling up a coiled spring in a dark room.

Kurt's face was haggard, and he lagged behind the rest almost as though he had not heart to continue. Wesley glanced over his shoulder at him from time to time and eventually dropped back to walk beside him. Wisely he said nothing, and for half an hour they climbed together in silence. At length Kurt sighed.

"I guess Lisa did her part."

"Uh-huh."

"And Mary too."

"Uh-huh."

"It's all over for them."

"Yeah, I guess so. But not for you, eh?"

Again Kurt sighed, and again they climbed without speaking.

At last Kurt said, "But *they did it,* Wes. I mean they didn't blow it or anything. I'm real glad for them both. But they're in the clear now an' I...."

"And you *and I....*"

"Yeah, you too. I keep forgetting that. But you're not scared. And you're like Lisa. You'll make out O.K."

Wesley searched for words. "It's not wrong to be scared, Kurt."

"I know. But Wes—if I fail, we'll all be trapped here. If I don't get rid of that creature.... An' it's not so much being scared that sickens me, leastwise not... oh, shucks, it sounds so dumb!"

"What does?"

"Wes, I'm scared of blowing the whole thing. What if I run away? I'm ashamed, Wes."

He looked so dejected that if Wesley had been the hugging kind, he would have put his arm round his brother's shoulder. But Wesley never could hug people and always stiffened up if anyone else tried to hug him.

"I'm scared I'll let everyone down, Wes, an' I don't want to. I really don't want to. Why ever is Gaal making me do it? You know what he meant by the 'sound that strikes terror and dismay,' don't you?"

"I suppose he meant the rooster."

"He couldn't have chosen anything worse. I mean—a *rooster!* Wes, he must know how scared they make me. Is he punishing me? Have I done something wrong?"

Wesley shook his head. "I don't know, Kurt," he said, and once more they fell silent.

"Wes?" Kurt said eventually.

"Uh-huh?"

"Could you—could you *stay* with me when it comes? It's facing it alone that, that scares me. I've been dreaming about it. An' each time I seem to be running toward it with the Sword of Geburah in my hand, hoping it will turn and run. But it never does. It screeches and runs *at* me instead. An' all the rest of you just watch. You don't do anything. I wake up screaming an' sweating like a pig. Come with me when I have to fight it, Wes."

"Sure I'll come, don't worry. It's going to be all right." But privately Wesley was beginning to wonder.

"What was it Gaal said in the letter? When you read the bit about the 'sound,' it was like being hit by a block of concrete. I didn't hear anything else." He paused. "If only I knew Gaal wasn't mad at me. Oh, Wes, what have I done? I must have done something."

Wesley was frowning. "Let's sit down a second," he said. "We can catch up to the others easily enough."

He pulled the parchment from inside his parka and unrolled it, pursing his lips. "Here it is—'Then the sound that strikes terror and dismay will fill your brother Kurt with fear. For the real guardian of Poseidon's Kingdom is the giant rooster with deadly spurs. Him must Kurt slay, if you are to escape. *Let Kurt remember that he whom Gaal pardons is pardoned indeed,* and let him strike his foe with the Sword of Geburah!' "

" 'He whom Gaal pardons . . .'?" Kurt began.

" '. . . is pardoned indeed,' " Wesley finished.

Kurt's face was blank. "Read that part again, Wes!"

Wesley did so.

"And again, Wes, please."

For the third time Wesley read the words, and then because they seemed to mean something to his brother, he read them yet a fourth time.

Kurt breathed in slowly. " 'He whom Gaal pardons is pardoned indeed!' Wes, I've kept thinking back to what Inkleth and I did on the island. I know he *said* he forgave me, and at the time I really believed him. But since then. . . ." He laughed shakily. "Pardoned indeed! Boy, that sounds good! Mebbe he's not mad at me any more than he was at Mary. Mebbe it's not a punishment."

"No, mebbe its some sort of test."

They sat for a full minute each wrapped in his thoughts. "Still scared?" Wesley asked at length.

"Yeah, I'm scared. But I feel a bit better. Listen, Wes, do me a favor. If we come across this thing—I know it sounds crazy—but if we come across it, would you stand right near me and read the letter out loud, especially the pardon bit. Would you?"

"Sure!"

"Promise?"

"I promise."

"You don't think it's dumb?"

"It *is* kind of dumb—but for you I'll do it!"

"Oh, Wes, thanks! You will?"

"Sure, I will!"

Unlike Wesley, Kurt *was* the hugging kind, and he flung his arms round his brother, burying his face in Wesley's shoulder. Wesley tried not to stiffen up, and if he did, Kurt probably didn't notice. Eventually he lifted his head and released his brother.

"Feel O.K. now?" Wes asked. Kurt nodded. As they got to their feet Wesley unfastened the sword belt that had been round his waist for many hours. He held it out, the sword and scabbard hanging from it. Kurt took it and buckled it on himself. He remembered his pleasure at doing so days before on their ride out of Nephesh. Then it was fun. But now he was arming himself for a reason.

"Ready?" Wesley asked. He nodded without smiling. Two minutes later they were both hurrying up the steps, their legs weak but somehow refreshed, to catch up with the main party.

27

He Who Is Pardoned

The curving stairway had grown narrower. It was now no wider than your basement steps; so the party had to proceed in single file. Most of them felt a little lightheaded. There was no rail to protect them from falling to a terrible death a mile or so beneath them. Happily the red dimness made it impossible for them to see what lay below. Even so their stomach muscles would tighten apprehensively from time to time at the thought of the emptiness under their feet.

It seemed strange to sit down to rest one above the other. Wesley, by this time, was at the head of the party. Kurt sat just below him, then Tiqvah and Kaas. Inkleth brought up the rear. Wesley called to the queen who was sitting below Kaas and above Lisa and Mary, both of whom were fondling the raccoons. "Your majesty is still able to continue?"

Suneidesis smiled. "What choice do I have? My limbs feel like water, but I have no doubt they will take me a little further yet. I believe, my lord Wesley, that we must be almost beneath the Kingdom of Darkness."

"Really?" Lisa sounded eager. "How can you tell?"

"By the feeling in my limbs! I know Gaal. He might make us go on *almost* until we drop. And I have now reached my 'almost'!"

"Me too, your majesty," Mary sighed.

Conversation lapsed. For several minutes they sat in silence, tired, yet heartened by a conviction they all shared, that their climb must be near its end.

Without any warning the silence was shattered by the crowing of a cock somewhere above them. It was a loud, shrill, piercing and terrifying sound which echoed emptily in the red obscurities around them. Kurt was not the only one to jump, but he jumped the most, and his legs began to quake. Mechanically he got to his feet. His legs, as Suneidesis had so aptly put it, felt like water— trembling columns of water. Carefully he pushed past Wesley trying to avoid his brother's eyes. He had the curious sensation that everything had happened before. It began to feel like a dream too, a dream in which he had no power to change anything. His feet moved by themselves as though he were a passenger inside himself and somebody else was driving. He mounted the narrow stair slowly, drawing the Sword of Geburah as he did so. He wanted to call to Wesley to follow behind him as he had promised, but though he opened his mouth, no words came, and he dared not turn round. Above him the stairway disappeared into red mist. There was no sign of the rooster.

Then he saw it—a gargantuan black shadow looming in the mist above him. It was several times as wide as the steps. He stopped, painfully aware of the narrowness of the stairway and of the limitless drop on either side. The shadow gave vent to a second trumpeted screech, and Kurt gasped as though somebody had thrown water over him. Even the sword, shimmering with blue light, was shaking piteously in his hand. Slowly he placed one trembling foot after another, moving toward the shadow, feeling his end had come and that he was powerless to escape.

The rooster's shape became sharp and the blackness turned to gleaming copper and green. Beneath a flaming crest one wicked black eye was fixed on him. He drew in a frightened breath, awed at the creature's magnificence, at the proud, puffed-out chest, the scornful toss of the head. His ascent became slower. He could see now that the stairway was a delicate bridge connected to a wall of rock beyond the rooster. Carved in the face of the rock a pathway proceeded up toward the Dark Kingdom. But to get to the rocky pathway they would have to deal with the rooster.

"You will not escape from Poseidon's Kingdom this way, little man," the rooster crowed. "State your business!"

Kurt stood still. To his surprise he found he had a voice. "I am a follower of Gaal."

The rooster crowed loudly again. "A follower of Gaal? You follow him only because you didn't achieve your wicked ambition to be a magician. You are still a follower of Shagah in your heart!"

So the rooster knew all about him! What hope of escape did he have? He was a phony. In the depths of his soul he knew it. In grim despair he pointed his sword at the rooster and with a pitiful cry began to run shakily toward it. It watched him until he was a dozen steps below and

then shot its long neck forward, spread its wings and ran at him.

Kurt screamed, closed his eyes and covered his face with his left arm. His nightmare was happening all over again, only now he was awake. He could hear Wesley shouting something repeatedly, but he was too frightened to listen. The terrible beak was about to strike him. He expected any moment that the awful wings would beat him and knock him off the staircase into the void. But they never did. Wesley continued to shout, and now he could hear the words, " . . . he whom Gaal pardons is pardoned indeed, and let him strike his foe with the Sword of Geburah!"

The expected blows never came. He dropped his arm and opened his eyes. To his surprise the rooster was farther back up the stairway, still facing him, still puffed and proud in its gleaming colors. He gripped his sword more firmly.

"A follower of Gaal?" the creature cried mockingly. "Do you suppose Gaal can forgive the insulting remarks you made about the only mother your cousin Mary had ever known? Or that you made it cruelly clear to Mary she was not wanted in Winnipeg?"

Once more in whimpering rage Kurt raised his sword. This time he rushed at the rooster, not caring, at least for a second or two, what would happen. But again when the long neck shot out at him, and the wings spread and the scrawny legs began to run, terror paralyzed him afresh. His wide eyes saw clawed feet sweep up above him for a moment and the cruel spurs come speeding down toward him. He covered his face a second time.

"He whom Gaal pardons, . . ." the words were hammering into his brain, " . . . let him strike his foe with the Sword of Geburah."

When he opened his eyes the rooster was still farther up the stairway, almost where it reached the pathway in the rock.

"A follower of Gaal?" it shrieked. "Gaal knows you inside out. How can he respect a boy who was too scared to go down the stairs into Poseidon's Kingdom—scared by his silly dreams?"

But Wesley's words were clearer, " . . . pardoned indeed."

The words acted on him like an electric shock. Kurt could never quite explain what happened next. Excitement and joy woke inside him. "Gaal pardoned me!" he yelled. "Listen, you dumb bird—*he pardoned me!*" He was running now, running and laughing toward the enormous creature, running and waving the shimmering Sword of Geburah as though it were a toy. "I'm coming at you! I don't care what you say or what you do! I belong to Gaal, and I'm going to strike you with the Sword of Geburah!"

He felt like yelling more, but he needed his breath to go on running. Again the neck shot out, but he never hesitated. The rooster began to spread its wings, but he cried, "Here I come, you big bird; you can't scare me!"

Then with a sudden sweep it turned round so that he found himself running into a curtain of shimmering green tail feathers. Laughing hysterically he slashed at them again and again, until the air was filled with floating pieces of feather as he steadily hacked away the rooster's tail, crying, "I'm a servant of Gaal! I'm a servant of Gaal! I'm a servant of Gaal!"

And well he might laugh. There are few funnier sights than a tailless, giant rooster, its rump wiggling in panic as it struggles to get its clumsy body onto a ledge that is far too small for it. Its claws scrabbled on the stairway.

It was trying to push its way against the wall of rock and to perch on the narrow pathway. But one of the feet slipped and the enormous body rolled sideways to topple into the void. With a squawk of terror it began to flap its wings to save itself. The last Kurt saw of it, it was flapping and twirling in dizzy circles into the darkness below.

He sat down, weary, breathless but hugely elated. Then the memory of the wiggling stump made him snicker. He tried to control himself as he saw Wesley looking at him, but soon he was laughing till he had to fight for breath. Wesley sat beside him still holding Gaal's letter and laughing too. "Oh, do stop laughing!" Kurt cried at length. "Whenever I stop, you start me off again."

The others were climbing up the stairs to join them and the amusement began to spread up and down the line with snorts and guffaws and chuckles and giggles and snickers and shouts and merry peals of laughter. Inkleth even held his sides and swayed perilously on the narrow stairway. The laughter subsided at length and one by one they followed Kurt and Wesley onto the ledge of rock. It was wide enough for three people to walk along it side by side. "But I'm going to hug the wall," Lisa said, and everyone felt the same way.

"Is this the 'rising finger of fire' the Lord Gaal spoke of?" Inkleth asked quietly, running the palms of his hands over it.

"Could be. I don't know why it would be called that though."

"The rock is warm," Inkleth continued. "Are fires from the world's core rising up through it toward the Kingdom of Cold Darkness?"

Tiqvah, too, was fingering the rock. "The rock trembles," he said with awe. "It is a living thing that breathes and moves."

I forget all the details they gave me about their climb through the floor of the Dark Kingdom. I know they felt frightened about the thought of fires from the world's core inside the moving rock on which they were traveling. I remember, too, that they mentioned there was a lot of water, where ice had melted from its contact with the warm rock, so that a stream ran down the sloping ledge and over the sides. Soon there was more ice than rock until everything was ice. They had a difficult time climbing half-melted ice steps in the near dark, but said that farther up the ice grew firmer and less slippery. What I couldn't quite understand was that they claimed they could see fire through the ice and the moving shadows of ogres, ghouls and goblins. I questioned them several times about it, but they all assured me it was so.

"Ruby-colored flames," Mary said, "rolling slowly and majestically up." Her own eyes rolled up when she described it, and I think she was rather proud of her description. "But you couldn't see anything clearly," Kurt added, "because the ice was so thick. But it was spooky, eh?"

Eventually they came upon a balcony overlooking the courtyard outside the throne room of the Palace of Darkness. Beyond the palace walls and down in the harbor below they could see the Thunderhead. A little exploration sufficed to discover an unguarded archway beyond the fiery gates, and they were soon on their way to the ship.

But Wesley and Mary waited beside the doorway to the throne room, wondering what they would find when they opened the door.

28

In the Palace
of Darkness

"There, your majesty, surely you must now see that Gaal has his hand on this ship!" Gunruth's eyes gleamed. Even Kardia was startled out of the hopelessness that had settled over him. In the harbor below the Palace of Darkness the Thunderhead was slowly turning round to point her bow toward Playsion.

" 'Tis more than an omen," the Matmon continued. "Gaal suffered us to be drawn in, and when the time is ripe Gaal will draw us out!"

They had arrived at their destination in the heart of the Kingdom of Darkness. Swiftly and silently the Thunderhead had been drawn through darkness over ruby-lit waves. Long after they crossed the enchanted circles they had entered the hollow core of the kingdom, sailing under dark skies of ice between black plains of ice until at last they entered a harbor below an ice mountain crowned with a glittering palace, whose walls and turrets glowed with inner ruby fires. The crew and men-at-arms still lay below decks in enchanted slumber.

"That then is the seat of her power," breathed Kardia softly as the Thunderhead gently settled along the quay-side, "and there, doubtless, the witch holds my queen and my son and heir. Yet there is something I cannot understand. If Gaal now calls himself Lord of ice, how is it that this woman hides herself in it?"

Gunruth, like the king, stared at the palace high above them, deaf to what Kardia was saying. His mind had gone back to when years before he had scaled the walls of Authentio Castle with Kardia, with Wesley and with his own son. But his son was now dead, and the walls that faced them this time were enchanted walls.

"How shall we penetrate walls of ice?" he asked slowly.

"Nay," Kardia returned, "do not say 'we.' This time I alone must go. You will be wanted here to aid us should we break free and need to sail in haste."

"Your majesty made use of my skills when we penetrated Authentio. Perchance I may aid you again. Once you are inside the palace I can return here. Give me but a moment to search below decks for a hook to throw, for in my sack I have a ladder of an elfin thread light as gossamer and strong as iron, by which you may safely scale the walls above us."

The pleading in Gunruth's voice was hard to resist. Moreover Kardia knew that the Matmon's skill might enable him to scale walls that otherwise would shut him out. In a few moments the dwarf was back on deck carrying in his hand a quantity of what looked like soft and glimmering gray silk and a triple hook. Kardia in the meantime had released two heavy rope ladders over the side of the ship.

He looked uncertainly at the gossamer in Gunruth's hands. "It looks as if it would part as quickly as a burning straw," he said doubtfully.

"No power in Anthropos could break it," Gunruth said. "It is emeth, and with it the High Emperor suspends worlds in time. It bears the weight of the ages."

When Kardia took the soft stuff in his hands and tugged, he gave a sharp cry of pain. Blood flowed from his hands where tiny threads had cut through the skin.

"You are satisfied, my liege?" Mischief lurked around the corners of Gunruth's smile.

"It is strong indeed," Kardia acknowledged, handing the almost weightless ladder back to Gunruth and wiping the blood from his hands. "But hist!" he continued, his eyes looking at the palace. "We may not need to scale any walls. Someone comes—and it may be Mirmah herself!"

A tiny figure was descending a long and curving flight of steps that came from the palace to the harbor. The light was too poor to see clearly, but as they watched they saw that the person who descended wore a tall, pointed hat and was wrapped with a cloak. It was Archimago. By the time he reached the harbor they knew it was not Mirmah for they could see the red cloak and hat, and soon they saw the skin of the long face, tight and smooth as parchment. Both Kardia and Gunruth descended the rope ladders to meet him as he crossed the quay. He reached the ship just as their feet touched the ice.

"Welcome to the future capital of the world!" the sorcerer said, bowing low. "I am Archimago, prime minister to her majesty, Queen Mirmah, Empress-to-Be of the Darkness that Swallows the World. Her majesty is pleased to grant an audience with Kardia of Anthropos."

If the sceptre in Kardia's hand had remained there,

the king would no doubt have replied. As it was his attention was absorbed with hanging on to the iron rod which for the fourth time began to twist and turn like a living thing. Having come through the Circles of Enchantment he had supposed his troubles with the sceptre would be over. But he was mistaken. A gasp of dismay escaped him as it was torn loose from his fingers, and flew into the hands of Archimago, who again bowed low.

"Her majesty bids me congratulate you on your wisdom. She takes your gift gladly as a token of your free submission to her sovereignty." Then he turned on his heel and walked rapidly away from them.

For a moment Kardia was stunned. It had happened so quickly. Neither he nor Gunruth had spoken a word, and within minutes of their arrival it was all over. Or was it? With a roar of rage he pulled his sword from its scabbard and ran after the figure in red.

Rage added speed to his limbs. If the sceptre had been important to him at the outset of their adventure, it was doubly so now. It meant more to him even than the fate of those nations whose safety lay in his keeping it. The fact that he had so nearly lost it three times in the enchanted circles had created in him a fierce desperation. In fury he ran, and as he caught up with the magician, fury made his sword arm rise up.

But in that same instant the magician swung round and struck the ice between them with the sceptre. There was a loud crack. A chasm opened to separate them. In a flash Kardia caught sight of depths below and the slow upward billowing of enormous flames. A wave of heat singed his beard.

Looking up he caught sight of Archimago beyond the chasm, running hard toward the stairway, and more enraged than ever Kardia leapt desperately across the fiery depths. Miraculously his leap carried him safely over. Consumed by a greater anger than he had ever known, he rushed madly in the magician's wake.

Once more he caught up with him and again Archimago turned and with Kardia's own sceptre opened a second split in the ice over the inferno far below. This time Kardia was unable to check himself. For a horrible second he thought he would plunge to his death, but thrusting his arms and chest forward he somehow succeeded in falling against the far side of the chasm with his chest and arms safely over the ice. For a moment he hung on desperately in terrible pain, his fingers scrabbling frantically on the icy surface. His sword had flown from his hand to slither away along the ice. With a frantic and convulsive struggle he heaved himself to safety, groaning with the pain of his broken ribs. Retrieving his sword he resumed his pursuit of the sorcerer.

Though he had lost considerable ground, his rage was still fierce. But it had become cold and determined rage. Slowly the distance between them decreased. They were mounting the stairway now, Kardia five or six steps below the magician. Twice more Kardia fell while Archimago slipped and fell once. Amazingly, neither of them slipped more frequently. Soon they were only three steps apart. Then two.

"He has to turn to work his magic," Kardia thought to himself, his mind quick and clear though his lungs were ready to burst. "This time I must plunge my sword into him the moment he turns."

As fast as the thought passed through Kardia's mind, the magician spun round. But Kardia was quicker. His sword arm drove forward as though a trigger had released it, and the sword plunged under the magician's ribs into his chest. Before his eyes Kardia watched a web of wrinkles weave itself across the parchment skin. Suddenly he was looking into the face of the oldest man he had ever seen.

The sceptre fell from Archimago's uplifted hand. It struck the stairway as Kardia caught it, and a third chasm yawned below the dead magician's feet. For one second Kardia felt the full weight of Archimago's body supported only by his sword over the abyss. Then the corpse slid from the blade, toppling and plunging like a rag doll into the fires below while Kardia, losing his balance, fell back from the chasm's brink, still clutching his sword with one hand and his sceptre with the other. But the danger was over. The sceptre, at least for the moment, was his.

Soon Gunruth reached the king and helped him to his feet. Every chasm had closed. No sign of them or of the conflict remained. Kardia and the Matmon chief were alone on a staircase of ice. Below them the Thunderhead lay silently at the quayside. From above, the Palace of Darkness looked down on them, glittering with lurid, inner fires.

It took them an hour to reach it. As they drew close, its walls, its turrets, its domes and its pinnacles stared down contemptuously at the tiny figures. What neither Kardia nor Gunruth had been able to perceive earlier they could now see clearly.

"The gates!" Kardia said, steadying himself on Gunruth's arm. "The gates! Look at them!"

Gunruth shook his head, wonderingly. "It is as well we brought the ladder of emeth," he said, for the gates consisted of leaping ruby flames.

"Gates of fire between walls of ice," mused Kardia. " 'Tis a strange welcome."

Apart from the leaping fire, there was no sign of movement. The palace might have been abandoned. Yet Kardia remained watchful as they made their way round the base of the walls.

"A building rises above the wall at this point," Kardia said, looking up. The outer wall formed part of a large building from which two rows of windows shone red. The windows of the upper row were tall and narrow. The row of small, round ones below them made it look as though a giant had written ruby exclamation marks across the wall.

Gunruth unwound a length of the gossamer ladder to which he had attached his hook and began to whirl it round his head. Kardia's mind, like Gunruth's a little earlier, went back many years to Lisa's perilous battle of wits with Ebed Ruach, the jinn, and to the moonlit night when he had watched the Matmon perform this very act below the rugged south wall of Authentio Castle. On that occasion Gunruth made several attempts before he succeeded. But this time, we don't know whether because of the magic emeth or because Gunruth was more expert, the iron hook rose like a bird to settle itself firmly in the ledge of the window far above. Below it, resting on ice walls, the flimsy gossamer ladder glowed faintly as though it were made of moonlight. Gunruth tugged fiercely, but the hook held firm.

Kardia embraced him. "Thank you, friend," he said. He tried to find words to tell him how fond of him he was. Gunruth's help in the Circles of Enchantment had written another chapter in the long story of their friendship. But no words came and the pain of his broken ribs made their embrace a tentative affair.

"Watch well for our coming," the king said, "and should we fail to return—then may Gaal protect you." For a moment his heart stood still. If he did not return,

Gunruth would have nothing to go back to. There would be no Kingdom of Anthropos-Playsion. Only dark and frozen night would remain, ruled by a witch.

Quietly he secured the sceptre in his belt, turned to the ladder and began to climb. "May Gaal go with you!" he heard the Matmon say. He climbed, feeling steely emeth threads under his feet. "If worlds can hang on a thread of emeth, then so may I," he mused wonderingly. In less than a minute he had pulled himself on to the ledge of the circular window. Below him he saw Gunruth's upturned face and knew that the Matmon, reluctant to leave, was waiting until he had disappeared from view. He waved and the wave was returned. Then he scrambled through the opening into ruby light to find himself standing in the throne room of the palace.

It was a wide room and tall. Steps, across the width of the far wall, rose steeply to a high dais. Behind the dais, the wall was covered with the same Tobath Mareh Tapestry he had already seen in the second Circle of Enchantment. Ruby flames from a hundred lamps threw wavering light throughout the chamber. But it was the light *below* the chamber that immediately caught Kardia's attention. Through the floor and the steps of ice he could discern shifting patterns of lurid light and shadow as monstrous silhouettes flowed endlessly beneath his feet. At one point he was sure he could make out a seven-headed ogre, and several times the shadows suggested that ghouls, harpies and giant bloodhounds were lurking among ruby fires under the ice. He shuddered, remembering the grim nights of battle on the Heights of Rinnar years before, and turned his eyes up to the throne.

It was vacant. Flanking it on either side, still rigid as statues, were the six sovereigns of countries surrounding Anthropos-Playsion. And when Kardia saw them it felt as

though a dark hand clutched his heart. He could sense the terror of evil power in the room. Until that moment he had never entirely lost heart. But now it seemed to him (though he could not have told you why) that his cause was hopeless. His mind grew torpid and lethargic. He plucked the sceptre from his belt and looked at it. Why had he struggled so hard to keep it in the face of such odds?

He tried to think of Gaal, to remember what he looked like or how his voice had sounded, but no memory would come. It was as though Gaal had never existed. "It was, after all, only a dream," he murmured, "while this is real, most horribly real, and I am undone." He struggled for several minutes against the almost physical power in the throne room, trying to visualize the forests and fields of Anthropos, or people thronging the marketplace in Nephesh. But the struggle was fruitless. Even the faces of his wife and son were impossible to recapture. His mind seemed trapped by flickering ruby light, by fearsome shadows below the ice and by six grim statues on either side of a crystal throne.

A door beside the throne opened and Mirmah, still in her dark robes and still bearing on her head the high and glittering Crown of Anan, passed through it and sat down. In her hand there was a scroll of paper. It was the letter of defiance that Kardia had written. Deliberately she tore it to pieces, smiling as she did so, and scattered the pieces around her feet.

"At last you have come." Her musical voice rolled from the throne down steps of ice to where Kardia stood. She leaned forward and smiled at him. "Kardia of Anthropos, you have slain a sorcerer who existed from the beginning of time. He served me well. You slew him because you were stronger and swifter than he. Hear me, you whose locks are gray but whose body is the body of a king and warrior. I have ignored the insult of your letter. If you will stay with me and take Archimago's place, I will teach you the deep secrets he knew and every magic art he practiced. What say you, ruler of Anthropos?"

Kardia was silent. The darkness of the place had eaten into him. Mirmah leaned back in the throne and watched him closely.

"I too come from the beginning of our world," she said. "I have known the Lord Archimago since he was a youth in my village. Men called me Mirshaath in those days. But I journeyed to the regions of darkness after men tried to kill me, and I became the bride of the Spirit of the North. Him I slew and him I devoured and now his power is mine. Serve me, Kardia of Anthropos, and this power shall be at your disposal."

Still Kardia said nothing, not because he was resisting her, but because his mind was blank and he had nothing to say. He stared stupidly at the sceptre, wondering what it was, no longer recognizing it. "What is this?" he asked her.

"You were bringing it to me," Mirmah said.

"Was I?" Kardia opened his hand. For a moment the sceptre seemed to balance itself upright. Then it fell, to roll and tumble up the steps to the throne where it lay at the feet of the Lady of Night. Kardia felt that something was wrong, but as he frowned and thought about it, he decided he must be mistaken.

"So you will stay with me," the witch said.

"Of course," Kardia agreed.

29

A Drop of Gaal's Blood

Wesley peered through a crack in the door on the throne room, but he could see nothing clearly. "It goes down in steps," he whispered to Mary. "It's like coming into the back of a concert hall, only there's no stage at the bottom. Give me your little bottle."

"You mean the phial Gaal gave me?"

"Uh-huh. I wasn't sure what you called it."

She passed it to him.

"Be careful with it—eh? Can you see the witch?"

"No. There's a man way at the bottom who looks like Kardia."

Wesley pushed open the door as quietly as he could and they crept through it. They were standing on the dais, behind the crystal throne and to one side of it. Vaguely they were aware of what they thought were six statues, but what were in fact the enchanted rulers. Below them at the foot of the steps stood Kardia. He seemed dazed, and gave no sign of recognition.

"Your name is Wesley, I believe. Come and stand in front of me, Wesley."

The voice (whose owner they could not see) came from the crystal throne. It was a woman's voice warm and musical. They walked round to stand in front of her. Wesley received a shock when he saw how beautiful and how splendid she looked. The Crown of Anan sparkled with lights he had never dreamed of. It reminded him of the crown jewels in the Tower of London—but it was far bigger and the jewels were beyond anything he could have imagined.

He wondered how to address her. Everything about her made him want to be on his best behavior. Yet one part of him knew she was evil and ruthless. He bowed, feeling that courtesy didn't mean you were siding with the enemy. The witch stared only at Wesley. As she smiled at him, he realized she must be the most beautiful person he had ever seen. Yet he didn't smile back, feeling that to do so would be disloyalty to Gaal.

"So solemn!" she said. "Yet I know you are of honest heart. Among all the servants of Gaal from worlds afar, you are the one who means most to me."

"But you don't know me, ma'am."

"I know you, ah, yes, I know you. I know your heart." The smile disappeared from her lips, and a look of infinite sadness replaced it.

"Don't trust her!" Mary whispered fiercely. "She just puts it on."

The witch ignored her. "It is not easy to govern," she told Wesley. "Decisions must be made that I find very difficult to make." She raised a delicate hand to her forehead and sighed. "I want you to take a message from me to Gaal," she said.

Wesley's face flushed. "Madam, Gaal has instructed me to place a drop from this bottle before your throne."

Did the witch start? Or had he imagined it? Certainly she seemed self-possessed immediately after he had spoken.

"You must do whatever Gaal bids you."

"I'll say he must!" Mary stamped her foot.

"I would not have you deviate one hairsbreadth from his instructions."

"Not much, she wouldn't! Don't listen to her, Wesley!"

Wesley was embarrassed, but he knew something of what Mary had been through. "Madam, I cannot blame my cousin. Your plans for her were . . . well, they were pretty awful."

"If Gaal only knew, . . ." the witch said with a look of pain and distress. "If he only knew what I have to tell him, there would be no need for a drop from the phial. All would be well."

Wesley hardened his heart. "I'm sorry, ma'am." He unstopped the phial. "I'm sorry. I just have to do it. We can talk about your message later."

"STOP!"

Wesley jumped. The witch's scream echoed throughout the throne room. There was no doubt now about her fear. Or was it fear? She rose to her feet, passionate rage distorting her face. "Let one drop of that blood be seen in this place. . . ." She held the sceptre above her head. For the first time Wesley saw that it was the Sceptre of Anthropos. "Know then, messenger of Gaal, that you have lost. Shed but one drop of blood and I will break this sceptre!"

"She means it!" Wesley muttered, frightened.

Mary said nothing.

"The power to darken the nations lies in my hands. But I will not take this final step if you will but stopper the phial and go back to Gaal bearing my message."

"But Gaal said. . . ."

"As you will," she was speaking more calmly now. "If the blood is spilled, I will break the sceptre and darken a whole continent. The destiny of a continent, nay, of a world lies in your hands, servant of Gaal."

"She's trying to stop you, Wes. Perhaps she knows that once the drop of blood is spilled she'll have had it!"

Wesley's hands were shaking. He looked at the bottle, and his mind seemed to be blank. He heard his own voice saying, "I'm sorry ma'am, but I've got to. . . ."

As he tipped the phial, the witch hurled herself forward to reach for it. Mary threw herself in front of the witch, knocking against Wesley's arm as she did so. The phial flew from Wesley's hand spilling blood on the ice. Mary lunged across the ice to seize it. The witch shrank back to the crystal throne. Mary, the phial in her hand, stumbled and slithered down the steps toward Kardia.

Wesley was dazed. He stared first at the witch who had dropped the sceptre and was sitting motionless upon the throne, and then at the spreading crimson before it. The ice beneath their feet shuddered, and Wesley could feel that it was sinking. His attention was arrested by the statues. One by one they began to move. The creature that looked half bear and half man shook its head. From nowhere a rod appeared in its paw. Groggily it began to lumber down the steps away from the throne. A graceful giant of a woman threw back her leafy hair and suddenly, alive with laughter, began to follow him while a dainty flower fairy in turn ran and danced to catch up with her. The other three rulers stared at Wesley and at the witch and with still greater surprise at the sceptre they found themselves carrying. No word was spoken. In a daze they began to follow the sovereigns of the trees and flowers and beasts.

The shuddering of the dais grew more pronounced. It was sinking rapidly. The steps that had once led up to the throne now began to lead down. Startled, Wesley turned and scrambled up out of the hollow into which the throne was sinking. He never noticed the Sceptre of Anthropos, still lying at the witch's feet.

While all this was going on, Mary had run to Kardia. "Your majesty!" she said. "It's me, Mary McNab!"

Kardia looked at her solemnly and his look puzzled her. Did he recognize her? She could tell something was wrong. "Take your boot off, your majesty. Your boot— *that* one!" She pointed to his right foot. *"Hurry!* We haven't got much time." Suddenly she realized the sceptre had been left behind. Whatever had happened to it after the blood had been spilled?

"Your boot, your majesty! Take it off, please!" He stared at her, not understanding. She knelt beside him, and tugged at his right leg. "Sit down," she said, "and let me pull it off for you." Kardia continued to look at her stupidly. "Your majesty, wake up!" She yanked angrily at his right foot, and he fell backward, pulling himself into a sitting position as she continued to tug furiously at his boot. With a considerable effort she succeeded in getting it off.

"Now, your big toe!" Carefully she smeared blood on it from the phial. "Now your thumb, please." This time he extended his right hand toward her, and she repeated the process, first on his thumb, then on the lobe of his right ear. As she did so she caught sight of Wesley standing beside them. "The sceptre," she said. "He doesn't have the sceptre. What happened to it? We've got to get it before the witch. . . ."

They both turned and were stunned by what they saw. The dais which had once been high up against the back wall beneath the Tobath Mareh Tapestry was now far below them, like the platform of a lecture hall. All the steps now led down instead of up. Facing them was a vast wall of green ice behind which the terrible shapes of slowly billowing flames and of ghouls and goblins filled them with fear. Wesley began to run down toward the witch. He could not remember seeing the sceptre but he sensed the urgency in Mary's voice.

But the king was quicker. A change had come over him. He had pulled on his boot and was racing down the steps, a new man. Suddenly he yelled with fresh zeal. Bounding and clattering down the steps, he spotted the sceptre. For the first time since he had been in the Kingdom of Darkness it seemed to want to join him and flew into his waiting hand.

It was only then that all three of them saw what the witch was doing. Standing before the throne she raised the Crown of Anan high above her head. They hurried down toward her, Kardia with the sceptre in one hand and his naked sword in the other.

"Gaal bade me slay her," Wesley heard him breathe.

As they reached the dais, the queen flung the crown down on the ice with such a force that it burst asunder, the glittering jewels spreading round her in a circle. From every jewel flames leaped high, surrounding her with a wall of fire. They stopped and stared in fascination. The queen's appearance was changing.

"She's melting!" Wesley gasped.

It was true. The beautiful face streamed down, dissolving. The robe, as though it were of wax, began to sputter and run. Only the mole on her forehead remained clear. Mary watched it as it grew darker and larger. The body was changing and shrinking, but from the middle of the melting wax something or some*one* was emerging.

"It's the old, old woman!" Mary exclaimed.

In another minute the familiar form was there—the rags, the sores, the matted hair, the rotting teeth, the filthy wrinkled skin, the great black warty growth and, more foul than ever, the smell that Mary would never forget.

Kardia gripped his sword tightly. He was about to step through the flames but she cried to him piteously. "See what I am, Kardia of Anthropos! Look upon my shame and my humiliation! Know that my punishment is upon me. The ice will open, the fires will scorch me and the goblins will devour even my bones. Does a man of honor need to slaughter an old woman whom Gaal has doomed?"

And even while Kardia hesitated, the center of the dais dropped down into the flames. The crystal throne and the hideous old hag disappeared. They stood before a circular hole that glowed red with other fires burning deep in the world's core.

For a full minute no one spoke.

"Is that the end of her?" Wesley asked.

Mary looked at him. "Horrid thing! I hope so." She was pale and trembling. Wesley, contrary to his usual way, put his arm round her shoulders. "I shouldn't say that. I feel sick, Wes. I wanted her to die—but to see what happened. . . ." She shuddered and hid her face in Wesley's parka.

"Hist!" Kardia said warningly. "Stand well back."

Even as he spoke a scaly head thrust itself from the hole, spouting flames from its nostrils and mouth.

"Run for your lives!" the king yelled. Holding his sword in one hand, he let Mary grip the sceptre which he held in the other. They turned to run up the stairs. Wesley seized Mary's free hand so that he and Kardia could drag her up the steps between them.

She could not resist the temptation to turn her head to see what was happening. "It's a dragon!" she gasped. "A great big dragon! Look out! It's flying!"

They turned to see. Wings filled the chamber as the creature flew above them. A pale circle showed up clearly on the scaly underbelly, and Wesley knew that the circle meant something, but could not remember what.

Then the dragon hurled its great bulk against the wall of the throne room through which Kardia had climbed originally. With a crash and a roar the ice wall burst asunder. For a moment it seemed as though the whole building might collapse, but it didn't. The dragon was gone, and through the breach they saw nothing but outer darkness. They ran to the wall.

"The ladder of emeth should still. . . . Thanks be to Gaal it is here!" the king cried delightedly. "Does the Lady Mary know how to descend it?"

Mary looked at the drop and her heart sank. "My dress!" she said in dismay. "I'll never make it with my dress!"

Kardia's sword was back in its scabbard. He handed the sceptre to Wesley. "Guard it well," he said, "though I sense the danger is at an end now."

He seized Mary, flung her over his shoulder, hardly feeling his broken ribs in the excitement, and with a merry laugh began down the ladder. For Mary it was far worse than a roller coaster. She found herself looking down, swaying and bouncing over terrifying empty space. She clung in panic to his leather jerkin.

But at length they were at the foot of the wall. The six sovereigns were now hurrying down the ladder above them.

Their descent of the hill was a dream of fright. The ice had begun to melt and was incredibly slippery. They never reached the stairway but fell several times, slithering and sliding uncontrollably down the hill. Mary, separated from them, glided at an ever-increasing speed toward the harbor.

"He-elp!" she cried. "I can't stop. Wesley, He-e-lp!"

But Wesley and Kardia were sliding, too. Fortunately the hill was not bumpy so that although the journey down was cold and wet, it was not painful. If you can remember your first toboggan ride on a long, ice-covered slope or even the first drop on a roller coaster, you'll have some idea of the sensation of not being able to breathe, of having left your insides somewhere above you—a sensation you try to recapture in later years but which is absolutely terrifying the first time you experience it. Well, Mary experienced it.

She could see she was traveling roughly in the direction of the Thunderhead. Dimly she was aware that there were people on the quayside pointing at her. But how ever would she stop? She was a human projectile doomed either to plunge into the icy waters of the harbor, or to crash through the wooden walls of the ship.

What she in fact did was slither onto the horizontal harbor area at the foot of the hill. Even there she failed to stop. On she sped, her momentum scarcely checked, nearer and nearer to the ship. She could see people leaning over the side and hear them shouting to her, but she was too scared to take any notice.

Miraculously her speed slowed. She struggled to stop herself, but the wet ice was treacherous. Suddenly she was there, shooting over the quayside, bumping against the wooden hull and splashing under the shockingly cold water.

For a moment she whirled in numbing cold darkness. Then arms were about her, and seconds later she was being hauled on board, wrapped in blankets, hugged, taken into a cabin, undressed, toweled, laughed over and forced to drink hot choking liquids.

Meanwhile Kardia stood against the stern, one arm round the queen's shoulders and the other around his son Tiqvah. He had been the last to climb on board before the rope ladder was hauled up. The three were staring up the hill at what was left of the palace whose ice walls were collapsing one by one. Ruddy flames rose majestically from among the ruins.

"I knew not, my father, that ice burned," Tiqvah said wonderingly.

"Look!" Kardia pointed above the hilltop.

"The dragon!"

It was circling slowly high above the flames.

"From whence did it come?"

"It rose from hidden fires beneath the ice."

Suneidesis said nothing but her face was drawn and pale. Dragon indeed. She knew at once what had happened. Their danger was far from over.

30

Playing Tag with Gaal

The hill was receding in the distance as drawn by invisible power they glided toward Playsion. They traveled in a broad channel now, away from the open water of the harbor and were suddenly startled by a thunderous crash on the starboard side of the ship.

"Your majesty, what is it?"

Kardia turned to see the ship's captain beside them, no longer the alert and confident skipper of the outer voyage, the man who had dared to upbraid the king for setting sail too hastily, but a shaken and wide-eyed sailor staring into the gloom, his pale face flickering with the fiery reflections from the channel. For the first time Kardia noticed the ship's company crowding the deck—sailors, men-at-arms, officers. Among them he saw the anxious stares of Chush and Qatsaph. Fear shone from every eye. Even the Friesens seemed scared. The three human rulers stared up at him dazedly. Kardia strode to the edge of the quarterdeck and called to them.

"Citizens of Anthropos-Playsion! Sovereigns of our beloved neighboring countries! Servants of Gaal from world's afar!

"Be of good cheer! Your terrors will soon be at an end. Gaal has broken the power of Mirmah, and draws us with a mighty hand out of the Kingdom of Darkness. You witness the death of a vanquished kingdom.

"Many of you have been lulled in enchanted slumber, but the power of Gaal and the blood of Gaal have released you. Therefore, fear not! Though the enchanted empire dissolve before your eyes, though caverns may crumble and seas may heave, the power of Gaal is about us and will bring us safely to Chalash harbor.

"To their majesties, the rulers of Klemma, of Mispach and of Chamash, and to the sovereigns of Chaiyah, of Perachim and of Elim I say welcome aboard my ship, the Thunderhead! Know by the sceptres in your hands that because of the courage of his servants from other worlds Gaal has set your peoples free.

"Let fires be lit in the galleys! Let food and wine be served! The journey is long and the dangers still are many. But eat, drink and quit yourselves like men, for Gaal is the ruler of all!"

There was a cheer—a rather feeble cheer it must be admitted—but a cheer nonetheless. A cloud of fear began to lift from the ship's company. It would have been better if everyone could have been given duties to perform. But the men-at-arms had no battles to fight and the ship's crew had no sails to hoist. Only the men who worked in the galley had work to do. The rest stood around in knots discussing their strange adventures or leaned against the bulwarks staring into the surrounding blackness.

The crash that had so startled the ship's captain had momentarily been forgotten until a thunderclap ripped the air. The ship lurched drunkenly, and they saw a ragged streak of ruby light extend from the edge of their channel into the distance. Unlike a lightning streak it did not disappear, but widened, filled with the same red waves as those through which they sailed. A perfect cannonade of crashing and roaring began. More streaks of ruby light split the ice into jagged fragments. Mary said it was like sailing over the surface of a thunderstorm and Lisa, that it was like a giant spider web made of red fire.

But the real terror began as the inky green roof above them began to disintegrate. If you have ever been in a hailstorm where the hailstones are the size of tennis balls, you will have an idea of what it was like. But these chunks of ice were of all sizes—from the size of cabbages to those of icebergs bigger than the Thunderhead.

At first nobody realized what was happening. They only knew that there were too many crashing sounds to be accounted for by the splitting of surrounding ice. Then from the channel astern and ahead of them, they began to see feathery plumes of fire-water, as the first few ice boulders plunged down.

"The sky is falling!" somebody cried.

There was a scramble to get below decks. Happily no one was hurt. What was a greater good was that so little ice hit the ship as she rode on tossing seas of fire among falling mountains of ice.

Lisa sat below the companionway. While it comforted her to have Mr. & Mrs. Raccoon in her arms, the arrangement was inconvenient for it left her without hands to steady herself. Her body was jerked to and fro by the lurching of the ship, and she kept bumping her left shoulder against the bulkhead. A soldier approached her bearing a bowl of broth, but she shook her head, trying to smile. Then as the ship lurched the man staggered and the bowl left his hands, passing over her head to splatter its contents on the bulkhead beside her.

"Your pardon, lady!"

"Oh, it doesn't matter. It wasn't your fault."

"Thank you."

Mr. & Mrs. Raccoon, frozen with fear, still clung to her.

"What a waste of good soup!" Mary's voice sounded above her. "You should try it, Lisa! I've never tasted anything like it. They serve tremendous food here!"

"How can you eat when the ship's tossing about like this? You don't even seem scared."

"Oh, I am. Mind you, after Mirmah, even *this* isn't too bad, eh?" Mary sat down beside her, chewing a hunk of cheese.

"Careful you don't sit on the broth."

Mary grinned happily. "Eating keeps my courage up."

As time passed the terrible cacophony of sound gradually subsided and they grew drowsy. Neither of them could remember lying down, but when hours later they awoke stiff, sore and chilled, they could see daylight filtering dimly through the portholes.

"Fantastic!"

"Incredible!"

Wesley and Kurt stood on the deck of the Thunderhead and stared directly overhead. Her masts and spars stood in sharp relief against high arching cliffs of blue-green ice. Here and there the vessel would glide beneath a patch of pale sky, but for the most part it threaded its way silently, sometimes along twisting gorges whose walls shut out the heavens, or else through tall and narrow caves with sides of delicate aquamarine. The shapes varied endlessly. It was as though a sculptor had carved an unending series of curving walls, a succession of cathedral-sized grottos where whales and porpoises might worship in the awesome silence. It was silent now. The gentle swish of sea water against the Thunderhead's sides was the only sound they could hear.

Like Lisa and Mary, the boys had fallen into a fitful sleep as the apocalyptic tumult of the night had subsided. But now morning had broken, and while the rest of the ship's company slept exhausted, some mysterious prompting had awakened the brothers to a strangely numinous beauty.

Footsteps sounded on the deck behind them, and they turned to see Lisa and Mary.

"Good morning!"

" 'Morning. Isn't this terrific!"

"Tremendous!"

"It's *way* better than Disneyland," Mary breathed.

"The colors!"

"Emerald!"

"Sapphire. Bet you can't think of any more fancy ones."

"Jade."

"Amethyst!"

"Oh, come off it. You just made it up. Where?"

Mary pointed below the waterline at a plunging chasm of ice.

"You're right. There's every shade from green to purply-blue," Wesley said slowly.

"Could you paint it?"

"I wish I had my camera. Those shapes are unbelievable."

"Like Henry Moore statues."

"Who's Henry Moore?"

Suddenly they stopped talking. Gaal was standing on the deck with them. Nobody knew what to say.

"Do you like it?" Gaal asked. There was a pause.

"You mean all this?" Kurt waved a hand at the scene they were passing through. "It's . . . it's terrific. It's like nothing I've ever seen. Did *you* do it?"

Gaal smiled. "I make beauty out of despair. There's nothing like a cesspool for growing white lilies. And I am, though you may have forgotten, the Lord of ice."

"But didn't *she* make the ice?" Wesley asked.

"No, I did."

"I don't understand."

"When I let her cover herself from light and warmth, my laws decreed that she must also suffer cold. So I gave her ice for her miserable kingdom. She did what she could with it."

"Her palace was *kind of* beautiful," Mary said, frowning. "Even the ruby flames. But it was different. This is something else." She shook her head, wondering at the difference. "The other was—phony."

"You carved it all out? And dreamed up the colors?" Kurt looked at him, amazement lighting up his face. "You're *terrific!*" Then the memory of the rooster came back to him, and the sound of Wesley's voice reading Gaal's letter when he had advanced for the attack. He looked at Gaal, filled with inarticulate gratitude.

"I've never. . . ."

"Say it, Kurt."

"It sounds dumb—but I've never. . . ."

"Never what?"

"I've never *touched* you."

"Try!"

Kurt moved shyly forward, and Gaal, smiling, backed away. "Come on. See if you can!"

All except Mary were embarrassed. How could you play tag with someone like Gaal? Kurt was blushing but he still moved forward. "Please, Gaal!"

Gaal reached out a hand, ruffled Kurt's hair, then moved out of his reach again. His movements were playful yet full of grace. None of them knew quite how it happened, but in a moment they were chasing him around coils of rope, or round the masts, or up and down the steps, now on the fo'c's'le and now the quarter-deck. At one point they climbed giddily up a rope ladder to the crow's nest and down another rope ladder to the deck. On a silent ship, beneath gothic arches of turquoise ice, four breathless and laughing children found it impossible to corner an agile, white-haired man in a long robe.

It ended when Kurt tripped and fell, and the others who were close on his heels collapsed in a heap on top of him. Gaal scooped them up in his arms and sat them on the quarter-deck steps around him. Kurt leaned against his right side with a sigh of satisfaction, and they all let their breathing settle as they watched the endless unfolding of majestic frozen architecture.

"There's a blue sky above," Lisa said.

"And sunshine!"

"Where?" There was certainly nothing but cool blue-green shade around the Thunderhead.

"Up there—look!"

High above them a crest of ice glittered with reflected golden light. Suddenly they realized how much they had missed the world of sunlight and air, and how long the night of their adventure had been. Day had come.

"I've never liked night—or winter," Mary said slowly, "until now."

"Winter's ugly in the city," Wesley said.

"When I first saw you in the snow and you gave me the Sword of Geburah, you *made* the snow beautiful."

A mood which I could best describe as one of contented awe rested on all of them.

Gaal had gone by the time the rest of the ship's company began to stir. Meals were served, and soon they were traveling in more open water between icebergs. The captain grew anxious, wondering whether they should hoist sail. He seized the helm but found that stronger and invisible hands were controlling it, guiding the vessel through the dangers of an ice field.

By noon they were driving through fairly heavy seas into a brisk south wind, and an hour later they had left the ice field behind and were in open water. But there was no sign of the Playsion coast.

The captain, Wesley, Kardia and the senior officers took council together. No one knew exactly where they were, only that they were heading in roughly the right direction. Either the whole Kingdom of Darkness had been drifting north, or because it was breaking up, all the normal landmarks were shifted. Wesley tried to ask about taking sights on the sun, but nobody seemed to understand. They decided that there was no point in using the sails since the winds were contrary, and since the ship was being driven and guided in the right direction by a mysterious power.

In the late afternoon they sighted the Playsion coast and the following morning they glided into Chalash Harbor as dense crowds watched, too awed to cheer.

For years to come the story would be told of how the Thunderhead entered Chalash Harbor, having sailed with her sails furled across the sea from the Kingdom of Darkness into the teeth of a strong south wind.

3^I

Because Kardia Didn't Kill Mirmah

The children stayed two more years in Anthropos. People told and retold the story of the Thunderhead's return. Songs were made about it, and minstrels went from town to town and from castle to castle singing them, not only through Anthropos-Playsion but through all the neighboring countries, even crossing the seas to distant continents. The fine ladies chosen to weave the new tapestry (the one to replace the Tobath Mareh Tapestry) insisted on beginning with a picture of the Thunderhead forging against the wind with furled sails into Chalash Harbor. They managed to complete a good deal of that part of the tapestry while the children were still in Anthropos.

The Thunderhead's return was only one story of many. There was the story of Goldcoffin's Palace, the story of Mary and the witch, the tale of the escape from

Poseidon's Kingdom, of Inkleth's battle with the ogre and many more. Mr. & Mrs. Raccoon became famous. They took up their quarters at the Palace Gardens in Nephesh. Mrs. Raccoon produced a litter of young during the second year and said she was glad to have another family because Timothy never came home to see them anymore. People were allowed into the Palace Gardens during the holidays (without having to pay anything) to watch them.

Twitterpitter stayed in the gardens too. She had a nest in a part of the grounds where the grass was never cut, and she often was heard singing high above the palace. Garfong along with the rest of the Koach preferred the woods while Strongbeak continued to live in the mountains. But once every few months each would come to pay a visit to Wesley, whom they seemed to regard as the true hero of the adventures they had passed through.

Tiqvah persuaded Kardia to let Kaas act as his gentleman-in-waiting. I think that what Tiqvah really wanted was someone to share his room, for it was a very big one. Kaas enjoyed the arrangement thoroughly.

Tiqvah and Mary seemed to strike up quite a friendship. Kurt wasn't sure what to think about it, and one day he talked to Mary. But all Mary did was to thank Kurt and tell him she thought he (Kurt) was cute. Children change a lot in two years. Mary grew tall and though she was never what you would call slim, she lost every one of her pimples, and had a glow of warm happiness that drew people to her.

The neighboring sovereigns, once Kardia's bitter enemies, now became friends of Anthropos. Their rescue from the Dark Kingdom had mended quarrels of many years, and Dipsuchos, gentle but healed of his shame and no longer timid, became an excellent ambassador-at-large.

However, all was not well. One day a minstrel came to Nephesh Palace bringing news (you see they had no magazines in Anthropos) and singing a new song, telling a long and dreadful tale of an enchanted treasure ship. According to the song, the ship was a pirate vessel from distant waters full of stolen treasure. It drifted, burnt black, into Chalash Harbor. On board were the charred remains of the crew. But no treasure could be found anywhere.

Then came rumors of dragons that flew through the night skies above every country in the continent. At first people felt there must be many dragons. Certainly the descriptions varied. But both Kardia and Suneidesis believed there was only one, and Suneidesis secretly felt that the dragon was really the witch in another form.

Winter brought more evil tales. The bodies of girls or women walking after sunset would be found charred and burnt in the morning. Always their jewelry was missing. Even the rings on their fingers would be gone. Usually there was a wild description of a flying dragon. How else could you explain the charred bodies? Fear increased. Women stayed home at night. But men were just as prone to die as women. Without gold or jewels people were safe. With them they would be burned and robbed.

"What would dragons want with gold and jewels?" Lisa asked Queen Suneidesis.

"Gold and jewels feed their inner fires, the fires that are the life of them."

"Their life is *fire?*"

"So say the legends."

"And gold and jewels are food for the fire?"

"That is what we are told."

So dead merchants would be found on the highways, their moneybags missing. Or the city gates would be opened at dawn to find the burnt wreck of a coach outside. Sometimes even the coins from the coachman's pockets would be gone.

Kardia grew moody and preoccupied. Wesley and Kurt had expected him to announce an expedition to search for the dragon, but the more he and Kurt discussed the matter, the less they were able to think of how one would go about a dragon hunt. How do you find a dragon? How do you approach it once you have found it?

"I really thought the fire-breathing thing was just a myth," Kurt said, "until Lisa explained the business about them being nothing but fire inside."

"I guess they're another form of life," Wesley replied, "fueled by metals and jewels in the same way we are fueled by food."

Spring came and went. One day Kardia invited all four of the children to accompany Suneidesis and himself to Lake Nachash where a royal lodge had been built since the children were last in Anthropos. It nestled at the edge of the woods above cliffs facing the Island of Geburah. There were steps cut in the rock leading down to a stone jetty on the lake.

"The fishing is good," he said.

His smile seemed forced, but the children thought little of it. They were puzzled that there was no mention of Tiqvah or Kaas but felt it would be rude to ask. However, the prospects of seeing Lake Nachash and perhaps of visiting the Island of Geburah were exciting.

Within three days they were on their way. No one mentioned dragons, but they were careful to travel by day. They journeyed slowly, spending the first night at an inn and the second at Chocma's Cottage. They arrived on the third day about noon.

Servants had prepared a midday meal, and from the table through the dining room windows they could look across a broad grassy space and a sparkling lake to the island on which Lisa, Kurt and Wesley had once spent a fateful day and a half.

"You can still see the tower," Wesley said.

"What's left of it!" Lisa laughed.

"Where?" Mary asked eagerly.

Lisa pointed. "See that sort of bump on the western tip of the island? I mean on the *left.*"

"Uh-huh."

"Well, that was where it stood until. . . ."

"Until what?"

"Oh, nothing. Your majesty . . . ?" Lisa had noticed Kurt's embarrassed silence and quickly changed the subject.

"Yes, your ladyship?"

"Could we, could we visit the island this afternoon?"

"It would be more prudent perhaps to wait until the morrow," the king replied gravely. If the children were disappointed, they gave no sign of it.

It was an uncomfortable afternoon. The king and queen seemed grave and spent many hours talking together, oblivious to their guests. If they had not known Kardia and Suneidesis better, they might have been tempted to feel they were being unmannerly.

"Something's bothering them," said Kurt as he and Mary watched the two walking slowly up and down the grassy clearing between the lodge and the cliff above the lake. They walked slowly, their heads bent. Sometimes they would sit and talk. Once or twice Kardia would take one of the queen's hands between his and the two would sit motionless for long periods of time.

"I guess we shouldn't watch," Mary said. "It looks kind of private and solemn."

Supper was a silent affair. Lamps were lit. Then to their surprise Kardia asked Kurt and Wesley, "Do the two of you still row well?"

"Not very well, your majesty. We can get by. But we're better at sailing. What do you have in mind?"

"Would your lordships do me the kindness of fishing with me this evening? There are eels in Lake Nachash as well as fish called stike that are best caught at night."

And so it was settled. Three hours later Kardia, Kurt and Wesley were drifting quietly in the moonlight, two or three hundred yards from the island. It was a night that under other circumstances would have intoxicated them with its magic. The moon was nearly full, and the water almost calm so that sometimes the broken fragments of the moon's reflection would jiggle themselves for a brief second into a round whole. The cliffs round the island no longer seemed ominous, only serene and peaceful. A beaver swam past them, his nose leaving a long V trail in the water.

Fishing was slow. In fact they caught nothing. At first the boys were excited but as time went on, whether because of the poor fishing or because they both slowly sensed that Kardia was not interested in fishing, they stopped watching their lines to stare furtively at the king. His eyes were never on the water but constantly scanned the skies. Suddenly he stiffened. The boys glanced at each other and looked to see what had caught his attention.

Kurt saw it first and inhaled sharply. "Look!" he breathed. "Circling above the lodge—like one of the Qadar, only bigger—see the red light at the front of it?"

Kardia turned. "Her majesty was right," he said.

For a while the creature, whatever it was, continued to fly to and fro above the lodge. Then it turned and with terrible speed began to approach them.

"Has it seen us?" Wesley asked in alarm.

"Aye, it has seen us."

"Then hadn't we better...." With terrifying clarity Wesley suddenly saw the hopelessness of their position and the futility of any attempt to escape. The flame-breathing shape grew swiftly larger, hurtling toward them. Kurt flung himself with a sob into the bottom of the boat. Wesley cringed, half crouching, his arm held over his head. Kardia alone remained standing, staggering a little, for Kurt's movement had set the boat rocking.

There was a sound of rushing wind as the dragon passed over them. Fearfully Wesley raised his head to see it rise in a powerful swoop over the cliffs that surrounded the island. It hovered for a moment above the castle ruins, then landed rather clumsily among them. They waited, letting the boat drift, but there was no further sign of the dragon. Slowly they began to row back, glancing over their shoulders from time to time.

"So the prophecy has come to pass," Kardia mused. "Her lair lies in the ruins of Geburah."

"*Her* lair. You mean it's a female dragon, your majesty?"

"No, my lord Kurt. The creatures are not male and female. They neither breed nor lay eggs as reptiles do but are as the salamanders, forged in flame at the core of the world."

"But didn't you say, *her* lair?"

"Aye, my lord, that I did."

"Then...."

The king sighed heavily. "It is she. It is none other than Mirmah whom Gaal bade me put to the sword. But I was loath to slay the pathetic hag, and I hesitated. And you, my lord Wesley, saw what happened."

"I saw her fall into the flames."

"You also saw her rise from them."

Dismay settled icily over Wesley's shoulders. Kardia's words were appalling. Had their mission ended in failure after all?

"Gaal told me," the king continued quietly, "that if I failed to slay her in the Palace of Darkness that she would return and slay me."

Wesley stopped rowing and stared at him. "Oh, *no!* But he wouldn't let it happen—he just *wouldn't!*"

It was too momentous. His mind struggled to grapple with what Kardia was saying. So this was what had made the king and queen so solemn. The picture of the children's arrival in the palace two years before flashed through his mind. He remembered the joy with which they saw the icy dagger melt when Kardia so boldly defied the challenge of the Lady of Night. It wasn't fair! Gaal just wasn't like that! What had Kardia done? *It didn't make sense.*

"Gaal wouldn't do that!" he said fiercely.

"It is not Gaal, who will do it, but the witch," the king replied. "Moreover, Gaal himself has told me that thus it shall be."

"But Gaal could stop her if he wanted to! What's the matter? Is he mad at you? Or doesn't he care?" The more he thought about the matter the more agitated Wesley grew. He had been sweating, but suddenly he began to shiver.

Kurt looked puzzled and dismayed. The king surveyed them both.

"Do not doubt Gaal, my young lords."

"But why does he have to let you *die?* You hesitated

for just a second. Does he have to let you get killed because of one second's hesitation?"

"Many a man has been killed for even less!"

"But couldn't he forgive you?" Wesley was shouting.

"He has forgiven me long since!"

"Then why do you have to die?"

"Because, my lord, I am mortal."

"No, that's not what I meant. I mean, if he has forgiven you, why does he have to punish you?"

"He is not punishing me, my lord."

Wesley seized the oars, dug them deep into the water and tugged angrily, throwing his body back in rage with each stroke until the boat fairly surged through the water. He was crying a little and his nose was running. For about five minutes he continued in this way until, exhausted, he let the oars drift again.

"You think he'll hear me if I try to send him a message?"

"Of course, my lord. Does he not always?"

"I'm beginning to wonder." He paused, deep in thought. Then he said, "I'm going to ask him to change his mind."

The king sighed. "Perhaps if I were not to die, a greater evil might arise. Gaal the Shepherd could easily prevent my death. But he could not—or he *will* not—change the past. What is done, is done. The witch *did* fall into the flames at the world's core. She *did* rise from them as a dragon. Would you have him undo all that? And how much else would he have to undo? Would you have him unmake that which *is?*"

Wesley stared at him blankly and Kardia continued. "Would you have him create fire that only is hot when we want it to be hot? That will cook but not burn? Or wind that will drive ships and windmills but never blow

371

dust in our eyes?"

Wesley frowned. He was struggling with a new view of the universe, and he shook his head wearily. Finally he said, "I still don't see why you should have to die."

Kurt said, "My turn to take the oars, Wes!"

Wesley sat next to Kardia in the stern and the king threw an arm round his shoulder. "Why so discouraged, my lord?"

Wesley stiffened uncomfortably. "What's the use of it all if you're going to die?" He shivered.

"My lord, you came not to save my life but to save Anthropos. That you have done. Your obedience to Gaal has brought deliverance not only to Anthropos-Playsion but six kingdoms more. My wife and my son are no longer in the clutches of an evil witch but are alive and free. Is all this of no account?"

Wesley sighed. "It's terrible to think. . . . I just can't. . . ." He bit his lip and shook his head. He wanted to ask when the witch would kill Kardia, but how can you ask someone when they are going to die? The king seemed to sense his embarrassment.

"The dragon will come tomorrow in the late afternoon. Gaal appeared to me in a dream a week ago and told me. It will come because it knows I brought the sceptre. I will fight it in the clearing before the lodge, and in the fight I shall be mortally wounded."

"And the dragon?"

"The dragon will be slain. But not by my hand."

"Who will kill the dragon, your majesty?" Kurt asked.

"That I know not."

"The queen, Suneidesis, . . . does she know?"

"She knows, my lord Kurt."

Kurt drew in a deep breath and shook his head. For several minutes no one spoke.

"It must be awful for her. Is there anything we can do?"

Again there was a long silence. Finally the king said, "No, there is nothing you can do for her. She must bear her grief alone. Your lordships together with your sister the lady Lisa and your cousin the lady Mary are to accompany me."

"Accompany you where?"

"As night falls a funeral barge will come to the landing to take me on my last journey. My servants will place me on the barge with the Iron Sceptre. You will sail with me."

"What about the queen?"

"She will remain here."

"Where are we going?"

"That I know not. Only that we go."

They had arrived at the landing and servants took charge of the boat. Wearily the boys made their way to bed. But they lay tossing and turning until dawn, Wesley trying to communicate in his mind with Gaal, begging him not to let Kardia die.

By late afternoon on the following day the news of the impending battle with the dragon had spread throughout the lodge. Kardia had chosen Wesley and one of the servants to assist him outside the house. Wesley handed him the reins of his horse and the servant passed him a long spear. He wore no armor except for a light metal helmet. His shield was slung over his back. He would use it only if he were unhorsed.

"Have you ever fought a dragon before, your majesty?" Wesley asked as the king prepared for battle.

"No," the king replied. "But every king of Anthropos has studied the technical points of dragon fighting. From ancient battle books and treatises on dragons, from histories of famous fights of the past came the lore I learned from boyhood."

"But how do you fight a creature so huge and strong?"

"It is not a simple matter, my lord Wesley," the king answered. "But there are three weak areas in the monster's armored scales—behind each foreleg and then, most vulnerable, on its lower underbelly. But the dragon will not expose this last area until it is assured of victory."

None of this conversation comforted Wesley; so he fell silent rather than continue. How could the king possibly last long against such a foe? As it turned out, Kardia's fight did not last very long.

The king stationed himself at the west end of the clearing where he would have the advantage of the slope, and where the dragon, a creature of night would be dazzled by the rays of the late afternoon sun. Wesley stood by his horse on the side nearest the lake. He felt ill and was badly frightened.

For an hour they waited. Then the dragon's disgusting black shape grew rapidly larger, flying toward them from the Island of Geburah. As it approached the cliffs it swept down steeply, hovered over the clearing at a level just beyond the lodge and dropped. The thud of its landing made the ground shake.

Wesley's mouth was dry. The creature that was slowly folding its wings was far larger than it had seemed the previous night. The tail, the neck and the body were all of about equal length, the tail being approximately the length of five horses standing nose to tail. Its folded wings were higher than the roof of the two-story lodge. The belly was pressed against the ground, while the angles of the jointed legs rose like those of a gigantic grasshopper thirty feet into the air. Flames rolled from its nostrils scorching the grass.

Wesley was totally unprepared for the creature's hatred. Malice characterized its every movement as it slowly crawled toward them. It intended to kill. But it intended to kill out of pure hate.

Suddenly Kardia left Wesley and galloped directly toward the dragon, his spear held horizontally in his right hand. He seemed small and fragile, pitifully defenseless against so terrible an adversary. At first it looked as though he would ride directly into the flames, but at the last moment, or so it seemed to Wesley, he swerved and began to gallop in a circle around it. But he had swerved too soon. The monstrous thing was able to turn as swiftly as he rode.

Without pausing, Kardia swung about and circled in the opposite direction cutting in more closely. It looked as though he had caught the dragon by surprise for it remained motionless for a second. As Kardia passed behind it, still narrowing his circle, the tail like a flying mountain flicked within inches of him.

The horse shied, almost throwing him. For a brief second he lost control. Then, wisely, he galloped back to Wesley and spent two or three minutes gently patting and talking to his charger. The dragon was by now immediately in front of the lodge, and Wesley could see white faces staring in anxious silence through the windows.

Again Kardia approached at a gallop, this time not swerving until it looked as though he were about to ride inside the creature's jaws. He swerved first toward the house and then to the left and in behind its right foreleg.

"Well ridden!" the servant shouted excitedly. Wesley had forgotten the man was there.

For two or three minutes it was hard for them to see what was happening since Kardia's movements were partly obscured by the dragon's foreleg. He seemed to be moving about in the safety area between the foreleg and hind leg, lunging again and again with his spear at the weak spot behind the dragon's foreleg. The dragon's legs were stamping viciously, its body moving now this way, now that, and the tail switching constantly to and fro. It could not see Kardia, but was attempting, by constantly changing its position, to maneuver him into a danger area.

Then so quickly that no one saw what happened the tail crashed sickeningly against the horse's rump, tumbling horse and rider head over heels and knocking them several yards toward the lake. Kardia was on his feet in a flash, bruised, but relatively unharmed. The horse screamed, struggling on its forelegs and floundering. Its back was broken.

But Kardia could not afford to attend to it. His spear was also broken. Drawing his sword he ran quickly into the safety area by the dragon's side.

"Kill it!" the servant cried to Wesley. "Take your sword and kill the poor beast!"

Nauseated and shaken, Wesley drew the Sword of Geburah and ran to the horse.

"I mustn't stop to think," he said to himself as he ran, "and I mustn't look at its eyes." He had no idea how to go about killing a horse with a sword, but he was not going to make matters worse by letting himself be shaken by its piteous fear. He was frighteningly conscious of the monstrous stamping, of the danger and the venomous hate of the dragon.

The horse was still struggling when he reached it. Disciplining himself not to hesitate, he drew the blade swiftly and cut deeply across the front and side of its neck. Blood spurted powerfully. In a few moments its struggles subsided and it lay on its side, its eyes wide and staring.

With a start he realized he was close to the dragon and turned to look at it as he jumped back. Close up it was terrifying. Its monstrous feet thudded against the ground and the whole scaly body was in heaving motion. He could hear the hiss of its fiery breathing. Kardia, dwarfed by its immense size, was struggling to extract his sword from the dragon's side at a point level with his own head, just behind the foreleg.

He had succeeded. He had pierced the dragon's side. Fire began to splash down on the grass from the wound. A cry of joy broke from Wesley's throat. Gaal must have heard him! Kardia was not going to die after all! The first great obstacle had been passed. Now it was only a matter of time, and of carefully staying in the safety area.

Wesley yelled with excitement. "Oh, *beautiful!* Oh, good for you! Oh, Kardia, you've done it! You've done it! You really have done it! Oh, Gaal. Thank you! Thank you!" He shrieked so loudly his throat was hoarse.

Then horrified he saw Kardia slip, lose his grip on his sword and fall. In what seemed to Wesley to be slow motion, a heavy foot descended crushingly onto the king's thigh and above the noise of the dragon's movements Wesley heard a gasp of pain. Wesley watched in horror, powerless to move or help as the foot was raised again to crash down a second time, this time on Kardia's chest and right shoulder, the claws tearing him mercilessly.

It knew what it had done. It rose slowly to its full height, swinging round at leisure to survey its victim. Wesley was appalled at the dragon's height, an armored tower about to plunge down on the wounded king below.

It was then that he saw the yellow circle and the words of Gaal's first message flashed through his brain. He had

come to Anthropos to plunge the Sword of Geburah to its hilt into a yellow circle *and the yellow circle was facing him.* In another second the dragon would fall on Kardia, crushing the life out of him.

He hurled himself forward, leapt over Kardia's body and with all the strength he could muster thrust the sword into the weak spot. A stream of liquid heat shot past him, singeing his hair, while the Sword of Geburah was pushed back out by pressure of the fires within. Wesley fell back, rolled over, narrowly avoided cutting himself in half with his own sword. He rushed to Kardia.

He need not have been afraid. With a thud that rocked the earth, the monster fell sideways. At first he could not grasp what had happened. It was in death throes, a wing flapping feebly and a leg convulsing sporadically. Liquid fire poured over the damp grass, setting it sizzling and smoking. But in seconds the glowing liquid had turned to gray ash and the dragon's black hulk was still.

But more was to follow. The enormous body began to shrink and to shrivel. It grew smaller and smaller until to Wesley's amazement it was only the size of a small human. It was a woman, a very old woman whom Wesley recognized.

"The witch!"

She was finally dead. Even as he stared at her, her flesh turned to powder and dropped from her prostrate form. Only her skeleton remained.

When he looked at Kardia, it seemed as though the king, too, was dead.

32

The Sceptre of Iron and the Sceptre of Gold

Kardia was not dead. But he was fearfully wounded, and it was clear that he was dying. Hiding her tears and smiling gently, Suneidesis washed, anointed and bound up his wounds. She wiped his face tenderly with scented oils, and she combed his hair and his beard. Then she raised his head letting it rest in the crook of her elbow while she helped him drink a wine mixed with pain-relieving herbs.

"Be not so cruel, my love. Though Gaal forbade it I shall yet come with you," she said, wiping his lips gently.

"Nay, it may not be so," he replied, his voice low but firm. "It will be my death barge. I go from this world and the children—are they not from other worlds?—will suffer no harm. But whither the barge goes, you cannot come. Would you die with me?"

"Most gladly, my dear lord," she replied.

The king sighed. "It shall not be," he said. "It grieves us to part. But your duty is here. Tiqvah will need your counsel. And the barge will pass through the veil of death. Do not continue to press me, heart of my heart. Have we not talked of this many times during the past days?" He sighed and the queen turned her face away.

They prepared a stretcher for the king, and his servants carried him by the steps cut in the rock down the cliff to the jetty, the queen and the four children following close behind. The night was well advanced. The moon floated high overhead sending its reflections to dance elusively on the black surface of the lake. There was little wind.

No sooner had they reached the jetty than they saw sailing toward them round the western tip of the island a boat with a square sail. As it came closer they could see that the sail was of the palest blue, bearing the cross of St. George at its center. When the barge settled by the quay, they marveled that nobody was sailing it. It had come by itself.

It was a stately barge, lined with pale-blue satin and furbished with blue satin cushions, edged richly with gold cord and tassels. The sail too was of satin and the mast overlaid with gold.

Kardia lay still as wax, only his eyes moving as he watched the queen. She kissed him tenderly on his forehead and held his hands between hers for several moments before laying them carefully across his chest. She placed the sceptre beside him so that it rested in the crook of his arm. Then she bade the servants to place him in the barge. Her eyes were dry and her voice was low and weary.

The children clambered on board too, sitting on either side of Kardia. But the queen knelt on the jetty clinging to the side of the barge, holding it against the rock. Her eyes held Kardia's.

"You must let it go!" he said faintly. She shook her head. They could see, now, her body was trembling. The servants had withdrawn and were standing behind her. "Let it go, my love. It is only for a little while."

For several seconds she crouched, still trembling, still clinging. Then with a supreme effort of will, she let the boat go and slowly stood erect.

At once the sail bellied out soundlessly by itself, filled with a wind they could neither see nor feel, blowing them toward the eastern end of the lake while the water lapped gently under the bow.

The servants drew away from the queen respectfully so that she stood trembling and alone on the edge of the quay, watching the barge as it moved away. Lisa lifted Kardia's head to let him see her, and the two looked at each other wordlessly across the water until the distance between them was too great for them to see anymore. As long as they could see her, Suneidesis stood erect like an abandoned statue. Kardia sighed and Lisa let his head rest back on the cushion. For a long time nobody in the boat spoke or moved.

"There is something more that one of you must do for me," Kardia said weakly at length, "and it shall be the lady Mary who does it. She it was sought to steal this sceptre from my side. She it was who by anointing me gave me power to get it back from the witch again. When the time is come it shall be she who flings it from me into the lake."

The idea sounded revolting to the Friesens. They had come to Anthropos so that Kardia might keep the sceptre. Now he was dying and so precious a thing was to be thrown away.

"Please, your majesty, why must it be thrown in the lake?" Kurt asked.

"Because it is fitting."

Mary was filled with awe. "Like King Arthur?" she whispered.

Kardia's face was blank.

"We have had no king by that name," he said slowly.

"He comes in 'Mort D'Arthur.' It's . . ." she hesitated, obviously troubled. "It's a long poem about him—er, dying—and his sword has to be thrown in a lake. Will an arm come out and catch it?"

Wearily the king shook his head, and seeing him Mary forgot King Arthur and was absorbed with the solemnity of her task.

For the next three hours they glided slowly and silently eastward. The Island of Geburah disappeared astern while the cliffs on both sides of the lake increased in height. The king's eyes were closed, and they supposed him to be sleeping. None of them spoke. They grew stiff and cold. Wesley felt they ought all to have been mourning or at least feeling very sad. He was a little dismayed to discover that he didn't seem to have any feelings at all. Their adventure seemed unreal, unbelievable.

After another hour Kardia suddenly said, "The time has come, lady Mary."

Mary started, and in the light of the moon the others could see her face was white. She got up from where she was sitting, leaned over Kardia and gently pulled the iron rod from where his forearm was folded over it. Then, her lips pressed together, she held it horizontally in her hands and looked at it as she had once done in the Palace in Nephesh. It was beautifully ornate, black and shining. She remembered the strange way it had been pulled back to Kardia. But it was not pulling toward him now. She felt a strange reluctance to carry out the king's wish. Kardia's dark eyes were fixed on her.

"Throw it, lady Mary. The moment is come."

It was heavy, and Mary knew she could not throw it very far. She was no good at sports. Nevertheless she tossed it with all her strength out over the water.

The throw was a far better one than she had expected. The sceptre shot vigorously upward. It seemed to draw light from the moon down upon itself. It continued to rise.

"What a throw!" Kurt cried.

The sceptre continued to rise.

"What's happening?" Lisa asked.

"It's still going up!"

Higher and higher they watched it rise, slowly turning as the moon caught it, until it twinkled like a star far above them. Then, gradually, they lost it from view in the sky. They strained their eyes after it. "Will it ever come down?"

"Who knows? Mebbe it was *meant* to go up!"

"Look at Kardia!" There was fear in Lisa's voice. His face was still, his eyes wide open, staring at nothing.

"Close them, Wes. It doesn't look right."

"Is he dead? How can you tell?" Kurt asked uneasily.

Wes knelt by Kardia's head. He had no idea what to do and was foolishly holding a pocket mirror over the king's mouth and nostrils. His hand was shaking, but after a moment he said, "I'm sure he's dead." Gently he drew the lids over the king's eyes, and held them closed, until they stayed closed by themselves. The face was like white marble under the moon.

"Oughtn't we to cover his face?"

"No, don't. He looks nicer like that."

For several minutes they continued to stare at him. But

Wes was bothered.

"I don't know why, but I feel we *ought* to cover him."

"Oh, no! Please don't. So long as his face is uncovered it seems . . . like he's not completely dead."

"I know. But I feel it's something we've *got* to do. Don't ask me why. We just have to."

Near the stern he saw a large folded satin pall, edged like the cushions with gold cord and tassels. He had not noticed it before, and he had no idea what it was. But clearly it would be ideal for the purpose. The children unfolded it as carefully as they could and very tenderly laid it over the king.

Dawn had broken ahead of them. They seemed to be approaching the end of the lake.

"What happens now?" Kurt asked.

"I don't know. But something special has to happen. What is there at this end of the lake?" Lisa asked.

"I've no idea."

"It's sort of misty. It reminds me of something," Lisa continued.

Slowly the eastern sky grew brighter until a golden flush illuminated the mist ahead of them. "I know what it is," Lisa said at last. "It's like the first time I saw the Bayith of Yayin."

"The *what?*" Mary asked.

"The Bayith of Yayin. It's a sort of palace—a real neat palace—where Gaal took me. I met Suneidesis there. And Theophilus."

The mist obscured the shoreline at the end of the lake. It seemed to have gathered the gold from the eastern sky and to be glowing with light. They moved into it. For a few seconds they were surrounded by a diffuse gold radiance. Then suddenly the air was clear and the barge came to rest at the foot of a marble staircase leading to the courtyard of a marble palace. Gaal was coming down the steps to meet them.

"*Gaal!*"

"The Bayith of Yayin!"

Gaal was smiling. In one hand he held a gold sceptre.

"Welcome!" he cried.

The children crowded to the front of the barge, and scrambled onto the marble pavement at the foot of the staircase. Mary was the first to run to him, while Wesley, Kurt and Lisa hung back a little shyly. He led her by the hand as he turned to greet the others.

"So you have not only overthrown the rooster, and jointly done my bidding in the dark places, but now you have slain a dragon. Well done, all of you!" He placed his hands on each of their shoulders in turn, shook hands with them and embraced them, laying down the gold sceptre to do so. "What's *that?*" Lisa asked, looking at it curiously.

Gaal picked it up to show them. "Don't you recognize it?"

Mary was the one who guessed first.

"It's—it's the same as Kardia's. Only gold."

"It *is* Kardia's."

"But it's made of gold."

"*Now* it is, yes. Why don't we give it to him?"

There was a shocked pause.

"He's—he's dead!" Kurt said.

"I have conquered death," Gaal replied quietly. "Death is my servant. It must do my bidding." He strode nearer to where the barge rested beyond the quayside at the foot of the steps and the children followed him, looking fearfully at the pale-blue satin pall covering Kardia's corpse.

"Rise, Kardia of Anthropos! Rise to reign with me!"

Gaal's ringing command echoed like a trumpet blast from the farthest corners of the universe. Wesley knew that distant stars were startled by that voice.

What happened next is not easy for me to describe. I questioned each of the children closely, and as far as I can make out it was like this. Kardia sprang *through the satin pall.* That is to say, he passed through it without disturbing it and without making any holes in it. The only thing the satin pall did was to sink back where Kardia's corpse had been and lie more or less flat.

For a moment Mary thought he must be a ghost, but she touched him and found he was solid and full of strength. He no longer wore the clothes that covered him on the stretcher, but a long linen robe, not unlike Gaal's, and a gold crown with zabach stones on his head. He was young again, young and vigorous, his hair and his beard jet black, and his cheeks glowing with health. He strode across the landing and up a couple of the steps to where Gaal's arms were stretched out, and bowed low before him. There was a new sword hanging from a gold belt round his waist. He showed no sign of age or weakness, and there were no wounds or injuries on him anywhere.

Gaal raised him to his feet, embraced him, and handed him the gold sceptre. "It is yours forever now," he said. Lisa, Kurt and Wesley watched them with awe. Mary went back to the barge to pull the pall aside, and later she told everyone Kardia's clothes were there, just as though he had also passed through them, like a ghost. They lay flat on the floor of the barge, clothing nothing. None of the children could explain it afterward. Yet on one point all of them were adamant. Kardia was *not* a ghost. He was, as Kurt put it, "more real and more solid than he had ever been." Mary said afterward that "all the old things, his clothes, his bandages and so on didn't have the same kind of *solidness* as things at the Bayith of Yayin."

From the courtyard above they could see crowds of people coming to meet them. Kardia turned to Gaal again. "My lord Gaal, what of the queen and my son? How will they fare?"

Gaal's arm went round Kardia's shoulders. "Suneidesis still grieves for you deeply. Yet her grief is not the bitter sorrow of those who have no hope. She knows she will join us soon. But first she must strengthen the hands of your son Tiqvah as he begins to rule."

The crowds had reached them. Many of the people knew Kardia and gave excited shouts of welcome. "Come," Gaal said to the children, "I have something to show you." They pushed their way up the stairs through the crowds, across the courtyards, past the Fountain of Dam, and in among the fluted and jeweled columns of the marble palace. Banners of gold and scarlet hung high above them.

"It's bigger than it was last time," Lisa said, puzzled.

"Maybe it's like Chocma's Cottage—changing size," Kurt suggested.

"My Bayith of Yayin has no size," Gaal said gravely.

They wandered among banqueting tables piled high with fruits and with all manner of food. Music, singing and laughter echoed from multitudes of men, women and children. At the far end Gaal led them to an alcove, and when they saw it, they stopped with a shock of recognition. In the wall of the alcove there was a trapezoid-shaped opening. It was eight feet high and about ten feet wide. The left side was vertical, but the right side sloped inward to meet—yes, perhaps you have guessed already —to meet the ceiling of the attic in Grosvenor. They were looking into the attic through a missing wall. The attic door in the wall farthest from them was slightly ajar. The television sets were still there and Mary's unmade bed filled the center of the room.

Kurt opened his mouth wide, and Mary began to laugh. They turned to say something to Gaal, but what they were going to say will never be known, for at that moment the sound of a familiar voice penetrated the Bayith of Yayin. "Get me some more nails! Where are you children? Where in the name of sense *are* you?"

The door in the far wall opened wide and Great Aunt Felicia, hammer in hand (and still wearing her flowered hat) strode through it. But when she saw them, she stopped, and rage swept over her face. She drew herself to her full height.

"I suppose *you're* one of those creatures they call a guru," she said addressing herself to Gaal, her cheeks flushed and her lips pressed together. Then as her eyes began to take in all that lay beyond them, the rage gave place to amazement. But Great Aunt Felicia was not one to let anyone know she was afraid.

"Why didn't they show me this part of the house before?" she demanded. She strode across the attic like a sergeant major leading a parade, stepped past Gaal and ignored the children. She was through the alcove and marching into the main banqueting hall before they could stop her, still gripping the hammer.

"Let her go," Gaal said. "She will soon have her fill."

They watched her progress as she strode among the people listening to the music and the sounds of happy laughter. Suddenly she planted her fists on a table among a group of feasters. "I want to know what's going on here!" she shouted. "Who runs this place? I know perfectly well that John isn't capable of organizing a setup like this."

It was as though nobody heard her. Conversations continued, and song swelled without a pause. Angrily she grabbed for a lute a young man was playing, but it was as though she had been a ghost. The lute player seemed neither to see nor to hear her, and though Felicia tugged fiercely to get it out of his hands, she might as well have been tugging a stone lute out of the hands of a statue. It was very funny to watch, but hard to describe. You could tell that the lute player never even felt her.

Angrily they saw her thrust her face to within an inch .of his. "Look at me, young man!" She had been going to say more, but somehow she began to realize that he might not after all be able to see her. Again she stood erect, a calculating look in her eye. Then raising the hammer high in the air, she brought it down heavily on a delicate crystal goblet on the table. But the hammer could have been made of air for all the effect it had on the crystal. And since it was *not* made of air, the hammer hurt Aunt Felicia's wrist. A look of pain crossed her face, followed by one of fear. Her glance swept the banqueting hall, yet still she looked neither at Gaal nor at the children.

"Where's the exit?" she shouted. "How do I get out of here?" She stalked in the direction of the courtyard, where she stopped and stared. When she turned round her face was haunted by terror. Then she ran back toward them crying, "Let me out of here! I am a citizen of the United States! Let me out of here!"

Catching sight of Gaal she ran past him, the hammer still gripped fiercely, crossed the alcove, ran through the attic and disappeared from view. Not one of them had moved. They were still standing at the entrance to the attic, Gaal's arms round all their shoulders again.

"This adventure is over now," he said. He pushed them gently. Suddenly there was silence. The music, the singing and the laughter ceased. Mary glanced back—but there was no Gaal, no banqueting hall, only an attic wall covered with faded blue wallpaper.

It was so sudden that for a moment they believed that Anthropos must still be just behind the wall. Mary even ran to the window to see if our own world was outside.

"It's no use," Wesley said as he saw her staring. "We really are back. We're even back to our proper ages and clothes." They looked at one another and it was so.

"I'd better make my bed. It looks a frightful mess," Mary said (which shows that some of the changes from Anthropos were permanent).

Lisa said, "Did we finish cleaning up the kitchen?"

But at that moment they heard Uncle John's voice calling from below. "Hello! Anyone at home?"

It was as though Anthropos had been a dream and they were awake now in the house on Grosvenor Avenue. Down the stairs they trooped, one after another, anxiously wondering what Great Aunt Felicia would say.

Uncle John was standing in the hallway. "I got your message about Felicia," he said. "I was back sooner than I thought, so I came straight over. Where is she? I see her bag's still here."

They looked at one another.

"When she left the attic, she looked as though she wanted to get away as fast as she could," Wesley said uncertainly. "I wouldn't be surprised if she's left."

"But her portmanteau's still here. What makes you think she would leave?"

Again the children exchanged glances.

Mary said, "Do you know anything about Gaal and the television sets?"

Uncle John whistled. "So *that's* what's been happening! Humph. Of course I know none of the details, but I can imagine. . . . Perhaps that was Felicia in the taxi that just pulled away!"

They went, as they often did at a time of crisis, into the kitchen for coffee. They were still talking at noon and sent out for pizza so as not to waste time cooking.

"Are television sets the only way to get to Anthropos?" Mary asked hours later.

Uncle John stirred his seventh cup of coffee thoughtfully. "I didn't even know that you could get there by television until. . . ."

"Until what?"

"Oh, never mind. I'll tell you some day."

"Have you been to Anthropos, Uncle John?"

"Well, yes."

"When? Tell us about it!"

But Uncle John would say no more. He has talked to me about it since then, but I'm not really free to tell you either. At least not now. Maybe in another book.

I can tell you that Great Aunt Felicia took the next plane back to Chicago and that she never again tried to adopt Mary McNab. There was a bit of a fuss at Winnipeg International Airport when she tried to go through security carrying a hammer. But in the end she gave it up, and they let her go on board, warning the flight attendant to keep an eye on her.

As for Mary, she settled down very happily at Uncle John McNab's, and most people who knew them thought she was one of the Friesens. She had become a thoroughly likeable girl, and when a couple of years had passed, though she was still a bit overweight, she had grown as warm-natured and attractive as she had been in the royal court at Nephesh Palace.

Appendix A
On Dragon Fighting

Anthropos dragons are powerful and extremely dangerous. In the air they travel at great speed. On the ground they are slower and clumsier, relying mainly on their weight, on the flames they shoot out from their nostrils and the lashing of their tails. Their tails are in fact their most formidable weapon, sweeping through an angle of 180° at unbelievable speed, to smash anything in their path. Full-grown dragons have been known to fell four or five large trees with one flick of their tails. It is therefore essential that if you fight an Anthropos dragon, you never approach it from behind, and that in a battle you never allow yourself to get further back than its hind legs.

While most dragon fighters are killed by being scorched to death, they die from a lack of technique. The flames from its nostrils can in fact be avoided fairly easily.

Anthropos dragons are what might be called stiff-necked. That is to say, the head, the long neck and the shoulders are almost immobile. They can move up and down but not twist from side to side. To spout fire in a certain direction, the dragon has to turn almost its whole body. The nose, head, neck, forelegs and thorax must all be in a line. Since an Anthropos dragon moves slowly on the ground it is possible to move to its side out of range of both its powerful tail and of the flames it spouts. In any case few dragons can spit fire for more than an arm's length. (A few can spout up to the height of a man.)

All of this is not to say that fighting Anthropos dragons is simple. A dragon is wily and cunning. It knows full well why knights on horseback ride around it in a circle. A dragon will automatically keep turning to face the rider wherever he is. The rider needs to maintain his position in the areas of safety on either side of the dragon between its foreleg and hind leg. To do this it is necessary to be fairly close to the dragon so the rider can move around the dragon faster than it is turning. Of course it is important to remember that the safety areas will move wherever the dragon moves. So one must constantly be asking, "Am I still in the safety zone?" even as you concentrate in finding the weak spots in the dragon's sides.

The weak spots themselves are few and far between. Dragon scales are made of a substance that is harder than steel, connected by a softer but surprisingly tough, leathery substance. Most books on dragon fighting recommend one seek to strike the area just behind and under the dragon's foreleg—the area corresponding to the armpit. The idea is to open a wound there large enough for the heavy

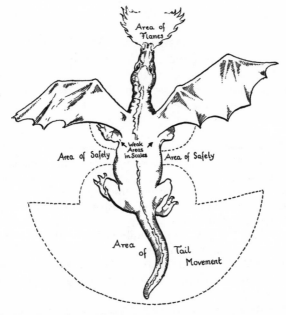

fiery fluid—the dragon's lifeblood—to flow out.

Dragon legs are not short and stumpy nor are they long and spidery. Yet they are limber and muscular. It is no fun to be stamped on by a dragon. Long steely claws curve under each foot to pierce any victim beneath them. In the safety area it is well to keep a close watch on the thunderously stamping feet. One mistake costs a life.

When a dragon overcomes an attacker, it commonly rises upright on its hind legs and brings its two forelegs, with the full weight of its body, on the attacker. The reason a dragon only rises up like this at the end of a fight is that in rising on its hind legs it exposes its underbelly. On the lower part of the underbelly is a large area, circular in shape and yellow in color—its largest weak spot. Behind this soft area is the heart of the fire fluid, where the heavy liquid is under tremendous pressure. The scales of this largest weak spot are notoriously fragile. A relatively small wound in this area will prove fatal since the inner fires are forced out so rapidly that the dragon cools and dies. The effect is similar to the effect of a bullet in a human heart.

In flight a dragon is careful to cover this area with its hind legs, folding its thighs inward for protection. On the ground it is careful never to expose the weak spot, staying close to the ground, unless it is sure its victim is unarmed and helpless.

Appendix B
A Guide to Anthropos

(Pronunciation notes: ch is pronounced as in loch unless otherwise indicated; long o is indicated by oe as in toe.)

A

Abaha (a-BAH-ha) a magical word woven into the hangings in the Bayith of Yayin.

Akrath (AHK-rath) an Anthropos dragon of the Northern Mountains that once captured Prince Galantash and held him for ransom. Slain by Guntug, father of Gunruth.

aman (ah-MON) a light, high tensile metal, peculiarly resistant to flaming darts; often used in shields.

Anan (ah-NAN) son of the Matmon Rathson and twin brother of Kashshaph. Given a magical crown by Shagah by means of which he seized and held the throne.

Ancient City *see* Bamah.

Anthropos (AN-throe-paws), the Kingdom of a magical kingdom planned and established by the High Emperor, by Gaal and by the pigeon.

Aphela (ah-FAY-lah), Hill of a hill west of Anthropos, whose exact site is disputed, containing caves (Caves of Aphela) reputed to lead to the regions of Deepest Darkness, and to be the lair of the Qadar.

Archimago (ark-i-MA-go) chief sorcerer and prime minister to Mirmah.

Arctic Fox, Mr. & Mrs. prisoners with Mary McNab in the igloo north of the Kingdom of Darkness.

Arctic Hare, Mr. & Mrs. prisoners with Mary McNab in the igloo north of the Kingdom of Darkness.

Atslah (AH-tslah) ancient chieftain, brother of Mirmah.

Authentio (aw-THEN-tee-oe; th as in *th in*) Castle ancient fortification, twenty leagues south of Nephesh; site of the famous Battle of Authentio in which Kardia and Chocma freed the castle from the power of Hocoino.

B

Bamah (BAH-mah) city located on the northwest edge of Nephesh which Gaal made into a lake after the defeat of Shagah; also called the Ancient City.

basar (BAH-sar) legendary leatherlike material discovered long ago on a desert journey. It is said that shoes made of basar never wear out.

Battle of Authentio *see* Authentio Castle.

Battle of Rinnar Heights *see* Rinnar Heights.

Bayith of Yayin (BAH-yeeth of Yah-YEEN) a mysterious palace which has been known to appear in any number of locations in Anthropos; here Gaal delights to feast his guests.

Behrens (BAY-rens) Matmon; son of Vorklund; brother of Visgoth; of the blond dwarfs of the north.

Bereth (BARE-eth) younger brother of the Matmon chieftain, Vilkung; also brother of Lechesh.

Bilith (BIL-ith) younger son of Gunruth; killed in a hunting accident.

Bjorn (B-yorn) first king of all Matmon who ruled over the Kingdom of Keshaph.

Blackness, Forest of a major forest in central Anthropos.

Bloggard (BLOE-gerd) captain of Lady Sheriruth's archers.

Bloglin (BLAW-glin) an ancient dwarf sword forged by the elves for Rathson, grandson of Bjorn. Lost for many thousands of years until rediscovered by Throssa, grandfather of Gunruth. It was completely without rust and was extremely sharp when found.

Blond Dwarfs a tribe of Matmon originally from the north who settled in Anthropos five hundred years before Kardia's reign; noted as sailors.

Bogedoth (BOE-gu-doth), Lord soldier under Mirmah's command.

Bolgin (BOEL-guin) elder son of Gunruth tragically killed in an attempt to rescue a wounded Koach trapped on the ledge of a high cliff.

Book of History and True Wisdom an ancient tome of obscure origin locked in the Tower of Geburah for many years until recovered by Wesley, Kurt and Lisa.

Book of Wisdom a book of various powers belonging to Cho_ma when read aloud a protective shield surrounds those nearby; composed of extracts from the Book of History and True Wisdom.

Borab (BORE-ab) son of Borglun.

Borglun (BORE-glun) father of Borab, Norab and Dorab all of whom took part in the Battle of Rinnar Heights. Borglun was said to be a descendant of the legendary Matmon Rogan.

C

Cave of Gaal *see* Gaal, Cave of.

Cave of Qava *see* Qava, Cave of.

Chaiyah (CHAH-EE-yah) the kingdom of the beasts.

Chakam (CHAH-kum) *see* Hall of Wisdom.

Chalash (CHAH-lash) principal port of Playsion on the Great Sea. From this harbor the Thunderhead set out on its mysterious voyage.

Chamash (CHA-mash) a kingdom sometimes friendly and at other times hostile to neighboring Anthropos.

Chazak (CHAH-zuk) a soldier under Nocham at the Battle of Authentio.

Chocma (CHALK-mah) wise woman living in the House (or Cottage) of Wisdom from before the beginning of time. Sometimes she appears to be very old and at other times young and beautiful. Adviser to King Kardia.

Chocma's Cottage located an hour's ride northeast of Authentio Castle; home of the wise woman Chocma; known to be larger on the inside than the outside; also called the House of Wisdom or the Cottage of Wisdom. Inside the Cottage are found the Hall of Wisdom and the Pool of Truth.

Chosek (CHOE-zek) a tall white pillar of rock on the side of the Hill of Aphela.

Chush (CHUSH) a knight in Kardia's royal court of Nephesh.

Circles of Enchantment three concentric circles within the Kingdom of Darkness: the Circle of Enchantment of Bodily Yearnings; the Circle of Enchantment that Dazzles the Eye; the Circle of Enchantment of Blasphemy.

Cottage of Wisdom *see* Chocma's Cottage.

Crown of Anan *see* Anan.

D

Dam, Fountain of a magical fountain with great cleansing powers located in the Bayith of Yayin.

Darkness, Kingdom of the realm of Mirmah north of Anthropos, under an ice mountain.

Darkness, Lord of master of Hocoino and Shagah; also known as Lord of Deepest Darkness.

Darkness, Spirit of *see* North, Spirit of the.

Deepest Darkness, Lord of *see* Darkness, Lord of.

Dilogos (DIE-loe-goes) treacherous lord and courtier at Kardia's royal court of Nephesh.

Dipsuchos (DIP-soo-chos) loyal but foolish courtier and knight in Kardia's royal court of Nephesh.

Dob (DOEB) a province in the Kingdom of Chaiyah.

Dorab (DORE-ab) Matmon son of Borglun.

Dragon, Ford of the a shallow crossing over the River Rure where in ancient times an enchanted dragon, magically controlled by the evil Lord Gannan, guarded the southern approach to Authentio Castle.
dryad (DRY-ad) a tree spirit.
Duin (DOO-in) the rarely seen elfinlike inhabitants of forests; curators and guardians of trees; allies of the Matmon.

E

Ebed Ruach (EH-bed ROO-ach) a sinister power known as a jinn. Servant-spirit of the sorcerer Hocoino. The jinn was confined inside a gold ring on Hocoino's little finger. When released, it could take the form of a yellow cat, a yellow serpent or an oppressive darkness. It was ultimately destroyed by light from the Book of History and True Wisdom.
El *see* Gaal.
Elim (EH-limb) a kingdom of walking, talking trees.
emeth (EM-ith) an elfin thread that is very lightweight yet extremely strong.
Empress-to-Be of Darkness that Swallows the World *see* Mirmah.
Envy, Sprite of a demon serving Goldcoffin; a green snake with a woman's head.
Ermine, Mr. & Mrs. prisoners with Mary McNab in the igloo north of the Kingdom of Darkness.
Evil Lord of the Castle Authentio enemy of Gaal who stole the Mashal Stone eight hundred years before Kardia's reign.

F

fenfinch a game bird with beautiful purple markings. Found principally in low-lying rivers and lakes in Anthropos, Playsion and Klemma. Occasionally found in marshy areas. Not a true finch, more closely related to grouse.
forest frights evil creatures of the forest attracted to powerful or magical objects; easily scared by a rousing song.
Friesens *see* Wesley, Kurt, Lisa.
furies evil, flame-throwing creatures.
Further Isles in the Great Sea, under the rule of Anthropos.

G

Gaal (GAHL) Lord of all worlds; Son of the High Emperor; Sender of the pigeon; Chief Shepherd of living beings; also known by the ancient names of Mi-ka-ya and El.

Gaal, Cave of in an uncertain location in the Forest of Blackness; a place of safety from evil forces with an opening in the roof through which events of the past and future can be viewed, known as the hole where time is no more. Like the Bayith of Yayin it could be found in the most unlikely places.

Gaavah (GAH-vah), Sir Gregorio (greh-GORE-ee-oe) a rebel nobleman who defected from Gaal's forces with seven hundred knights to fight against Kardia in the Battle of Rinnar Heights.

Galantash (gah-LAN-tash) last surviving member of the Matmon royal family. Galantash never married and had no descendants. Never ruled as king since the Matmon had divided into separate tribal groups.

Gannan, Lord an evil nobleman of the ancient family of Gannanim; rebel against the throne of Anthropos and possibly responsible for the theft of the Mashal Stone.

Garden of Peace birthplace of the first sovereigns of Anthropos.

Garfong (GAR-fong) Koach leader, twin of Whitefur.

Garfong, Son of son of Garfong, who assisted Wesley, Kurt and Lisa during their second visit to Anthropos.

Gasus (GASS-us) a flying horse, twin brother of Peg and son of Theophilus V.

Geburah (geh-BOO-rah), Castle of ancient fortress built on the Island of Geburah.

Geburah, Island of the principal island at the western end of Lake Nachash.

Geburah, Sword of a magical sword made of logos-tempered steel, but reputed by some to be made of tiqvah and by others to be forged from seven thunderbolts allegedly buried in the Garden of Peace and made magical by elf runes. Kept in the Tower of Geburah for hundreds of years. Also called Imrah. Early history obscure.

Geburah, Tower of the keep of the Castle of Geburah.

ghoul a black, scaly, red-eyed, winged creature serving powers of darkness.

Goblin of Hatred *see* Hatred, Goblin of.

Goblin of Murder *see* Murder, Goblin of.

Goldcoffin a wicked Matmon who built an enchanted castle, known as Goldcoffin's Palace, on the Low Way under the Northern Mountains. Murdered Rathson, favorite grandson of Bjorn, first king of all the Matmon, who banished Goldcoffin for the deed. Survived many thousands of years by the practice of black arts.

Goldcoffin's Cave *see* Goldcoffin's Meadow.

Goldcoffin's Meadow an open area in the western Northern Mountains with a cave (Goldcoffin's Cave) through which one may enter, once every one hundred years, the Low Way which passes through Goldcoffin's Palace. Also known as Goldcoffin's Glade.

Goldcoffin's Palace *see* Goldcoffin.

Great Northern Pass a pass making travel possible through the Northern Mountains from the Canyon of the Rure to Playsion.

Great Sea large body of water north of Anthropos-Playsion.

Greed, Spirit of a demon serving Goldcoffin; a huge yellow bird.

Gunruth (GUN-ruth) Matmon chieftain, son of Guntug, grandson of Throssa, and descendant of Bjorn. Expert in scaling walls to penetrate castles. Deadly swordsman and expert with the axe. Once slew two giants in single-handed combat with a short sword. Ally of Kardia.

Guntug (GUN-tug) son of Throssa, a descendant of Bjorn. Mortally wounded in his battle with the dragon Akrath, whom he slew with Bloglin. Father of Gunruth.

H

Habesh (HAH-besh) son of the Matmon Inklesh. History records almost nothing about this younger twin of the renowned Inkleth. Fought under Kardia in the Battle of Rinnar Heights.

Hall of Seven Pillars *see* Hall of Wisdom.

Hall of Wisdom a large meeting hall in the House of Wisdom (Chocma's Cottage) which is supported by seven large trees; also called the Hall of Seven Pillars or Chakam.

halls of darkness abode of dead goblins and other evil creatures awaiting judgment. Also known as Halls of Deepest Darkness.

Halls of Deepest Darkness *see* halls of darkness.

harpies flying creatures serving powers of darkness.

Hatred, Goblin of a demon serving Goldcoffin; a massive black beetle.

Hocoino (hoe-COY-noe) an evil sorcerer who, though originally called by Kardia to act as his chancellor, plotted to depose the king and rule Anthropos. Finally overthrown after the Battle of Rinnar Heights.

hole where time is no more *see* Gaal, Cave of.

House of Wisdom *see* Chocma's Cottage.

I

Imrah *see* Geburah, Sword of.

Inklesh (INK-lesh) son of Klingall; chieftain of the Red Dwarfs who was succeeded by Inkleth, his son.

Inkleth (INK-leth) son of Inklesh; High Chieftain of the Red Dwarfs

and descendant of Kolungall, founder of the Red Dwarfs. Kolungall
descended from Bjorn and was distantly related to Gunruth.
Iron Sceptre *see* Sceptre of Anthropos.

J

jinn *see* Ebed Ruach.

K

Kaas (KAH-ss) friend of Prince Tiqvah, and son of the treacherous
and brutal Lord Ramah.
Kardia (KAR-dee-ah) ruler of Anthropos; father of Tiqvah.
Kashshaph (KASH-shaff) Matmon twin brother of Anan and son of
Rathson to whom Shagah gave a richly jeweled crown which lacked
the magical properties of the crown Shagah gave his twin.
Keshaph (KEH-shaf), Kingdom of kingdom established by Bjorn,
first king of all Matmon.
Klemma (CLAY-mah) a kingdom for most of its history hostile to
Anthropos until the defeat of Mirmah.
Keshaph (KAY-shaff) ancient Matmon kingdom that once separated
Anthropos and Playsion.
Klingall (KLING-all) Chieftain of the Red Dwarfs; son of Lenglesh;
succeeded by his son Inklesh.
Koach (KOE-ach) an intelligent species of wolf; loyal to Kardia;
found only in Anthropos.
Kolungall (kau-LUN-gall) first ruler of the Red Dwarfs who insisted
on a coronation and the title of king. None of his successors claimed
the title so they were called chiefs or chieftains. Kolungall was a
descendant of Bjorn on his father's side and of goblins on his mother's
side.
Kurt brother of Wesley and Lisa, sent by Gaal to Anthropos in times
of great need; known as Kurt Friesen in his own world.

L

Lady of Night *see* Mirmah.
Leanshanks a Koach scout who served Garfong, the white Koach
prince.
Lechesh (LEH-kesh) younger brother of Bereth and of the Matmon
Chieftain Vilkung.
Lenglesh (LEN-glesh) first-born son of Kolungall and ancestor of
Inkleth; refused to be called king, defying his father's claims. Slew

his own father and became the first Chieftain of the Red Dwarfs.

Lesser Rocks three rock formations between the Heights of Rinnar and Bamah.

Lightening a Koach scout, who together with Leanshanks, served Garfong, the white Koach prince.

Lisa sister of Kurt and Wesley, sent by Gaal to Anthropos in times of great need; known as Lisa Friesen in her own world.

logos a hard metal.

Lord of Deepest Darkness *see* Darkness, Lord of.

Lord of ice and snow title used for Gaal especially in contrast to Mirmah.

Low Way a passage under the Northern Mountains running from Goldcoffin's Meadow in the west to Chalash in the east.

Lower City *see* Nephesh.

M

McNab, Mary sent by Gaal from another world to aid Anthropos in time of great need; cousin to Wesley, Kurt and Lisa Friesen.

Magician's Falls created by Shagah when he made the Canyon of the Rure to punish the mountain tribes of the north, thus reversing the flow of the Rure so it emptied into the Great Sea.

Marah, (MAH-rah) Lady wife of Sir Chush.

Mary McNab *see* McNab, Mary.

Mashal (MAH-shull) Stone much of the history of the Mashal Stone is obscure, though it is described in the earliest listings of the royal treasury of Anthropos. Stolen from the treasury eight hundred years before Kardia's reign, during a time of civil war, by the Evil Lord of Authentio Castle, it reappeared in the castle during Kardia's rule, only to disappear again and be recovered from Goldcoffin just prior to Kardia's death. The wearer of the stone is able to perceive the truest forms of reality while remaining invisible.

Massah (MAH-sah) southern port of the Kingdom of Darkness.

Matmon (MAHT-mun) dwarfs found only in Anthropos and neighboring countries. Most Matmon live between three and four hundred years.

Medusa (meh-DOO-sah) a giant sea anemone with snakelike tentacles streaming from her head; a daughter of the old gods; servant of Mirmah, guarding the cave prison in Poseidon's Kingdom.

Medusa's Stairway created when Mary McNab destroyed Medusa by throwing Mirmah's crystal ball into Medusa's mouth; leading from the sea bed of Poseidon's Kingdom to the Kingdom of Darkness.

Migtar (MEEG-tar) -of-the-Heart-of-Ice *see* Mirmah.

Mi-ka-ya *see* Gaal.

Mirmah (MEER-mah) ancient witch; sister of Atslah; bride of the Spirit of Darkness and would-be conqueror of the world. Also called the Lady of Night, the Empress-to-Be of Darkness that Swallows the World, Migtar-of-the-Heart-of-Ice and Mirshaath. For a time she dwelled in Goldcoffin's Palace. Was 6,601 years old when finally destroyed.

Mirshaath (MEER-shath) *see* Mirmah.

Mispach (MIS-pach) kingdom having trade agreements but tense diplomatic relations with Anthropos.

Morpheus Lake below the Northern Mountains in the middle of which is Goldcoffin's Palace which blocks the Low Way.

Murder, Goblin of a demon serving Goldcoffin; a great red lobster with a human head.

N

Nachash (NAH-kash), Lake an oblong lake in southeastern Anthropos emptying into the River Nachash; most noted for the Island of Geburah which dominates the western end of the lake.

Nachash (NAH-kash), River main tributary to the River Rure.

Nanta beautiful but vain goblin princess forced to marry the Matmon Kolungall.

Nephesh (NAY-fesh) capital of Anthropos and site of the Royal Palace (Nephesh Palace); also called the Lower City.

Nephesh Palace the royal residence in the capital city of Anthropos.

Nocham (NOE-chum), Lord knighted at the Battle of Authentio and subsequently made Earl of Authentio. Close friend and loyal servant of Kardia.

Norab (NORE-ab) Matmon son of Borglun.

North, Spirit of the also known as Spirit of Darkness, husband of Mirmah.

Northern Mountains mountainous region between Nephesh and the Great Sea.

Numa (NOO-mah) the bright star which is within one degree of true north in Anthropos.

nyriad (NI-ree-ad) a flower fairy.

O

ogre a seven-headed, man-eating creature with long fangs and red, hairy body.

Oqbah (OCK-bah) a traitor in the court of Nephesh, sole descendant of an ancient and at one time royal family in Anthropos.

P

Pachad (PAH-chud), Sir Percy a rebel knight, ally of Hocoino, whose followers bore enchanted spears that created terror in any man or beast wounded with them.

Peg a flying horse; female twin of Gasus and daughter of Theophilus V.

Perachim (peh-rah-CHEEM) kingdom of singing and dancing flowers.

Playsion (PLAY-zee-on) kingdom surrounding Anthropos on the east, south and west; united to Anthropos by the marriage of Suneidesis and Kardia. Prince Tiqvah was the first ruler of the united Kingdom of Anthropos-Playsion.

Pool of Truth a deep pond of water in the House of Wisdom which reveals things as they are and gives true form to those who pass through it. The pool also has powers to heal ills caused by deception.

Poseidon (poe-SIE-dun) majestic god of the sea beneath the Kingdom of Darkness; in reality a huge, doll-like creation filled with and run by goblins.

Poseidon's Kingdom found directly beneath the Kingdom of Darkness, ruled by the god Poseidon.

Prison of Greed where Goldcoffin lures victims in his palace.

proseo comai (pro-SAY-oe KOE-my) precious jewels blown to all parts of Anthropos at the dawn of history; under certain circumstances they can bring answers to the yearnings of the inhabitants of Anthropos; given by the shepherd's father; also called proseo stones.

Q

Qadar (kad-DAR) emissaries of the Lord of Darkness who roam the night skies on huge batlike steeds; also called the night warriors.

Qatsaph (KAT-saff) an impetuous courtier in Kardia's royal court of Nephesh.

Qava (KAH-vah), Cave of located at the northern end of the Rinnar Heights, once holding five hundred knights enchanted by Hocoino.

Qosht (KOESHT) woven material from ancient crystalline fibers quarried in the same mines from which the legendary Mashal Stone was mined. Like the Mashal Stone, the fibers give a blue light in the darkness though in sunlight they appear to be red.

Quashash (KAH-shash), Oak of landmark rallying point in the northern end of the Forest of Blackness.

R

Ramah (RAH-mah), Lord member of Kardia's court and traitor, handing over Queen Suneidesis and Prince Tiqvah to Lady Mirmah. Drunkard and brutal father of Kaas.

Rathson (WRATH-son) Matmon favorite grandson of Bjorn; murdered by Goldcoffin; father of Kashshaph and Anan.

Ratson a royal family with a distant claim to the throne of Anthropos.

Red Dwarfs Matmon tribe first ruled by Kolungall.

Reflection Ford along the road between Nephesh and Chalash; so named because the beautiful but vain goblin Princess Nanta spent all her time combing her hair there, watching her reflection, until she was seized by the servants of Kolungall, and forced to marry him.

Rinnar (RIN-ar) Heights a vast rocky eminence just west of Nephesh; site of a fierce and bloody battle won at great cost by Kardia over the forces of Hocoino.

Rogan (ROE-gun) a blue-clad Matmon cheiftain with reddish-brown hair who arrived on the shores of Anthropos many hundreds of years before Kardia's reign. Some believe that Rogan was the ancestor of Vilkung as well as of Borglun although tradition holds that Bjorn is the ancestor of all Matmon.

Rure (ROOR) principal river of Anthropos, originally flowing south into a swamp, but made to flow north into the Great Sea by Shagah's enchantment.

Rure (ROOR), the Canyon of created by Shagah to punish the mountain tribes of the north, thus reversing the flow of the Rure so it emptied into the Great Sea.

S

Sceptre of Anthropos given to Kardia by Gaal shortly after the Battle of Rinnar Heights as a sign of Kardia's true kingship over Anthropos.

shade an inky green, batlike creature known for inducing nightmares in humans.

Shagah (SHAH-gah) Ambassador-in-Chief of the Lord of Deepest Darkness; awakened from his enchantment in the Tower of Geburah by Kurt and Inkleth before meeting his ultimate doom at the hands of Gaal.

Shepherd *see* Gaal.

Shepherd's father the High Emperor.

Sheriruth (SHARE-ee-ruth), Lady an evil enchantress who could assume various forms; joined forces with Hocoino in the Battle of Rinnar Heights. Slain by lord Wesley.

Sleeper *see* Shagah, so-called because of the state of enchantment he was under in the Tower of Geburah until he was awakened by Kurt and Inkleth.

Spirit of Darkness *see* North, Spirit of the.

Spirit of Greed *see* Greed, Spirit of.

Spirit of the North *see* North, Spirit of the.

Sprite of Envy *see* Envy, Sprite of.

stike a kind of fish which frequents the waters of Lake Nachash.

Strongbeak an eagle; servant of Kardia.

Suneidesis (soo-nay-DAY-cease) rightful Queen of Playsion, wife of Kardia and mother of Tiqvah VII. Learned in lore of Anthropos.

Sword of Geburah *see* Geburah, Sword of.

T

Theophilus Gorgonzola Roquefort de Limburger V flying horse who referred to himself as an equine angel; sire of the twins, Peg and Gasus, and of Theophilus VI.

Throssa (THRAW-sah) discoverer with Prince Galantash of the ancient sword of Bloglin, found in a cave following Throssa's successful battle with a serpent.

Thunderhead man-of-war of Anthropos commissioned during Kardia's reign.

tiqvah (TICK-vah) a precious metal.

Tiqvah (TICK-vah) VII son of and successor to Kardia as King of Anthropos-Playsion.

Tobath Mareh Tapestry a history of early Anthropos was depicted in this tapestry—showing the construction of the Tower of Geburah, the murder of Gaal by the Cave of Gaal, the arrival of the boy John Wilson from another world, and many early battles surrounding these events; destroyed in a fire in Nephesh Palace twenty-one years after Kardia was restored to the throne of Anthropos.

Twitterpitter a skylark who acted as scout for the Friesens on the journey to the Kingdom of Darkness.

V

Vakan youngest son of the Matmon Rathson; founded his own dynasty in defiance of his older brothers Anan and Kashshaph. His subjects wore garments of a distinctive blue dye.

Vilkung (VILL-kung) Matmon chieftain; descendant of Vakan (though some believe he descended from Rogan). His younger brothers Lechesh and Bereth fought in the Battle of Rinnar Heights.

Visgoth (VIZ-gahth) son of Vorklund and brother of Behrens.

Vorklund (VORK-lunt) chieftain of a fair-haired, blue-eyed tribe of dwarfs who wore helmets similar to those worn in our world by Vikings. Their origins are unclear. Most believe they arrived by sailing ships many hundreds of years before the Battle of Rinnar Heights. Father of Visgoth and Behrens. His clan was expert in metalwork.

W

Wesley brother of Kurt and Lisa, sent by Gaal to Anthropos in times of great need; known as Wesley Friesen in his own world.

Whitefur Koach twin of Garfong; a scout.

Wilson, John an English schoolboy and the first person from our world to visit Anthropos. He rescued the Book of History and True Wisdom from an enchanted well, and placed it along with Imrah, in the Tower of Geburah.

wood spites evil creatures of the forest attracted to powerful or magical objects, easily scared by a rousing song.

Z

zabach (ZAH-bach) legendary fiery red crystals mined in ancient times and still existing in Anthropos jewelry during Kardia's reign. Believed to have been originally formed from organic matter subjected to enormous pressure and heat.